# CALIFORNIA PROMISES

---

## ERIN SPINETO

SEA PEPTIDE PUBLISHING

*To Mom,*
*For having the foresight to marry a man*
*who would become a stellar example of*
*what a real romantic hero looks like.*

# READ ME
# DIABETES

Diabetes can be a confusing disease that has a language and behavior all its own, just like most chronic conditions. It plays a role in this novel, but, because Charlie thinks about it so little, it is explained only a little.

If you want a deeper explanation of her diabetes—Your Diabetes May Vary—or you are confused, the Diabetes Appendix in the back of the book will catch you right up or introduce you to the would of type 1 diabetes if you haven't experienced it yourself.

It is arranged by page reference so you can read it all beforehand or flip to an excerpt as needed.

# CALIFORNIA PROMISES PLAYLISTS

There are several songs listed in this book. Charlie also plays her Anit-Love Playlist in Chapters 6 and 7. I have compiled those on Spotify. If you would like to listen to either playlist while reading, just scan the QR codes below with your phone.

### CALIFORNIA PROMISES PLAYLIST

### CHARIE'S ANTI-LOVE PLAYLIST

# CALIFORNIA PROMISES

# 1

## CHARLIE

Tomboy. The expression is a cheap shot, a jab at a girl's ability to play the Feminine Game. But, in that word, I've found my hidden superpower. The freedom to peek behind the fortifications of Guyland, to discover the side they'd never show a "real" girl.

Of course, that label also means that I can't use any of that insight to find a man of my own since no worthwhile guy in his right mind would date a tomboy.

A text flashes on my phone next to a picture of Principal Dick Vernon from The Breakfast Club.

**Glenn: Need Confirmation by Tomorrow!**

I don't know why I ever surrendered this number to Glenn Kratzcy, the man in charge at Big&Lime, the tech startup I slave for. Though, at a super-juvenile twenty-nine, I'm not sure he can be called a man. Maybe the under-ripe chief of a band of milk-fed imbeciles?

Another message lights up my screen.

**Glenn: Dirk is going to take the lead on pushing ahead with the reminder app that he proposed at our last meeting.**

That he proposed? Glenn actually thinks Dirk's mansplaining my proposal in our last meeting was him coming up with it.

Beyond the computer on my bedroom desk, out the row of wood-framed windows, is a sky painted with giant swaths of neon pink and purple, fading into a darkening navy opposite the sun as she waves goodbye before slipping beneath the saltwater.

The hot cyan skies that bled into my upstairs bedroom when I sat down at my computer this afternoon have drifted off without my notice. I've been entrenched in trying to "work the problem." Though I only proposed Nudge to Big&Lime this week, I've been developing the project for years.

My phone buzzes again. God, I hate every-sentence-texters.

**Glenn: We think Dirk has the best perspective and familiarity with the subject to guide the project in the right direction. I want you to work with him on it.**

I pound out my reply.

**Charlie: Perspective and familiarity? You mean he has a cock. Because that's the obvious prerequisite for knowing anything about sports or fitness. Forget the fact that the app was my creation or the fact that I have played more ball than he ever has, unless, of course, you count playing with his own marble sack. He is male, so, obviously, he's the one you put in charge.**

Rereading what would be my resignation, I slam it down on my charcoal-stained desk. I need this job, no matter what kind of misogynistic quips I have to put up with.

"*I, I love the colorful clothes she wears, And the way the sunlight plays upon her hair,*" the Beach Boys tune wafting in through my open window entices me from this funk and towards a party mood, but I have to stop this Kamikaze flight before it tanks my future at Bad&Lime.

My phone blares again.

Seriously, Glenn? For a tech genius, you sure don't grasp texting.

**Glenn: Let me know ASAP. Dirk is going to start work tomorrow at first light.**

Of course, that asshat would go in early Saturday to hijack my baby.

Working with Dirk is a total shitfest, but enduring it means Nudge would exist in the real world. How cool would that be? Something I've been working on for years, helping people.

To bring it there, though, I would have to work with that troglodyte every day for months. I'm not sure I could take the constant stream of douchey humor without going all "bitch mode" as they call it.

"*I'm picking up good vibrations, She's giving me excitations,*" the song continues.

"Charlie! Get down here. And put on your dancing shoes, pronto."

I lay my hands on dingy white paint covering the window sill and peer over them. On the weathered deck below, my roommate, Indigo dances wildly to the music that's been breezing in my window.

Erasing my last text, I slip the phone into my pocket. I wonder if Greyson has shown up, yet. He always gets my head spinning in the right direction.

I drift over to the walk-in closet I share with my roommate, Bex, though share is an overstatement. Bex has allocated a quarter of the space for storage of my limited wardrobe and paltry shoe selection. The other three-quarters houses her extensive clothing collection.

My dirty blue and white checkerboard Vans in front of the closet stare at me. These are not dancing shoes. Tonight's a Fancy Vans kind of night.

My Fancy Vans aren't your normal everyday shoes. They are the color of Napili Bay at the west end of Maui and made from the softest canvas I have ever touched. When I slip them on, they lend me a twinge of confidence and a snippet of joy.

Toiling non-stop in the cramped bedroom all afternoon, I've shed most my clothes. Since no one would appreciate me coming downstairs in my cutoffs and an old sports bra, I slip on a white tank-top with random flecks of aqua to match my dancin' shoes and toss a blue and black checked flannel over it. I take out my ponytail, bleached the lightest shade of blond from too many hours in the salt water, and run my fingers through my hair. Good enough.

Pausing for just a moment at the top of the stairs, I rehearse my opening lines. Smile. "Hi. How are you involved with the film? How do you know Indigo?"

Small talk with large groups of new people has always been difficult. I am way more at home in small groups, but I work hard not to show it. I've found that a couple of opening lines are all I need. Once I get people talking about themselves, I don't have to do much more than listen.

Downstairs, I search for Greyson in the throng of people filling the dated kitchen of our beach shack. Unrecognizable bodies fill the seats at the handmade table in the adjoining dining room and pour out onto the deck and further onto the sand.

Our shack was built in the 1930s in the side yard of a beach-front mansion in Del Mar, California, the same strip of land that hosts the multi-million-dollar homes of Bill Gates, Theodor Geisel, and half of the current NFL and MLB stars when they're not killing it on the field. It was designed for the original owner as a workshop to shape surfboards.

In the '60s, the new owner converted it into a guest house with a kitchen, dining room, and small living room downstairs, two tiny bedrooms upstairs, and the most glorious back deck I have ever seen. It hangs over the sand with the surf only sixty yards from its back railing.

It hasn't been updated since the '60s and it shows in the chipped exterior, faulty plumbing, and noises it makes with every step, but moving into the dilapidated bungalow with Indigo and Bex means I can write 2830 Ocean Front as my address.

Ocean. Front.

Every morning I eat breakfast and drink my first Diet Dr Pepper of the day with my feet buried in the dew-drenched sand. Each night, while I drift off to sleep, I listen to the sound of waves dancing on the shore. And at night, as I slumber, the salt air invades my dreams and draws me away to islands filled with warm uncrowded surf, boundless tropical fruit, and dazzling golden sunshine.

Tonight Indigo is hosting a party for the cast and crew of the third indie film she wrote, produced, and directed solo. Later on, she'll show the movie on the giant screen anchored at the edge of the deck.

I make my way through the crowd of Victoria's Secret model

wannabes to the cooler and pop out the Diet Dr Pepper Indigo hid for me under the bottles of Stone and Lagunitas beer. I hadn't known Indigo when I moved in a few months ago, but she has tuned in to my habits faster than most people I've met.

I quickly pour the soda into a pint glass so some cheesy dude doesn't come up with the bright idea to ask me the oh-so-clever and super-insulting, "So why aren't you drinking tonight? You get too wild when you do?" Nothing makes me want to jump in bed faster than a sleazy pickup line.

Trying to shift mental gears, I meander to the splintered railing. Indigo has strung what must be hundreds of tiny white lights in the Banyan tree, their light pouring over the railing and out onto the sand. She is always telling me how superb lighting can change a scene, and tonight she has set the stage for a celebration worthy of her accomplishment.

"How are you ever going to entice a man in those sorry excuses for shoes?" Bex yelps so the guy she's been eye-banging won't hold my appearance against her.

Bexley Liddell isn't naturally pretty, with legs too short to be considered sexy and a face too forgettable to make up for it. But she does know how to maximize what little she has. She's a whiz with makeup and only wears what will show off her well-earned bum. After ninety minutes of preening and painting, she'll turn every guy's head with the sheer volume of hotness she's able to amass.

"Because that is my goal in life, Bex," sarcasm dripping from my lips.

I appraise her victim for the night. He's not a bad choice, wavy blond hair probably styled with the salt from a surf earlier, shoulders hardened by years of paddling. Maybe I should give Bex's shoe theory a try if it could win me a guy like that.

"So I have decided on our Summer Goal," she exclaims gleefully without taking her eyes off Surfer Boy.

Bex and I have been friends since we were seven, and every year since we had a Summer Goal. Bex would come up with a goal by the last day of school and we would devise our battle plan at my house on the first night of summer. I think it was a way to distract herself from the dark void her father left when he bailed on seven-year-old Bexley, and the overbearing shadow her mom radiated when demanding Bex behave the way a proper lady should, withdrawing her love when she didn't comply.

When we were eight, our objective was to ride our bikes to the store every single day for a triple-decker scoop of ice cream at Thrifty's. At ten, we reached for the heavens and attempted to dip our feet in the ocean each and every day.

By the time we were twelve, our focus shifted. That summer our target was Timothy and Michael Holmes, the cutest twins in our grade. It didn't matter to Bex that I was more interested in Bryce Taylor; the only acceptable goal that summer was to date twins.

She developed a three-pronged plan. First, we had to become as thin and tan as possible. For Bex, that meant counting every calorie that passed her lips and loafing in the sun for hours on end. For me, that meant surfing every morning while she was still snoozing.

The second part was to ride our matching, yellow cruisers past their spectacular, two-story home every day in our cutest cutoffs and bikini tops, hoping they would invite us in. For the last step, Bex would orchestrate a game of Spin-The-Bottle, decrying, "All boys can be swayed with a steamy kiss."

A spark of hope at what this summer could bring lights my chest. "Summer Goal Number Nineteen. It better be a good one."

Bex tears her eyes off her man, grabs my hands, and bounces with anticipation. "I am so super excited about this one, Charlie."

I try to match her elation, but that level of girliness is hard to mimic. "Okay, Bex. Hit me."

"So, this summer, I am going to find us boyfriends so we can both be married by spring and then start having matching babies that can totally grow up together."

Her hands flit all over the place, emphasizing each and every point. "And we have to make sure our men like each other so we can take family vacations and barbecue in our backyard."

"Our Backyard? We're gonna share a house with our broods?" I laugh.

Logic is not Bex's strong suit. That was always my part—

to figure out the details—taking her crazy ideas and developing rational plans to bring them to fruition.

"No, dummy. You'll live in the house directly in back of us and we can rip down the fence in between so we can share a yard and your kids can swim in the pool that my independently wealthy husband will have custom-designed for me."

Bex may be my polar opposite, but she's great at noticing my weaknesses and pushing me to work on them, like my lack of drive to find a husband. Over the years, I've become a better version of myself because of it.

"And all this is going to happen this summer?" I take a sip of my soda. "You can just will it to happen?"

"Looks like I already did." She nods towards her Surfer Boy, now talking to an equally hot friend. "Remember not to settle on either one too soon, just in case the one with the long hair is into me. You know how I love long hair. And best friends never take each other's sloppy seconds."

With that, she drags me towards Step One of the plan.

"So what's your deal?" the brunette one says to me, his efforts focused on his consolation prize now that he lost his battle for Bex's attention to his long-haired friend.

"My deal?" I shoot back hoping for a better question. Of course, I'm stuck with the champion conversationalist.

"Yeah. Like, what do you do? What're you looking for? What turns you on?"

I put on my best ditsy accent. "Well, like, for fun I drink. And I totally love to conversate. And boys turn me on. What about you?"

Waiting for him to catch on is an exercise in futility. He perks up and hums, "You turn me on."

I glance over my shoulder hoping Greyson will come save me from this disaster.

Bex considers the gaping smile on her guy's face and gives my arm a squeeze of approval. If only she knew.

After a lifetime of vapid questions from the boys, stellar flirting from Bex, and what can hardly be called proficient flirting from me, I've had enough. I excuse myself to grab another drink, but with Bex hanging on both boys now, they don't miss me.

Leaning on the wobbly railing, the salt air from the water playing in the darkness beyond the reach of our deck comforts me. What I wouldn't give to pick up a board and be out there now instead of trying to play nice with a bunch of strangers. And making my current social stress worse, deciphering the predicament at work is diverting my mental energy from pretending to enjoy small talk.

"I just met the man I'm going to marry," squeals the leader of the throng of girls behind me. "He has the most beautiful blue eyes that just sing out that you are the only woman for him. He has super thick brown hair and the perfect stubble," she says motioning to each body part like her friends have no clue where his hair or eyes or stubble go.

"And he is totally ripped, biceps as big as my head, and a shoulder tattoo, which is, like, totally my favorite."

A grip of nooowaaay's and ohmygaaaawd's ring out like the squawking of seagulls.

"He bumped into me inside, and he looks deep into my eyes, so my heart, like, almost stops, and then, after he touches my arm, he says, 'Sorry about that babe. I didn't see you there, but I do now.' But. He. Does. Now," she proclaims punctuating each word with a bob of her head.

I scan the crowd for the man they've all been oohing and ahhing over; that 'But I do now' line sounds familiar.

"Briiiiiii. You are so lucky!!!" I swear they all cry in unison.

"And get this, he's a fireman. A real-life freakin' hero fireman."

And, at that, I know Greyson's here.

Greyson Steele and I have been friends since I was fifteen when his cousin invited him to hang with our group of friends during our regular Friday Night Pizza and Bowling.

He had the same effect on the girls back then, too. I hate to admit it, but even I was drawn in for a hot minute. I'm not usually a masochist; I don't enter fights I can't win, and I cannot win any girly competition.

That night, I studied him as he navigated the crush of girls fawning all over him while we ordered our pizzas. I grabbed my cup from the cashier, filled it up with Dr Pepper, and slid into the large round booth at the far end of the restaurant like we did every Friday night. The girls were buzzing around, waiting until Greyson chose a seat so they could dive into the booth after him to monopolize his attention, until the strangest thing happened.

He walked over to where I was sitting at the edge of the booth and said, "Wanna slide over?"

Dirty looks exploded from the girls signifying their plans to get a leg up in this game had just been thwarted by the girl they didn't even consider competition. For a brief moment, I thought a guy actually chose me over a mob of girls way prettier and certainly more well-versed in the art of flirting. Don't worry, though, it didn't last long.

A few minutes later he leaned over, motioning like he wanted to tell me something.

Only me.

I leaned in, awaiting the sweet secret, and he whispered, "You remind me of my sister."

Gravity concentrated beneath me drawing me back into my seat. It only took him ten minutes to figure me out.

I was defeated, but at least he saved me the embarrassment of flinging myself at him before he realized he would never want a girl who can out-surf him, out-think him, and who probably spent way less time getting ready than he did.

Although I didn't win the girly showdown that night, I walked away with a much better prize—Greyson Steele as my best friend.

# 2

## GREYSON

Thirty-two emergency calls in twenty-four hours—almost a firehouse record. Thirteen medical aid responses, four hazardous material responses, eleven fire incidents, and four other incidents. In the last twenty-four hours, I've spent less than ninety minutes in the sleek modern Del Mar Firehouse.

We responded to three of a series of nine fire alarms pulled in one hour by Dallas Leeks who we found passed out under the ninth one. We even had a ninety-year-old woman who called in a house fire because she said she knew we wouldn't come if she told us the real story; her dog was stuck under the dog house.

The last one was my favorite, though. Moments after stepping out of the rig into the cavernous cement bay right after the doghouse run, we get called out for a medical aid response at Moonlight Beach.

"Encinitas lifeguards are requesting assistance at the Main Life Guard Station for a shark attack," the dispatcher relayed.

We jump back in the pumper and are wheels turning in under forty seconds. I've gone on a shark call before. A fifty-year-old triathlete was open water swimming a half-mile off Pillbox Beach. He was struggling behind the pack of swimmers when a fourteen-foot Great White came up from the depths and took off his entire leg above the knee in one bite. The saltwater and the open artery made for a bloody beach.

I prepared my guys for what we'd encounter at Moonlight—the crowds and cameras and the bloody sand. When we roll up to the beach, a lifeguard comes on the loudspeaker, "Ladies and gentlemen, there has been a shark sighting in the water. Please exit the water."

We're the second unit on the scene and I am searching for the victim, but only find a mid-forties male, burnt to a crisp, wearing a soaking white tank top and elastic-wasted trunks two sizes too small. He's sitting on the curb behind the main lifeguard tower surrounded by tanned lifeguards looking much too calm to be at the scene of a shark attack.

Larry Piles, Marine Safety Captain is in the mix.

"Larry, what's the situation?"

He steps back from the victim to chat. "Oh, you won't believe this one," he laughs.

Larry has been the Marine Safety Captain in Encinitas for the past eighteen years and it shows in his leathery skin folded in neat diagonal patterns on the back of his neck and a hairline requiring more and more sunscreen every year.

I study the victim and realize his white tank top is simply the part of his skin that was covered by a tank top yesterday when he burned the rest of his body on day one of his vacation.

"I'm coming in from a swim, when I hear him screaming, 'A shark bit me!'"

"So it is a shark bite?" I scan the man for any signs of injury.

"Not exactly. I drag him to shore, but there's no injury. No blood. Nothing."

"Nothing?" The man's current state is starting to make more sense.

"By this time, people in the water told the guard on shore there was a shark attack, so he calls it in, clears the water for two miles, starts posting signs, and talking to everyone onshore."

The news crews gathered earlier start wrapping up their gear and head back to their vans.

"So I ask him what happened and he says he was trying to catch a wave and he kicked something big. It was huge, like a monster.'"

At this, my guys behind me lose it. I shoot them a look to keep it professional. There will be plenty of time to laugh back at the station.

"Why's he still here?" I ask.

"Turns out he thinks he sprained his ankle on the monster so we're gonna transport him to Scripps Encinitas," he says, looking back over the sand crowded with pop-up tents and umbrellas. "Looks like tourist season is in full swing already."

Maybe it's the start of summer bringing swarms of tourists ignorant of the ocean's power, or the multiple days of Santa Ana winds making the residents of Fire Town, USA call the moment they see anything resembling smoke rising in the sky, or maybe it was just bad luck, but that was the worst shift I've had in a long time.

Well, except for *that shift*.

But this one is still wearing on me, even twelve hours later.

I glance in the rearview mirror of my navy Tacoma to make sure fatigue isn't visible. The quick nap and shower helped wash it away and there's nothing my old Station 6 shirt won't cure.

I muster up every ounce of energy I can and force it into my burnt-out shell of a body. The only reason I'm here is to help Charlie navigate the soiree Indigo is throwing at her place. Sometimes I think socializing is the only thing I can do better than Charlie, cause, damn, I captivate the shit out of partiers.

I bound up the stairs and slip through the door, bumping into some girl as I do. "Sorry about that, babe. I didn't see you there," I say giving her a smile. "But I do now."

She gazes up at me and the faintest smile raises the corners of her mouth before I pass her by.

I drift past the groups of strangers to the backyard. If I know

Charlie, she will have found the most remote place possible to weather the social storm.

The lights on the Banyan tree shine around her like a spotlight, not that she needs any help, she floods a room with warmth and vibrancy all on her own. Charlie Sands, hands slipped into the back pockets of her jean shorts, is surrounded by Indigo and a few surfer types who are basking in that warmth. Her long blond hair, usually tied up, is flowing over a tank top I am sure is showing way too much for the boys chatting her up.

Indigo waves me over.

Charlie turns, bracing herself for who she'll have to talk to next until a broad smile washes across her face when she sees it's only me. I'm sure it's the first real smile she's held since this night started.

"Indigo, this place is almost as beautiful as you tonight," I say throwing my arm over her shoulder. "Thanks for letting me crash this shin-dig."

Indigo is extravagant and loud, but she's also a brilliant filmmaker. And she's sharp; she never gives any mind to my flirtation. "Will you tell Charlie she should sing on the soundtrack of my next film?" Indigo prods.

Charlie only moved in a few months ago, but, God, I love Indigo's influence on her. It almost makes up for the fact that Charlie now lives with Bex, too.

"I tell her all the time she should do something with that voice of hers. But you just can't fix stubborn."

Charlie smiles and rolls her eyes at me.

"I'd pay to hear you sing," the blond kid who didn't even bother to change out of his wet trunks says to Charlie. "How does dinner tomorrow sound?"

Wow. He's just going for it, but Charlie laughs him off, "Sure thing."

My gaze drops to the faded wooden planks as I try to wipe away the fatigue only to spot Charlie's bright blue shoes and part of the tattoo sticking out from beneath them. It took her four years to pull the trigger on the design she created when she was seventeen. Four years, a trip to Ensenada, and a few more beers than she typically drinks.

The tattoo is her take on the Luther Rose, the symbol designed for Martin Luther during the Reformation, with a black cross on a red heart laid on a white rose inside of a blue sky and gold ring.

Charlie's always had a thing for church history. She, of course, replaced the rose with a Gerbera daisy. And, yes, I know how lame it is for a guy to know the name of a flower, but I've heard it enough times for it to be burned in my brain.

Four of the Five Sola's, Latin phrases summarizing the Reformers' theological convictions, wrap around the border with the fifth, *Sola Reformada,* in script below the circle. I never thought church history could be so sexy until I saw that tattoo.

A high-pitched voice brings me back. "Wow, Indigo. This is so exciting. A real premiere. Are you excited?"

The woman I bumped into earlier has wriggled her way between the blond kid who hasn't taken his eyes off Charlie since blatantly asking her out and the other surfer dude who's only slightly smarter.

Clearly, Charlie is bored with this woman because she starts a conversation with me, without saying a word.

*Hard day?* she asks with a look.

I thought I was covering well, but it's hard to hide anything from this girl.

*The worst.*

*Talk about it later?*

*That would be really nice.*

She leans over and, using actual words, says, "I've got to talk to you about work, too. Glenn wants me to work with Delta Bravo."

For a woman who kicks ass in a man's world, she still can't bring herself to curse. She tells me she swears like a sailor in her head, but I seriously doubt that. She's got all sorts of code words she uses instead. Like Delta Bravo, her version of Douche Bag.

"Occy, here, played the soldier," Indigo interrupts.

"Occy? Like Mark?" Charlie asks, suddenly interested in small talk.

"Yeah, kind of. My real name is Okemos, but everyone's always called me Occy," he says with a grin.

Charlie is now beaming with the second real smile I've seen tonight.

*I know Okay-mos is a ludicrous name, Charlie, but you can't laugh right in his face.*

"So are you as good a surfer as the real Occy, or are you just a blight on the name?"

Occy's got a matching smile.

"I'm okay. I don't get as much time in the water as I'd like cause of work."

"So, your agent's got you booked all the time?" she asks.

Wow. She's smiling at *him,* not his lame-ass name. It's as if she actually likes the guy. A guy who shows up to a party in trunks and a wrinkled Reyn Spooner. A guy who probably hasn't brushed the dirty dishwater-blond mop on his head for weeks.

I look to Indigo to explain the tennis match of flirting going on in front of us. She is happily following the banter back and forth like she's encouraging it. Maybe I don't like her influence on Charlie after all.

"We've got to get you out there sometime. I bet you look great in a bikini," he says looking Charlie up and down like a melting ice cream cone he's trying to decide where to lick first.

What a dick. And she's eating it up.

*Shit, Charlie, I thought you had better taste than that.*

I'm going to need way more alcohol in my system to watch any more of this.

Leaving Charlie to fend off the sharks, I open the fridge in the kitchen, put my hand on a beer, and pause. With fatigue washing over my body every ten minutes, I'm not gonna make it home if I have even one beer.

Probably time to call it a night. Charlie seems to be doing just fine without my help and I could use an early night.

"Oh, goodie. You're getting me a drink!" that same high-pitched voice calls out to me.

I don't have the energy for my usual games tonight. "Here have mine. I'm gonna call it a night."

"Hi 'Gonna Call It A Night'. I'm Briiiiii."

It sounded like her name would go on forever.

"Good to meet you Bri, but I'm headed out."

"I'll walk you out."

I think I've become the melting ice cream cone, the way she eyes me. Not that I'd mind her spending a little time on the spot her eyes have paused on.

"Sure," I cave.

I wouldn't want to deny her any fun.

# 3

## GREYSON

Wait. You sent her home without sealing the deal?" Mick says as if it's an impossibility. In front of the large engine bay flanking the firehouse, Mick drags out the dumbbells and lays them next to the weight benches.

Mick Witter is the only guy at the Del Mar station besides Captain Jameson who's been here longer than I have. He may be all too willing to use his fireman status to benefit his game with the ladies, but he's the guy you want at your side when you go on direct attack at a structure fire. He's also the one guy who spends more time in the gym than I do, which is exactly why you want him fighting alongside you.

"Charlie get up in your head again?" he says.

Mick knows the deal with Charlie, but he likes busting my balls.

I stretch out my left shoulder, preparing it for my workout. "She didn't get in my head," I say, emphasizing the *get*.

Charlie is always in my head. She's the voice pushing me through the front door of every structure fire I've fought, the one reminding me to treat women kindly, and the voice screaming at Fuck Stick when he torments me.

Mick lifts a set of fifty-pound dumbbells and starts a set of step-ups with hammer curls.

"There aren't any bonuses for biggest biceps, you know," Junior says.

Junior Braddock is a rookie, but he can play with the big boys and he'll be one hell of a firefighter if he stays humble and keeps learning.

Without stopping, Mick calls back, "At thirty-five, I've got to have something to offer the ladies you lazy twenty-five-year-olds can't."

"How about a little chivalry and compassion?" Patrick tries to play. He's a kind soul but he'd probably never earn a girl's attention if it weren't for his Irish accent.

Junior and Mick look at each other and then bust up laughing.

"Yeah. And then we'll go braid each other's hair and talk about our feelings," Mick teases.

I give Patrick a conciliatory glance. "Mick. Get over here and spot me," I call out.

Laying back on the bench, I pop the bar off the rack and start a set of bench presses.

"Daaammmnn," Mick says leaning back for a better view around the garage door frame.

The firehouse sits on the edge of a bluff overlooking the San Dieguito Lagoon, Del Mar Fairgrounds, and the Pacific Ocean beyond. But the ocean is not what captured Mick's attention.

I finish my rep and sit up on the bench, glancing at where Mick is collecting fodder for his spank bank. When a blond woman prances up the driveway dressed in a short, red skirt and skin-baring black top, I jump up and try to cut her off before she gets too close to the unruly swine I work with.

"Bri. What are you doing here?" I say trying not to sound too annoyed.

"I think my phone is broken. It won't send texts to your phone. Like there's something that's eating up texts, but only to, like, certain people?"

It's not broken. I've received all eighteen of her texts over the last twenty-four hours ranging from friendly to angry to exasperated to, uh, let's just say, provocative.

I still haven't responded to a single one. I spent my whole Saturday doing absolutely nothing, trying to recover enough to make it back into work today.

"So I decided I'd bring you lunch instead." She holds out a picnic basket and bottle of wine.

"I can't really take lunch right now. We have to go over some more training and stuff."

I throw my arm over her shoulder and walk her back to her car before she can see any of their shenanigans. I put her in her car safely and send her off, promising I'll call when I want to see her again.

Returning to the bay, I lay back on the weight bench to finish my next set.

"You could have at least given her a ten-minute tour of the sleeping quarters." Mick's not the most subtle of guys.

"Shut up and spot me." I pull the bar off the rack and finish two full reps before my phone rings.

"Another booty call?" Mick asks.

I rack the weights when a photo of two sea turtles lazing in crystal blue water greets me. Charlie refuses to let me take a picture of her for my contacts. Instead, she insists on setting hers to random things she says will make me smile.

"You up for lunch? I never got to tell you about that new project." Charlie never bothers with the usual pleasantries to start a phone conversation. She gets to the point and gets off the phone with the fewest words possible.

I throw the phone on speaker, lay it on my stomach, and finish my set. "Just finishing a workout, so, yeah."

"I can grab some burritos and head over."

I push out a couple of reps while trying to figure out how to avoid that catastrophe.

"Tell her to bring one of those one-pound California burritos from Roberto's. I'd love to watch her eat that burrito nice and slow."

"Fuck off, Mick. That's Charlie." He's lucky my hands are busy with weights or he might have been reeling from a retaliatory junk-punch for that comment.

21

"Exactly." He covers his crotch, knowing what his comment might bring.

"Damn, Greyson. Two girls bringing you lunch in one day?" Junior says. "I don't know what you're doing in bed, but you've got to teach me, Sensei."

"What's all that about?" Charlie asks.

"I'll tell you at lunch. Kealani's in 20?"

"Sure." My phone turns black as she hangs up.

Mick assesses me, deciding if he should assist as I struggle to finish my last rep. "Good plan. Best not to let her get a look at me or your shot at bedding that girl would be gone forever."

I rub my shoulder trying to erase the building pain. "I'm not trying to bed her. Just don't want you anywhere near her."

I do my best to keep Charlie away from the Station. Away from the boys. It would be like throwing a baby seal to the sharks. It's not in the Rule Book, but protecting her from the dregs of the male species is definitely a precedent I try to follow. And, yes, that's Rule Book with a capital R and capital B.

Charlie came up with the Rule Book shortly after we met, and it's always been more of her thing. I don't think she has it written down—with a mind as sharp as Charlie's, she probably doesn't need to—but she references it often. It contains the policies we have to follow to keep our relationship going.

Oh, wait.

Rule #14. Never call it a relationship. People—*read, me*—might get confused. We are just friends or as she likes to say, Poe Friends.

Charlie thinks the meaning of Poe Friends should be blatantly obvious to anyone, but she forgets most of us aren't playing with the same IQ she's been blessed with. Most of us are mere mortals destined to walk this planet with mediocre brains and, thus, I've had to explain the cryptic phrase more times than I am willing to count.

A reference to Edgar Allen's most famous poem, The Raven, she says we're friends, "Nevermore" or Poe Friends for short. She thinks she's so clever. I think naming a friendship is the stupidest thing I've heard.

But it works. We've been friends for twelve years and not once has there ever been any confusion.

Which is exactly like Charlie. She comes up with these crazy ideas that are just out of this world, but they always come from this really sweet place and are always based on some scientific study or theory she has analyzed.

And they always, always work.

After doubting a few of her ideas, then seeing them turn out exactly as she had predicted, now I just go along with whatever nonsense she comes up with because Charlie is always right.

Not that I'd ever admit that to her face.

Five minutes early, I pull up to Kealani's a block off Highway 101 in Encinitas and wait inside where the rain forest mural and lava rock waterfall transport me back to Maui. Charlie and I found this place the week after our Maui trip a few years back. They serve plate lunch, which consists of the teriyaki meat of your choice next to one scoop of white rice and one of macaroni salad.

Charlie bounds in the door just moments later.

"The usual, guys?" Lelani, the owner, asks.

Lelani moved here from the Islands ten years ago with her husband who got stationed nearby in Oceanside. It was the first time she had left the islands and she was miserable. One year later, she opened Kealani's, named after her mother who taught her to cook, and I have yet to see her without a grin.

I nod at Leilani, passing over a twenty. After ordering, we slide into a table on the dirty sidewalk out front where the sweet scent of meat cooking mingles with the salt air.

"So, Bri shows up today at the station with wine and a picnic basket I'm sure was filled with handmade sandwiches with the crusts cut off and strawberries dipped in chocolate. Like I could just bail on work and have a picnic."

Leilani sets my plate of teriyaki steak and rice in front of me, and Charlie's rice and fries in front of her.

Charlie glances at her plate, then raises her brows at me.

"You mean because eating food outside on a sunny day during work is not allowed?"

"Okay, fine." I raise a forkful of teriyaki steak. "But after eighteen unreturned texts in twenty-four hours, nothing in her head said maybe I'm not interested? It's not like I slept with her or anything."

The onshore breeze flows down the small street, cooling us from the unusual heat which has come too early this June.

"Of course she's gonna do that. The way you treat her?"

She smothers her plate in four containers of teriyaki. She has to smother that stuff in sugar and soy to make up for the fact it's missing the most important part of plate lunch, meat.

"It is hard to resist these lips," I tease.

"Ugh. It's not that."

She shovels a huge bite of dripping rice, not bothering to finish chewing the bite before she starts back in on me. "You make yourself out to be the perfect man, all charming and slick. It's not their fault they fall for him and then wake up the next morning to find..."

"This loser?"

"Is that Fuck Stick talking or you, Greyson?" she admonishes, finally done with her mouthful of rice.

Fuck Stick is what Charlie's named the voice in my head that tends to spin out of control with anxiety at times. She says it's easier to tell it to shut the hell up if I give it a name. Who am I to argue with her wisdom?

As an added bonus, hearing her actually curse out loud makes me smile with delight.

I steal the only fry that escaped her teriyaki deluge from the corner of the plate and pop it in my mouth.

"They don't find a loser, Greyson, just a real guy who may be different than the guy they imagined you'd turn out to be when they met you. It's like seeing a carton of Ben and Jerry's on the worst day of your life. You see the marshmallow fluff and salted caramel and little chocolate chunks shaped like trouts," she says, almost moaning out the words in ecstasy. "So you buy it and you take it home and slip out of your work clothes and into your most comfortable trunks."

"So, for you, just a different pair of trunks than the ones you went to work in?"

"Whatever." She gives me a look of exasperation. "So you dish it up and sit on the back porch to eat it while watching the sunset over the water and hope of better days."

"So, I'm a bowl of ice cream? You're nuts, Charlie," I say throwing a dripping fry at her.

She dodges it. "That's exactly my point."

"You have a point?"

"I would have gotten to it already if you weren't so eager to discount it."

A car pulls into the street-side parking only a foot away from the table. Charlie laughs as the driver takes four attempts to wedge his yellow VW bus into the spot.

"Go ahead." I wave my hand over the table like I'm granting her my royal permission to keep bashing me.

"So this ice cream is going to change the day for you, really turn it around. And you finally take a bite."

"Finally."

"And it's Peanut. Butter. Ice. Cream!" she says trying to hold back her gag reflex. "You can't even swallow it."

"Oh, they always swallow."

"God, Greyson, gross." She hits me as hard as she can, but her hand hurts more than my shoulder if the grimace on her face is any indication.

"So I'm peanuts?" I ask.

Glad to know how she sees me—Charlie absolutely, vehemently, passionately, thoroughly hates nuts.

She says it started in the third grade when she was clueless enough to buy a peanut butter sandwich from the cafeteria after forgetting her lunch at home. Within minutes of polishing off the sandwich, she stood, took two steps, and launched the whole thing into the huge grey trash can in the middle of the cafeteria.

The rambunctious crowd fell silent, four hundred incredulous eyes gawking at little eight-year-old Charlie. It's no wonder she's not keen to recall the taste or even the smell. I had to give up eating peanuts within an hour of seeing her; even the smell on my breath was enough to make her crinkle up her nose and run for the hills.

"Hey, some girls like peanuts," I counter.

"But if the carton promises marshmallow and caramel and chocolate, it sure as hell should not be wrapped in Peanut. Butter. Ice. Cream. That's criminal."

"They're the ones putting all that RomCom, picture-perfect fantasy on me. I make no promises. Ever."

"I know you don't, but just make sure the peanut butter is in large enough print so they're not so shocked to wake up the next morning with the scent of peanuts all over them."

"Don't be ludicrous. I'm a gentleman. I always offer to let them shower after," I tease.

"God, it's always sex with you."

"What do you expect? I'm a guy."

"Oh, you're such a…"

Her voice drifts off as a business suit and heels walks by. One of the perks of this particular lunch spot, the Starbucks next door hosts a steady stream of execs from down the block.

I tip my head, taking in the full show as she heads down the sidewalk back to her office. I wonder if she has a couch in that office of hers. I could make excellent use of that.

I turn back to the table to find Charlie patiently waiting.

"You back on earth?" she asks to make sure I'm tracking with her. "Good. So I decided to take on the new project at work. It was my--"

I gather the trash, stand, and with a nod, ask, "walk?"

She stands, not missing a beat, "idea in the first place. I'm not going to let that Delta Bravo finish it."

We walk to the overlook at the end of D Street beside the stairs descending to the beach at the base of the cliffs.

"You have got to stop taking their shit, Charlie. You don't have to put up with it to be able to use your talents."

"I guess so," she tries to placate me.

"No, Charlie. You can't stay in a place like that forever. There's going to come a time when you have to demand it stops or just get the hell out of there."

She knows I'm right, but she thinks she's got to blend in at work. Like, if her colleagues figure out she's a girl, she'll never get ahead. So she puts up with way more shit than I'm comfortable with her encountering.

"And promise me you won't roll over every time that dick tries to walk all over you."

"I won't."

Two boys with tiny surfboards and giant smiles bound up the stairs chattering about the 'giant' waves they just carved. I guess when you're four feet tall any wave is overhead.

"You know what you should do? You should go into Glenn's office and demand to finish Nudge by yourself. It's your project, Charlie. You came up with the idea. You developed it for years. You deserve to finish it without that nut-packer."

"I know."

I raise my eyebrows to ask, *Do you?*

"I already committed. I can't go back on my word."

"I know. I know. Charlie never lies."

The overlook at the edge of the cliffs gives a clear view of every surf break from Swami's to the south up through Beacon's to the north. Not much but walled-up slop coming through today.

I turn, leaning my side against the railing. Even with crappy surf coming in, Charlie's filling with joy at the sight of the water.

"So, have you sung for your supper yet?" I ask, raising my eyebrows.

She scrunches up her nose and shakes her head. "Sung for my supper?"

"You know. The stoner from Indigo's party. He asked you to dinner if you sang for him."

A local guy in trunks and flip flops drags a wagon full of beach chairs, games, coolers, and toddlers to the overlook. Parking the wagon, he begins piling his paraphernalia onto his back in hopes of making it down the eighty-two stairs in one trip.

"He wasn't asking me out," Charlie purports.

"Uhh. Yeah, he was. Right there in front of everyone. And you laughed in his face. Boy's never going to recover. I think you turned him into a Monk."

"Whatever."

She seriously has no clue how guys look at her.

"How long did it take that other guy to try his luck?"

"What guy?"

"Octavio? October? O'Kylee? The guy you were making googly eyes at all night?"

"All night? You were there for twenty minutes before you bailed with, what was her name, Briiii," she says in an ungodly squeal while flipping her hair and making a face that would put Zoolander's Blue Steel to shame.

"So how long?" I repeat.

"He wasn't into me," she says with a completely straight face.

"All that, 'look at me, I'm a cool surfer dude', and the grinning and the 'let's get you into a bikini so I can check out the goods', not like he wasn't already doing that while you were fully clothed."

"Yeah. In my cutoffs and Vans. Super sexy. He was just being polite, trying to make small talk."

"And The Rationalizer is back," I tease.

This girl could explain away anything. Think you have some strange disease? She'll talk circles around you using research and statistics until she's got you convinced it's simple dehydration. You say you're dehydrated? She can convince you you should go get some blood work done to rule out cancer, type 2 diabetes, or some other crazy-ass disease I've never heard of before.

And when she turns those powers on herself, they go into overdrive.

"How come it is you can identify within seconds when a chick is into me or even when a guy likes Bex, but you can't see when a guy, or in this case, multiple guys, are into you?"

"Because I know guys don't see me that way."

She motions to the trunks that are long enough to cover her ass, but short enough to keep you thinking about what they do cover and the slate grey tank clinging to her chest enough to make it difficult to focus on her face.

*You have way more going on than you realize, Charlie.*

Motioning for us to walk back, I tease, "Whatever you say, Professor Sands."

# 4

## CHARLIE

*I*t has to have a kick-ass name, not some wishy-washy, girly-ass, flower-child name like Inspire or Whisper," Dirk says in a mocking, wilty voice.

"It does have a woman's voice, you know," I fire back.

After three solid weeks of working non-stop with Dirk, I can say with certainty it has been the low point of my career.

I look up synonyms for 'remind' to scrape up other ideas. "Fine. What about Jolt, or Hint, or Twit," I suggest.

We've been working on names for the app for the last three days and we haven't even verified this thing works.

"More like Twat," he says with a howl, standing behind the podium in front of the large screen in the Media Corner.

From his dominant position on stage, you'd think he was talking to a room full of colleagues, but I'm the only one sitting on any of the six lime green Pottery Barn Teen sectionals lining the one wall this room has.

"What about Urge?" I growl.

"The only urge I want to hear from a woman's mouth is the urge to suck my cock."

From his poorly executed sexual jokes, you'd think he was

leading a Chapter meeting at the Alpha Pi Alpha house discussing which pissy-yellow domestic beer to serve at their next house party.

"I need a break."

When I interviewed for this job, Glenn asked if I could handle the testosterone-filled workplace without them having to make changes. I rambled on about how I had grown up working in all-male surf shops and that most of my friends were guys and how I'm not easily offended.

Little did I know, he meant he encouraged the frat house antics in "his bros." What kind of boss, no, what kind of man, over the age of twenty-two even uses that word?

On my way to the bathroom, I shuffle by Brad and the Thad who—there's so many of them, I can only distinguish by them by their strange traits—the one who is the spitting image of the big asshole brother from Weird Science.

He's lost in a game of Grand Theft Auto in the School Yard, an open room with a gaming system surrounded by chalkboard walls meant to record the grand ideas we would generate while tuning out with video games. Most of the time, though, chalk drawings of boobs and giant penises fill the green walls like some seventh-grade textbook.

Big&Lime is in an open warehouse just half a mile from the water in Carlsbad decorated like the ideal bedroom of a millionaire, teenage sports fan. The entire thing resembles an old gym with exposed wood beams and a row of enormous windows below. TV's playing every single televised sporting event in the world cover one wall.

The Thad who only codes at his treadmill desk wrote a program to automatically tune each TV to a different sporting event, from the familiar basketball and football to the more obscure sports like Ultimate Frisbee and springboarding, a bizarre example of athleticism where athletes use axes to chop wedges into totem poles that they use to climb higher only to chop the next wedge. That's just one of the completely useless sports facts I've learned since working here.

I cross the floor of the warehouse scattered with desks occupied by more bros and more Thads. When I notice the scoreboard on the far wall displaying download stats of every one of Big&Lime's apps, I flinch. Not because of the stats, but because of my checkered history with this particular scoreboard.

Glenn designed it to wail every day at exactly 3:11, declaring it Push Up Party time. I know it's coming, but every single time it buzzes, I jump and scream like the grim reaper has savagely appeared before my desk. And every time it happens, an entire warehouse of guys howl, mocking my scream like they haven't done it sixteen-thousand times before.

But when I pound out my requisite seventeen push-ups and am back at my desk working again while they struggle to push out number five, I find it in my heart to have pity on their poor, weak souls.

I lay my hand on the bathroom door and knock on the cherry-red sheet of paper over the Women's Room sign saying, "THAD's ROOM."

Since there were more Thads working here than women, they thought it only fair the Thads get the small, second bathroom. I learned quickly this wasn't an impotent threat designed to make my life more unbearable, when I walked in to find one Thad on the pot with the bright orange stall door wide open, chatting with another Thad, junk in hand, pissing in the sink.

When no one responds to my knock, I enter, snatching a latex glove out of a box I stashed behind the full-size Ms. Pacman arcade machine against the far wall and turn on the sink.

"Braver than you believe. Stronger than you seem. Smarter than you think," I mutter to myself in the mirror and take a slow, deep breath.

When I came up with the idea for Nudge, I had envisioned using AI to listen to the environment around me looking for signals indicating my willpower might be challenged soon. The app would then send texts to encourage me to stay the course.

If I was trying to watch what I ate, it could listen to Jenny tell me Sweet Treats, the bakery next door, "has totally orgasmic cupcakes." It would sense she might invite me there soon and text me a line to help me decline politely.

**Nudge: You could tell her, "I've heard those cupcakes are absolutely delicious, but, I cannot eat another drop of food. Now tell me about that new puppy of yours."**

Or if it hears you mention an ex's name...

**Nudge: You're allowed to miss him, but I promise you're better off. Now go conquer the world. There's nothing sexier than a woman who doesn't need a man to be happy.**

Then it would send you a pic of when you felt most fierce and one last text.

**Nudge: P.S. Rebounds are great when you're ready.**

After just three weeks, Dirk has turned Nudge into something that will remind me to do push-ups every hour or pound out a nine-mile run. If I miss a scheduled workout, a Drill Sargent screams in my face, calling me a douche junkie, pube nugget, or scrotum stain, phrases that took Dirk three full workdays to settle on.

In the synthetic turf-lined counter shaped like a rolling golf green lie three giant holes for sinks. I scrub my hands in the middle one as I glance above the mirrors to the carefully stenciled, "Keep your eye on the ball."

At least this quote is pertinent, unlike the one in the gym emblazoned over a mural of the Malibu lineup filled with seven surfers on the same wave. "One drop in is an accident, two is rude, but three is a twatable offense."

What Dirk and I have come up with is not exactly like what I envisioned Nudge to be—hell, it couldn't be any farther from its original intent—but it technically came from my idea. And if it gets big, I can use it to buoy me up to the next level.

I turn off the sink with the glove, dry my hands, toss everything into the green trashcan at the bottom of a golf flag. and take a slow, cleansing breath before opening the door to return to the jungle.

Not two steps out the door, Weird-Science-Asshole-Thad knocks into my shoulder on the way to Thad's Room.

"Glenn said Lowest Man had to do a PCWC going back to 2012," he says while trying to smother a laugh. "Oh wait, you're not even on the totem bowl, you're just a chick."

*Totem Bowl.* I don't know how a guy this brainless manages to tie his shoes, let alone earn his living programming, and yet he is Glenn's Go-To-Guy.

"Really. And what's a PCWC?" I play along.

"Post Comment Word Count. And you call yourself a coder? Damn, Charlie. How do you not know that?"

He turns to Treadmill-Desk-Thad and shouts, "Dude, this chick doesn't know what a PCWC is."

A cacophony of Thad laughter echoes across the warehouse. I work with a whole gaggle of dipwads.

"Well, since you're so good at them, Thad, can you explain it to a simple girl like me?"

"You count how many times a word appears in the comments in each of our posts on Instagram going back to the start of the account. Shouldn't take you more than eight to ten hours," he says pushing Thad's Room's door open.

He turns back to me. "Oh yeah. Glenn wants it by midnight tonight."

A deep rumble and a loud, "Shiiiit yeah. Just in time," comes from the bathroom before the door finally closes.

And that's my cue to go to lunch before I explode on these guys with a lot of what Thad just exploded in there.

I swipe my bag from my desk and climb the stairs to the roof-top deck. We share it with the whole building, but most days it lies empty. With bright turquoise striped cushions on the rattan outdoor sofa and barstools pulled up to a counter at the railing with an ocean view, it is my quiet respite from the testosterone-infused sports world below.

When I have projects of my own, I do most of my work up here for some peace and quiet away from the frat house, but Dirk would turn lobster red after seconds in the sunshine. So in the past three weeks, I only get to enjoy lunch up here.

I slide my phone onto the counter and dial Greyson. "Tell me I'm smart enough," I plead.

"Charlie, you're the smartest human I've ever met. Don't let those dickheads ever make you think differently."

Hearing him say that helps a little, but how can I take his assessment of intelligence seriously since he is so far off about his own brain power?

Greyson's one of the smartest humans I've ever met, but his struggles with school painted a different picture in his mind. He struggled in classrooms filled with forty students and teachers who hadn't changed their teaching methods since Tom Curren was the World Surfing Champ.

Knowing Grey had to keep a 2.5 GPA to remain eligible and lead a struggling baseball team to the C.I.F. championships for a record fourth season in a row, the coach threw tutors at him left and right, but none of the tutors took long enough to find out what was making school so challenging.

When you have a constant stream of self-flagellatory thoughts running through your head all day, it's difficult to hear what the teacher is saying.

"Thanks, Grey. I just needed to hear it."

"What'd they do now?"

"Nothing more than what their very nature constrains them to do, but I'd love to forget about it, if only as long as lunch."

I take a big bite of my tuna sandwich and, damn, it is superb. I took the time to add some diced red bell peppers and fresh parsley like Greyson suggested yesterday. "You are so right," I say.

"No shit." He laughs. "But what, specifically, was I right about?"

"The sandwich. It's turning around my day."

"Nice. You up for a run tonight?"

I throw back a Diet Dr Pepper to wash down the handful of pretzel sticks I shoved in my mouth while he spoke. "I've got to go out with Bex tonight, double date at some bar, but I'd really rather go for an LSD if you're up for it. Let me see if I can get out of it and I'll buzz you back as soon as she bothers to text me back."

An LSD is a Long Slow Distance run. Well, long for me. I'm not really a runner, but the cardio helps my paddling endurance when the waves are small or crappy. Most of our runs are the longest of my week, but they are simply recovery runs for Grey, a short slow run to loosen up his muscles after the real miles he runs alone.

"Let's do it," he exclaims.

"I have six minutes left to polish off this sandwich, so—"

"I'll let you go."

"Don't be crazy. I just wanted you to know why you're only getting uh-huh's while you tell me about your morning for the next six minutes. Fires, the boys, resting heart rate, go."

"I hit fifty-two this morning. A new low and a house record. Mick's getting close, but he has no patience for crawling to the heart rate monitor in the rig. That guy has no patience for anything. Kills him with the ladies, too. He's so eager he comes off as an ass. I keep telling him, you've got to play the long game, but he tells me he gets plenty."

"Mmm." I polish off the sandwich in four bites and throw back the rest of the DDP.

"You sound worse than a reef shark at a feeding frenzy. Seriously, Charlie, it may be time to pick up some manners."

"I'll put it on my To-Do List first thing when I get back downstairs."

"I'll swing by at four. That give you enough time?" he asks.

I collect the remnants of my meal and toss them in the trashcan on the way to the stairs. "Yep."

Phone in my pocket, with my hand on the door, I pause, take a deep breath, and head back into the frat house. Stopping at the first landing, I tap out a quick plea to Bex.

"Hey. Work's really beating me up today. I don't think I have it in me to be around people tonight. Raincheck?"

I hit the bottom of the stairs and decide to go right back up for a quick workout. After two more sets of stairs, and making sure no one has a basketball in hand, I drop into my desk to figure out the whole Glenn PCWC thing.

My desk sits right under the basketball hoop against the back wall of the building. If you move all the desks to the side, you could play, but the bros will often shoot from anywhere, anytime so it helps to check before sitting in the rebound zone.

The wall behind my desk also holds the dartboard. Most of the time I'm safe from the line of fire, but when the Thad with the black horn-rimmed glasses stands up to throw darts, I take a well-timed snack break. I don't need a video of me with a dart sticking out of my head posted online, and they would totally be the guys to grab their cameras instead of trying to help me out.

I pick up the mango-colored piece of coral from my desk and flip it around in my fingers. There's an excellent chance Glenn didn't actually ask me to do a PCWC or that a PCWC doesn't even exist.

No way I'm wasting eight hours on a futile task. I'm tempted to bail on it, but if he really did ask, and I don't do it, I can wave aloha to this job and I need this job and a good reference to ever get ahead in this male-dominated world.

I plunk the coral down next to a silver dollar-sized drawing of a sea turtle I made from Shrinky Dinks last weekend. The trinket is the only other decoration on my desk, in accordance with Rule #47 of the Fitting Into the Male Programming World; avoid displays of femininity of any kind. This encompasses desk decoration, wardrobe, and the severely mocked displays of emotion or "being hysterical."

Why on earth would I count words for eight hours when I can write a program to do the work for me? In under an hour, I've finished the code and run it.

Glancing at the results, I quote Luke 6:9 to myself. "Someone takes away your coat, do not withhold your shirt."

I rewrite the code to do more, much more, then compose a message on Slack to Glenn with my results.

> To: Glenn Kratzcy
> From: Charlie Sands
> SUBJECT: PCWC assignment from Thad B
>
> Thad B relayed your instructions to do a Post Comment Word Count on the @Big&Lime Instagram account. I attached the results.
>
> I also wrote a piece of code making the job no longer necessary. It will run nightly and post results to a private channel on Slack called PCWC. I can adapt this to also include our Facebook and Twitter pages if you find that info useful.
>
> Charlie

With that, I am out the door.

Tomorrow, I will have to deal with whatever hair-brained ideas Dirk comes up with working by himself this afternoon, but I can't do another productive thing today.

# 5

## CHARLIE

My drive home along Highway 101, with its views of the water and local shops, provides a calming distraction from work stress. Bex finally texts.

I pull over at the parking lot at Dip-In-The-Road to read it.

We call it that for obvious reasons. Highway 101 goes from atop cliffs to sea level and back up to another cliff creating a...

Dip. In. The. Road.

It's a fun little surf spot, though I avoid it when Greyson's around. Not one of his favorite places.

**Bex: NO WAY!!!!!!**

Always the over-user of the grand exclamation point, that one. Her tone, even through the phone, says there's no way I'm getting out of this one.

**Bex: You're NOT bailing on me**

I check out the surf for a while before succumbing to my fate. The waves are blown out this late in the afternoon, but there might be enough swell to be fun tomorrow morning when the winds have died down.

**Bex: Like it's that hard to be around people Charlie**

She doesn't understand she can write more than one thought

in a text. Or maybe she thinks so slowly she's not convinced she'll have another.

**Bex: Besides, I have a surprise for you**

Hopefully, I'll be in a better mood after my run with Grey.

**Charlie: Fine, I'll go if you're gonna be so demanding**

I tap out, but then erase it. It will only make the night that much worse if Bex is in a nasty mood.

**Charlie: Looking forward to the surprise**

The drive down the 101 isn't doing its job of de-stressing me with summer in full swing now. I got stuck behind four, count them, four, different cars who decided the fastest way to the beach was waiting in the only lane of traffic for a parking spot currently occupied by an entire family of tourists trying to shake every grain of sand off each toy, bathing suit, towel, and foot before getting in their car to leave. They could have walked from a spot a mile away in less time than they spent waiting for this one.

When I finally make it home, I run in the front door, throwing a, "Sorry. Two min," to Greyson, who is already charming Indigo's group of beautiful friends in the kitchen.

"Take your time. I'm happy here."

Such an attention whore.

I strip and tug on a pair of black running shorts and a black and white, floral print sports bra. I redo my ponytail, gathering all the stray hairs who wriggled free during the day, as I jog down the stairs, passing Grey on my way to the back door.

"Let's do this," I say without slowing down.

"Well, ladies, I have to go put in some miles. I do hope you'll be here when I return," Grey coos to the girls.

I stop at the steps and turn, waiting for him to finish being Public Greyson and become Private Grey.

He drags his shirt over his head, putting on a show for his new admirers, and tosses it on the railing before turning to flash them his winning smile while every single girl stands frozen gaping at the beautiful architecture of his body.

He has a well-earned swimmer's body, that beautiful V-shape, wide, chiseled shoulders and back, a solid chest over strong abs, and a thin waist. He's always been lean from the countless miles he ran getting ready for the major league draft, but the thousands of meters of swimming he added after he stopped playing baseball have turned his body into a perfectly shaped mass of muscle.

The only visible imperfection is the alabaster white stripe on each thigh right below his running shorts. He spends most of his time in the sun surfing in longer trunks, so his tan resembles a reflective band runners wear at night to make them more visible, but his reflective band is blinding in broad daylight.

"You have got to buy longer running shorts," I tease.

We warm up with a solid half-mile of jogging in the soft sand.

"I like the way these breathe." He flips the edges up revealing the slit rising all the way to the waistband.

"You are such an old man."

We transition to the more compacted wet sand near the water for at least a mile or so.

"I got a good one for today," he says over the sound of the wind.

"Song of the day?"

"Yep. This one's perfect."

"Don't hold out on me."

I hop over a piece of sharp green glass. Last thing I need is a lecture from my Endocrinologist on how dangerous it is for a diabetic to run barefoot on the sand.

"*Mmm Bop*."

I nearly trip as the laughter doubles me over. "*Mmm Bop? That's the song?*"

"It's funny and happy and guaranteed to make you laugh. Isn't that exactly what the Song of the Day is for?"

We've been doing the Song of the Day since the first 5K I ran with Grey years ago. Around mile two, I was ready to quit, bitching about why people do this on purpose, why they think torturing themselves is fun, and why on earth I had now become one of those stupid, stupid people.

Grey started singing, "*When I wake up, well I know I'm gonna be, I'm gonna be the man who wakes up next to you.*"

Runners next to us turned their heads, searching for the man singing in the midst of such pain, which of course brought out Public Greyson, so the singing got even louder. *"And if I get drunk, well I know I'm gonna be, I'm gonna be the man who gets drunk next to you."*

I couldn't help but laugh, and that laugh took away a bit of the pain. The cadence of the song quickened my pace and soon, I wasn't cursing the day I signed up for this race. I was smiling and pushing forward.

When he got to the line, *"But I would walk five hundred miles,"* every runner around us was singing as loud as their labored breathing would allow. After that, it became a habit. I even wrote it in the Rule Book.

Rule #36: It is imperative Greyson never show up to a run without a Song of the Day.

For every run since then, he has come prepared with a new song. Some he would share at the beginning of a run so I would have something to look forward to. But for the really good ones, he would wait to surprise me right when I needed it.

"Where on earth did you come up with that song?" I raise my stride to avoid a wave.

"This girl I went out with last night. I asked her what kind of music she listened to and she says Hansen. Hansen!"

"The blond mop heads?" I say trying not to lose my breath laughing.

"Right? And she goes on and on about how *Mmm Bop* changed her life when she first heard it."

"How old could she have been when it came out? Seven or eight? How life-changing could a song be at eight."

"I said the first time she heard it. She wasn't even born when it came out. She saw it on one of those Remember When shows a year ago."

"Another infant scholar, I see."

"She may not have had stellar taste in music, but her taste in lingerie was phenomenal."

"Ewwww." I bump him midstride and it takes a few paces for him to recover. "You screwed around with a girl who thinks Hansen is revolutionary music? Don't you have any standards?"

"It's not like she had to have it playing in the background while we did."

We run a few paces while I picture Hansen singing like Marvin Gaye, their blond hair flowing back and forth, matching the timing of their swaying hips. Not something I want to conjure up again.

"We were, you know... and I bend down to suck the inside of her elbow and she just went nuts. I didn't know that was such an erogenous zone for you girls. Did you?"

I swear he tells me those details just to embarrass me. Like a little game for him, let's see how quickly I can get her to blush and hit me.

I am a fierce competitor, though. I'm excellent at not showing my discomfort. Most of the time, I can distract him with a question about the girl he doesn't know like, "Why'd she have to leave in such a hurry this morning?" or "So what did she say she does for a living?" Sometimes, it's as easy as asking, "What did she say her first name was again?"

"Seriously, Charlie. Is that an erogenous spot for you?" he prods.

*Uhh, how the hell would I know?*

As the stairs at the base of 30th Street come into view, or, more specifically, the corner of the stair's handrail, the official finishing line of our 5K run, we both instinctively speed up dropping the subject I desperately want to avoid.

I guess today took more out of me than I realized because Grey beats me cleanly. At least this means I didn't really lie to Bex about being tired. I hate not being honest with my friends.

At the top of the stairs, the beach shower stands in a river-rock wall. I turn it on and we dip our feet in the stream.

Greyson "mistakenly" bumps me, making me stumble full-on into the shower stream.

"Tex!"

I tear Tex, my insulin pump, from my shorts and shake the water from his screen. He's waterproof—he could even take a full dip in the pool with no problems—but I don't think Greyson knows.

He hurries over to assess the damage. "I'm so sorry, Charlie. I totally forgot. Does it still work?"

With his back to the spray, I force my eyes to tear up.

"Aww, Sands. Please don't cry."

"Tex is a Gremlin, Grey," I say in a menacing voice. "You get him wet and he goes crazy."

I put both my hands on his chest.

And shove.

He stumbles back into the spray, but not before capturing both my wrists dragging me back into the water with him. He lumbers through the water and up against the bumpy river rock embedded in the wall, catching me as I crash into his chest.

My eyes shoot up to his face, trying to discern why he hasn't dropped his hands from my waist yet.

His gaze flickers down to my mouth momentarily before I'm able to push myself off him.

"We should go. I'm sure Bex is freaking out that I'm not dressed and ready for our lovely date tonight."

I slide my hand down the tubing coming out of my shorts, until I hit Tex, dangling from the end of his leash. Securing him again in my waistband, I try to avoid reliving the water dripping off Grey's chest.

We make our way down the alley leading to my house in an arduous silence. This is the exact reason we have the Half-Foot Rule. Any girl gets within six inches of Grey and he's thrown off balance, compelled to mount them, and he doesn't know how to halt it.

Whether he likes them or not. Whether he thinks they're a decent person and they might have a future or not. You get within half a foot, you get ambushed.

"*Mmmbop, ba duba dop,*" Greyson busts out more Hansen.

I finish the chorus with him.

"I hate to admit it, but I actually like that song," I say.

We walk, dripping, along the alley, laughing with the endorphins of a hard run coursing through our veins.

In front of us, the door of an obsidian black Tesla opens skyward. Bex's voice hits me before she even gets out.

"Seriously? We are supposed to be at The Nolan in like four minutes. You know how I like to be the first one there on a night like this. Gives me time to size up the competition before settling in on my guy," she instructs.

"Sorry. I needed to work out some stress with a Greyson run."

"Isn't that what sex is for?" she asks.

"Hey, I'm good either way," Greyson offers up.

"I think I'll stick with running," I say rolling my eyes at him like an annoyed teenager.

I lead them through the front door and bound up the stairs to shower and change.

"Put something cute on, Charlie. How you look affects my chances of success tonight. And not just a t-shirt from the floor. An actual top," she yells as I shut the door behind me, pretending not to hear.

After a two-minute shower and spending at least four minutes arguing with myself about what constitutes cute and why I even care about it, I put on a lightweight, steel grey top covered in a pale grey palm-tree-and-parrot print with a conservative v-neckline. It hits slightly above my hips and is the only "top" I own.

Glancing in the mirror, I squeeze some tinted moisturizer onto my fingers, wiping it on my face like sunscreen.

Sitting in an open, black canvas tote on the counter, a black tube with NARS written in skinny white Serif font catches my eye. I've seen Bex apply it gingerly with a brush to her cheeks or eyes or some part of her face before. She wouldn't mind if I borrowed some. She did say look cute.

Pulling off the lid, I swipe it across my cheeks, blending with my fingertips. My colorless eyes. Why not? I swipe it there also, remembering to blend.

"Good enough," I say as I breeze out the door.

Coming down the stairs, I am greeted by flirty giggling that can't belong to Bex; she can barely stand to be in the same room as Greyson. I pause two stairs up as Indigo and her star-struck actresses file out. "Bye, Greyson," they chirp in unison.

"Sorry to interrupt your rehearsal," I whisper to Indigo as she trails behind them.

"If only I could get them to read lines with the enthusiasm they show for flirting with Greyhound over there."

Without his eye candy fawning over him, Grey rests against the island with nothing to look at but me.

I turn back to Indigo, "That bad?"

"I may be looking at recasting," she shrugs and follows her thespians out the door.

As I take the last few stairs, I slip my phone wallet between my hip and the waistband of my neon yellow shorts. I learned the hard way, after two shattered screens, the pockets on these are so worn out they couldn't hold a slip of paper, let alone my phone.

Greyson mutters something under his breath that sounds a lot like, "Damn, that's sexy," but there is no way he just said that.

I check behind me for one of the stunning actresses returning because she forgot her purse or her three brain cells.

"That's your idea of cute?" Bex scolds, halting my search for Greyson's eye candy.

I turn and tug at the hem of my shirt to show it off. "I put on a top."

"I wouldn't throw her out of bed for eating crackers," Greyson tries to defend me. He will say anything to contradict Bex.

"No wonder you haven't kissed anyone since eighth grade. Would it really hurt to put in a little effort?" she pokes.

Greyson's face is in wild disbelief. He can't conceive of a human lasting that long. He certainly never has. Unless you count the two months he was MIA while recovering from Aubrey Graves, though, I suppose, he could have found plenty of willing participants on the road.

I glare at Bex as if to say, "Thanks for sharing that embarrassing detail."

I didn't want it this way, the barren wasteland of my love life, the opportunity just hasn't presented itself all that often. I may not have chosen for it to be this way, but, now that it is my reality, I like being able to tell my future husband he is the only man I've kissed since I was thirteen. I think it's kind of sweet.

However, even if I may view it as a strength, there's no way I'm letting Bex know that.

"At least it didn't take me till eighteen to start," I shoot back at her trying to take that look off Grey's face.

"Eighteen, really?" Greyson takes the bait.

"Whatever. I'm making up for lost time and I'm taking you with me," she says linking her arm in mine and dragging me to the front door. "We have boys to meet. I've hooked us up with a double date guaranteed to check off this goal for us."

I turn back to Grey with a plead for him to save me from the impending shitshow.

He throws up his hands and shrugs.

Dammit.

I'm going to have to go through with our most ludicrous Summer Goal yet.

# 6

## CHARLIE

By late August, we have made no progress on our Summer Goal. Unless you count going on unending, horrific double-dates as progress. Bex has doubled down in her efforts to succeed and decided it will all come together at Brendon and Delilah's wedding in Santa Barbara this weekend.

Brendon was in Grey's class, two years ahead of Bex and I, at Los Al High School and was the guy who would do anything. Dare him to streak the C.I.F. Finals baseball game in only a sock and some body paint? He'd do it. Ask him to rub a plate of sardines all over his chest and climb in the shark tank at Sea World? Yep, he did that, too.

When senior year got too stressful and everyone started idly talking about skipping the whole college thing and running away to seek an endless summer of warm water and unparalleled waves, he bought a plane ticket that evening. None of us expected it would take ten years on the road and a very special woman to bring him back home.

As I'm perched at the kitchen table, halfway through my bowl of Honeycomb cereal, a loud rhythmic thumping interspersed with cursing comes wafting down the hall.

"What is going on?" I shout as I take another bite.

"Blimey O'Reilly. This bloody suitcase won't make it down the stairs. It's all cocked up now," Bex shouts.

Bex has come under the insane impression using British expletives is somehow more refined. I think it just makes her sound like the local hobo off his meds.

She gets to the bottom of the stairs with one final thud, and a suitcase large enough to hide a body appears in the hall.

"We're only going for two days, Bex. How could you possibly need so much stuff?"

Bex drops the handle, letting the luggage flop to the floor, and saunters to the counter to pick up an orange. She leans back against the counter as she drags her acrylic talons through the rind.

"Well, duh. I need one outfit to change into when we get there; I hate the feel of stale car on me. Then two dress choices for the wedding. In overcast light, periwinkle is so my color. But the red is perfect in the sun or any blue-based artificial indoor light." She splits the orange in half and pulls off the first wedge. "Then there's the whole next day and makeup and shoes and my straightener, curler, dryer."

She pops an orange wedge into her mouth, looking around for my bags.

"I can help you bring yours down?" she says.

I size up the faded, olive green backpack sitting in shame in the shadow of her mammoth "overnight bag."

Bex darts over to the bag and begins rifling through its contents. She stands and takes a deep breath before turning to me.

"Charlie, we're really far into August. And, yes, I know that, since we graduated, the final deadline to accomplish our Summer Goal has been extended to the sciency end of summer instead of the start of school. But, still. We only have four weeks left. Four. Bloody. Weeks."

"I'm confused," I say, shoveling the last few bites of Honeycomb into my mouth.

"Charlie, a wedding is the perfect place to meet a marriageable man. Which means you need to look like a woman. And a woman needs way more stuff than that tiny, army-reject bag you drag with you everywhere."

I take my cereal bowl to the sink and rinse it.

"I totally knew you'd do this," she sighs. "So I packed a dress and shoes for you, too."

I plaster on a big smile and say thanks, then turn back and set my bowl on the drying rack.

"Bex," I say, still hiding my face from her. "Is it weird? You know, going back after..." I let my words fade.

"After what?" she says clueless.

I would love, just once, for Bex to understand what I mean without having to actually say it.

"After visiting her there so often? This will be the first time I've been back since..."

"Not really. It's gonna be so much fun scouting for boys, fueled by free champagne."

She bounces to the trashcan to toss the orange rind before the energy drops out of her voice. "Oh, hey, Greyson."

Greyson nods his head in return and wanders over to me. "You okay?"

I school my face before I spin around, "I'm fine. Why?"

He searches my face for my tell. "You want to leave her here?" he whispers.

I brighten at his plan and the comfort of having at least have one friend who can read me without explanation.

"Can you imagine the fallout?" I ask.

We both laugh.

By the time Greyson guides his truck north onto the 5 freeway, I've left all my gloomy thoughts behind. We have a wedding to celebrate, an old friend to hang out with and I'm planning on having a great time.

"Here. Plug this in so I can play some music," Bex pleads, passing her phone forward.

"No. Way," Grey and I say in unison.

I hit the Charlie button on Grey's radio to connect my phone and pull up my music. Donning my most mischievous smile, I say, "I made a playlist."

"Please tell me it's not filled with stupid '60s rock and punk," Bex whines as she slumps down in the back seat, pouting.

"It's not filled with '60s rock and punk," I parrot.

I crank up the volume and hit play.

"*Well, it's been ten years and a thousand tears, And look at the mess I'm in,*" the stereo croons.

"Always the sentimentalist, Charlie," Greyson says as the Social Distortion song continues.

"*Take away, take away, Take away this ball and chain, I'm lonely and I'm tired, And I can't take any more pain,*" Grey and I sing along while Bex moans.

When the song ends, I am convinced this will be an amazing trip. "I thought a themed playlist would be just what this road trip needed," I say.

I turn to Bex in the back seat. "Don't worry, I put in some Justin Timberlake just for you."

She perks up. "Thanks, Babe."

I didn't bother to tell her it was *Bye Bye Bye* from when he was with *Nsync; I want to see her disappointment firsthand when it blares from the speakers.

The green hills and wildflowers bordering the freeway in San Diego fade into cold cement soundwalls and unimaginative buildings crowding the road as we enter Orange County. When stop to pick up Connor, another of our high school friends, he is sitting on the porch of the 1950s ranch house set right in the middle of two mega-mansions.

Rossmoor is an older tract-home neighborhood, but it was built before HOA's and matching house colors. In the ensuing decades, a lot of money has moved in and, without the regulations of an H.O.A. board's oversight, they have rebuilt a good portion of the houses into god-awful palaces without any regard to style or taste. An Italian villa sits right next to a sleek modern estate. The older homes in between remind me of the old man's house in *Up* wedged between the houses time didn't leave behind.

"Connor still lives with his mom and dad? Like in the basement?" Bex scoffs as she slides on her black, strappy heels and pours out of the truck.

"They don't have basements in Rossmoor, Bex. And you should probably wait to judge Connor," Greyson scolds, walking around the front to greet Connor with a manly, back-slapping hug.

"You know what I mean, though," she continues as we step out of the truck. "Is he all holed up in the garage with his Apple 2E and Star Wars dolls surrounded by hamster tubes running all over the rafters?"

"Who has hamster tubes in the rafters?" Connor asks taking his time appraising what five years have done to Bex's body.

"Uh, you." She snickers, pointing to the garage. "You may want to put away your big boy dolls before your mommy makes you clean your room."

Somehow I forgot how polite Bex can be.

In the ten years since high school, Connor has gone from insecure surf rat willing to do anything to garner a girl's attention to a confident, well-built version of the action figure Bex is so eager to denigrate him for owning. Now, he doesn't have to do a thing except exist to command every girl's attention.

"Bex? I don't live with my parents," he says patiently. "I figured since I was in town I should stop by and visit before we left."

"Sure you did," Bex says unconvinced.

Connor shrugs, no longer a slave to her opinion of him.

Bex studies him, trying to decide if his knockout looks and king-sized biceps are enough for her to overlook his lack of earning power.

Greyson leans over to speak in her ear. "Connor just closed on a huge house right on the beach in Wilmington."

This catches her attention.

"You have a picture?" Bex asks, not wanting to be lured in with a plastic worm instead of the genuine article.

Connor pulls his phone out and taps the screen a few times, then holds the phone out for her.

Bex lays her hand on his bicep as she leans over to check out the pic of Connor on the broad front steps of a three-story, waterfront home with his arm around his Rhodesian Ridgeback dog. Her gaze moves to the scruff on his face as he swipes to the next pic. In return, she pops her chest into his eye line.

"Easy there, Bex. He's got a fiancé," Greyson admonishes.

Connor returns his phone to his pocket and hoists his duffel bag onto his shoulder. "Ready?"

Greyson and Connor move to the truck as Bex, ever the opportunist, looks like she swallowed the entire Cheshire cat. "It's all fair game until there's a ring."

I don't think she realizes his fiancé is the girl he's been in love with since the fifth grade and dated since the seventh. They grew up together, did the grown-up thing of letting each other go off to chase their own dream, and then came back together when they both, independent of the other, took their dream jobs in Wilmington.

He proposed a few months later.

Bex doesn't stand a chance, though I suspect she was only playing with him to prove she could.

Connor and Bethany's story only makes me feel more lost in my own life. I pray he doesn't ask me what I've been up to in the last few years. My answer would be pathetic.

Let's see. I have a job I hate with people who treat me like I am brainless, no love life to speak of, and no hope of ever finding one. Hell, I can't even figure out how to wrangle a second date with any of the dozen or so guys Bex has roped into a first date with me this summer.

I open the pickup's back door, but Bex shoves me into the front seat so she can have the back with Connor.

"You'll have to forgive the music, Connor," Bex apologizes. "Charlie has built her anti-love playlist and won't relinquish control to anyone."

"*Girlfriend in a coma, I know, I know, it's serious,*" Morrissey belts out.

"The Smiths. Nice choice, Charley," Connor applauds.

We spend the first hour catching up and listening to my playlist of anti-wedding songs. *Kiss Off* by the Violent Femmes, *I Hate Everything About You* by 3 Days Grace, *I Wanna Be Sedated* by Ramones, and, just to show I'm not entirely heartless, a little sappy, Sinead O'Connor with *Nothing Compares*. I'm leaving it up to Providence to play that one when the moment is right.

"I can't believe Brendan's getting married." Greyson slows a bit in the ever-present LA traffic. "Hell, I can't believe you're getting married, Connor."

"I know," Bex spins a piece of hair in her fingers as she stares out the window at the passing Ron Cook VW billboard. "I always thought I'd be the first in our group to get married."

She smacks her gum. "At least I know I won't be last. That's Charlie's gig."

*Tell me how you really feel, Bex.*

Connor and Greyson avoid that landmine. I doubt they want to jump in the middle of a chick fight.

Or maybe they just want to watch.

But there will be no fight today. I've stopped letting her comments rile me up a long time ago. I tend to follow Mark Twain's advice, "Never argue with an idiot. They will drag you down to their level and beat you with experience."

"So, is that what the Summer Goal has been about?" I turn to gauge the extent of lying in her answer to my question. "Making sure you don't leave me behind in your race to the alter?"

"No way. It's been about finding men we can both be around without killing ourselves." She tips her head towards Grey.

With a silent head shake, I try to persuade Conner it's not like that, without throwing fuel on the Bex-Grey feud.

"So, let me see if I have this right," Connor teases. "Your goal this summer is to find a thruple? Or would it be a quadruple?"

I cringe. "Ugh, Connor. Too far."

Greyson flashes me a teasing smile. "They have decided in the span of twelve weeks to each find a husband they both approve of."

"Any luck, so far?" Connor asks.

I turn to Bex, pleading with her not to bring up last night.

"Oh. Em. Gee." Bex punctuates each word by patting Connor's thigh. "So last night, we're at Finnegan's with Jack and Bobby. And Jack is--"

Greyson cuts into her words. "Jack and Bobby?"

"That's what I said, Greyson," Bex fires back. "Jack. And. Bobby."

"And there's nothing you find funny about that?" he asks.

"Whatever. So Jack is totally into me and we're flirting and sending vibes back and forth and Bobby is really into Charlie, like grinning at her and touching her." She lays her hand on Connor's arm demonstrating. "Real flirty stuff. And that rarely happens for Charlie that quickly, you know. It usually takes a while for a guy to find her attractive or be into her."

"Shit, Bex. You are such a good friend for dragging Charlie along with you," Greyson growls.

"That's not true at all, Bex." Connor takes her hand off his arm and places it back on her lap. "What about Juan?"

"Juan?" I ask.

"The guy who senior year, shows up to bowling and is instantly infatuated with you. Remember, he bought you those flowers from the shop next door and brought them back to you."

"Oh, yeah." The memory starts flooding back. "And he started writing me those super creepy love notes."

"And, there was the guy, what was his name? He kept showing up at Bible study early when you'd be warming up for worship. And he'd bring fish tacos for everyone." Grey threw air quotes around everyone.

"And what about Grey?" Connor asks.

I squint my eyes and tip my head, straining to figure out what he means.

Greyson shoots him a look in the rearview I can't gauge.

"Greyson probably has a ton more stories," Connor says.

"Well, whatever. This guy's into her." Bex flips her hair over her shoulder. "So, after dinner, we walk outside and I'm giving them the signal like, how about Jack takes me home, hint, hint." She leans forward to emphasize her point. "And Charlie's eyes go really big. She's terrified to be alone with this hottie."

"That wasn't fear. It was 'please don't make me spend another second with this numbskull,'" I clarify.

"Sure, Charlie. So I pull Jack's arm and walk him towards his car and look back to nudge Charlie to do the same. And Bobby leans in to kiss her, and she steps back."

She waits for Connor and Grey's reaction.

When they don't oblige, she repeats, "She. Steps. Back," just in case they didn't hear her the first time.

"The guy was obnoxious. I asked him what he did. He says, just like this," I bring out my best stoner guru voice, "'I'm a deep thinker.' Then he pauses to rub his chin and think, and I'm waiting for something interesting to follow that and he goes, 'I think about things, like, a lot.'"

"Okay. So not really husband material," Greyson says.

"Not even close," I agree.

Bex lays her hand on my shoulder patronizingly. "Charlie, you are so picky."

"Only if wanting a guy to be able to hold a conversation without telling me Florida is an island cause it has beaches."

Connor laughs. "He actually said that?"

"Yep. Even when I stared at him like he was joking, waiting for him to laugh too, he had no clue."

# 7

## CHARLIE

By the time we stop at In-n-Out in Ventura for lunch, the heat is oppressive. Bex takes this as a directive to whip off her shirt, leaving her neon lime triangle bikini top barely covering the girls. She adjusts it to draw even more attention to her chest.

"So this place we're staying. Whose place is it again?" Connor says as he slips into the round concrete table on the patio.

"Chad, who I screwed but never loved, but he still loves me, so he gives me whatever I ask." Bex flips her hair behind her shoulder, as she basks in the attention of the crew of young surfers fueling up after a morning surf. "He rents out his place to the UCSB college kids during the year, but it's empty in the summer."

Chad is one of Bex's college conquests she keeps stringing along for the last few years. She pulls him back up when she's tired of having to go fishing for fresh meat. She's learned that, although she doesn't have enough depth or character to keep a guy on the line with her personality, she can keep them there with other, more physical, means.

"And his place has four beds?" I press for the particulars

she's been a little dodgy with. I desperately want to avoid the who's sharing a bed with whom thing.

"Well, like three, probably," she says.

I tip my head back and take a deep breath. I knew I should have pushed her for more concrete details when she promised this place would be great.

"So, Bex, you're taking the couch?" Greyson suggests.

"No way. I told Gemma and Trix they could have the beds. And then, of course, I get one."

"Who are Gemma and Trix." Greyson snarls, more of a demand than question.

"They went to UT with me and Brendon. I told them they could stay with us. I was being nice."

"To who?" I say under my breath, shaking my head.

This is so like Bex, I don't know how it still surprises me.

"Chad has some couches, and he said he'd leave out some sleeping bags. It's not like you'll have to sleep outside."

After we've settled into the two-story row home at the top of the cliffs overlooking the water, Bex dons her second outfit of the day. I try to squeeze into the minuscule, mold-covered bathroom already packed with girls, trying to take a quick peek at myself in the mirror.

"Charlie! That dress is perfect," Bex squeals. "And you curled your hair! But... let's do something with your face."

Bex flips the toilet lid closed and guides me onto it.

I weigh my options.

I could argue with her and deal with her outrage now and her throwing it back at me for the rest of the trip and probably the rest of summer, or I could bury my pride, sit for ten minutes, and let her work on my face and maybe even learn a little something. After all, I've seen the expert work she does on her own face with her bag of tricks.

"You're going to look so hot tonight," she announces.

She wipes my face with primer. The last time I used primer was when I repainted our bedroom last year.

"Can I give you some advice, Charlie?" she asks.

Like I could stop her from spewing whatever nonsense she has bottled up in that head of hers.

"Close." She motions to my eyes.

I obey.

She swipes something across both lids.

"If you want to meet someone and have him stick around for a while, or maybe forever... You can open."

I open my eyes to find Bex with an uncommonly serious look on her face.

"You have to start distancing yourself from Greyson. There's no way you will ever land a boyfriend with that behemoth of a man blocking the way for all other men."

She brushes something pink across my cheeks.

"Here, go like this." She purses her lips together and shoves them forward.

I copy her as she holds a tube of lipstick next to my lips.

"I don't think you can pull off..." she flips the tube of blazing red paint, "...Ruby Woo. Maybe something a little lighter."

Digging through her bag, she pulls out a tube of sparkly pink lipstick. She snatches my chin, lifts my head, and dabs my lips with the tube working from the middle to each side.

"He's not blocking anyone," I say, trying not to move my lips.

She lets my chin go and hands me a tissue. "Blot."

I put the tissue between my lips and press.

"I just think that when a guy sees you with Greyson, he's going to assume you two are together." She shivers at the thought. "And he won't even try."

She lifts me off the toilet, pushing me to the mirror.

"I don't think anyone thinks we're a..."

My face.

It looks good. Thinner maybe. Or more defined.

And my eyes, they're... perceptible. Someone might actually notice them.

Bex does have a talent for this.

She gives me a final once over, making sure I pass muster, before pointing to the insulin pump tucked inside the band of my underwear, only slightly visible under the material of the dress.

"Can you take that thing off? It's so ugly. You don't really need it, do you?"

I've explained my pump to her hundreds of times, but expecting her to remember would require her to actually pay attention to someone other than herself.

"Only if I feel like living. But that's not what's important tonight, is it?"

"I guess you can keep it on."

*Thank you, Bex, for permission to take care of myself.*

We arrive at the pre-ceremony cocktail hour a few minutes after it starts. This is the only way to attend a wedding, thoroughly liquored up and well-fed. Or, in my case, after half a beer and a few slices of cheese to slow down the alcohol.

Today is more high school reunion than wedding with all our high school friends gathered to celebrate Brendan and Delilah.

We're joined by Sam-n-Eric, twins who were unfortunate enough to have a book-loving mom with a mean sense of humor. Sam is handsomely graying a little around the temples, but Eric has put on forty pounds and fifty years. He looks like the astronaut twin who stayed on Earth while his brother slowed down his aging in space.

"No, it's true. Starbucks spends more to cover health care for employees than they do on purchasing coffee," Eric explains.

I guess if I had worked in insurance for the past ten years, I might look older than I should, too.

As we wait to take our seats, I catch the flower girl reaching up to the cake table, her hand on a donut hole platter beside the cupcake tower wedding cake surrounded by dozens of, you guessed it, mason jars.

I know what our drinking game should be tonight.

When the flower girl sees me, she freezes. I smile and give her an approving nod. She takes three donut holes in that Lilliputian hand of hers and flees.

Greyson, standing among all these old high school friends, dressed in a well-fitting, dark grey suit and flip flops—Brendon mandated them for all the guys—is the only one who looks even better than he did in high school.

Tonight, every inch of him is solid, manly. He looks like an adult. Like a man.

When you see someone every day, you miss the big changes happening right before your eyes. When I first met Grey, he was barely seventeen, scrawny, angry, and a mess of energy and testosterone. He would flit from girl to girl, basking in their attention.

Back then he was almost always Public Greyson, life of the party, the guy everyone wanted to invite out because he made everything more fun and he made everyone feel like the center of his universe. The guy who could charm the stink off cow pies. But it always made me wonder if he was trying to make up for some deficiency, trying to keep the light off his faults.

And, even though he still gives off this super-suave, player vibe, charming the pants off girls and their mothers alike when he's not saving the world as a fireman, when it's just the two of us, he's anything but slimy and arrogant. He's sweet and scared and, most importantly, real.

I spy the Lilliputian fleeing the cake table again, sugar dusted across her cute face. How many donuts can she fit in that tiny belly?

When Brendan's brother begins to play his guitar beside a woman singing some country love song, we take our seats, Grey sliding into the chair next to mine on the aisle.

I've never been one of those girls who planned my wedding since I was five, but if I was, Brendan and Delilah's wedding on the sand in front of the Santa Barbara Yacht Club would be exactly what I would have imagined. With a flower-wrapped arch framed by palm trees in front of a few rows of white chairs in the sand, it's the simple affair weddings should be.

The little flower girl in her bright blue dress makes her way down the aisle, scattering fresh white rose petals. Every eye is on her, most beginning to tear up at how cute this little bugger is, as she makes her way over the bamboo aisle runner framed by teal abalone shells.

"She is so darling," the granny behind me whispers to her husband.

The girl smiles at me and stops right next to my chair.

"Keep going. All the way to the front," I whisper, pointing her to her final destination.

The smile vanishes from her tiny face, replaced by a momentary look of horror. Then she bends at the waist and deposits a stomachful of donuts in the sand next to my feet.

An audible gasp can be heard, and then complete and total silence.

The sound of waves becomes perceptible. One palm frond scratches against its neighbor. A seagull squawks over the sound of rigging clanging against the masts of million-dollar sailboats in the nearby marina.

Tears flood her eyes and she peers up at me, pleading for help.

"Well, it's all out now," I say, shrugging.

Removing the napkin from the cheese still in my hand, I wipe her tiny mouth.

From under my chair, I take the shoe Bex forced on me earlier and use it to bury the little girl's present in the sand.

"There. Now no one will know. Now go on and rule this wedding." I point to the flowered arch. "All the way to the front. You'll be fine. I promise."

She smiles and continues her march.

I look at Grey to reassure myself I wasn't hallucinating. After a moment's pause, we both bust up laughing.

Halfway through the hour-long service, he leans over and whispers, "Shoot me if I ever have a wedding this long."

"Seriously. Ten minutes. Tops."

"Do you? Sure. Do you? Why not? Okay. Man and wife. You may tongue your woman."

"Really? Tongue your woman? On your wedding day?"

"You prefer swapping spit?"

I shake my head, bringing up the hand-lettered, pink wedding program and groan. Leaning closer to Grey with a modicum of discretion, I read off a litany of the torture we still have left to endure.

"Candle lighting. Reading from the mother of the bride. Reading from the mother of the groom. Reading from Monica Geller-Bing read by Tina, M.O.H."

I reread that last one in credulity. "I think they're reading a wedding speech from Friends. Like the TV show, Friends."

I turn to him to smother another laugh.

He points his finger further down the program. "What the hell is a beer blending?"

"I guess we'll find out in another eighty minutes."

# 8

## GREYSON

*I*n the reception hall inside of the Santa Barbara Yacht Club, an over-the-hill fratbag with his suit collar popped saunters up, leering at Charlie. Someone should tell this guy that dressing like that when he's a few decades out of college is just sad.

"Only four weeks left for our Summer Goal," Bex whispers to Charlie and it lands like a jab to the center of my chest.

This has got to be Bex's crowning achievement, using their longstanding tradition so Bex comes out with all of Charlie's attention and me as just a hellion she exorcised from Charlie's life long ago.

"You're gonna dance with me, honey," the creep demands of Charlie.

"Nah. I'm good." Charlie gives him a conciliatory smile.

Bex may be making headway in her extrication plans, but I don't have to sit around and watch.

"Oh, I know you're good," the sleaze says.

I step forward until I am inches away from his face. "Does it look like my friend wants to dance? Read the room, Fucko."

"Chill out, Chief, I was just--"

I step into his words. "Leaving. You were leaving."

He lets out one last moment of bravado before sulking back to the swamp he crawled out of.

Bex gives Charlie a look that says, "I told you."

What the hell has she been filling Charlie's head with?

"Thanks, Grey. That guy was such a..." She searches for a word strong enough to describe him, but clean enough to mutter out loud.

"A Delta Bravo?" I suggest.

"Exactly. A Delta Bravo," she repeats.

"You think you can ward off all the other Delta Bravo's for a couple of minutes? I'm out." I hold up my empty bottle.

"Yeah. They're really lining up for me," she says with a chuckle. She has no idea.

Standing next to the open bar is Brendan's mom, Fiona Jacobs. Brendan made more friends in high school because of his mom than he'd ever like to admit. An invitation to his house in the summer was an automatic yes.

It was guaranteed she'd be laying out in a red bikini with the tiny strings holding it on her captivating body looking like they might burst at any minute, giving us the real-life version of a fantasy we had all played a few too many times in our heads.

"Look at you, all grown up." She has every appearance of debating whether her husband would notice if she took me upstairs to their hotel room for an hour to find out just how grown up I'd become.

"And you somehow managed to look better and younger than ever." This earns me a smile.

"You have Stone?" I ask the bartender while Fiona revels in a fantasy of her own.

I wonder if it plays out anything like mine used to. Likely not. A woman like that, with all her years of experience, has much more fodder to pull from than a horny, inexperienced fourteen-year-old.

I snag the beer the barkeep places on the counter and throw her a knowing smile as she finishes her daydream, then cross the room and settle back in my chair, drained from a long afternoon of charming the world.

Apparently, Bex succeeded in finding a guy Charlie deemed acceptable enough to dance with. He is eagerly trying to impress her with his dance moves. She is too busy enjoying the music to even notice.

Bex will have to try a lot harder than that to extricate me.

Charlie tugs at the hem of the little black dress Bex dressed her up in with nothing covering her back except for lace straps forming a picture of the Eiffel Tower. Not at all Charlie's style.

Unlike most typical girls, Charlie has never once expressed interest in anything Parisian. She'd much rather be on any beach in the world with warm water, plenty of sea turtles, and enough clean waves to keep her entertained.

The dress may not be exactly her style, but she wears it well, and every guy in here from thirteen to eighty-nine has been noticing. It's long enough to let her dance without a worry, but highlights her body with its skin-tight fit. Delicate straps and a deep-cut neckline expose her collarbone and the curve of her chest beneath. The lace Eiffel Tower on her back may be gaudy, but it leaves the rest of her back entirely bare.

Bex finished dressing her up with a pair of black strappy heels that show off her tan, toned legs. The shoes made it through the pre-ceremony cocktail hour with Charlie teetering on the unfamiliar height, but the second we took our seats at the ceremony, her feet were bare again and I doubt those shoes will make a reappearance anytime tonight.

Mr. Longshot tries to lay his hand on the soft, bronze skin her dress reveals, but Charlie spins out of his grasp, dancing over to Bex who's preoccupied with her current mark.

*That's my girl, Sands. Don't play into Bex's scheming hand.*

He shimmies after her, displaying his White Man's Overbite as he turns up the volume on the uncomfortable display.

She appears oblivious to how hard he is trying, and I'm certainly not going to tell her. No need to push her any farther into Bex's grasp.

A light tap on my knee alerts me to a toothless grin lighting up the flower girl's face. The grin's owner couldn't be more than eight, her blond hair in curls framing a face full of freckles.

"Excuse me, would you care to dance?" she says, holding her hand out palm up.

She turns to her dad. "Did I say that right, Daddy?"

He nods his agreement.

I guess they've gone all equal rights at Cotillion, teaching the girls to be as polite and bold as the boys.

I look to him, brows raised for permission and he nods.

Letting her take my hand, we step onto the dance floor as *Rock the Casbah* comes on, persuading us to boogie.

She spins and flails her arms. I try to match her enthusiasm.

I glance over at Charlie to make sure Douchey McStupid hasn't made too much headway. I must be adorable right now because she smiles at me the same way she gazes at one of those sea otter pics she's always texting me.

Looking down at my dance partner, this little girl is the spitting image of Charlie, all blond and freckly. If I didn't know any better, I'd swear this was her long-lost daughter.

The girl spins around and around until she falls to the floor.

I bend down and offer her my hand. "You need some help up?"

She takes my hands and I pull her back to her feet.

"Owie," she says, falling back to the floor, holding her ankle.

The seat her father occupied earlier is empty.

"Can you walk on it?" I ask.

"Nuh-uh."

"That's okay." I scoop her up in my arms and search for her dad. Stepping off the dance floor, I hope he'll find me before I have to wander through the crowd like this.

Her dad materializes with a full beer in hand. The moment he spots us, he sets his drink on the nearest table and hurries towards me, concern plastered all over his face.

I've seen that look before. The one people give me when I approach them outside a burning house or a traffic accident. The look that says, "Please tell me everything is okay, that everyone is alright."

I glance down to find the girl, eyes closed, limp in my arms. She's not moving.

"Jenny!" her dad calls out.

She pops her head up immediately and says, "Did you see me dancing, Daddy? Wasn't I beautiful?"

He walks to me, lifting her out of my arms and says, "Of course you were Sweetie. But more importantly, you looked like you were having the best time."

My hands refuse to lower.

Instead, they fill with another tiny body.

*Her* body.

*It was your fault, Steele.*

The music dissolves into howling sirens as the caustic scent of gasoline mixed with wet asphalt seeps into me.

*It was your job to search.*

In my arms, *her* body lingers.

Limp.

Lifeless.

*You missed her.*

My muscles burn from the load.

The thrashing of my heart overpowers the sirens.

Some guy bumps my shoulder on his way to the dance floor.

*Need to leave.*

I scan the room for the nearest egress.

Double doors. Straight ahead.

*Boom.*

I shove them open.

*Shit.*

More people.

And in the midst, *her* father.

Beggin me for good news.

But then knowing.

Without me having to say it.

*If you just fucking looked harder, she'd still be alive.*

A door ahead leads to the deck.

I fling it open.

It slams against the wall.

The cool air blasts my face.

I check for *her* father.

He's not here.

*You should have known.*

My breath stalls.

I stumble to the railing overlooking the ocean.

But the little girl won't leave my arms.

I force in a breath.

And release it.

Her once blond curls, now crimson, stick to her face.

*Breathe in.*

Her father lifts her weight from my arms.

*Breathe out.*

My hands left camouflaged the same color as her hair.

*Breathe in.*

*Breathe out.*

*In.*

*Out.*

I grip the railing as I try to slow my breathing to match the speed of the waves wandering up the beach beneath me.

C. S. Lewis commiserates with me, "No one ever told me that grief felt so like fear."

He couldn't be more right.

# 9

## GREYSON

*W*hen my body has finished freaking out on me, I take one more long, slow breath and stagger inside to the bar.

"Whiskey, neat."

I slide the glass off the bar.

The weight of just a glass too much for my arm, I let it hang as I drift back to a table at the rear of the room.

It's pretty fucked up that *that day* gets to invade my life whenever the hell it wants to.

Who knows what sets it off?

Sometimes a face, one that reminds me of that girl or her father. Sometimes a smell, like gasoline fumes. Sometimes nothing at all.

I can't stop it from happening or predict when it will, but when it comes, it comes full force.

Charlie spies me from the dance floor and instinctively knows what happened. She strides across the room to sit next to me.

"Whiskey?" she says, motioning to my near-empty glass.

"Yeah." I run my finger along the rim.

"Fuck Stick decide on a lashing tonight?"

I nod my head.

She turns her head back to the dance floor, giving me a moment to breathe.

Bex is in the center of a group of guys who are all gyrating like idiots, trying to out-ass the guy next to him for her attention.

Charlie slides my glass off the table, looking at the last few drops lingering next to the ice.

"What triggered this one?"

She lifts the glass to her mouth, polishing off the last sip.

The last drops of deep amber let go of the ice and fall onto her tongue.

"That little girl who asked me to dance? I had to pick her up."

"Damn," her voice trailing off.

I shake my head.

Charlie doesn't ask for a play-by-play or if I'm okay, and I don't need to explain it to her.

She just knows.

She sits next to me and we have precisely the nonversation I need; Charlie never feeling like she needs to fill the silence with useless words, and me not having the words I would need if I tried.

A few minutes later, she motions to the plates still on the table, the dried-out wedding chicken barely picked over. "I think the chicken died in vain."

Her Jimmy Buffett reference provides a splash of joy to my weariness. She always knows how to pull me out of a funk. That's what she calls it, at least to my face. She refuses to call it PTSD, and she gets pretty fired up when other people do, too.

She doesn't have a problem with the sudden disruptions PTSD inflicts on our day. She takes issue with the actual D in PTSD.

"You say disorder and it makes it sound like it's your fault. Like you somehow made your brain process this way, react this way. Like you are broken somehow. Disordered. You call it Post Traumatic Stress? All of a sudden, all the blame is on the trauma where it should be. The trauma causes the stress, not you," she once explained.

Weird thing is, it helped.

For the first time, after hearing her diatribe, I realized the stress is not my fault. It's just shit we all deal with on the job.

That little difference, knowing it was stress and not my disorder, gave me the confidence to start working on my reaction to it.

"Wanna hit up Roberto's for a late-night burrito? I saw one on the way in. I think we have thirty minutes easy before anyone even notices we're gone," she says.

She's as eager to get out of here as I am.

I scan the room, looking for an exit, slower this time.

"You need your shoes?"

She cocks her eyes as if I just asked if a shark needed a snorkel. She shrugs. "It's a beach town."

When we return home that night, Bex escorts her college friends up to our beds without so much as a word.

I throw down my jacket on the small round table in the kitchen, unbuttoning my shirt.

"You up for another one?" Connor holds out a bottle.

"Why not?" I take the bottle and raise an eyebrow at Charlie.

"I think I'm gonna crash," she says. "You guys mind if I take one of the sofas?"

"Unless Bex has them reserved for another five friends she didn't tell us about," Connor answers.

I don't know how the most considerate girl I know became longtime friends with that thoughtless narcissist. If Charlie weren't so loyal, Bex would have been left behind years ago. But Charlie and her rules.

I follow Connor out to the back deck.

It's mind-blowing, that this strip of real estate became ground zero for the herd of drunk, wannabe scholars at UCSB. It's one of the most amazing swaths of land on the California coast. On a high tide, the waves crash up against the cliffs below the back decks and each night students are treated to a spectacular display of lights and colors as the sun sets if only they would glance up from their books and phones long enough to appreciate it.

"Hey, sorry about back there in the car," Connor starts.

"The car?"

"The whole, guys finding Charlie attractive immediately thing. I figured she would know by now."

"Oh that. Don't worry about it." I tip my beer into my mouth, hoping he'll move on.

"Does she not know?" he presses.

I shoot him a quizzical look, not wanting to give away anything.

"That you were crazy about her when you first met," he continues.

Does this guy not take a hint?

I regard him, assessing if he's serious. "Crazy's a bit of an overstatement."

I was seventeen. Anything even remotely female was enough to drive me crazy.

It didn't take long for me to figure out Charlie was smart enough to see right through my games, and that I was way too intellectually deficient for her to even consider dating.

"Besides, that was years ago. It's not like that for us now."

"I'm not convinced that's true," he says, gauging my reaction over the top of his beer.

I refuse to give him one.

"So, two months 'till you walk the plank?" I ask, trying to change the subject.

"Alright, alright, I'll stop pushing it," he says with a laugh. "I'm gonna hit the rack. You want the couch or the floor?"

"You can have the couch. We can't send you home to Bethany with a crimped-up back. She may well leave you if she realizes how old you really are."

I take another drag from my beer.

From this vantage point, Point Conception to the north, Point Magu to the South, and a few specks on Santa Rosa Island more than twenty miles out to sea all light up the horizon.

I turn and glance through the open sliding door to the living room where Charlie is settling into bed.

*Does she not know?*

Connor's question reverberates in my mind.

I doubt it. If she ever suspected it, I've seen no indication. But, then again, Charlie's a master of keeping her cards close to the vest. Is it possible she knew?

I finish my beer and throw it in the can at the corner of the deck with a loud clank. I take one more breath of salty air before heading in to change out of this monkey suit.

In the stuffy bathroom, I slip on a pair of navy sweat shorts and wash my face, looking at the dark swollen skin under my eyes. It's been well over two years since I've had a proper night's sleep.

I reach for a shirt out of my faded canvas duffel before reconsidering. The August heat is in full force, and, although this place has million-dollar views, it has no A/C.

When I step out of the bathroom, the living room is dark. As I lean to snag the sleeping bag leaning up against the couch Charlie is sleeping on, her eyes open slightly. She gazes from my arms to my bare chest to my abs and hovers just below the waistband of my shorts for brief a moment.

The feel of her eyes moving over me is intoxicating. I scan her face for any sign of enjoyment, but she simply closes those glowing green eyes, her face indecipherable.

I lay out the sleeping bag on the floor next to the stained, brown couch and climb in. Laying back with my hands under my head, I replay the reception as I try to drift off to sleep, a struggle for me lately.

Just like the panic hits at random moments during the day, it creeps up at night, too, and I'm not too keen on having to explain to Connor why I tend to cry out while thrashing around for no apparent reason.

Charlie shifts on the couch, flopping her hand off the side, and, for a fleeting moment, I want to reach for it.

When she is nearby, the panic isn't as insurmountable. When it hits, I'm on a boat capsized by a rogue wave; I have no idea where the deck is, which way is up, how to get out. But if she's there, everything rights itself and, sure, it still takes a while for the water to drain out, but I know where I am. And I know it will all return to normal if I can only force myself to breathe.

Bex has no idea what it would do to me if she were successful in driving me out of Charlie's life, and I don't think she'd care even if she did. But there's no way I'm letting that happen.

I turn my head, giving a second thought to holding her hand, but she's tucked it back under her pillow.

In this light, laying there with her guard finally down, Charlie seems peaceful with blond curls falling over her cheeks and the freckles that appear on her nose each summer in full force. She's... pretty.

I smile as the thought fills my mind, until she bolts upright, scooting until her back abuts the armrest. She pulls her knees to her chest, her breath short and fast.

The look on her face? I've seen that look on the face of every rookie before he steps through the door of his first real structure fire. It can only be described as fear.

I do for Charlie what I do for every rookie in that moment. Throw my arm on his shoulder and tell him, "You fight fear with action. Let's go."

I slide onto the sofa next to her and put my arm on her shoulder, but before I can say anything she peers up at me with the saddest, puppy dog eyes and says, "This place looks just like hers."

She buries her head into my chest and begins to sob quietly.

I wrap my other arm around her, pulling her into me, hoping to drive the pain out. I want to fight off everything that would ever make her this sad.

I take stock of the nondescript Isla Vista row home, trying to place what brought this on when it hits me. Lizzy lived in one of these nondescript homes when she went to UCSB.

Elizabeth Blade was Charlie's best childhood friend. She was that first childhood friend that made her feel like she belonged.

One foggy February morning, at the base of the cliffs of Hendry's Beach, they found her in a heap. Some people speculated she fell one morning while checking out the surf. Charlie knew better.

She lifts her head off my chest and looks up at me again.

"It was my..."

She stops breathing and bites on her lip, straining under the weight of what she is afraid to say. Afraid to admit.

"It was my fault."

Once she lets the words out, she disintegrates into me.

I remember watching Charlie in the days after she found out. Word took a while to reach her. Though Charlie and Lizzy were inseparable as kids, they traveled in different circles in high school and, by the time they both left for college, they only kept in touch through email, catching up once in a while when they were both home from school.

She didn't find out until two weeks after it happened. By then Charlie had missed the funeral, missed her chance to say goodbye. She never really grieved for Lizzy. She just went numb.

I think the numbness just wore off.

"I should've been there," she adds.

I was so selfish not to think about that before I brought her here. I've seen how death can weigh on a person. I've seen it in my family and in my brothers at the station. When they think it was their fault, even though it isn't, it is so much worse.

And, recently, I've seen it in myself, when it was my fault.

But this wasn't her fault, and there was no way I will let her take on the added trauma of thinking it was.

I bend down to whisper in her ear. "There were things in her life she didn't know how to handle."

Loosening my grip on her, I draw back. I need her to see my face when I tell her this.

Her eyes lift, connecting with mine.

I take my time with each word so she knows it's more than empty platitudes. "It was not your fault."

She smears the back of her hand against her cheek like she's angry her eyes betrayed her with all these tears.

In all the time I've known Charlie, I've never seen her cry. Not once. I'm sure she's done it, she is human after all, but, around me, she has always been Fierce Charlie, an expert at hiding away her feelings, her pain, never wanting to broadcast her weaknesses.

I think it' came from spending so much time in a man's world.

She's learned the same things little boys are taught growing up. Men don't cry. Men don't show emotion.

If she were to cry at the Ref's unfair call when she was the only girl in the boy's football league, she would have lost the respect of her teammates that she spent the entire season developing. If she were to become emotional at work, those guys would double down on the ridicule they already showered her in.

"She called me that Christmas. I was supposed to meet up with her."

She shakes her head in regret before continuing. "I knew she was hurting, that she needed someone to talk to. And I?"

She buries herself in my chest, hiding from what she must be thinking.

This girl in my arms tonight? This is not Fierce Charlie.

I rest my hand on the back of her head.

"The waves were firing. It was a perfect day. I wanted to catch a few more," she continues.

With her finger, she traces the lines of the tattoo on my chest, trying to distract herself from her ill-conceived shame for a second.

This is Tender Charlie I'm holding, and all I want to do is fend off anything and everything that would ever seek to hurt her.

She drops her hand from my tattoo. "I failed my best friend on this whole earth for a few more fucking waves."

Speaking the words allows her to begin the grieving process she has held off for far too long and she gives in to the tears.

I don't stop her or try to convince her that it's not her fault. She needs this right now. I pull her into me and run my fingertips along her shoulder over and over, tracing the lines of her muscles while she sobs quietly.

I hate that I let her go for six months without realizing she was hurting like this. She's always so tough, sometimes I forget she has feelings. I'm so wrapped up in my own needs, I barely notice hers. I have to do a better job of recognizing the small signs she can't hide; when she retreats to Quiet Mode if she's angry, when she shoves her tongue into her lower lip and hardens her face to fend off impending tears, when she turns her back to hide all traces of emotion.

When her breathing steadies, she lifts her head. She may have figured out how to put makeup on for the wedding, but she still hasn't figured out how to take it off before she goes to sleep. Her face is a mess of charcoal sinking from her eyes and smeared over her cheeks.

I push a strand of curls out of her face and run my thumbs over her cheeks to clean her up. Leaving my hands on her neck so she won't try to hide again. "Even if you met her that day and you were the absolute best friend that I know full well you can be, it might not have changed a thing. This is not on you."

She listens to my words, absorbs them, like she is borrowing my strength.

Charlie sees me as an expert in dealing with death. This may be the only subject on earth I know more about than her and it feels amazing to be that for her.

I run my thumb over her cheek, wiping her last tears away and glance down at her lips. I have to hold myself back from leaning down to kiss them. To cover her mouth with mine. It may be exactly what I need right now, but it is not what she needs.

And so I hold her.

As her breathing slows down, growing more even, her eyes eventually close.

I let her fall into me as sleep finally takes over.

And her pain is finally gone.

# 10

## CHARLIE

*I* wake to find Greyson wrapped around me.

Shirtless.

His face is nuzzled into my neck, my cheek resting lightly on his forehead.

My leg is draped over his hips as his hand rests on my lower back, fingers tucked under the hem of my shirt, touching my bare skin.

I breathe in the intoxicating scent of chlorine and summer nights. And, somehow, it is the sexiest thing to ever have been inhaled.

Every inch of my body is using all the neurons at their command to send my brain messages.

Messages I don't want to be receiving.

*Fuuuuuuuuuuuck.*

This can't be happening.

I have to make this not be happening.

And I have to do it before anyone else sees.

Before Greyson sees.

I gingerly lift my leg off his hip and check for movement.

Nothing.

Unwrapping my arms from his back, the sharp lines of his shoulders capture my attention.

*Not the time for that, Charlie. Stick to the mission.*

I roll my hips away from him, missing the way they fit perfectly against mine.

He doesn't notice their absence.

Almost fully extricated, I realize my arm is trapped under his head. With my neck further away now, he has nuzzled into my arm, his lips resting on the bare skin of my inner arm. They're soft and—

*Oh my god, Charlie, moooove.*

This is so not okay.

I slide my arm ever so slowly from under his head.

He doesn't even stir.

I lift myself off the couch and over his body and I'm free.

Slipping out the back door, I sprint down the stairs at the edge of the yard to the sand below, to the sound of the waves that can wipe away the imprint of his body on mine.

A north swell pushes the waves up to a clean four-foot, right-handed break. A few waves roll in as I picture myself riding each one, up to hit the lip, racing ahead only to do a sweeping cutback and hit the reform hard, and then off to hit an air as the wave closes out.

It almost clears my mind.

Almost.

*What was he doing?*

Chlorine mixed with the scent of his skin fills my mind again and I miss the warmth of his hand on my back.

It was late.

It was late and he was just consoling me.

It was late and I was crying like a baby.

It was late and he fell asleep. Just like I did.

It doesn't mean anything.

It doesn't change anything.

He might not even remember.

A brown pelican scrapes the face of a wave with his wings,

the bird far better than I am at painting the waves with his movements. He pulls up and continues his sunrise search for breakfast.

*But what if he does remember?*

*If it does mean something?*

*If he wants more?*

The thoughts force me to move, anywhere, as long as I don't have to think those thoughts again.

As I return to the bottom of the steps, something catches my eye: a tiny plastic dinosaur.

"You're coming home with me," I tell Dino while scooping him up.

Up on the back patio, the crew is just sitting down to breakfast, Greyson at the grill, leaning over the shoulder of Trix with Public Greyson face on, and I let out a laugh at my silliness.

What was I thinking? He's woken up next to so many women before. Naked women, even. This is nothing to him.

Less than nothing.

He hasn't even spent one second considering it. What a damned waste of energy.

When I reach the top of the stairs, Trix has taken her place between Bex and Gemma at the faded picnic table.

Greyson is flipping flapjacks on a pan atop the barbecue with a dish towel hanging out of this back pocket like a gangster throwing colors. Watching him like this, so incredibly fluid and skilled when he cooks, it makes sense that Trix would pull out all her tricks to get his attention.

I stand next to him—well, a proper half-foot away—and the pain from last night washes over me again.

"Captain Crunch?" he asks as he pours three pancakes onto the pan and sprinkles the crushed cereal on top.

I don't know another soul who likes Captain Crunch in their pancakes, which means he brought them especially for me.

We stand for a while, watching tiny bubbles form on top of the batter. When the perfect number pop, Grey flips each one, landing them in the perfect spot on the pan.

He shakes the spatula at me. "It's all in the wrist."

"The wrist. Got it."

When they're done to perfection, he deposits the cakes onto a plate and hands me a mug filled with ice, a can of DDP sitting on top, and slips my Dexcom receiver into my back pocket.

"You left it this morning," he says without even a twinge of awkwardness.

He leans in and whispers in my ear, "When you're done, there's something we need to do."

His cheek brushes past mine.

I lean in, needing more of it.

And it brings up the one question I have been too afraid to ask.

What if *I* want more?

We pull over on a street running alongside hills covered with well-manicured grass and scattered coastal oaks. I might mistake this for a golf course if it weren't for the neatly aligned, three-foot-tall stones standing in wavy lines, matching the incline of the hills.

I angle in my seat towards Grey. "You take me here to kill me? A little easier to dispose of my body around a place filled with them?"

He turns towards me and rests his hand on the back of my seat. "You told me a lot last night."

He points out the window. "I thought it might help to tell her."

I study his tropical-ocean eyes, trying to avoid the thought of doing what he suggested. If I can just sit here and watch his eyes, I won't have to turn and...

"You might be surprised how good it feels to just say the words." He gains a mischievous grin. "And I can promise she won't argue back."

"Oh. Come on, Greyson," I say, letting a small laugh slip.

"Too morbid?"

I nod. "Too morbid."

"Go on." He nods his head towards the lush hill.

84

I cover a full six rows before coming to the spot where they stashed her body.

I was eight when my grandma died. Lizzy was there to help me process. I remember her saying how weird it was that people came to a cemetery to talk to their loved ones. How, when she died, she would be out riding the waves of her favorite break, never again having to jockey for a wave. No one would ever realize she snaked their wave if she were a ghost.

"Hey, Lizard," I say to nothing. "I know you'd be laughing at me standing here, talking to an empty box in the ground, but it... I don't know... Greyson said it might help."

With my finger, I trace the letters engraved in stone.

ELIZABETH BLADE. 1994-2020.

*Twenty-six years was not enough.*

"You were the first real friend I ever had. Do you remember the time we got your brother's BB-gun out to shoot birds? We thought we were so cool. We'd practiced all day on empty soda cans and we were finally ready for something bigger. Faster."

I study the ground. Wet, but not soaked, so I sit.

"When you hit that bird and its tail feathers went flying as it took off? We felt so bad. I don't think either one of us thought about what it would mean if we actually hit the bird. We swore off meat that very day. Killing an animal became a little too close to home."

I laugh at the thought of Lizzy throwing the gun to the ground and looking at me like she needed me to reassure her she wasn't Satan.

"I think every bit of trouble I got into as a kid, you were there. Every great thing too. On the beach in Hawaii, when you dared me to kiss Rich Cooper, my first kiss. The day I got that beat-up surfboard from your brother and rode my first wave. And that summer camp for gifted kids—that label still infuriating—when I realized for the first time there were others like us, girls who would rather sit around and do logic puzzles than go shop at the mall."

I look back to Greyson stretched out in the bed of his truck, soaking up the solitary ray of sun managing to poke through the marine layer and breathe in his strength.

"You were always there for me. Even when we drifted into different social spheres, you made it a point to check in with me, to write me birthday cards every year just to make sure I was still okay. And then I... God, Lizzy. I am so sorry."

My voice, eaten up by the tightening in my throat, goes silent. *I should have been there for you. I flaked when you needed me the most. And for what? A couple more waves?*

*I got so wrapped up in myself I forgot to be a good friend, to abide by the contract we wrote when we became Ketchup Sisters. Even back then we were too smart to be Blood Brothers like those stupid, pathogen-spreading boys.*

I poke at a dried leaf on the grass next to me, listening to it crackle as it breaks under the weight of my finger.

*I failed you, Lizard.*

Trying to hold back the tears is futile.

*I wish I could have done better. Listened. Asked the right questions. Just been a better friend. You deserved that.*

As I place my hand in the tall grass, the dinosaur in my pocket pokes at my leg. I take it out, hoping to distract myself for just a moment. Anything to escape the sheet of guilt draping over me like the past-due June Gloom overhead.

"You would have loved the surf this morning. It looked just like that morning at Ala Moana Bowls, the one where you pulled your first floater. It was nearly perfect."

I lean forward to place the tiny plastic beast on her headstone. "I love you, you Terrible Lizard."

Standing, I give her headstone a pat. "I'll do better," I assure her.

Greyson's head pops up from the back of the truck. He must somehow sense I am done here.

As I make my way to the truck in the growing brightness of the clearing August day, my current best friend fills my mind. I may toy with the idea of more with Grey, but there's no way I could handle jeopardizing what we have now for the chance of more. I can almost hear him scolding me, about how we can't break The Rules, how he just doesn't see me that way, and how I was so stupid to mistake that gesture of friendship for anything more.

And he's right.

I know he's right.

There have only been two people in my life who have truly known me—known me *and* accepted me— and in my twenty-seven short years, I've already lost one of them.

*I will do better, Lizard.*

I have to do better.

I won't let my selfishness drive away the only real friend I have left.

An old man brings the most beautiful arrangement of Gerbera Daisies towards the edge of the grass, stopping just shy of the road. "Here you go, My Dear. Sunday morning flowers for you, just as you like."

He knocks a dead leaf off the headstone where he lays the flowers. As I walk by, he greets me with a smile.

I turn back to return the smile and catch her headstone which reads, "My Dear Martha McKinney. Devoted Mom, Superior Human Being, and My Forever Friend."

# 11

## GREYSON

By late October, we have fallen back into our old ways without ever bringing up that night.

Too cold to run barefoot in just shorts now that the weather has cooled considerably after the Indian Summer heat lingered through late September, our weekly runs have moved back onto the streets with much more clothing involved.

Charlie still calls daily at lunch to bitch about her colleagues and steel herself for the afternoon of harassment. She fills me in on the never-ending stream of double-dates Bex keeps setting up. They decided, or, more likely, Bex decided, that they would extend their Summer Goal through the holidays, Bex unable to bear the thought of another holiday, gasp, without a boyfriend.

Charlie's beginning to realize that Bex is incapable of choosing a guy who is remotely smart or interesting enough for her. She is pushing to find her own men for these dates, but Bex is difficult to persuade.

Things are back to normal, but it doesn't feel the same. Like a favorite old pair of jeans you pull out in the fall after spending the summer in trunks. When you put them on again, they just feel odd, like there's no way you could have loved them so much. At least for me, that's the way it feels.

For Charlie, it's like she never took those jeans off. She's reveling in the normal as if she's driven any memory of that night from her mind.

"Another nightmare?" Mick grunts from the next bunk over.

The light from the sole window in the firehouse bunkroom brightens his face enough for me to see he's more concerned than mad that my thrashing woke him.

I shrug and roll over, pulling my blanket over my shoulder. My bed next to me a cavern of emptiness, adding to my late-night anxiety. I would give anything to have Charlie work her calming magic right now, to yell at Fuck Stick for me.

In high school, when my anxiety really started taking off, she would trap my head in her hands, tilting it down so she could talk to the top of it. Putting on her best tough guy Brooklyn accent, she'd yell, "Hey, Fuck Stick. Time for you to shut up. All you do is tell my boy here lie after lie after lie. Knock it off or I'll make you sleep with the turtles," her sweetened version of the common mafia threat.

She's always been my stabilizing force. Just having her nearby is enough to slow my heart rate and the racing what-ifs. Coming from a home where nothing was predictable and everything could go to shit without warning, Charlie's consistent kindness was a breath of fresh air. The only way I made it through the toughest times in my life was with Charlie standing by my side.

When my parents split up and I had to move out on my own senior year.

When my dreams of playing pro ball got fucked and my world went to shit.

When Aubrey...

Charlie was always there for me, calming me down through thick and thin.

Which is why the only thing I want is for her to crawl into bed next to me, for us to be wrapped around each other again. For her to tell Fuck Stick to go to hell, the thought alone bringing a smile to my face.

I want her cheek on my chest, her hips pressed up against mine, her leg draped over my thigh. I could fall asleep to the sound of her breathing in and out.

It makes me realize, for the first time ever, how much I want her to be here with me.

How much... I want her.

The thought rattles me.

I try to shake it off, but as I drift back to sleep my mind spins with everything we could be.

When I wake up the next morning, thoughts of Charlie still rattle in my mind, but now they bounce around alongside another thought.

What if?

And this is not the joyful kind of What-If.

This is the What-if-the-world-wrenches-open-along-its-seams-liberating-a-legion-of-Satanic-Leaf-Tailed-Geckos-to-ravage-the-world-and-all-of-it's-inhabitants-because-I-had-the-simpleminded-impulse-to-try-to-pursue-Charlie-Sands kind of What-If.

If I'm going to cross that line with Charlie, to test those waters, it has to be something small. So small I could deny it at the first sign she doesn't want me.

Which I already know to be true.

I know that.

It's written in every line of her Rule Book.

She wrote it out clearly in black and white because she wanted me to know it so thoroughly I would never screw things up like I am contemplating doing right now.

Like I was contemplating.

The smell of potatoes swimming in grease wafting into the bunkhouse persuades me to head downstairs.

I fill my plate with the hash browns and pancakes Patrick whipped up this morning.

Mick scrubs the last piece of pancake around on his plate to sop up the remaining syrup. "You good?"

I don't think I'm at 'good' yet, but I am getting closer.

"I'm fine. Syrup?" I point to the bottle.

Junior slides it across the table to me. I pour it over my

pancakes as Charlie's voice tells me, "Go easy, G-dog. Just cause you have a working pancreas doesn't mean you need to provoke it with that much sugar."

I put the syrup down and dig into the potatoes.

Mick taps Junior on the shoulder, then points to me. "There it is again."

"What's there again?" I ask, feeling like I missed the joke.

"That smile that's been popping up on your face randomly ever since you got home from that wedding? What exactly happened there? You finally get Charlie into bed?"

The more the days pile up between us and that night, the more thoughts of Charlie randomly invade my mind. I think about holding her in my arms, the scent of bananas and possibility surrounding us. When we sat outside of Roberto's instead of in that stuffy reception hall because she knew I couldn't keep up my life-of-the-party act, but needed to just be myself with her by my side.

The look on her face when she finally let go on the dance floor. I've never seen Charlie come alive like that, dancing so freely. She had every pair of male eyes on her all night, maybe even some female ones.

"Shit no, I didn't sleep with her." At least, not in the way he's asking. "And I'm not trying to. She's my best friend. I don't want to screw with that. How many times do I have to say it?"

"Until you actually look like you believe it." Mick clears his plate and heads towards the conference room. "Morning meeting. Let's go."

I can't seem to shake the thoughts of Charlie, though, and they do make me smile. They hit without warning and linger for as long as I can keep them there. I don't plan to do anything about them. They're just great thoughts to have. They make me smile when things around me don't.

Like tonight.

Board & Basin, the pub acting as my watering hole for the night, is crowded and noisy and decidedly Charlie-free.

I was foolish enough to make yet another first date, this time with Crystal Glass. And, yes, that is her real, God-given, on-the-birth-certificate name. Her parents must have been hoping their little girl had stripper ambitions.

As I lean on the barstool waiting for our table, I roll up my sleeves and try to listen to Crystal tell me about her dog. I think she said it was a Something Corgi, but it's hard to absorb anything she says when she turns every sentence into a question, raising her tone at the end of each and every sentence.

"The Queen of England had thirty Corgi's in her lifetime?" She sips at her bright green drink.

I shake my head over the top of my IPA. "I don't know. Did she?"

"And I, like, taught Duke Fenton Gulliver to fetch in only six days? He's like so smart?"

She pulls her phone out of her white leather purse.

Please, no. The last thing I want to see is pictures of her MENSA pooch.

When they say God doesn't give with both hands they must be thinking of Crystal because what He didn't give her in brains, He more than made up for in looks.

She's wearing a white linen blazer dress with four pairs of tan, turtle-shell buttons going down the front. I only know this because she spent the first twenty minutes of our date tonight explaining how L-Space, the company that gives her free clothes including this dress, was up in arms that she didn't mention the buttons in her paid post on Instagram.

The dress reminds me of a trench coat a girl might wear to win back her lost love with a little surprise. As she sits, it rides up, revealing tan, toned thighs I'd love to run my hands up if only I didn't have to listen to her voice trail up at the end of every sentence while I did.

I can hear it now. "Kiss me, Greyson?" and "Harder? Faster?"

That's not gonna do it for me.

As she leans forward to show me the fiftieth picture of her mutt, her blazer pulls open revealing a tattoo in some ancient script gracing the curve of her chest.

"What language is that in?" I ask, trying to change the subject.

She pulls her blazer open even more, looking down surprised, almost as if she had no idea she had a tattoo.

She giggles. "I don't know."

Is it wrong to leave a date before we're even been seated?

The waitress swishes by. "Your table's ready."

Crystal slips off her barstool and follows the waitress past the swarm of people near the bar still hunting for dates, to the tables in a somewhat quieter side of the restaurant.

On my way, I whip out my phone and tap out a message before throwing it back in my pocket.

**Greyson: I think I'm on a date with Deep Thinker's twin. She's got a script tattoo and doesn't even know what language it's in.**

I grab a stool at the bar height table while Crystal stares at the menu, slowly putting the letters together to form words. I pick the first burger on the menu in two seconds, so, while I wait for the beautiful scholar to decode the menu, I entertain myself watching people passing by on the sidewalk just outside the colossal window at the end of our table.

A buzz from my phone pulls me away from the forty-something woman screaming at her twenty-something boy-toy as she slaps at his chest.

**Charlie: I think they might be triplets. Told Chad tonight that I wanted to surf Australia one day, and he deadpans, completely serious, "I, like, don't even know where that is."**

I let out a howl which spooks Crystal.

"What!"

So it goes in both directions; sentences become questions and questions become sentences.

I shake it off. "You know what you want?"

"I can't decide. Should I get a Qwesa-Dilla or the chicken sandwich?"

"A Qwesa-Dilla?" I say, repeating her awful pronunciation.

Our waitress approaches before Crystal can figure out I'm mocking her and spits out the standard speech. "I'm Delia. I'll be helping you out tonight. Do you guys know what you—"

"So is the Qwesa-Dilla made with cheese or...?"

The waitress, unsure if she's kidding, turns an eye on me for clues.

I shake my head in shame.

"It's made with Asiago, Monterey, and an artisanal cheddar made on an organic farm run by the chef's brother."

"So, like, can you make it without all that cheese?"

I silently apologize to Delia, whose long-suffering surpasses mine.

"I'll have to go ask."

Maybe I should try that. I'll tell her I have to go ask the chef something and never come back.

Faintly, behind the sounds of guys trying to impress women with their predictable lines, Joan Jett belts out a song.

I pull out my phone, hit record, and then send.

I follow it up with a message.

**Greyson: Another for the Anti-Love playlist?**

I amuse myself with the sight of the girl at the next table trying to give her suitor the cold shoulder until the vibration in my hand pulls me back.

**Charlie: I can't make it out. You should sing it to me.**

**Greyson: Ha. Not likely. I'll give you a hint. Joan Jett.**

**Charlie: I am seeing the jet black hair. Leather pants she pours herself into. I'm listening for it...**

**Charlie: Do You Wanna Touch Me? I Love Playing With Fire?**

Stumping Charlie lightens my mood.

**Greyson: Nope. Try again.**

She does.

**Charlie: Run Aw NO I GOT IT!!!! I Hate Myself For Loving You.**

I peek up at Crystal, who is shooting daggers at me. "I'm not wasting another second on a guy who isn't smart enough to give me every second of his attention," she snaps.

So she does know what an actual sentence is supposed to sound like.

She slams down her paper menu on the table and glowers at it. "Ugh. That was supposed to make a bigger sound," then she storms out the door, shoving the hostess out of her way as she goes.

Outside she passes the open window next to me, flipping me off with both hands which flings her purse from her shoulder in the process. She stumbles a few steps before recovering and then stomps off.

"So, just the check, then?" Delia asks hesitantly.

"Actually, can I get a Barbecue Burger with the, uh, what was it? Artisanal cheddar? It sounded amazing. And another RuinTen, please?"

"Sure." She tucks her pen behind her ear.

"Thanks, Delia. And sorry about her." I point my thumb over my shoulder where the prodigy disappeared.

"I'm just surprised she's the one who left first." She runs her eyes down my chest as if proving her case.

"What can I say, I think everyone deserves a fair shake." I throw her my best Good Boy smile.

When she leaves to put in my order, I take the last sip of my beer and enjoy the cool breeze coming through the wall of open windows while I try to recover from yet another disheartening date.

I have completely lost my tolerance for dating, lately. It's all so much work. Pick out clothes that make me great, but not intimidating. Put all sorts of product in my hair to make it look like I did nothing to it. Trim my stubble so it screams 'I shaved this morning like a responsible man, but I am so much man I can grow a shit load of facial hair in mere hours.'

Then I'm forced to listen to vapid beauties drone on and on about shit I really have no interest in. And, when I'm not fortunate enough to pick the place, like tonight, I begrudgingly eat food at pretentious restaurants serving Frightened Monkfish Jam with Farfalle or Kraut Puree with Fingerling Shell Bean and Bison and where the waitstaff calls you Sir or, even worse, Chief.

Honestly, I'd rather be at home eating fish tacos and watching a stupid chick flick with Charlie, but she, too, is torturing herself with another Bex-approved tool. And if her response time to my texts is any indication, she would rather be on the couch next to me, too.

I should do a better job of saving her from that fate. It would be the right thing to do after all. And trying to nudge her over that friendship line will be much easier to recover from if I do it via text.

I take a huge bite of the dry-aged burger Delia dropped at the table and tear off a paper towel from the roll thrown at the end of the table.

**Greyson: If I had known your standards for intelligence on a date were so low, I'd have asked you out myself.**

I try to convince myself I'm really not trying to sabotage her date.

**Charlie: Hey! He's a Bex pick. Can't blame me for this.**

I'm only trying to save her night because, honestly, what we have is better than a shitty date. Hell, it's better than a good date. And Charlie deserves that.

**Greyson: Probably time to pick your own dates, don't you think?**

**Charlie: I'm starting to. Not sure how many more Bex rejects I can take.**

I stuff a truffle oil and Parmesan fry in my mouth and wash it down with a few gulps of my IPA, never taking my eyes off my phone.

**Greyson: Just don't give him your first-in-a-decade kiss. That one's reserved for me.**

I stare at the screen before sending. Am I asking my best friend to kiss me?

*Too far?*

Erasing the second sentence, I debate my next move.

**Greyson: Just don't give him your first in a decade kiss.**

That reads nothing but protective friend.

*Not far enough?*

I retype the original second sentence and send it before I have a moment to reconsider.

*Shit.*

*It was too far.*

*Too far, Steele!*

Someone really needs to come up with an app that will take back texts cause I would pay about a million bucks right now to have it.

Three dots jump on my screen.

Up and down and up and down and up.

My stomach reels with their every climb and sinks with each drop.

Then they disappear.

And nothing.

I think the nothing is worse than the dots.

Am I not being clear?

Or is that simply her answer? Trying to be kind while rejecting me. Trying to let me down without shaming me.

I wish I had the guts to just ask her what the hell she feels about me, but if I do and it's bad, once that's out there, it screws everything up. Once you mention the pink gorilla in the room, you'll never stop thinking about him.

It will forever stain every interaction we have. She'll wonder if there's a hidden agenda behind every word I say. She'll question if I'll ever got over those feelings or if I have some ulterior motive for taking care of her and protecting her from all the Delta Bravos out there.

You can't take the cyanide out of the cupcake once it's baked in there.

Not that, I'd do it that way, in case some judgmental blond I know ends up dead and smelling like almonds.

I finish off my burger and leave a few bills with the check, making sure I leave a quick note on the receipt, followed by my number. "Thanks for making a rocky night a little easier. Grey."

Outside, the nightly onshore winds have brought the scent of campfire with them. Waiting at the corner for the light to change, I spot Kealani's all closed up for the night. The plastic tables are stacked on one another inside the plate-glass windows, lush rain forest plants painted around the edges.

*Holy shit.*

*Did I seriously just ask my best friend to kiss me?*

I pull out my phone as the light changes and I cross. I'm only fooling myself, but I open the messaging app and reread my last text. Just in case.

Nope.

I'm a complete dumbass.

Apparently, I don't meet Charlie's new lowered standards of intelligence in men after all.

I take in another deep breath of roasted marshmallow when my phone finally speaks to me.

**Charlie: There's no way I'd ever kiss this buffoon.**

Tension in my neck I hadn't noticed before dissipates. Not sure if it's because she promised not to kiss him or because she's decided to keep talking to me, but either way, I'll take it.

I guess text wasn't the best way to push the boundaries after all.

I need to be able to see her react, to read her body, see her eyes as she processes the change. Text will never be a reliable substitute for real conversation; too many ways to miscalculate.

# 12

## GREYSON

The following Tuesday night, Delia is sitting on my distressed leather armchair giving me her best version of Come-Hither eyes. She's playing coyly with her straw in the scotch she requested but hasn't even tasted.

She's been sending those looks my way since I slid into the booth across from her at dinner, but now that we're back at my place and she can do something about it, she is putting on the full-court press.

Trying not to engage her from the other end of the sofa, I study the dust piled up on the signed baseballs on the bookshelf across the room and finally understand why Charlie is always busting my balls to dust the collection.

Delia is pretty enough, and she has a nice ass, for sure. I'm just not convinced there's enough between her ears to entertain me in the long run, but for tonight, she'll do.

Before I realize it, she springs on me like a ravenous lion. At least she's a decent kisser. All that aggression is well-tamed as she presses her mouth to mine.

Buzzing from my pocket cuts into our activities.

I try to pull my head away to check, but she has me pinned.

I press my hand to her shoulder to gain some distance, but she lays her hand on top of mine, giving it a little squeeze.

This is going to take more force than I expected.

"Hold on a minute," I say into her open mouth.

"Don't worry, I have one." She pulls a condom out of her pocket.

"Nope. Not where I was going." I slide out from under her and check my phone.

**Charlie: Fish Taco Tuesday. Be there in ten. U have Lagunitas?**

I text her back a beer mug and a shaka and set my phone screen-side down on the coffee table.

I turn to Delia, who is ready to resume her attack.

"Work. What can you do?"

"Oh." She gives me her version of puppy dog eyes, which come out more like an emaciated child on one of those Feed the Children commercials. Definitely more depressing than alluring.

"Do you haaaave to go to the fire station?" she whines.

"Yep. So, you've got to go. Sorry."

I offer my hand to help her off the couch and hopefully hurry her along.

"I can help you change into your uniform."

This woman cannot take a hint. "Nope. Don't need any help. Been getting dressed by myself for decades."

I pull her to her feet.

She steps into me, laying her hands on my chest, inching closer and lowering her voice just above a whisper. "I can come visit you there tonight. Bring dessert for the boys."

"Ahh. That's alright. We'll be working, so I'll just call you."

I rest my hand on her back and start walking her to the door.

She's finally convinced this date is over and, with a way too forceful kiss, is out the door.

I carry her scotch glass to the long kitchen island, polishing it off on my way. No sense in letting a quality scotch go to waste.

I wash the glass and throw it in the stainless steel dish rack to dry, then wipe the counter with a rag.

Shuffling back to the couch, I straighten the pile of surf mags on the coffee table Charlie always leaves here. I smack the pillows on the couch trying to remove the impression of Delia from them, not sure why I am fussing over couch pillows and magazine stacks.

I check my phone to see how long it's been since Charlie texted. Six minutes. Enough time to brush the taste of Delia's scotch out of my mouth.

I lean against the exposed brick wall next to the bathroom sink and scrub my teeth.

Returning the brush to the rack, I take a quick glance at my face in the mirror.

No trace of lipstick, but I really should cut my hair. The loose waves at the top become a full-on curl if I leave it too long.

The clink of a key in the lock pulls me out of my self-assessment.

I wipe my mouth on the still damp towel on the back of the door on my way out and, where I expect to find Charlie, there is only a plastic Rubio's bag in place of the magazines now scattered on the floor beside the table.

I follow the intermittent crunching to find Charlie sitting on the navy floor runner covering the length of the galley kitchen. She guzzles a bottle of Dr Pepper in between throwing handfuls of Lucky Charms at her mouth.

Some of them even make it in.

She's wearing ripped black jeans and a tight grey tank top, probably shed her modest button-down work shirt in the car.

"A bad one?" I ask as I scoop up the fallen pieces of cereal and toss them in the sink.

With cereal spilling out of her mouth, she mutters, "How can you tell?"

"You look..." I hand her a paper towel for the Dr Pepper now spilling out the side of her mouth, "...food aggressive."

"Food aggressive?" She laughs out an entire mouth full of marshmallows.

I peruse the scattered, half-chewed cereal surrounding her.

She tries to gather them off the rug quickly, spilling more out of her hand.

"Sorry, Grey."

She's so heartbreaking I can't muster an ounce of anger at her destroying my pristine kitchen.

"You got enough sugar?" I ask.

"Uh-huh."

That one came out without a hitch.

"Come recover on the couch."

I lead her past her wreckage to the couch. She pulls her legs up and rests her head on her knees.

Flipping on the game, I set up dinner, and retrieve one Lagunitas from the fridge; after a low like this, Charlie won't want to go back to a fuzzy brain from beer.

Leaning back against the couch, I lay my hand on her back, trying to make the pain of a bad low go away. My hand runs over her tank top and onto her bare shoulder, still deeply tan even in late October. My eyes follow the lines of her toned shoulder up her neck, willing my hand not to follow my gaze.

It's the first time I've touched her since we woke up together. When she's low, she doesn't enforce the Half-Foot Rule, some sort of weird exception or something, so I think I'm safe with a friend-approved hand on the back.

A few minutes later, she lifts her head, a baby bird spreading its wings for the first time to see if they are capable of flight. She lowers each leg tentatively and, when fully assured she is functional again, she digs into her fish tacos like nothing ever happened.

Knowing my small rule-free window just closed, I lift my hand and shift forward to hang my head over the taco wrapper. I never could figure out how to eat these things without dripping all over myself.

Charlie has some Kung Fu master technique for doing it without spilling a single drop, but that's Charlie. She has engineered her way out of any little annoying thing she encounters.

After she polishes off her first taco, she turns to me, full of energy again, and blurts out, "Delta Bravo is such a Dirk."

She tells me about his skill in taking anything she says and making it sexual and how he has systematically taken every valuable part of Nudge and redesigned it so it resembles "a stinking swath of blue whale poo. Except their poo at least creates pastures for krill to feed on. His poo won't bring a single positive thing into this world."

Leave it up to Sands to know the life cycle of whale poo.

"Why do you put up with it? You've got to do something about it?"

I fold up the taco wrapper and lean forward to put it in the bag at the far end of the coffee table. When I shift back, I let my leg rest against hers.

Instead of satisfying a need, the feel of that small bit of her skin only increases my hunger to touch her. To touch all of her.

She may not be low anymore, so I won't be able to break her Half-Foot Rule straight out, but I can see how far I can push it before she flinches.

"I just want to get through this project so I can go back to not having to work so close with Dirk."

She wraps up her trash to add to the bag, but when she slides back onto the couch, she comes back to the same spot without shoving my leg out of the Half-Foot Zone.

Interesting.

I lift my beer, stopping halfway to my mouth. "You know what they're doing is illegal. I've been looking up sexual harassment law and you could sue. You should sue."

"Then I can't use Big&Lime as a reference or take credit for making Nudge."

"Sounds like it's not really Nudge anymore. And do you really want to be known for making The Prick?"

"No, but..."

"I'm telling you, you should do something about it. Go to HR. Tell your boss. Do something."

"Whatever. Let's talk about something else."

She wrangles the beer from my hand, takes a long draw, and asks how my day was.

I tell her about dinner with Delia and her predatory skills.

"That was tonight? You order the Blue Hair Special, you old man?"

She hands back my beer after peeling the corner of the biscuit-colored label down a bit.

"We went out at a normal time."

She checks her watch, then looks to me to clear her confusion.

"When you texted, we were..." I hoist my beer and sip, hoping the suspension of words will help her fill in the details.

"And, what? When I texted, you told her to get out?"

She surveys the couch like the imprint of our bodies remains. Reflexively, she scoots over, leaning back on the armrest, pulling her leg up to widen the distance between us.

"Not like that. I was nice about it," I rumble.

Standing to throw away our trash, I see her defensive distance and raise her an entire room.

"I wasn't really into her," I call from the kitchen. "She wasn't the sharpest tool in the shed."

"So, you're not interested in her, but you'll still bring her back here and screw her?"

"Who said I brought her back for that?"

She doesn't know it's been years since I slept with a girl. And I don't mean that figuratively. I mean literal years. As in two-and-a-half years.

And all because of something she said.

You know that line in Office Space where Peter tells his therapist since he started work, every day of his life has been worse than the one before, so every single day you see him, that's on the worst day of his life? Charlie says that's the opposite of how she envisions her future sex life.

In a rare moment of openness, maybe spurred on by the second beer she had that night, she shared how, on her wedding night, she'll be able to have sex with her husband without any comparisons floating around in the back of her mind.

She won't have to think, "Oh, Bobby did that better," or, "Jimmy would do it like this." For her, everything he did that night would be the best she ever had. And it would only get better from there. So on any given night, she would be having the best sex of her life.

That thought, that way of looking at sex changed something in me, and I haven't been able to shake it. It always stops me in my tracks when I'm with a woman, well before I get to the good stuff.

"And since when is it okay to call a woman you're with stupid?" she roars.

Charlie's usually the first to disparage the women I date, and now she's getting all huffy because I say one's dumb? She was the one to tell me to stop promising I'm a great guy. To warn them they'll end up with a Cretan if they stick around, and when I do, I'm the bad guy? That's total crap.

I run my hand along the polished concrete atop the kitchen island while Charlie shifts uncomfortably.

"You're mad, Sands? Really?"

She rolls her eyes at no one in particular and shakes her head. "I'm not mad."

Oh, yes.

She is.

And why exactly is she getting so mad at this? Was it my lack of manners or the thought of me fooling around with a woman?

A woman who is not her.

I lean back against the end of the island, arms crossed in front of my chest, resting one foot in front of the other. "You sound mad," I say letting a little cockiness seep into my voice.

"Whatever. I should probably get going anyway. That was a rough low."

She crosses the living room and stands inches from me.

I place my hands behind me, leaning back on the counter. "You're leaving?"

She studies my face like the answer to my question is written there.

I study her lips like I want to know if they'll taste of lime and IPA and heaven.

She leans forward and I am immovable, all my brash confidence failing me right when I need it.

We're not those people who hug when we leave. We certainly don't kiss goodbye. So what is she doing leaning in like this?

As she moves closer, her hand brushes past mine on the counter, sending fire raging up my arm, but she is still considering my face.

Considering my eyes.

Considering my... lips?

My head will not budge.

*Move, you insubordinate traitor! Move!*

A jangling stirs me from my tirade as she reverses her course.

She flips her keys around her finger. "Good night, Grey."

# 13

## CHARLIE

*I* close Greyson's front door behind me a little too loud. I won't convince Grey I'm not mad by doing that. I turn back and stare at the door praying to see right through it, replaying our last conversation to distill why I am so heated.

How did a simple hang-out become a fight?

The closed door won't share any of its secrets, so I hop in my tin-can grey Jeep and slide the key into the ignition.

Why was it so weird when he brought up Delia?

I've heard pretty much all of his escapades with girls in great detail, oftentimes way too much detail, and never felt my stomach twist like that.

I mean, did I really need to know about the one girl who couldn't keep her hand out of his pants whenever they ate in a restaurant? Not really, but it didn't drive me to bash him like I did tonight.

When he told me another girl was a colossal fan of near-public fornication, I didn't bat an eyelash. I spent three years hearing the endless stories of Aubrey's giggle, her dreams of following him around the country when he got to the majors, and their plans to raise a little baseball-loving family. Grey once told me he had memorized every single curve, scar, and mole on her body and his goal was to kiss every single one.

I never overreacted like this.

Not once.

So why did this one bug me so much?

With no answer showing itself, I turn the ignition and drive home in a complete stupor. By the end of the short drive home, the only answer I have come up with was that the low made me cranky. That's one of the symptoms listed under the horrible clip art drawings on those posters in the doctor's office. Symptoms of low blood sugar may include: shakiness, making it very difficult to get cereal *into* my mouth; hunger, no shit; sweating, so gross. And confusion and irritability.

Maybe that was it, just lingering symptoms.

Once in bed, I have to go through some breathing techniques to persuade my muscles to relax and my heart rate to slow. As I hit the dreamland between awake and fully asleep, Grey scoots closer on the couch, letting his leg rest against mine, and I feel the same pull that almost dragged me under in Santa Barbara.

The next morning, I clear my head the best way I know how, with a full dose of saltwater. The water was prematurely cold and the solid strip of overhead clouds prevented the sun from mitigating the cold, but the waves were solid and the cold kept the crowds away.

Returning to the back deck, I strip out of my wetsuit and slip it onto a hanger. On my way to the screened-in sleeping porch extending from the deck around the side of the house, I set the hanger on the industrial metal pipe rack I set up the first day I moved in. Though this shack is old and creaky, it does have the most amazingly hot outdoor shower, and, on a cold morning, when my toes are nearly numb after a two-hour surf session in fifty-degree water, there is nothing more heavenly.

I jump in the shower in my bikini—it is outdoors after

all—and there are still people wandering by on the sand. My phone notifies me of a text from atop the daybed Greyson and I dragged home from a garage sale up the street when I first moved in. Grey knew how much I enjoy an afternoon nap in the sun, and I have more than gotten my money's worth from the ten-dollar price tag.

I wash the salt out of my hair using the small set of shampoo and conditioner I leave on the wooden shelf outside the shower as I ignore yet another notification. After a quick scrub with body wash, I stand under the water, enjoying the deceleration of my thoughts brought on by time in the ocean. Either someone is blowing up my phone right now with some sort of emergency or it's one of my favorite every-thought-texters, but either way, there is no way in hell I am leaving this shower until I am completely thawed.

Another ten minutes of overusing our state's most sparse natural resource and I'm sufficiently defrosted. I tug a fluffy pink towel from the hooks next to the shower and wrap it around my waist. Drying my hands on it, I lift my phone.

**Bex: What are you wearing tonight?**

*I don't know Bex. That's six hours away.*

I roll my eyes and then continue reading.

**Bex: Guys will judge you within the first five seconds of seeing you and take at least five days to change their mind about it.**

I wonder what scientific journal she read that in.

**Bex: You're a good person. Nice. Funny. Even though I don't get half of your jokes.**

I rub the drips of water from my eyelashes and reread that. Wow. That was almost nice.

**Bex: And you're smart, though you may want to tone that down in the beginning. You know how insecure guys are.**

I toss the phone onto the bed again and pull the towel from my waist. I wrap it around my hair, squeezing to remove as much water as I can, then resume scrolling through the never-ending stream of Bex's thoughts.

**Bex: And you always forgive so fast when I screw up.**

Huh. I assumed she was oblivious.

I walk to the scratched-up bar top at the far end of the deck and set down my phone so I can brush the ocean tangles from my hair while I keep reading.

**Bex: But guys can't see it before they write you off cause you dress like a dude.**

And there it is, Bex being her authentic Bex-y self.

**Bex: They won't stick around long enough for you to show them who you really are.**

That sounds a lot like what I have been trying to explain to Greyson with the peanut butter ice cream.

Maybe Bex is right. Changing my packaging is the only way I will catch a guy. I have to use the right bait. I can always cut him loose later on if he's not right.

**Bex: Nevermind. Come upstairs and I will help you pick something out.**

I towel off the ends of my hair once more and then hang the towel back up to dry. On my way through the kitchen, I nab an apple to tide me over until I can cook lunch. Choosing clothes with Bex can be a test of endurance, and I'm already hungry.

I meet Bex in the closet as she is whipping my clothes from one side of the closet to the other.

"Where do you keep your nice clothes? Like, the ones you would wear in public?" she asks, totally serious.

I point to the clothes she's currently scrutinizing.

She laughs and shakes her head.

"Hmm. You look good in white..."

She spins to her side of the closet and pulls out three different tops, then shoves them into my hands.

"And put this on." She pulls a short, black wrap-around thing with laces up the side. I swear it's a dried puddle of paint someone cut up and tied together with a string.

I glance at the clothes and then at her, brows pulled together like she just handed me plans for the DragonX and said, "Go in the other room and whip up a little rocket for me."

"Just try it on," she encourages.

Rounding the corner, I try to hide as I change so she doesn't witness my incompetence. After four attempts at wrangling the skirt onto my lower half, I slip on the translucent white blouse, buttoning the front.

I check out my new self in the mirror. I'm surprised Bex has a skirt with such a conservative length. It hits just above my knees and the blouse hangs loose around my hips. Not awful, if I forget about the fact it is so tight I can only take three-inch strides.

Bex exits the closet holding a huge bright pink box and sizes me up as she twists the skirt around me, setting the ties on my hip instead of dead center like a fly, and pulls it from sagging on my hips up to my waist. There goes the conservative length.

I run my fingers along the front seam of the shirt, looking for the other buttons. "Your last date a little too eager to get you out of this?" I joke.

"What?" She holds a gold chain with a giant round gold medallion up to my chest.

"It's missing the top buttons. I can sew some on if you need," I offer.

She laughs.

"It has all its buttons, Charlie. It's supposed to show off your cleavage. You have a great rack. You should show it off."

She holds up another thin gold chain, this one with a square medallion. "Here, put these on. I'll find some bracelets and earrings."

"Bex, it's freezing out." I pull at the thin blouse. "Do I at least get a long jacket?"

"That's what these are for." She holds up a pair of black boots that have to be at least three feet tall.

She actually wants me to strap myself into those.

*Use the right bait, Charlie.*

I breathe out a sigh of abdication and slip on the boots, meeting Bex in front of the wide mirror above the double sinks in the bathroom that opens into our shared bedroom.

"Charlie, fashion is about more than the bare necessities needed to cover your jubblies and jay-jay. It's about the extras, the flourishes."

She hands me two necklaces and a pair of dangly earrings.

"The bracelets, earrings, shoes that showcase what you have. Show it off."

I press the earrings through the closed-up holes in my ears with more than a little pain, trying to absorb Bex's Style rules. Maybe I should add them to my rulebook under appearance. Or maybe I test them out and verify they work first. They are from Bex, after all, a girl who thinks the moon can only be out at night.

My phone buzzes against the pink linoleum-covered counter. Bex swipes it. "You've been holding out on me, Charlie. Who is Untamed Stallion and why is he flirting with you?"

"It's Grey. And he's not flirting with me."

Greyson thinks it's hilarious to go into my phone and change his contact info and ringtone. He's renamed himself Incredible Hunk, Prince Charming, and Deep Water Horizon, whatever that means. He once changed my ringtone to *Why Don't We Get Drunk and Screw?* which, unfortunately, I wasn't smart enough to change before I got a call while having lunch with my grandma.

I now keep a very close eye on my phone when I'm anywhere near Grey.

Bex squeals with derision dripping from her voice, "Oh. Em. Gee. He's like totally pledging his love to you."

Bex scrolls through my texts over the last few days.

"Let me have that, Bex."

She pulls it out of my reach. "I'm sorry, what? 'Just don't give him your first in a decade kiss. That one's reserved for me'?"

She stares at me like her whole world view just exploded.

"He didn't mean it like that. It was a bit we had going about all the stupid people we keep ending up on dates with."

But the incredulity won't leave her face.

When I first got that text, even I had to read it through a few times to figure out what he really meant. With text, you miss so much punctuation. And you know what they say, punctuation saves lives.

Let's eat, Grandma.

Let's eat Grandma.

I started reading it out loud in every way possible to figure it out. I must have sounded like a Swedish robot.

Save. That one for me? Save that one for? Me! Nope. Not that way!

Save that. One. For me. Save that one. For me? Yeah. That one. As in, "do this enormous favor that I know you don't want to do. Please do it for me since you value our friendship so much." Save that one. For me? He was just looking out for me. He wouldn't want me to waste something I value so much on a dork.

I rescue my phone from her grasp. "There's no way he meant it like that. It's not like that with us."

"Oh, I know. Poet Friends." She hands me foundation and a wedge of sponge. "Like I showed you," she nudges.

"Poe Friends." I take the foundation and lay down a thin coat.

Bex sets down the pallet of eye colors she's been smearing all over her face and whirls around to scrutinize me. "You don't have feelings for Greyson, do you, Charlie?"

Usually, I can answer that question without hesitation. I've had to answer it hundreds of times over the years from friends and family and even well-meaning complete strangers, and each time it has been the simplest question to answer. Like one plus one is two.

But lately, that question has been a bit fuzzier. Like what is infinity divided by zero. No real clear answer exists, and asking me to articulate why is painful.

Even if I have no clear answer, I won't let Bex know it. She'd take one little admission and run with it, inserting herself in places she doesn't belong.

"I don't have those kinds of feeling for him and he doesn't see me that way either."

"I wouldn't be so sure. You heard him when you came down the stairs before our date with Jack and Bobby."

She moves back to painting her face, like focusing on me fully for over thirty seconds is beyond her ability. "He almost dropped his jaw on the floor and was like," Bex drops her voice to Marvin Gaye levels "'She is sooooo sexy.'"

She bursts into a rendition of *Let's Get It On* complete with a striptease.

I laugh at exactly the wrong moment, streaking eyeliner out towards my ears.

"You are reading way too much into that, Bex."

I snatch a makeup wipe from the counter and erase my blunder.

"Don't worry, Charlie. I'll figure it out. You'll know how he feels by the end of the week, one way or the other."

That's exactly what I was trying to avoid, Bex inserting herself in the middle of things.

"I don't want you talking to him about this, Bex. He won't take it well. Especially from you," I demand.

I finish my eye makeup and turn to her, even putting my arm on hers to reinforce my point. "Promise me you won't talk to him about it, Bex."

"I won't say a word, Charlie." She finishes blotting her lips, tossing the tissue in the trash.

She spins on her toes and nearly prances out the door. "But I'm still gonna prove it to you," she calls over her shoulder.

I don't like the sound of that.

# 14

## CHARLIE

*L*ater that evening, I arrive home sans Bex, who decided to stay out with Walker, the more ambitious of our two dates tonight. I lay my boots at the base of the stairs on my way to the kitchen.

Indigo is using the dining room to rehearse a scene from her next short film with a guy who was built for a leading man's role. His chocolate hair lays over a finely chiseled face, rippling muscles bulging from beneath a tight tee.

I slide my earrings onto the counter as I silently load my arms with a spoon, bowl, milk, and a box of Honey Nut Cheerios; after nine p.m., I like to go a little healthier with my cereal. I slide open the door to the deck and am greeted with a gust of frigid wind. I'll need a swim parka over this outfit to eat outside.

"You don't have to eat out there. You can stay in here if you want," Indigo says.

"Thanks. I'll be quiet, I promise." I slide into the seat at the island and begin reading the back of the cereal box. I still think they should print SAT words on the back of these things, the way kids incessantly read them while chomping on their sugar nuggets floating in milk.

"Charlie, you think you could do me a favor?" Indigo asks.

*As long as I can get back to my fourth meal before it gets soggy.*

I swipe the milk dripping down my chin with the back of my hand, careful not to drop it on the thin blouse or Bex's skin-tight skirt-thingy. "Sure. What'd you have in mind?"

"Could you run this scene with Wells? Jennie didn't show tonight, and it's too hard to get a good sense of what he's doing when I'm also reading the other part."

I rise and tug down the hem of my skirt. "I can read it, but I can't really act it."

"That's fine. He just needs someone to work against."

I approach the dining table where they're seated. "Do I sit down here?"

"Yeah. You can start from here." Indigo points to a line at the top of the third page.

I hesitantly read out the first line. "What are you thinking, Johnny?"

Wells turns into a whole new person when he begins. He is oozing confidence and charm and looks at me in a way I am totally unfamiliar with.

"At Quantico, they train us to read people, to figure out what they're thinking. And I've got to say, Sutton, you're pretty easy to read."

His attention brings color to my cheeks. I know he is reading from the page, but my body reacts anyway.

Indigo taps the script in my hands.

"Oh... sorry... Umm." I check the script. "Oh, yeah?" I prompt Wells waiting for another dose of his scripted flirting.

"Yeah. You meandered up the stairs- not really in a rush to get home. You have your keys in your hand, but you haven't made a move for the door. You're not quite ready to leave me out here."

I pick up on my cue. "You're not that hard to read either."

I flash him a cocky smile, really getting into it. "You walked me home slowly like you're in no big hurry to return to that party. You brought up this conversation that's a little provocative, but not too committal, so you can figure out where my head's at.

And now you can't look me in the eye. I may not be trained by the government like you are, but I think that usually means you're trying to hide something yourself."

Wells locks his eyes on me and lowers his voice, "So, Sutton, where is your head at?"

"That's what I'm talking about. The back and forth. Playing off her." Indigo beams. "Can we do it again?"

She swivels back and forth between Wells and me.

"Sure. That was kind of fun," I say.

I read through the last line one more time. The first two are easy enough, but I want to get the last one down.

We read through a few more times while at the table.

"How about we try it at full speed? And outside? We need stairs."

Indigo rises and moves us into place on the steps leading to the sand, showing us how we'll move as we go through the scene.

I have the lines down pat and have some fun moving around. Pretending I'm someone completely different is a total trip.

When Wells gets to his last line, he climbs the two sand-worn steps bringing his face just inches from mine, and whispers, "So, where is your head at?"

I am so into this alternate reality I lean in a little before catching myself.

"That's perfect. Let's keep that just like it is. What did you think, Wells?" Indigo asks.

"It's a lot easier with...," he pauses, letting me fill in my name.

"Charlie."

"It's a lot easier with Charlie. She gives me something to work with."

Indigo studies me. I can tell her head is spinning with ideas. She jots down a few things in her notebook before looking back up at her watch. "Why don't we call it a night. We can work more on Thursday?"

As she walks Wells to the door, I clear my cereal mess and melt into the bench on the deck, rubbing the arches of my foot.

Indigo slides onto the bench next to me, carrying a pear with her. She's clearly as exhausted as I am, but she has her director's face on. "So, what would I have to do to convince you to be Sutton?"

"I don't speak Hollywood. What does 'Be Sutton' mean?"

Indigo eyes me like I am her only life raft in a sea full of rolling waves. "Jenny's not really working out and we start shooting in about eight weeks. We shoot in Maui, so a free trip. You'd really be helping me out."

"You want me to act?" I laugh. "I really don't want to ruin your next movie, Indie."

She tosses the pear from one hand to the other. "Your chemistry with Wells is off the charts, Charlie. You'd be saving my film."

"Wait. You're serious?" I lift the script from the bench next to me and thumb through it. Only fifteen pages—I could memorize that in a day—and it was really fun pretending to be someone I'm not.

"So what's the role like? What's the story?"

Could I really do this? Act? In front of people?

It's one thing to play around when no one is watching, but to do it for real with a camera and people staring at me is a whole other animal.

"After saving Sutton, Johnny, an FBI agent, is assigned to shadow her to keep her safe. But the real danger they face is in falling for each other." Indigo sounds like she's rattled off this summary more than once.

"So Sutton is the main character?" I toss the script back onto the bench. "There's no way I could pull that off."

"You'd be perfect. Come on, you'd really be saving me. If I keep Jennie as Sutton, I'd rather not make the film at all."

"So, how'd you get into making Indie movies anyway?" I say, trying to change the subject.

I have always been so in awe of Indigo's fearlessness. She has some studio credits from early on in her career—I looked her up on IMBD when I first met her—but she struck out on her own in a way I could never have done.

"I spent a hundred grand on an education I am still paying off only to be told I would have to work my way up from the scuzzy bottom, starting with retrieving coffee for talented dick heads who propositioned me twice daily, as if that would teach me anything about making movies except for how I didn't want to treat people."

She lifts the pear and bites into it before continuing. She pops the pear piece out of her mouth and takes a second bite of it, leaving the skin in her hand. "And we were making total crap. Soulless, heartless movies people would forget before they even walked out of the theater. I would come home each day and start blaring punk rock music—Ramones, The Clash, Blondie—just to wash the assholes out of my head."

She uses her teeth to peel the rest of the skin off in chunks, leaving them in a neat pile on the bench before biting into the pear like a normal person. "Punk rock back then was more than just a music genre. It was a set of values. They had something to say, and they wouldn't let a lack of technical ability prevent them from saying it. They loved doing it on the quick and on the cheap. They weren't in it for prestige or for the Sunday Paper reviews, and they would not waste any time talking about it. They were doing it."

I lower my right foot and lift my left, working out the knots those black boots created in it tonight. "I never thought about it like that."

"I realized these artists I looked up to my entire life were doing art the right way. The way I wanted to do my own art. I looked around and realized I had all the tools I needed to make my own movies instead of the bullshit Hollywood has been pumping out by exploiting the cheap labor of future filmmakers. I could pick up my iPhone and a bootleg version of Final Cut Pro and finally make my own movies. Movies that said something. I quit my PA job the next day and never looked back."

I still can't believe she had the guts to strike out on her own with no one to help her or fall back on.

"Making movies your way is cheap, right? But not free. Even cheap movies are like hundreds of thousands of dollars to make. How do you pay to make them and pay yourself on top of that?"

"A cheap Hollywood movie is hundreds of thousands of dollars, but my last feature was only a little over nine grand."

She slides her pile of pear skin pieces from the bench beside her and tosses them into the trash. "Hey, throw on the fire pit, would you?"

I lift the seat of the bench and retrieve a long lighter from the storage bin below. "Is it really that cheap?"

"Sure. If you have something to say, you find a way to say it. Money should never stand in the way of art."

That may be how it is for art, but what about for creating other stuff? I wonder if the same could be true of all creative things? Even creating an app?

"Okay. So how do you come up with $9000? Trust fund? Rich parents? Rich boyfriend?"

Indigo disappears into the kitchen to retrieve a Kombucha from the fridge. She returns to the bench with a fuzzy pink blanket emblazoned with a large mohawked skull and chugs down half of her drink in one gulp before going on.

"I find investors. People who love good films or companies who are interested in a certain topic in my film. They're willing to shell out money for a passion project. Whatever money I make on one project, I roll over into the next one."

Investors.

Could I do Nudge by myself, my way, if I had investors?

"And it works? I mean, aren't you afraid of losing someone's money or going bankrupt or something?"

"I don't make any promises when I ask for money."

I turn the knob on the propane tank in the storage bin and lower the lid.

"They have to understand that it's art. You can't predict how it will be received by an audience. And I sure as hell will not censor my own voice to make more money for them."

I wish I had that kind of faith in my own creations. That kind of artistic integrity.

"You thinking about striking out on your own with Nudge?" she asks.

I hadn't seriously thought about doing Nudge on my own before tonight, but she has made a strong argument.

I don't need fame. I don't need reviews or BuzzFeed to write about me. And I certainly don't need a lot of money as long as I can keep living here for so cheap.

"Not really. I am just inter—"

She steps on my excuses. "Why not? You've got a killer idea there."

"Wait. How do you know about Nudge?"

I've never talked about it to anyone but Greyson.

And my asshat boss.

"I've seen the plans."

I wrinkle up my forehead, trying to think of what plans she's talking about.

"The yellow paper. Next to your desk," she explains.

"Oh, that."

I can't visualize all the parts of a new idea on a computer screen, too confining. So I've been adding thoughts on features and ideas for the user interface to a colossal piece of sunny yellow butcher paper. Blue lines and arrows swipe from place to place, connecting the ideas floating around in my head.

I try to keep it rolled up tight when I'm not working on it. It would make anyone who got a glimpse of it seriously consider calling the FBI to turn me in as a serial killer plotting my next murder.

"I swear I'm not crazy. I need the space to organize my thoughts."

She laughs. "You should see the glass doors after I take a bath."

Okay. Crazy is relative, after all.

"The glass doors?" I prod.

"I never take a bath without a dry erase marker. I always get my best ideas in there."

She moves forward on the bench awaiting the heat coming as soon as I can focus enough to light the damned thing.

"That's so true. I can't tell you how many times I've jumped out of the shower, dripping wet, to write things down on paper only to find it soaked and illegible afterward."

"Right. And if I wait until I'm finished bathing to write them down, they're gone. So I write them on the doors," she adds.

"That's brilliant."

Dry erase pens go on my mental shopping list immediately.

"What's brilliant?" Greyson's voice booms before he appears in the doorway.

He's dressed like he's returning from another date, dark grey pants slung low on his hips held up by a broad black leather belt cinched in a flat buckle. His plain heather grey tee is made less plain as the light from the moon lays in highlights and shadows against the planes of his chest and stomach.

"Having Charlie star in my next short," Indigo plays the only card she has left; convincing Greyson to sway me.

I fix her with a stare that she either doesn't see or simply ignores.

"That is brilliant." Grey would take her side.

He sits on the bench behind me while I tighten the last bolt inside the fire pit and close the door.

"Not happening," I vow.

Greyson leans forward, resting his elbows on his knees. "Why not?"

"Because I don't act? Because I am not anywhere close to what that role needs? Because I don't want to ruin her movie?"

I turn the knob on the fire pit and touch the lighter to it.

*Whoosh.*

Flames jump up almost engulfing my face.

I lean back to avoid the singe and turn to see if they saw how close it was.

Greyson's eyes are wide.

Indigo is so invested in convincing me, my narrow escape from a fiery death barely registers.

"You'd be saving my movie. We film in eight weeks. There's no way I could find someone as good as you in that time," Indigo pleads.

"Sutton's like the lead, right?"

I sit between Indigo and Grey, pulling half of her blanket over my legs before putting the finishing touches on my indisputable argument. The one they have all overlooked.

"She's the sexy girl on all the posters, the one who convinces all the boys to go see the movie. There's no way I could pull that off."

"Guys would line up to see you do that, especially in that outfit," Greyson says with a sly smile.

My cheeks warm and my heart speeds up like they did from Wells's scripted flirting.

I take in the sheer white top with its non-missing buttons and the short, black skirt. Maybe dressed up as someone else, I could pull it off.

I school my face to hide the smile threatening to bare itself. "Yeah. To see me embarrass myself," I try to play it off.

Indigo slides the rest of the blanket onto my legs and stands. "It's been a long night. I'm gonna hit it. Greyhound, convince her to do it for me."

Greyson flashes Indigo the same sly smile. "I'll do my best."

Indigo's cheeks don't turn pink. Her heart, I'm sure, doesn't speed up. She's smart enough to recognize a player's smile for what it is.

Usually, I'm better at it, too. I think all this play flirting with Wells has made me lose my edge.

Greyson pulls the blanket to cover his legs and for a moment, we both take in the delicacy of the vaulting waves of light and heat emanating from the fire pit.

"So." He pulls his eyes from the flames. "We gonna talk about it?"

Shit.

I avoid his inquisitive eyes, not having an explanation for why his story about Delia got me so pissed last night.

"I was kind of hoping we wouldn't?" I plead.

His voice grows gentle and rusty, "What the hell was that, Charlie?"

Over the velvety blanket, I let my finger trace the golden earring in the skull's ear. Or, rather, the place his ear would be if he had any flesh remaining.

"I overreacted a little," I say, hoping my small admission will satisfy him.

"A little?" He laughs. "And the 2020 Australia wildfires were just a little campfire."

"Okay. Fine. I freaked out."

I cross my arms in front of me.

He bumps his shoulder into mine.

"You did freak out. Didn't you?"

# 15

## GREYSON

O kay, I can't do this any longer." Charlie stands up, tossing aside the blanket we had been sharing.

I pull my eyes from the fire and scan her face for any indication which way this is going.

I replay the past few days while waiting for my best friend to rebuke me. I told her she is sexy enough to be a leading lady. I broke the Half-Foot line a few times and she didn't send me packing. I joked via text about her kissing me.

Okay, fine, I outright asked her to kiss me.

I could have sworn she thought about kissing me in my kitchen the other night.

But then there's the fighting and the leaving and the radio silence for days on end.

Reading Charlie is getting harder and harder, lately.

I take a deep breath and ready myself for whatever she throws my way. "Can't do what?"

She holds her arms out to each side, revealing the laced-up side of her short black skirt and the miles of cleavage her sheer white top reveals as if I'm supposed to know what that means.

"You may have to use words on this one, Charlie."

"Wear this costume. I feel like I'm playing dress-up in someone else's story."

She runs upstairs, returning a few minutes later in a pair of cut-off jean shorts and her favorite heather red Pinky and the Brain shirt. She wraps her hair into a bun on top of her head, and somehow, like this, she is even more beautiful. Though that last outfit showed off the best aspects of her body, there was something unsure in her demeanor. Now, in her favorite shirt with her hair pulled back and the ease with which we sit together, she is radiant.

I put on my best British accent and ask, "Gee, Brain, what do you want to do tonight?"

She growls back menacingly, "The same thing we do every night, Pinky...Try to take over the world."

Back in high school, it somehow became a bit we would do every time she wore the shirt.

"Where'd you find it?" I ask.

She tugs at the hem of her shirt making the picture of the two cartoon lab rats on the front lie flat so she can take it all in. "Can you believe it was at my parent's the whole time? You and I spent like five hours looking for it."

It isn't the first time her favorite shirt has gone missing. She was wearing it the morning she found me passed out in my own vomit after the worst call of my career.

After sitting through a debrief at the station and counting down the minutes for my shift to end, I spent the rest of the night searching for the numbness that would make everything go back to normal. When the first three beers didn't do the trick, I moved on to whiskey. By the time I missed our run the next morning and had forgotten to reply to Charlie's six texts and four phone calls, she was getting scared.

I still cringe at the thought of her opening my front door to find me motionless, face down on the charcoal grey planks of the hallway leading to my bedroom. She ran to my side and shook me like a great white trying to kill a baby seal.

I rolled over and, like the total shit I was, pointed to her shirt and said, "Gee, Brain, what do you want to do tonight??"

She didn't reply.

It was a bit we had done a hundred times before, but it wasn't what she wanted to hear after thinking she found her best friend alone in his house, dead.

When I finally looked past her shirt, I saw Charlie leaning up against the far wall of the hallway with tears streaming down her face.

*Steele, you asshole.*

Rubbing the back of her hand over her freckled cheeks, an enraged growl escaped her lips. "What..." was all she could manage in her fury.

She spots the Alex Rodriguez-signed baseball stuck in the new hole in the wall, the pile of beer bottles I polished off once the whiskey ran out, and back to the puddle of vomit I used as a pillow last night.

She leaned forward on her knees and pulled my arm from the ground. She ran her fingers up to my hand, folding it over hers and trailed them over the dried blood covering my palm and the open wounds camouflaging my knuckles. Her anger evaporated.

She knew something had gone wrong. Really wrong. But she didn't ask.

She stood and left the hall, returning with a full glass of water and a bottle of ibuprofen. "Think you can sit up?"

She helped lift me to a sitting position, slowly, not knowing if the puddle beneath me contained the totality of my stomach contents or if I had more to add.

Pouring out two pills, Charlie looked at me and said, "It's an eight-hundred-milligram kind of a day, isn't it?"

She shook out two more and handed them to me with the water, then leaned back against the other side of the hall again, not pressing me for information or demanding anything. "The same thing we do every night, Pinky," she whispered.

I let out a small laugh before the thing I tried so hard to drink away last night slammed into me again. I dropped my head to my knees and started a cry that didn't let up for several days.

Charlie stayed with me the whole time. She made sure I ate and showered and when I was ready, she listened while I told her the story of my greatest failure. She didn't leave once. She ate my food, showered at my place, and stole my clothes when she got sick of wearing her favorite shirt for the third day in a row.

I never told her, but I slept with that damned shirt of hers for the next month. The smell of bananas and sunshine were the only light in the dark days that followed.

By the time my next shift was to start, I had gathered enough strength from her that, after my mandated shower, I got dressed in more than dirty sweat shorts for the first time in four days. I still wasn't sure I would have the strength to venture outside my front door, but I knew getting dressed was the first step.

"Ooh. You look good." Charlie scooped three banana-and-chocolate-chip pancakes off the griddle and slid them onto a plate for me. "You finally ready to leave this place and venture outside?"

The concept of leaving the safety of this house, the safety of her presence, stared me down like a forty-foot clean-up set at Jaws. I scrubbed my hands through my hair, contemplating the task that just a few days ago never would have given me a moment's pause.

She dropped the plate onto the placemat across the island from the six-burner stove she was working on.

I forced as much false bravado into my voice as I could muster. "I don't know if I'm ready, but duty calls."

I slipped behind her to the fridge, fighting the urge to wrap my arms around her and never let go. I pulled the apple juice from the fridge and poured myself a glass.

"You don't work for another week, Grey."

I closed the fridge and tapped on the schedule held to the door by the Southernmost Point magnet Charlie brought home from her last sailing trip in The Keys.

She shook her head at me. "Nope. Captain Jameson called two days ago, asking about you. I told her how you were doing—"

"You didn't."

"Don't worry, I left out the embarrassing parts. But she said she'd get someone to cover your next shift."

"Was she mad? She was mad. Did she sound pissed? Like she was planning on firing me, but needed some time to get the paperwork in order? Or was—"

"God no, Grey. She was concerned about you. She told me to make sure you kept talking about it. That when the guys stopped talking is when we really have to worry."

Silently, Charlie asked if she needed to step up her worrying. As long as she stayed by my side, she wouldn't need to worry about a thing.

"I'll keep talking, if you keep listening, Sands."

I slid into the barstool at the kitchen island and, as I ate the greatest pancakes ever, thought for the first time in days, that I might have the courage to leave my front door.

Charlie's sweet voice breaks me from the memory. "I swear this shirt has a life of its own when I'm not looking."

She pulls the blanket back over her legs on the bench next to me. "I sometimes wonder if it goes out for beers with the boys or goes for a surf. Or it takes long, relaxing, tropical vacations without me."

"Maybe it has to go comfort all the other little boys and girls who need him."

I hardly see Charlie for the rest of November or December. I bury myself studying for finals in my Fire Behavior and Public Fire Protection classes. Charlie buries herself in learning the finer points of acting. We both make it home for Christmas, but magically are too busy to hang out back home. By the time January rolls around, I have settled into my early morning study routine for the last two classes in the Bachelor's of Occupational Safety I'll need to one day become Captain.

I don't love hiding the fact I'm working towards my Bachelor's, but if I tell her, she'll offer to help me study which will only make me feel dumber. She picks up more info by quizzing me than I do after hours of reading and studying.

The only way I even passed High School was because of all the tutors Coach Ford lined up for me. That and the pressure he put on the teachers to inflate my grades. Charlie tries to convince me it's not true, but when I blew out my shoulder at USC and I lost the tutors and inflated grades, I couldn't pass a class to save my life.

Thank God these classes are easier, but only because if I don't learn this, someone dies. Just that simple. With those kinds of stakes, I have to learn.

After four hours straight pouring over Fire Prevention Management and Fire and Arson Investigation, the rumbling in my stomach is making it hard to focus. I toss my books to the coffee table. Pulling my legs from the leather couch sounds like peeling off a wet condom.

I stretch them, taking long strides to the kitchen to find something to stave off the hunger. I pull open the fridge and stare. Studying has used all my brainpower for the day, and figuring out what's edible is nearly impossible.

I'm saved by my phone buzzing back on the coffee table. Charlie will for sure want to grab food somewhere and with her making the decisions, I won't have to strain another brain cell. I tear across the kitchen and check my phone. Lighting up my screen is a picture of Kathy Bates in Misery hoisting that sledgehammer.

Why the hell is Bex calling me?

"Becky?" I tease. Bex hates being called that, so of course, I try to use it as much as possible.

"Uhh.. Greyson?" Did she seriously forget who she dialed only moments ago?

Might as well go with it. "Nicole?"

"Wait. What?"

"I know who it is, Bex. What do you need?" I grumble while underlining, *Structures, environment, and other failures are inextricably intertwined in Deepwater Horizon.*

"You have to come get me, Grey," she whines.

"Come where?" I continue marking my textbook, *These forensic incidents are very rarely an accident.*

"Moonlight Beach parking lot. Like, right now. There's this really creepy hobo who keeps smiling at me."

I must have missed some crucial info. "You don't have anyone else you can call, Bex?"

"You're the only one with a truck. And my bike won't fit in Charlie's Jeep."

"Why don't you ride your bike?" I say like I'm talking to a three-year-old, which really isn't too far off for Bex.

"I told you. I got a flat tire. Are you gonna help or not?"

My phone says 11:30. How did I lose six hours studying?

I need lunch anyway. I can pick up a burrito on my way home. "I'll be there in fifteen."

# 16

## GREYSON

When I arrive at the parking lot at Moonlight Beach, I walk to the railing overlooking the water and check the waves. I haven't missed anything by studying this morning.

"Greyson, my hero." Bex throws her arms around me like she doesn't hate every bone in my body.

"Bex," I say coldly.

I step out of her arms and pull my shirt away from my chest which is now emblazoned with two wet triangles where Bex pressed her bikini top into me. "Where's the bike?"

"Down there." She points to the bike rack at the bottom of the hill. "Can you carry it? It's too heavy for me."

I retrieve the bike, fully expecting her to be dried off and dressed when I return. No such luck.

I toss the bike in the pickup's bed and round the tailgate to slip into my seat.

She lays a towel on the seat and bends to grab her bag from the ground, making sure to angle her barely covered ass my way.

I turn away to check out the waves.

She drags her giant, yellow-striped bag into the car, setting it between her feet before pulling them onto the seat, tipping her knees towards me. "That was so heavy for me. You make it look like it doesn't weigh a thing."

She rests her hand on my arm.

Okay. Now I know she is up to something. She better not have a sledgehammer in that bag of hers.

I pull my arm from her grasp and turn around to back out. When I turn back to drive, she is still inches away, staring at me and smiling coyly.

I keep my eyes plastered to the road, trying not to encourage her. She doesn't get the message, running her hand up and down her thigh, pretending to be fidgeting. She is pulling out all the Bexley stops.

Making a right onto Highway 101, I try to distract her from her scheming. "So how is the Summer Goal going?"

"I don't know GreyBey."

GreyBey? Since when does she have a pet name for me.

"I can't seem to find the right guy. I keep picking these childish boys. I need a man. A real man."

"Uh, huh."

Why can't Del Mar be closer to Moonlight? Why couldn't Charlie have bought a truck instead of her stupid Jeep? Why did I ever agree to this in the first place?

"I don't know what I'm doing wrong. I go to all this trouble to get ready for a date, pick out the perfect outfit, jewelry, makeup. I always wear my killer stilettos and my best lingerie." She flips the visor down and runs lip gloss over her lips. "And they never call me the next day. After all that. Nothing. And I do everything a guy wants."

She puts her hand on my arm again for emphasis, and mouths, "Everything."

I stare back at the road, thanking God there is no traffic this late into fall.

She puts on a fake pouty face. "Maybe it's the lingerie. I think I pick out the wrong ones."

I turn onto Charlie's street.

"Do you think I could try them on for you? Get a real man's opinion? No one will be home for a couple of hours."

I pull up to her house and throw it into park. Her problem is she doesn't know how to take a hint. We've been barely civil with each other for years—the only reason I put up with her at all is because she is Charlie's friend—and now she thinks I'll follow her up to bed?

There is one girl I would love to see try on lingerie in that bedroom, but it isn't Bex.

I don't bother answering her, instead, I hoist her bike from the truck bed, and walk it to the side of the house.

Bex follows me, tugging at the sides of her bikini.

When I turn to walk back to my truck, she has me cornered in the narrow walkway. Striking a pose, she leans against the gate, then pulls it closed behind her, trapping me. "So, can I get your opinion?" she moans.

"Nope."

She steps closer to me and runs her hands along my chest. "But GreyBey, I need a real man to show me what I'm doing wrong."

I pull her hand from my chest. "You're barking up the wrong tree, Bex. I'm not interested."

She stares at my pants and licks her lips. "Mmm. I'd like to climb your tree."

"What the hell, Bex. Stop."

I try to walk past her, but she shoves me up against the gate with such force the lock busts off and I fall backward through it. Thankful for the escape, I hurry back to my truck and speed off.

I spend my drive home trying to erase the sight of Bex coming on to me by wondering what kind of lingerie Charlie would wear in that fantasy try-on session. Probably a neon g-string. Neon yellow is amazing against her skin when it's tan. And a matching lace bra, thin enough to not really cover anything. Or something in black during the winter when her tan has faded and her skin is polished satin. A black teddy. Maybe a matching garter. And one of my white button-down shirts hanging open over it all with her hair down and wavy and falling in her face.

Does Charlie even own stuff like that? A whole drawer of things I'll never see?

When I pull up to my driveway, I realize I've spent the last twenty minutes daydreaming about Charlie in a way she would execute me for if she ever found out. She just might have to spank me for my devious thoughts.

*Dammit, Greyson. Get your shit together.*

I plop on the couch and try to resume studying, but flashes of Charlie sauntering out of my hallway, leaning up against the wall, showing off another outfit for me prevent me from focusing on the politics at play in fire department administration.

I have to see her.

I pull out my phone, open the messaging app, and my last failed attempt at text-flirting slaps me in the face. My stomach seizes at the memory of seeing those dots bouncing and disappearing on my screen. My thumbs hover over the keys, waiting for inspiration.

How do I say I want more with her? And how do I say it without freaking her out and losing everything we have already? Am I being greedy to want the crazy, giddy kind of together where we giggle uncontrollably while wrapped up in each other's arms?

During one of my study breaks this morning, I scrolled past a picture of two sea otters on the sand. One is sitting upright against a rock, the other otter rests her head on the lap of the first, his paw resting on her hip. The sight of it shot joy through my entire body because it reminded me so much of that quiet comfort Charlie and I share.

I pull up the picture and send it to Charlie with a message.

**Greyson: Want to hang in the sun today?**

I know I said text wasn't the best way to push our boundaries, but a picture of otters isn't really a text.

Dots appear on my screen, then disappear. I set my phone on my books and pace the room.

*Come on, Charlie. Type something.*

I grab a Corona from the fridge. It's too early in the afternoon for anything heavier if I still want to study and retain anything.

I check my phone. Now I remember why I swore I wouldn't try to text flirt again. No feedback. And the waiting is killing me.

Did I say too much and she's pissed? Did I say too little and she doesn't sense the shift? Did I say the right amount and she is so overjoyed by my advances she is speechless?

Yeah, doubt that.

I hold the beer bottle to my head as the heat from my face leeches into the glass. Back to Financial Management and Purchasing in the Fire Department.

After another thirty minutes of dead air from Charlie, I try again. I find a picture of the cutest baby sea otter in a wicker basket hanging his head over the edge with the saddest expression on his face.

**Greyson: Radio silence makes me a sad otter :(**

I give her another twenty minutes to reply while I read and reread the same paragraph to no avail. I dial her number. "What's with the lag in texting?" I demand.

Silence passes for a long minute. Faintly, Ramones play in the background, and two seagulls squawk while fighting for some sap's sack lunch left lying on the sand while he swam before I hear her mumble, "I didn't know how to reply."

"I just wanted to see you. I always feel better when you're right next to me."

I sketch out a picture of the two cuddling otters on my paper. "Okay..."

She's already pulling away.

"Come on, Sands you can't say that otter wasn't the cutest thing you've ever seen."

"It was cute," she admits.

There. I have her on the hook.

"I saw it and it reminded me of you, the most adorable thing I've ever seen."

The line goes slack. I've lost her again.

*Charlie, you're not only adorable, you're the most beautiful woman I've ever seen.*

*Say it.*

*Just say it, Steele.*

I don't have the balls to force the words out of my mouth.

"If I'm the cutest thing you've ever seen, you've lived a truly sad and sheltered life, Grey."

It kills me to hear her talk about herself so brutally like she's not on every guy's radar. She is fearless in every other area of her life, but when it comes to this one thing, I swear Bexley must have done a number on her over the years. The constant stream of undermining comments must have chipped away at her confidence until there was nothing left but a pile of confidence dust.

I can't find any other reasonable explanation for why a woman as stunningly gorgeous as Charlie wouldn't know beyond a shadow of a doubt any guy would be thrilled to have even one scrap of her attention.

I try another tack. "Want to go grab some lunch and soak up this January sun?"

"I can't. Bex is dragging me shopping."

"Bex is with you right now?"

Bex wouldn't be stupid enough to tell Charlie about being rejected. Would she? She can twist any story to make her look like the victim.

"Yeah. She was in the middle of telling me every single detail of her day. Did you know she ate six m&m's for breakfast and then had to ride her bike fourteen miles to work them off?"

"Fourteen miles, huh?"

Does that mean I happened to call right before she was about to share the part where she trapped me into picking her up?

"And then she tells me she broke the gate. Just one more thing I have to fix around here."

Shit.

Bex told her.

But what version of reality did she dispense? I have to know what lie I will have to erase. "How'd she say it happened?"

"She brought some guy home, and he stripped her down right on the side yard and went to work."

There's irritation in her voice, but I don't think it's directed at me.

"He pushed her up against the gate so hard he pushed her right through it. I bet it didn't stop them from finishing up, either," she says snidely.

Bex kept my name out of it.

"Yeah. That happens, I guess."

"That happens? Really?"

Her previously Bex-centered irritation is now squarely focused on me. "You've been so hard up to get some you couldn't wait until you were inside?"

*With you lately? Yes.*

"I've had that urge with—"

She steps into my words before I can confess. "Let me guess. With Aubrey. You wanted her so badly you had to strip her down on her front porch, where anyone could walk by, and just have your way with her."

Her words slam into my chest.

"Fuck, Charlie. You really need to go there?"

Charlie knows exactly where to throw the knockout punch.

"Whatever. I don't want to talk about this with you," she roars.

I match her thunderous volume. "You moved way past talking a couple of decibels ago."

"Sorry I shared. I thought you'd understand, but I guess not. What can I expect from a guy who will hump any female with a pulse and two brain cells to rub together?"

"When did this become about me? I thought this was about Bex's out-of-control libido."

I can picture Charlie's head shaking, the same furious head shaking I've seen hundreds of times before. She goes from yelling to head shaking to silence. And I think I'm about to get a huge dose of that silence.

I pick up my Alex Rodriguez ball from the shelf and spin it in my hand, giving her the time and space she needs to formulate her next sentence. But it never comes.

"Sands?" I say softly.

More silence. I figure more head-shaking, too.

"Talk to me, Charlie."

Her hand is rubbing back and forth across her forehead, trying to rub away the anger.

"I should go," she whispers.

The line goes dead. How did we go from otters to me being

a manwhore? Thank God I didn't tell her I've felt like doing that to her in the middle of that whole thing.

I just don't understand her lately. When she was pissed about Delia, I thought she might be jealous. But this time it wasn't even about me. Bex was the one telling her made-up sex stories. And she still got pissed.

It isn't jealousy at all. I think she just noticed the pink gorilla who's been following me around, eating a giant, cyanide-filled cupcake.

# 17

## CHARLIE

By the time January swallows up the last breaths of fall heat, I'm a seasoned actress. With rehearsals and costume fittings and a crash course on acting, having an entire production depending on my acting skills doesn't entirely terrify me.

Or at least that is what I have been telling myself repeatedly in the mirror each morning.

After being groped by a TSA officer because my diabetes gear can't go through the x-ray machine, and sprinting down the terminal to board the flight taking off in six minutes, I spy Indigo and Greyson standing next to the closed boarding door. "I'm so sorry we missed it, Indigo. They usually don't take that long at TSA."

She lifts her hand to the marquee above the boarding desk with the word DELAYED in bright red letters.

"Perfect. I didn't have time for coffee this morning." Greyson hoists his bag onto his shoulder. "And you look like you could use a BAS," he says looking to me.

After spending most of the last three nights lying awake trying to sort out my recent foray into explosive anger, I could use a Big Ass Soda.

We walk back down the terminal to an Einstein's Bagel shop and stand in line with our new third wheel: Absolute Silence.

Greyson orders and pays, handing me my soda cup to fill at the fountain. When the barista hands him his coffee and our bagels, he nods for us to start our walk back, only this time it's more of a stroll. "Once again, Charlie, I'm back here asking, what was that all about?"

He tips his cup into his mouth, letting out, "Ack. What possesses people to make coffee so hot if they know no one likes to actually drink it that way?"

I slug down a belly full of soda, hoping my stalling will make him forget his original question.

He tosses a piece of bagel into his mouth and raises his eyebrows to me, waiting for my reply.

"I don't know. I think I was just in a mood. Work sucks."

He withdraws his gaze from me and redirects it to the coffee swirling in his cup. "Work, huh?"

I go on, trying to prove my point. "Nudge is failing and of course Dirk blames it all on me even though he won't listen to a word I say. And then I have to take off for this shoot and he's gonna take over even more."

It sounds logical. It was the only explanation I could come up with during three restless nights.

Or possibly it was the only excuse I was willing to entertain.

I busy myself with calculating my insulin dose, knowing Grey always pauses to let me focus on it. Flying complicates my morning calculation, so I take as long as I believably can.

When I'm done, Grey's sullen mood has suddenly evaporated.

"Can you do anything about work over the next four days?" he asks.

"Not a thing."

"Then you don't give it another thought. Right?"

He pulls a slice of bacon from his bagel sandwich and pops it into his mouth. "We're about to be in Maui. Let that sink in, Charlie. Maui. Get your head straight and let's enjoy the shit out of this trip. Okay?"

He's right. Our sparring, my stupid freakouts. They're in the past. We are here, now, about to hop on a plane that will land in Maui, the one place on earth I am guaranteed to be so totally, absolutely, completely, brutally relaxed and happy.

I can't help it. The smell of the hibiscus as it greets you the moment you step ouy of the airport. The rain that falls even though somehow there are still rays of sun on your skin. The feel of the warm salt water as you melt into it even though it's January. I have been waiting for a winter trip to Maui for years and, now that it's here, there's no way I'm wasting it being pissed off.

"Heads straight, Grey. Thanks." I throw him a smile and pick up the pace, excited about this trip for the first time in a while.

When we get back to the gate, Indigo is waiting, camera in hand. She snaps off a few shots, showing us the best ones.

Indigo is a genius when it comes to writing and directing movies. I had no idea that talent extended to photography as well. She tips the camera down to us to show us a black and white shot of Greyson and me walking towards her. My head is dipped, but my wide smile is still visible. He is watching me with a look I don't have a name for yet.

Even though the photo is in black and white, somehow his blue eyes shine a deeper hue of aqua. The ridges between his brows, deepened so much with the anxiety of the last few years, are barely visible now. For that matter, all the muscles in his face looked relaxed. And he's wearing a gentle smile that rounds out his cheeks a little more than usual.

It could be his Pleased Face? Or his Relaxed Face? Maybe it's his... Content Face?

I think that one's it. He's content. Like a cup of coffee and a bagel sandwich are all he ever needed in life.

When our turn to board arrives, I slide into my window seat, Greyson filing in beside me. Indigo sits a few rows behind us and leans over the rows of chairs to hand me a half-sized copy of the script. "I changed a few words here and there. I wanted to give you a chance to learn the new stuff."

"You can do that?" I ask, freaking out at the thought that, at any minute, she could change anything she wanted.

It took me eight weeks to get comfortable with exactly what

Indigo wrote on that page and now she can change it with only a day or two to relearn the scene?

*You are Braver than you think, Charlie.*

*Or stupider than you realize to agree to this,* the Rationalizer replies.

I sink into my seat and look to Grey, who is now two shades paler than I am. He almost looks the color of his namesake. "How did we come up with this stupid, stupid plan?" he stutters while checking his seatbelt for what I am sure is the eighth time since sitting down thirty seconds ago.

"You're not that bright." I laugh as I slip my buckle into the receptacle.

Greyson leans over and tugs it snug against my hips. "Seriously, how are we gonna fix this?"

He wraps his hands back onto the armrests.

"We're not going to fix it. You're going to man up and endure it. I still don't know how you can run into burning buildings with no problem, but you're terrified of a plane."

"The building is on the ground." His hand goes from the armrest to his mouth where he commences removing every bit of nail visible.

"Well, what about the huge ladder thing? When you have to climb up into buildings."

"Still on the ground," he says.

The flaps on the wings make a clang as they move up and down, the captain testing them briefly.

His hand flies back to the armrest. I think it might splinter under the force of his grasp.

"So, it's the air? You're afraid of air?" I tease, taking my headphones out of the bag I've tucked into the seatback in front of me and sliding them around my neck.

"It's the falling thousands of miles into the ocean, drowning, and having my body picked over by sharks."

"Oh, the sharks won't pick at you. They'll take entire limbs off in one bite, then move on to the next limb until there's nothing left for me to identify."

I think this Greyson is my favorite Greyson. I enjoy Public

Greyson—the full of energy, quick with a story, life of the party, panty-charmer, the one everyone gets to see—but I cherish Private Greyson, the periodically depressed, consistently anxious, occasionally terrified Greyson he only shows me.

The one who sits down next to me at the end of a long day, while he peels the label of his beer, and says, "Charlie, my heart hurts." That's the Greyson that has kept me standing by his side no matter what he goes through, no matter how obnoxious people may say he is at first sight. It's the Greyson I have called my best friend for twelve of the hardest years of our lives.

We back out from the gate. His gaze shoots to me, checking if this is normal.

I just laugh as this six-foot-two, normally courageous hero is about to piss himself from the feeling of rolling down the runway.

He clutches my hand and nearly crushes it in fear.

I give him a pass on the Half-Foot Rule. It's an acceptable breach of protocol. And what kind of heartless woman would I be to deny him a little touch when he's in this state.

Besides, there's no way his mind is in any shape to read anything into it.

Once we're airborne, Greyson tries to distract himself by watching Tommy Boy. It's a lot harder to stress when you're laughing uncontrollably, but he still manages to gnaw his fingers to the bone.

I throw on my headphones and fire up the *She's a Punk* podcast. Ever since Indigo told me about the punk ethos, I have been obsessed. I cannot believe how many leaders, entrepreneurs, and artists have subscribed to this theory and used it to make incredible things and alter everything around them.

This episode is an interview with Cindy Whitehead, a former pro skateboarder and top-ranked vert skater in the 70s when being a female skater was a rarity. A lot like being a female coder today.

She discusses having to deal with comments from the boys and being included in a man's world. When the mostly sexual comments started coming from the boys when she was skating vert, she would tape headphones to the outside of her helmet—

this was in the days before earbuds—turn on some music, and tune them out.

I may have to try that.

When the boys she skated with her whole childhood started excluding her because they thought it would be too rough for her to, say, illegally go skate an empty backyard pool where the cops could show up forcing them to run and hop fences to get away, she had to find ways to insert herself into the situation.

She said she realized at that point that no one was going to just hand her a place at the table. You have to make a place for yourself.

I could do that.

With Nudge.

I could make it happen in my own time, exactly the way I originally conceived it, as something to help women increase their drive to accomplish their goals.

One of my favorite tenets of the Punk Movement is their D.I.Y. culture. Punk rock musicians would not wait around for someone to hand them a record contract. If they had something to say, they wouldn't let a lack of training or tools stop them. They usually found along the way, other people wanted the same thing and were willing to lend their talents to the project.

I could start Nudge and pray I meet the right people to help make it a reality. For the first time, quitting my job to give Nudge my full attention doesn't sound insane. If I crash and burn, it wouldn't be the end of the world. I could always find another job in tech. Big&Lime is not the only tech company in the world. I might even find one who values women and treats them with respect.

And if I lose it all and become homeless, Grey would totally let me sleep on his couch as I recover. He still owes me for crashing at my place after the great Post-Injury-and-Aubrey Road Trip of 2012 when he disappeared for a month to recover from Aubrey unceremoniously dumping his ass when she realized her chances of becoming a famous MLB baseball wife were no longer on the table.

Grey bumps my arm to point out his favorite scene in Tommy Boy playing on his phone. I don't need headphones to know what is about to happen. Chris Farley will put on David Spade's coat and sing *Fat Man in a Little Coat* before ripping it straight down the back with his enormous size.

Grey's already seen it a million times and acted it out every single time he sees a small coat, but he still laughs as hard as the first time he made me watch it ten years ago.

He closes his eyes and leans back, and the smile spreading across his face kicks off a matching one on mine. He lifts the bottom of his shirt to wipe the tears from his eyes, giving me a full view of a stomach chiseled by years of hard labor battling burning buildings and I am struck by the profound lunacy that drove Aubrey to walk away from this incredible man.

# 18

## CHARLIE

*J*ust as I turn over another page in my leather-bound journal to jot down more notes from *She's a Punk*, a pretzel flies across my field of vision.

At the origin of the projectile Greyson's motioning for me to take off my headphones.

With his head atop his arm propped on the tray table, he turns to me and whispers, "I think this guy is snoring in Morse Code."

I listen for a moment. He snorts five grinding inhales. Then lets it out in three loud puffs. His next breath is two long wheezes in and four grating rattles out.

I whisper back, "MI6, I think. Signaling his partner about their target."

I point inconspicuously to the balding man in the opposite aisle dressed in shorts and a short-sleeved button-down shirt, both in matching blue Hawaiian print.

Greyson swivels his head to scout the haole, then turns back to me. "He'll make the drop when we touch down."

"Drugs?" I ask scandalized.

"Live eels in empty bottles of lube, freshwater crocodile

babies inside croissants, and bright blue poison dart frogs inside hollowed-out avocado skins."

My laugh stirs the MI6 agent and his breathing steadies for a moment before returning to transmit more crucial information to his partner.

"How do you come up with this stuff?" I ask between laughs.

Greyson laughs then drifts away somewhere in his head. The corner of his mouth twitches.

"Fuck Stick singing his songs again?" I ask, my voice startling him back into this realm.

"No. He's taking his smoke break. He really worked hard this morning."

I turn my headphones off, put them back in their case, and retrieve a Ziplock full of apple slices doused in cinnamon and sugar. When I lean back, his head is still resting on his hand and he's got on his Content Face again. "Christmas is over. Is it official?" he asks the moment I fill my mouth with an apple slice.

I swear he derives pleasure from tempting me to be a foul-mannered pig.

*Not this time, Grey.*

I finish chewing before I answer.

"Is what official?"

"Did you guys DNF? On your Summer Goal?" He's so excited, I think he might have bet money on it.

Probably gave me 100 to 1 odds.

"Did Not Finish is not in my vocabulary," I counter.

"Bex granted you another stay of execution, huh?"

"Till Spring Break," I concede. "Whose spring break, I don't know, but whichever school has it latest, I expect."

"So what's the latest horror story?"

"We went out with Tanner and Hunter last Friday. They're both 'in finance'," I say, using air quotes.

"Did they both show up in suits?"

"Blazers and skinny cut pants three inches above their sweaty, sockless feet stuffed into shoes that probably cost more than my rent."

The flight attendant offers us a basket of snack choices.

Greyson picks a bag of trail mix for himself and Rold Gold pretzels for me and tosses his napkin onto my tray table. "Why does Bex still think that's your kind of guy?"

He tosses a red m&m from his trail mix onto the napkin, saving the peanuts and raisins for himself.

"It's more like it's the only friend the guy she's currently obsessed with can wrangle up for a blind date with me."

"She should show them a picture of you. They'd be lining up for a chance to date you."

There it is again. The guys lining up for me thing.

He adds a blue and brown m&m to the red one, then watches me like he's trying to gauge my reaction to his last comment.

I pop all three in my mouth and almost finish chewing before going on. "So I ask them, 'What kind of short-term financing would you recommend to fulfill my cash needs for a tech startup?'"

"Are you striking out on your own? Finally. I am so—"

I step into his words. "I'm not striking out. I just wanted to see how far they'd take their lie."

"And?"

"Before they had a moment to fake an answer, Bex drags me to the bathroom for a pep talk. I wasn't executing on the game plan she had in mind."

"That was her first mistake. She should have just given you the Double Dating with Bex Rule Book. You'd follow that to the letter."

"If it worked nearly half as well as my Rule Book, I might consider it. But her rules suck."

I should start writing them down.

Bex Rule #9: Believe anything a guy tells you without asking any follow-up questions.

And Bex Rule #22: Play dumb because stupid boys are easily intimidated.

I know I suck at playing the dating game, but if we all keep playing this game where we hide so much of ourselves hoping to find the right person, no one will ever find a real relationship.

How are you supposed to identify your person if everyone on a date is pretending to be someone they're not?

"Do you know what she said to me, right before we walk in to meet the guys?"

"I can't wait to hear this." He crumples up his trail mix bag and stuffs it in the seat back and tucks his tray table against the seat.

"She's looking in the visor mirror, putting on her fifth coat of lipstick."

The memory makes my throat squeeze my next words like it's trying to stop me from releasing them from my mouth.

"She says, 'You wear so little makeup, it makes sense guys think you're one of them.'"

It was the worst thing she's said to me in a long while and the perfect thing to put in the front of my mind right before a date.

She thinks the only way a guy would like me is if I become a Bex replica. It made me even more disappointed with myself for letting her dress me up that night.

"What was that?" Grey taps on an imaginary hearing aide. "Sorry, this thing doesn't always pick up bullshit."

I am so glad to have Grey to balance out all the Bex bullshit. Sometimes, I get so wrapped up in what she says, I start to believe it. Hard not to when she has so many guys flocking to her.

"So, after drinks, the guys get the grand idea we should go to the batting cages. I was not dressed for batting cages."

"Was that the night you wore that amazing black skirt with the laces up the side?"

When did Greyson start taking stock of what I wore?

"And thigh-high boots with heels at least three inches tall. Standard Baseball Uniform."

Greyson rubs his hand across his forehead and shakes his head. He gets how ludicrous it was for me to play dress-up like that.

Bex Rule #14: Wear totally uncomfortable clothes, don't let you enjoy your date, and leave you shivering in the cold because, otherwise, guys won't give you a chance.

"So Bex jumps in Hunter's car, leaving me to drive Tanner, and the whole way over he can't answer one simple question about himself. What do you like to do? Where do you want to travel? Where'd you go to college? He answered that one like he had been rehearsing all day."

"Maybe he was just too distracted thinking about what might happen if he pulled on the end of the string holding that tight black skirt to your body."

"Maybe."

It's been helpful over the years to have an inside glimpse into the mind of a guy from Greyson. I get to hear all the running commentary right below the surface in every man's head. The things guys think that would shock most women, I know are simply normal white noise.

The fact that, in any given moment, the guy you are talking with is probably undressing you and picturing what he could do to each and every orifice on your body? Standard procedure. He's also doing that to any good-looking woman walking by. Or the one he sees on TV. Or on Instagram.

And he can do it, at least most of the time, while carrying on a conversation that has nothing to do with sex. It's like he has two channels, both operating simultaneously.

"So Hunter and Tanner won't be getting another serving of the Bex-Charlie double scoop?"

"Let's just say Tanner was not that into my Fish Food. But Bex is crazy for Hunter. She went home with him that night and hasn't stopped talking about him since."

It's like Bex has no idea guys are putting on a show for her. She's suckered into every one of their enhanced realities.

I swear, sometimes I feel like the interpreter for Bex in the Land of Boys. It's as if she's never visited there before and has no understanding of their culture. She's like the foolish haole paddles out at Pipeline on a foam rental board, no clue how many customs she's just violated and how much she has endangered everyone else in the lineup.

Bex thinks playing the game this way is the best approach to finding a husband. To finding true love. I think that game only ensures they will find a one-night hookup and nothing more lasting or real than that.

I'll pass on that game.

From the car rental place at the edge of the airport, it's only a quick drive to the house we'll be staying in for the next few days. The aroma of guava and rich forest soil fly in through the open sides of the white Jeep Indigo rented.

We drive through the tiny town of Paia with cheerfully painted shops in bright blues and deep greens along Highway 36, stopping for some pizza at Flatbread Company in the middle of town.

With our bellies now full, we make our way along the one-lane Hana Highway as it snakes along the ocean. Huge waves crash on the rocks beside the road, sending mist into the Jeep.

We cross a few rivers as the foliage becomes more abundant, turning up an even narrower street covered in a canopy of green trees, winding its way uphill past yards filled with palm and eucalyptus trees. The road turns into a dirt path right before it ends in front of a two-story main house on what I can only describe as a compound. The rest of the cast and crew who are waiting for us on the wrap-around porch amble out to greet us.

Surrounded by a canopy of lush green foliage, the grounds go on forever. I may be a little biased, growing up in yards small enough to touch your house and your neighbor's house at the same time, but it is expansive enough to host an Ohana—the Hawaiian equivalent of a granny flat—and a sunken fire pit surrounded by beach chairs nestled snugly in sand and still have enough land to have a tropical fruit orchard full of fresh mango, banana, guava, and papaya trees surrounding a raised vegetable garden.

"How did you swing this place, Indigo? It's beautiful," Greyson asks as he kills the engine.

"It's my buddy Finn's place. He's back on the mainland visiting his parents. He needed a dog-sitter, and I needed a place to shoot."

A reddish mutt runs up to greet us. I bend down to pet him while Greyson hauls our luggage from the Jeep and Indigo introduces us to the cast and crew, Tank, Trina, Wells, and Sonny. It's a small group, everyone filling multiple roles.

Wells wraps me in a warm hug and whispers in my ear, "It's great to see you again, Charlie."

With this much flirting coming my way, he must be into method acting.

Indigo leads us through the front door to the house that will function as our sleeping barracks as well as our set. "I think it'd be best if Trina and I take the master upstairs so we can review footage each night without keeping you all up."

Indigo tosses her bag on the stairs leading to the landing outside the second-story bedroom. Trina wraps her long brown hair into a pile on top of her head and takes Indigo's bag with hers up the stairs.

"Finn's asked us not to go in his room or his office, but the couch folds out into a bed and he borrowed two roll-away beds."

We toss our bags down in the living-room-turned-dorm-room.

Indigo walks to the open kitchen abutting the room. "Help yourselves to any food in the kitchen. I had Finn set us up before he left. The beach is two blocks further down the main road we came in on. Feel free to explore the city or just hang out."

Tank is out the side door in seconds. "That hammock's got my name on it."

He tosses his wrinkled Hawaiian shirt on the wide-planked wooden floor on his way out the back door.

"I was hoping to work with Charlie and Wells for a while, walk them through blocking on site so they can make the necessary adjustments. Call time is 7:30 tomorrow. Until then, have fun."

By the time we finish walking through almost the entire script, except for the scenes in the hotel room, Indigo giving us notes on our marks and where she saw each scene happening, fatigue and the amount of info I have absorbed have me ready to pass out.

"It's nine now," Indigo says. "We'll film scenes three, seven, and ten first. Try to be ready with your costume and makeup for those by 7:30."

"Sounds good," Wells says.

"And by 'try to be ready', I don't mean sitting around the

table finishing up breakfast before you decide to go throw on some clothes. Have your shit together, on your mark, and ready for me to call action at 7:31."

Director Indigo is a beast.

It makes sense, though, with everything she is responsible for pulling together over the next four days, but it's a little startling to see her go from free-wheeling artist ready to have long meandering conversations about the meaning of life to hard-ass director ready to have us jump whenever she calls.

Everyone is asleep when we sneak back into the house. Tank and Grey have claimed the queen-sized pull-out bed, Wells takes the sofa next to them, and the two roll-away beds were left for Sonny and me.

Sonny is asleep already, only the top of her blond head visible under the white sheet.

I dig into my army-green bag sitting on the empty roll-away bed and plug in my phone after setting an alarm. It's only nine, but with the time change, it's almost midnight back home, which makes this fatigue much more reasonable. It also means I should change the settings on my insulin pump to better match my current time zone.

I whip out Tex and try to muffle his beeps as I scroll through the menu. Sonny is rustling in the rollaway bed next to me.

I set the time zone to halfway between home and Hawaii, knowing I won't be here long enough to adjust fully and that the earlier work schedule will change my morning insulin needs, too. I bring up the bolus screen to correct for higher than usual blood sugars due to my nerves about being able to perform tomorrow and disappointing Indigo.

Sonny rolls over and rustles under the covers.

All my diabetes crap makes it difficult to sleep in the same room with me.

"No way!" Sonny's face is lit by a small screen in her hands.

I glance up from my pump. "I'm so sorry my pump woke you up."

She turns the glowing light my way, revealing a matching Tandem insulin pump. "Tandem for life, baby."

Tank shifts in his bed at her proclamation.

"You have diabetes too?" I ask.

She shines the glowing pump screen on herself as she lifts her shirt to show me the Dexcom sensor on her belly wrapped in a tropical print oval of tape.

I roll away from her and lower the top of my sleep shorts an inch or two, revealing a matching Dexcom surrounded by the Hawaiian flag.

Sonny sits up, fully awake now. "Don't you just love Expressionmed tapes? They make everything so much brighter."

We stay up far longer than we should, chatting about our diabetes technology and where to buy the best stickers to jazz it up, trying to stifle the laughs and excitement in our voices at finding another from our tribe.

Tex beeps in my hand, upset I didn't finish giving myself my last correction bolus before I got distracted by Sonny, and it is one beep too many.

Tank rises from the far side of the sofa bed. "Hold on, Mom. Gawd. My hot pocket is done."

Sonny and I gape at each other and then dissolve into a laughing fit.

Tank walks to the kitchen, opens the microwave, and retrieves an invisible hot pocket.

We're glued to the set of this incredible new TV show.

He takes a bite, then hangs his tongue out of his mouth like a St. Bernard in the heat of a Florida summer. "You'd think someone would tell you your Hot Pocket is gonna be hot."

Then, his arms drop to his side as he is pulled back towards bed. Only he's not headed towards his bed.

He's headed straight for mine.

Before I can slide out of the way, he falls onto me, trapping me below his heavy arm and is immediately snoring again.

I tap his shoulder with my free hand. "Tank, wake up."

He doesn't move.

I shake him. "Tank."

He is so deep in dreamland a tsunami couldn't wake him.

I try to lift his arm off my chest, but there is a reason he's earned the name Tank.

I shimmy lower in bed until my face is smooshed by the weight of his enormous arm. Struggling until I wriggle free of him, I stand and check if I woke him.

He jerks his arm back towards his face, smacking himself in the jaw.

I squint at Sonny to ask, *did that really happen?* And we again bust into a giggling fit.

"Looks like you're sleeping with Greyson," Sonny whispers.

I feast my eyes on Greyson, lying on his stomach, shirtless. The low angle of the moonlight drifting through the bare windows delineates his back muscles and I want to trace the lines of each one. I can't sleep next to that without a repeat of the Santa Barbara Spectacle. "I don't think so. You can hop in there."

"Haven't you guys shared a bed since you were zygotes?"

"No way. We have rules," I explain like it's common knowledge.

Sonny's face lights up. "If you're not going to share a bed with that...," she motions to Greyson with his arms tucked under his head, putting his giant biceps on display, "...you don't have to ask me twice."

I sit on Sonny's bed as she slides under the covers next to my Grey and there's a strange pull in my chest as she lays her head down next to him.

She rouses him just enough for him to turn his head towards me and give me a sad smile before closing his eyes again.

*Shit. He didn't hear me. Did he?*

# 19

## GREYSON

Charlie's Dexcom wakes me up a few times during the night. And once the thought lands in my head she's low, I can't keep it from spinning out of control. She doesn't always wake up to her alarms immediately which scares the crap out of me and reminds me of all the things that could happen to her.

Back when I was an EMT, we got called to the house of a young boy with type 1 diabetes. We made it through the open front door to find his mom sitting in the entry hall holding the boy in her lap, weeping over him.

My partner threw down his trauma bag, retrieved a glucagon emergency pen, and slammed it into the boy's leg. When the boy didn't move immediately, I thought we hadn't made it in time.

His mom started rocking the boy slowly. With agony in her features, she lifted her eyes to me, and through her tears, she muttered, "I broke the needle. I broke it."

On the ground next to her was a small orange case with a full vial of glucagon.

"How low was he?" I asked trying to distract her from her admission.

"Twenty-four."

Low enough to end his life.

As I surveyed the scene, the broken syringe rolled out of her hand.

The little boy stired.

It's not like they show on TV where one shot and the kid is up, fully conscious, and happy. He was groggy and confused.

"Hey, Boogie. I'm here. You're going to be okay."

After witnessing the despair and sense of failure in that mom's face because panic made it impossible to complete the eight complicated steps to administer that old-fashioned glucagon kit to her dying son, I made sure I always carry a Gvoke HypoPen.

Two steps: take off the cap, slam it into any available patch of skin.

I bought an armload to store in hiding spots wherever Charlie normally is. In her house, downstairs and upstairs, at her desk at work, in her car, in my car. She even keeps one at her parents' house now.

As I wait for the alarms to wake Charlie tonight, I am mentally running through my action plan should she need it. I know she keeps a HypoPen in her black diabetes bag in her suitcase, but I don't want to have to search for it in case she put it somewhere else in the house while we're here. Mine is in the outside pocket of my backpack so I can remember to bring it when we're on location.

Charlie's phone wails the fire alarm signal, the more serious and loud alarm declaring that she is quickly approaching the line of losing consciousness and having a seizure right before... she's no longer my Charlie.

I slide my foot from under the covers and kick her bed. She wakes up, silences the alarm, and downs two juice boxes without even becoming fully awake.

She's back to sleep while I'm left with my What-Ifs to keep me company in the darkness, making it impossible to go back to sleep.

And of course, there was the Charlie and Sonny talking and giggling, and Charlie's absolute horror at the suggestion she share my bed to keep my mind occupied.

It's no wonder then when we gather around the fire pit to

start shooting in the early morning light, I am having a hard time with the easiest job on set.

Indigo was so sweet when Charlie asked for me to come along so she'd have the confidence to do the acting thing. When I told her I had no experience on a movie set, she said, "You've held a fire hose for years. I'm pretty sure you can hold a boom pole," squeezing my bicep in lieu of an interview.

By the time we break for lunch, my arms are burning and my dogs are barking.

Sonny has placed a table on the porch with special order sandwiches, chips, and cookies. We each scoop up lunch and kick back in the beach chairs surrounding the fire pit in the middle of the yard.

"No. One. Gets. Burnt." Indigo barks out as she tosses Charlie a black bottle of Sun Bum zinc sunscreen. "Everyone puts it on every exposed bit of skin and even the ones that aren't. One burn will destroy this whole picture."

Charlie obeys without a word and passes the bottle on to Tank in the chair on the other side of her.

"Hey, Sonny," Tank croons as she slides into the seat across the empty fire pit. "Can I get some help putting this on the parts that aren't exposed?" He wags his eyebrows at her.

"Not a chance, Tank."

I elbow Charlie. "What odds you running on these two getting together before this shoot is over?"

Refusing to remove her eyes from the script in her hands, she mumbles flatly, "Yeah, totally."

I elbow her again.

She's close to cutting her lip wide open the way she's gnawing on it. "What's up?"

Her quiet mode is starting to worry me. She shakes her head and stares back at the script.

"Hey, Indigo is going to kill you if you cut up your lips."

She squints up at me like I just asked that in the dialect of the Cook Islands.

"You're biting your lip, Charlie. What's up?"

She rises from her chair and nods her head for me to follow her to the shade of the porch.

When we reach the top of the stairs, she laces her hands behind her head. She wrings her hands free and deflates against the house. "What was I thinking, Grey? I can't do this. I can't do any of this. I can't act. I can't do seduction."

I lean back against the porch railing opposite her. "What are you talking about? You're killing it."

"I have to kiss him." She flips the script around and beats it with her finger. "Right here. Indigo changed it last night. I have to kiss Tank to piss off Wells—sorry—Johnny."

My heart hurts for her. Most people wouldn't think twice about a stage kiss, but Charlie's different. It means something to her.

When Charlie first told me she hadn't kissed anyone since eighth grade, or, rather, when Bex blurted it out, I stayed up all night trying to figure out if she was really serious or just screwing with me. If it was some kind of Bex and Charlie inside joke.

She's never talked to me about kissing anyone before, but we don't really talk much about her sex life, or in my mind, a complete-lack-of-sex life. But not kissing anyone since eighth grade? That couldn't really be true. Could it?

When she confirmed it to me a few days later, the only thing I could think was *virgin lips*. Charlie had pristine, untouched, virgin lips. It took all the restraint I possessed to not reach across the table and kiss her right there.

And now she has to throw away something pretty special to her for an acting gig.

"This must be killing you." I shove my hands into my pockets, frustrated I can't fix this for her. "Have you talked to Indigo?"

"No. I can't."

"I can try if you want," I offer.

"Please don't." She gives her lip a break and begins chewing on her thumbnail. "I committed to doing this for her and if she thinks that's what the story needs I don't want her to water down her art cause I'm such a freak."

"You're not a freak, Charlie." I run my hand along the dark ipe wood railing. "All that physical stuff means something to you. It's rare, for sure, but it doesn't make you a freak. It makes you sweet."

She laughs. "Sure, Greyson. It's sweet I haven't kissed a guy in a decade."

She rubs both of her hands up and down her face. "I just can't believe after all this, after making such an enormous deal about it, that Tank is going to be the guy to break the streak."

She points to the fire pit. "The sleep-walking, smart-assing, perma-adolescent."

I glance over my shoulder to find a shirtless Tank dancing wildly around the fire pit, brandishing a bamboo pole like one of the hunters from Lord of the Flies.

"That guy is going to be my First-in-a-Decade kiss," she scoffs.

She runs her tongue over the spot she's been nervously nibbling for the last twenty minutes as her eyes grow glossy. She doesn't want to ask Indigo to change the script. She doesn't want to break her streak with an imbecile like Tank. She's between a rock and a hard spot. There's only one solution I can think of to help.

But... it's crazy.

She shuffles across the porch to stand mere inches from me, looking out to the fire pit.

I turn my head to watch her. Her long, blond hair blows across her back in the balmy trade winds as she scrutinizes the buffoon she will soon have to kiss.

Maybe... it's not... *that*... crazy?

It could be just the thing to shock her out of her rule-following paralysis. Slowly pushing our boundaries wasn't getting me anywhere. I need to drop a nuke on that damned wall of hers.

I take in the delicate, daisy-yellow strap holding up her silky tank top as it lays over her collar bone and the ridges of her back muscles. I follow the sunny silk to the bottom hem fluttering in the breeze atop the tarnished leather belt holding tiny jean shorts on her body.

She lays her hands on the railing and leans her hips against it, her face declaring her disappointment, before flashing me those melancholy blue-green eyes. "It won't be that bad. First-world problems, huh?" she says unconvincingly.

I will do anything to stop those innocent eyes from filling with tears again.

As she searches my face for reassurance, I notice her lip is slightly swollen where she laid her anguish into it. She's as close to me now as she was the night in my kitchen where she chose her keys over my lips. It may be crazy, but, if it saves Charlie from one more second of pain, it's worth it.

My hands still plastered to the railing behind me, I lean my head towards her and, before she can blurt out a million reasons why this is the most imbecilic thing I have ever done, I press my lips to hers.

And her lips kiss me back. A sweet, gentle kiss that is completely Charlie.

I pull away slowly unsure if she will view it as another stupid Grey mistake or a sweet gift from a friend trying to ease her pain.

"There," I whisper. "Now it's not Tank breaking your streak."

Charlie studies the chipping sky-blue paint on the edge of the creaky porch from over the railing.

"Break's over!" Indigo yells from the yard.

Charlie lifts her head.

"You're back on the clock. Let's get shooting before we lose the light," Indigo commands.

Charlie tips her head closer to me and whispers back, "What was that Grey?" then rushes off the porch towards Indigo and an afternoon of macking on Tank.

Of washing me off her lips.

As we walk the path to the beach up the road to finish off shooting for the day, Charlie does a good job of distancing herself from me, making it clear kissing her was totally, absolutely, completely, brutally not the right choice. Halfway there, she turns back to me, her face plastered with confusion.

Shit.

She's pissed and clearly did not enjoy that. Why do I keep doing this? You'd think I would know how to follow the rules by now.

The coastline on this side of the island is rugged, mostly cliffs, but Indigo finds one cove with a swath of black sand to film on for the remainder of the day. She waits until the golden hour to shoot the dreaded scene.

Charlie is draped in Tank's sweatshirt, her character borrowed it from his earlier to taunt Johnny, Wells' character. Charlie fiddles with the sleeves as she delivers her line, "You can do better than that."

Tank marches up to her and dives for her face, mashing his against hers.

Indigo, Wells, and I all flinch at the impact.

"Cut!" Indigo calls.

Tank steps back and wipes his face proudly. "That was awesome, right?"

"Maybe a bit too passionate?" Indigo the Diplomat replies. "Let's take it down a notch and try again."

On the second take, Charlie flinches when he makes his move. Visibly flinches. The third take is only slightly better.

Indigo gives the actors a break, pulling Charlie aside. They chat for a few minutes by the waterline before Indigo waves me over.

I'm not sure how I can help, but if I have to act as her kissing dummy for rehearsal, I will gladly sacrifice for the project.

"You have any insight here, Greyhound?" Indigo pleads.

"What's the problem, Sands? Besides Tank kissing like a German Sheppard in heat."

Charlie laughs. "So, it's not just me?"

"No way. Tank attacked you," I assure her.

Indigo turns around, sizing up Tank. When she turns back, her frown has been replaced with wide eyes busting forth with ideas. "How about we have you kiss him instead? That way you're not flinching every time he makes a move."

Charlie draws a circle in the sand with her foot. "That would be better... but, I don't really know how..."

She surfaces a small shell with her toes.

"How to make a move?" Indigo asks.

Charlie nods.

Indigo grins at me.

*Not gonna happen, Indigo. Not again at least.*

Indigo heeds my silent plea. "Try to imagine he's someone

else, someone you enjoy kissing. Like, your best kiss ever. Remember that."

Charlie suppresses a smile as she visualizes her best kiss ever.

Please let that be me. I have to be capable of out-kissing an eighth-grader.

"You got it?" Indigo checks.

Charlie lets her lips sneak up a bit. "Yeah."

"When you go to kiss Tank, picture that kiss."

"I can do that," Charlie says, full of confidence.

Indigo explains the plan to Tank and we're ready to shoot again.

"Tip the reflector a little to the right, Greyhound." Indigo points to the happy couple. "Keep it pointed at Charlie's face even as she moves in."

"Got it, Boss."

The golden reflector casts a warm light on Charlie's face, highlighting the freckles on her nose. The white reflector Wells holds behind her lights up her sun-bleached hair making her into an angel.

She delivers her line perfectly, then slowly leans in and rests her hands on Tank's chest before she gives him one of her perfect Charlie kisses.

"Dammit, Greyson! The light!" Indigo's scream wakes me from my nightmare. "That was perfect and you dropped the light!"

"What?" I snap.

She sighs as she stomps over to me. "Sorry, I yelled," her voice calmer now. "I know it's a tough scene for you to focus on. You want me to get Sonny to finish the scene for you?"

Was I that transparent?

I check if anyone else heard what she said. If Charlie heard.

They are all staring at us, but the sound of the ocean waves probably covered her voice.

"I can do it. I'm really sorry I ruined your shot."

"I know. And for your punishment?" she says coyly. "You have to watch them do it again."

This time, I focus like it's the seventh game of the World Series. I have the light squarely on Charlie's face the entire time so I don't have to watch Charlie lay her lips on that clown ever again.

After three full days of shooting on Finn's compound, Indigo moves us to the Grand Wailea Resort to finish shooting the last few scenes. At the southern tip of the island, it is a beach-front maze of pools, tiki huts, and palm trees with an amazing sunset view over Kaho'olawe, the smallest of the eight volcanic islands about seven miles off the coast.

We check in to the Wailea Suite and Indigo tasks us with rearranging the whole place to fit her vision. After three hours of heavy lifting and moving one particularly heavy koa wood desk in front of the window and then away from the window and then back again, we are ready to explore the nine connected pools on six different levels.

We jump in the whitewater rapids outside our tower and ride it to the activity pool complete with a Tarzan rope swing, waterfalls, caves, and a water elevator.

Tank and Wells are competing for Charlie's attention on the rope swing, trying to outdo each other with flips and belly flops. Charlie is pulling off some pretty great flips of her own. Usually, she'd be oblivious to the attention she attracts, but tonight, she is fully aware. And enjoying it. She's even flirting back.

I can't drag my eyes from them. This must be her way of sending me the message she didn't think that kiss was as electrifying as I did. What more do I need to know to convince me I was right all along? There is no way she will ever see me as anything more than her best friend.

Her Poe Friend.

"Hey, Grey." Trina slips her hand into mine and tugs. "I found the coolest cavey thing over here. You have to check it out."

With nothing holding me back, I might as well check out the cavey thing Trina finds so incredibly amusing. I take one last glance Charlie's way to find her wrapped up in Wells' arms as she tries to shoot a basketball in the hoop at the edge of the pool.

*Message received, Charlie.*

I glance up the arm tugging me towards the opposite end of

the pool. Trina's fit body is only covered by small white bikini bottoms held up by several white strings on each side and a tan top with white trim and one large white flower on each boob, like she's only wearing pasties.

She pulls me into a cave surrounded by palm trees and saunters towards me. "Isn't this amazing? It's like we're in our own little world."

She lays her hand on my chest, leaning in closer to whisper in my ear. "Where we can do anything."

Trina doesn't hold me at arm's length. She won't chew me out for thinking I might be good enough for her. She won't become furious with me for wanting to have her.

I wrap my finger in the strings of her bikini bottoms and draw her closer.

She presses her shimmering lips to mine. I try to lose myself in it, but my mind won't take the bait.

With my eyes closed, I realize I couldn't pick this girl out of a lineup. I can't tell, by this late in January, the freckles on her face have faded until there are only a few scattered across her nose. Or in the dark of this cave, the green in her eyes would outpower the blue and they would be nearly the same shade as the bamboo forest we drove through yesterday. Or her ears have a little crease in the lobe that showed up a few months after she graduated from college.

I am in serious danger if I'm picturing my best friend while I'm kissing another girl.

I pull away from Trina and force a smile on my face.

She drags her thumb across her lips. "Mmm. I hope there's more where that came from." She turns and bounces away.

I lean my back against the cave, grateful my stupidity has been concealed from the world by the fake rock walls. Some girl decides she likes me, and I fall right into it without a second thought. Maybe Charlie's right.

What am I saying? Charlie is always right.

A girl comes within six inches of me and I am forced to maul her. I am completely unable to control myself.

# 20

## CHARLIE

*I*ndigo has saved the hardest scene for last. I have been dreading this scene since I first read the script back in November. It is the emotional payoff of the whole short and I know, if I don't nail it, the entire piece will suffer.

Indigo rearranged the room yesterday so all that is left is to set up sound, lights, and the camera. Indigo and Trina perfect their lighting scheme and place the boom mic on a stand, invisible in the shot.

"Alright. Tank, Greyhound, Sonny, and Trina, you're wrapped." Indigo calls out. "Head out to the pool. We'll be down to celebrate when we finish this last scene."

By the time we finish the scene, I am completely spent. I debate skipping the whole pool scene and crawling into bed instead. The beds here are heavenly and after a few nights on the roll-away bed with a fat bar poking at my back all night, I could use a nap before having to power up and make it through dinner out and a night of celebration.

But I know how much Indigo has put into this project, and I don't want to be a wet blanket.

I wander down to the pool and sit on the edge, watching Wells and Tank in another pissing match on the rope swing. I slip my feet into the warm water hoping to wash away some of the pain.

To my left, Kaho'olawe sits on the horizon, framed by a deepening rainbow sherbet sky below blue and purple clouds, the light of both reflecting on the turquoise ocean below. Three shirtless Hawaiian men enter the pool area to begin their nightly tiki lighting ceremony. The first man blows into a conch and the sound rings out across the forty-two-acre property while the second man begins playing his drum. The last man trots around the pool, lighting tiki torches as he goes.

I glance back towards the jacuzzi. Trina is sitting next to Greyson with her legs laying over his lap and she decides during a sacred Hawaiian tradition is the perfect time to make a move. She slides her legs off his lap while she leans into him and kisses his neck, then climbs onto his lap resting her hands on the edge of the jacuzzi behind him. His hands slide up her sides, confidently, like he's done it a million times before. She lowers herself to him.

I don't really want to watch the rest of this. It's hard enough listening to Greyson tell me stories of his escapades, I don't really want a live demonstration.

I turn on my heels and head for the room. A quick nap is in the cards after all.

After a luxurious soak in the marble-lined tub full of bubbles that smell like guava and mango, I throw on some shorts and a tee and slip beneath the velvety blankets in the King-sized bed. Drawing the heavy down comforter over my head, I sail off to Napland.

"As Steven Spielberg has said, 'All good ideas start out as bad ideas, that's why it takes so long.'"

Indigo raises her glass of champagne to her band of misfits who have momentarily calmed for the first time tonight in the living room of our suite after dinner at Benihana and a little too much Saki. "I wanted to make this film for over six years. It has taken the talent and vision and sacrifice of everyone in this room for it to become a reality."

I take in the eight of us who, over the course of five long days, have created something entirely new. Something that has never existed before. Something uniquely ours. If any one of us hadn't been here, it would have been a different project.

"I have to say, and I'm pretty drunk already, but, I really do want to say, I love you all. I really do. Thank you. Thank you for sacrificing your time and energy. I really wish I could pay you what you're worth. Thank you for believing this film could be something."

She raises her glass and we raise ours in response. "Now let's party!" she hollers.

The room breaks out in hoots.

I take a swig of my Diet Dr Pepper and let the sense of accomplishment wash over me.

Tank, already two sheets to the wind at dinner, is close to letting out his third. He jumps on the hundred-year-old, hand-carved dining table, starts a drumbeat on the chandelier with a wooden spoon, and with all the power in his enormous lungs, puts on his best Freddie Mercury. "I've paid my juice. Time after time."

Wells joins in. "And baked me steaks, I've made a few."

They haven't gotten a single line right but the chorus.

Greyson roars into his upper register, "I've had my share of fat chicks in my bed, but I've come through,"

And with that everyone has picked up the torch and is ringing out the loudest rendition of the overplayed Queen song ever.

"We are the champions, my friend."

Needing a moment to myself, I bring my soda to the round table on a lanai bigger than my entire house. On the horizon, the outline of Kaho'olawe is barely visible beneath a sky brightened by a full moon. The sounds of Hawaiian drums and ukuleles drift up from the Luau below as the sweet scent of night-blooming Jasmine wafts over on a tropical breeze.

Greyson slides open the glass door, joining me at the table.

"So what do you think? You gonna quit Big&Lime and run away to L.A. to pursue your acting dreams?"

"I don't know about that, but I did love it. It felt amazing to let it all go and entirely be another person. I didn't have to analyze who I was or what I should be doing, because I wasn't me anymore. I was this sexy girl Johnny wanted. I want that feeling more often."

Greyson rests his head on his hand as he watches me, fully absorbed. "I get that."

I drag my eyes from him to the horizon before it becomes obvious what I'm imagining. "I'm always so focused on doing the right thing. I consider every word I say before I say it. I get upset over silly things that don't even matter. I wish I could just *do* instead of contemplating everything."

"So why don't you? Tonight. Let loose. Have a little fun. Break your half-drink limit around people. I'll watch your back."

That sounds so perfect. I can't remember the last time I did that.

Oh, yeah... because I haven't ever.

"You'll watch my back?" I can't believe I'm actually considering this. "So if I am going to do something embarrassing, you'll stop me before I make a fool of myself? You promise?"

"I promise."

He hands me his bottle of Stone IPA.

I put on my best pouty face. "The one time I'm gonna drink and my only choice is beer?"

"It's either that or the bottles of the hard stuff in the mini-bar. But I suggest you should walk before you run, Sands."

I lift the bottle to my mouth and drain it, ready to let loose in a big way.

As soon as that first beer hits me, Tank sprints onto the lanai with Wells following immediately. He has to rip Tank from the railing while he screams, "I could totally hit the pool if I jumped."

Dex interrupts my cackling, announcing I'm low. I have juice boxes and Gu energy gels in my suitcase, but, right now, a Three Musketeers sounds divine. Knowing it's not the smartest idea to wander off alone when I'm low, I scan the room for Greyson. He's cuddled up on the couch with Trina.

Dex's siren screams. I am dropping fast.

Explaining word things to Greyson sounds really hard-like.

Stomach howling and heart bent on the fluffy, whipped nougat wrapped in decadent chocolate, I sprint to the vending machine down the hall, only to find it empty.

Dammit. I have to have nougat.

The store downstairs has some.

Taking the elevator to the little store by the front desk, I jerk the shiny silver wrapping from the sugar, stuffing half of it in my mouth.

I slap a five-spot on the counter and mumble, "fanks" from behind a mouthful of sweetness.

I collapse onto a flat foot-stool thingy and polish off the rest of my treat. When the sugar finally seeps into my blood, I am enticed aloft by the most beautiful thing in the world.

A waiter in the bar across the hall is carrying a giant fishbowl filled with blue liquid and topped with a slice of pineapple.

I have to have one of those.

I saddle up to the bar and wait for the hot bartender to come take my order. He's scruffy and so stinking strong, muscles bulging under a tight white tee.

"What can I get for you, darlin'" he drawls.

I never thought I was into the whole southern thing, but it's really working for me right now.

"What are those big blue ones?" I point to another one whipping past.

"That's a Blue Hawaiian."

"What's in it?"

A yellow and green fishbowl flies past me. I spin around to follow it. "Wait, what's that one?"

"That's a Maui Wowie. That's coconut rum, melon liqueur, pineapple juice, and orange juice."

I may love the way coconut smells, but I can't stand the taste.

"Maybe I don't need to go all tourist..." I turn back to Hot Barkeep. "I'll have a margarita."

"Good choice. I'll go grab that."

He wipes down the sticky bar in front of me before leaving.

"I'm Billy." He flashes me a smile that makes me consider moving to wherever he's from. "In case you need to get my attention," he amends.

"I'm Charlie. No, in case."

*Oh my God, Charlie. You really do suck at flirting.*

Billie slides a coaster in front of me and anchors my drink on it as I continue attempting to flirt.

"I just realized Maui Wowie is really fun to say. I almost want to order one just to say it. Maui. Wowie."

Billy leans his elbows on the bar and gives it a try.

"Maui. Wowie. Maui. Wowie," he says into the air. "It is pretty fun."

"It's pretty fun watching you say that."

*That's not flirting, Charlie. That's just creepy.*

I raise the glass to my mouth, trying to hide my embarrassment.

He flips his bar rag over his shoulder with a cocky grin. "It's the most fun I've had tonight, I'll tell you that."

He nods down the bar to a couple of slow-moving tourists, bright red from their first day ever in the sun, waving their hands, demanding to be served. "See what I mean?"

I laugh as he slogs down the length of the bar to placate the manatees, glancing back at me a few times as he continues to serve other people along the length of the bar.

As I polish off the last of the lime concoction in front of me, I lick the remaining salt off the rim of my glass and recall the past week. I can't believe I actually pulled it off. I must have kissed Tank convincingly enough since Indigo never moves on with a scene until she is absolutely sure it is perfect. Maybe I do have some natural instinct with this stuff and won't be a total disaster when it comes to guys after all.

Except for guilting Grey into a pity kiss. That is the definition of a disaster. One that needs to be cleaned up sooner rather than later.

With a few drinks in me quieting The Rationalizer, I can think clearly about it. I have to tell Grey I know that kiss was only a favor. That I haven't given it a second thought.

And we must. We must, must, must remember the Rules. They keep us safe and not confuselly.

I need to get this out before the words run out of my brain. I tap my phone, lighting it up with a picture of an eighteen-year-old Greyson in his USC baseball uniform.

I trudged my way through horrendous traffic to the heart of Los Angeles to watch his first college game and had to exact my revenge for it.

Before his first game, I made him stand outside his dorm room door, holding up a little chalkboard sign like those overbearing moms do to their kids on the first day of school. It said, "Greyson, Age 18, First day of Big Boy Baseball."

He wasn't a willing participant, but it wasn't hard to compel him after mentioning I would tell Aubrey about Mr. Ruggles his Winnie the Pooh baby blanket that he still slept with on rough days. At one point it had a cute little picture of Pooh and Piglet walking among the forest trees with the quote, "Sometimes the smallest things take up the most room in your heart." After so many years of being cuddled, most of the letters had faded. Now it simply said, "The thing up in your fart."

"You had to go and kiss me," I scold Big Boy Grey on my screen.

When he doesn't defend himself, I open up the email app, type out my thoughts in a logical fashion, and hit send.

Perfect.

Now that I got that out of the way, we can go back to normal. And I can party.

I slide the phone next to a full margarita glass—Billy's a good bar dude—then spin around on my stool to watch the tourists as they eat their fancy meals and drink their giant blue fishbowls, trying to infuse their lives with a year's worth of fun in ten short days on the island.

The straw makes it really easy to down my drink, after I shake off the ice cream headache, that is.

"We have a room upstairs," a deep voice causes me to spin back around towards the bar.

Some creep has perched on the stool next to mine. He runs his hand under the strap of my yellow tank top.

"I'm good here," I reply, shrugging his hand off my shoulder.

A hand wraps around my right arm, lifting me to my feet. I reach for the bar, but it is swaying worse than the floor. Behind the bar, Billy hauls a shotgun into view. At least I think it's a shotgun. At this point, it could be a chair leg. It's hard to keep my eyes on any one object for too long.

"I believe the lady said she was good here," Billy says.

"Whatever, jackass," the voice curses.

Gravity turns up a notch as I fall onto my stool.

Alone.

"You have a phone?" Billy asks.

I wave my hand in the direction of my phone still on the bar.

"Open it."

He asks sweetly, so I do before resting my woozy head on the bar for a second to steady it.

"She's in the Ulua Tap Room. I think she's gonna need some help getting home. Can you come get her?"

The skinny, bleach blonds at the end of the bar wave their hands, trying to gain Billy's attention.

"I'm Billy. I tend bar here," he says.

Guess he tells all the girls that.

He holds out my phone. "Put this in your pocket so you don't forget it. I'm gonna go help those girls before their heads explode, but I'll come back to finish our chat."

"Sounds like a plan, Stan. Wait. You're Billy. Sounds like a... I can't think of anything to rhyme with Billy."

"That's okay. You tried."

He shuffles to the end of the bar. I can't actually hear what they are saying, but I swear I know it.

"Oh my God. Don't you know I am the most importantest person in the whole world," the skinniest one says.

"She is. She, like, totally is," in a chorus, her minions pipe in.

"And I, like, totally needed a drink, like, five minutes ago."

Over her shoulder, Greyson steps inside the door, scanning the room. Maybe he got my email?

"You still doing good, hon?" Billy's voice makes me turn back to the bar.

"Yep," I say slurping the last of my margarita through my straw. I lift my glass for him to have a closer look. "But I am out of this."

He doesn't even glance at my glass. "You Greyson?"

I follow Billy's eyes to Greyson standing right next to me.

"Greyson! You came to drink with me," I shout.

"Get your stuff we're leaving," he gruffs.

"No way. You've got to have one of these. They are like the best in the whole, wide, big world."

I show him my empty glass, but he won't look at it either.

"Thanks for calling," Greyson says to Billy.

"She really should be more careful. I had to use my Lesson on Civility to get them to leave?"

Greyson's brow goes all wrinkly.

Billy raises enough of the gun above the bar for Greyson to understand.

"Did she settle up?" Greyson asks.

He glares at me. I smile, but he won't smile back as he hands the bill to Greyson.

"Where's the rest?" my Grey asks.

"Yeah. She's that wasted on three drinks. I was gonna cut her off after two, but, I mean, who gets cut off after two drinks?"

Greyson lays some money on the bill and says to me in his grumpy voice, "Let's go."

"Where to?" I slur, hoping he has a big night planned.

He lifts me out of my chair. "Back to the room."

I fall into him, laying my head on his chest. It's warm and so strong. "I could sleep forever just like this."

"Yeah, right. The other night you were avoiding my bed like the plague, but now you want to sleep in my arms?"

He takes a hold of my hand and starts towards the door. "Let's go."

It's hard trying to keep up with Greyson with the ground pretending it's the deck of a sailboat in a huge-like storm.

Greyson wraps his hands around my waist. It helps and feels so nice, like a toasty, safe hiding spot.

And it makes other places heat up, too.

The balmy island air smacks my face when we exit the bar. Greyson keeps my feet moving on the path to our room.

The cutest old couple walks towards us. The man yanks his wife closer like he's scared of someone. I wonder who. I turn my head, but that makes the floor rise up swiftly and then drop out from under my toesies.

I fall into a patch of grass bordered by banana-yellow, strawberry-red, and orange-orange flowers. "It's so pretty, Greyson. I just want to sleep here for tonight. We can go back to the room tomorrow." I pat the soft grass for him to join me.

Greyson tries to make me stand, but I'm not having it. "Fine." It comes out like a growl.

He scoops me up, carrying me towards the pool.

Damn. He's strong.

I nuzzle into his neck. "You are so hot like this," comes tumbling out of my mouth.

"That's enough, Charlie." He plops me down on a round daybed next to the pool and sits down on the side farthest away from me.

I roll over towards him. "Greyson?"

"Yeah," he growls.

"Are you mad?"

He spins towards me. All the anger that scrunched up his face earlier is gone. It's just my sweet Greyson. "What is going on with you, Charlie?" He lays back and rolls over so I can see his face.

"Yesterday. I was watching you. At the pool. With her."

"Trina?"

"Yeah. She had pulled you behind the trees over by the rocks where she could have you to herself. And she ran her hands along your chest." Maybe he'll get it more if I show don't tell. I put my finger on his chest just like she did.

He peeks at my finger and grins. "I don't think I've ever seen you this sloppy."

I've never been this sloppy.

"She whispered in your ear, right here," I say as I run my finger along his ear, tugging at the bottom, just in case he doesn't know where his ear is.

"And you kissed her." I run my thumb across his lips stopping in the middle. They're softer than I remembered.

And so damned close. I would only have to move an inch and we'd be kissing.

I fall into the memory of him kissing her, pulling at her lips until it fades into the memory of the quick kiss he gave me, the one that made me want so much more. "I was so..."

He scrunches up his brows all high. It's his Tell Me Now face.

I search my head for the word.

Nope.

It's not there.

"Jealous?" he prompts. "Angry? Sad?"

I find the words. "Turned on."

His eyebrows fall and his lips fall open. "Really?" he whispers. "Turned on?"

He smiles a little, only with the edges of his mouth like he's trying not to, but it slips out anyway.

"And when she straddled you in the Jacuzzi, that was it. I had to leave."

Greyson mulls this over for an hour-long minute. He starts to say words and then stops. The little muscles in his jaw flex and relax over and over like he's chewing the words.

"Can I ask you something?" he says when he finally does make words come out.

"I got tons of honest juice in me. You're gonna get a really good answer." I tip my forehead down to his and try to match the seriousness on his face.

"When you went back to the room..." He stops and rubs the back of his fingers along his jaw.

I draw back to watch his fingers move. It seems fun, so I run my fingers along his jaw, too, before he takes my hand and lays it on my leg.

He sucks in a gigantic breath and blows it out, slow-like. "Did you..." he continues, even quieter.

Either this boy is talking really slow or the booze has made my brain skip to an alternative time plane.

"...finish things up?"

"Huh?" I yelp. Sometimes that boy is so confusing.

"You know," he continues. "Did you play DJ Hero? Do a Meg Ryan?"

Meg Ryan? He's gone bonko.

"Do a little handiwork?" He adds a gesture this time and I get it.

I totally get it.

*And I got it last night, too.*

The memory of it slaps a grin on my face.

"I slipped into a warm, bubbly bath," I admit.

He lowers his voice and starts to speak slower like he's worried one wrong syllable might toss him in fiery-hot volcano lava.

"Was..." He pulls his eyes away from my lips and dips his head to hide his face. "Was *I* there?"

I take a moment to relive the fantasy of Grey reaching into the silky, bubbly water and helping me out.

He lifts his eyes to mine, drawing out the answer I am powerless to stop. "You... were... amazing."

The corner of his mouth ticks up as his lips part. He lets his eyes drift to my lips as his head closes the last bit of distance between us.

But before he can...

I hiccup.

Then explode into giggles. I know, in cartoons, drunk people always hiccup, but I didn't know it was real.

When my giggles subside, the heavy pull of sleep begins to wash over me. When the last waves of sleep threaten to take over, I'm hit by a blast of panic sending my eyelids flying open.

I have this churning feeling I made Grey involuntarily watch as I recklessly erased a thousand invisible lines tonight, and I need to fix it fastly. "You'll always be my friend. Right, my GreyGrey?"

His yes is enough to wash away my fear and I fall into the deepest, darkest sleep I have ever known.

# 21

## GREYSON

The warmth of the sun spreading along my face is nothing compared to the warmth in my arms. The scent of her banana shampoo swirls around me before I even open my eyes. My hand runs along the small of her back as I try to pause time, holding her this close to me.

Her white jean skirt wriggled up her body as we slept now revealing the curve of her ass, nothing more than her bikini shows off, but somehow so much sexier in the early morning light, in my arms, within my grasp.

*You. Were. Amazing.*

She thinks of me like that. Hell, she fantasizes about me like that.

I guess that makes me less of a creep for doing all sorts of sordid things to her in my own mind over the years.

She moans languidly and lifts her chin, bringing her lips to my neck. They're silky and supple and I want to cover them with mine, to make her moan with passion instead of sleep.

*You'll always be my friend, right?*

Fuck.

She said that, too.

The thought of it drives me to put as much distance between her and myself as possible. I roll to my back while she traps my arm underneath her.

Charlie may like my body enough to pleasure herself while picturing it, but it's clear my intellect is not enough to satisfy hers. My idiocy is exactly why she has permanently assigned us to being Poe Friends.

She deserves more.

She knows it.

And I know it.

A jellyfish-shaped cloud slips away from its slap and drifts, foretelling of the hasty demise of all of them as the sun evaporates them into nothing.

I turn my head back to take her in one last time before she's had a chance to call that ship back to port. Before she turns on the rage, or sarcasm, or whatever the hell she will use to hide the fissure in the firewall she maintains to keep us from burning one another.

For one brief speck of time, we are us. It may be the only speck I ever capture of us, so I plan on taking it all in. I turn back to her, sliding my hand over her waist to her ass, but my movements jostle Charlie enough to welcome the first wave of a hangover.

She rolls out of my arms to the opposite end of the lounge to empty her stomach.

*Welcome back to me-and-her land, Steele.*

I push off the lounger and take a few steps to prepare for what will soon be surging from her mouth. And I don't mean last night's dinner.

When she finishes her purge, she asks in a strangely soft voice, "Where am I?"

You're with me. You're *with* me. "By the pool at our hotel," I tell her.

"Oh, thank God it's you. I thought I just woke up next to a stranger."

What!

A stranger?

A fucking stranger!

And there we have it.

Well, at least it wasn't the typical sarcasm or rage. I never thought she'd go with the straight-up, blacked-out, no-memory shit to patch up the crack, but, then again, a lot of what I know about Charlie hasn't been on point lately.

I spin around to face her, ready to throttle her. "Did you hear what you just said?"

The smile on her face flees.

Good, she knows I'm pissed. Now, let's see just how pissed I can get. "Do you know what it was like to get that call last night? And to see you drunk off your ass like that?"

"What call? What are you talking about?"

*Don't play dumb, Charlie. We both know that's bullshit.*

"The bartender had to grab a bat to run off the two asshats trying to get you to go home with them. Any of this ringing a bell for you?"

"What? When was this?"

*Right before you confessed you want me. Before you told me you could sleep in my arms forever. Before you decided it would be fun to fuck with my heart and then play like you don't remember a goddamned thing.*

I want to shout at her how screwed up it is to tell me I turn her on, sleep in my arms, and then pretend it never happened. And she expects me to play along. It's clear we won't be talking about it today.

Or any day for that matter.

She may not want to admit to it, but I sure as hell am going to make her pay for it. "You went out drinking alone," I take two steps towards her, towering over her as she cowers on the chair. "Alone, Charlie. You know what could have happened."

Fuck. How did I let her go drinking alone?

No. Screw that.

She did this. Not me.

"Did you even check?" my voice rising to a roar. "You sat in that bar for hours. No one would have thought you were anything but a drunken chick, sweating and slurry."

The thought of her going low alone in a bar is almost enough to break me.

She slides her hand into her back pocket, retrieving Tex. Her head drops lower as she clears the alarm and slides it back into her skirt while pressing the buttons on the side of her pump with her other hand, trying to hide it from me.

Like I don't know exactly what she's trying to fix.

The picture of her drinking with diabetes, of what could have happened, what still could happen at any moment, just adds to my rage and makes me into a total asshole. I watch it happening from outside my body, but I am powerless to stop it.

And so the fiery darts keep flying.

"If you passed out, no one would give it a second thought as you lay there with the sugar rushing out of your blood, starving your brain of any fuel. Until you started seizing, they all would have stepped right over you as the life poured out of you. What then, Charlie?"

I wait for an answer.

*Anything, Charlie. Give me anything.*

*Tell me you remember what you said last night. How you said it. How you looked at me like you had to have me.*

*Something. Anything.*

"God, you don't even remember," I scold her. "Get your stuff. Let's go."

I don't wait for her to catch up. She trails behind me far enough that her footsteps are silent.

And I'm glad. I don't want to hear her. I don't want to see her. I don't want to want her.

But I do. And no matter how much I scream and attack her, I can't stop wanting her.

She catches me as I wait for the elevator, her eyes swollen and red and... glistening?

Is she crying?

Because of me?

She's swaying next to me like the foxtail palms behind her. The urge to steady her, to take away the sting of my words, breezes through me, but it's driven out by a stronger force.

*Charlie passed out on the beer-stained carpet, dying.*
*Another funeral.*
*Another loss.*
*Me.*
*Alone.*

Charlie's shoes dangle from her hands as she contemplates the gravity of her actions.

Or maybe only the swirls of the carpet.

The elevator doors swing open. She steps in, standing right next to me, yet miles away, counting the seconds until those damned doors open again. I push the button for the seventeenth floor and ride up in silence, except for the screaming in my head, which has got to be loud enough for her to hear.

Is this a once-off? Will she never let me behind that wall again? What kind of heartless woman would—

My phone buzzes.

**Trina: We're grabbing brekky downstairs. Meet us there?**

Right above us now, their voices float down the elevator shaft. I hit the button to the fifteenth floor to stall us.

The doors open and Charlie takes a step out. I wrap my arms around her waist. "Not our floor."

The ten seconds it takes for the doors to close again last an hour as I slowly remove my hands from her hips, the voices getting louder.

The doors swing open on the sixteenth floor. Charlie makes another move.

"Not ours."

The voices quiet as they pass in the elevator shaft next to ours.

We reach the seventeenth floor and the doors resume their ways. Charlie doesn't move.

I step out without a word and slip my hand into my pocket searching for the key. It's not there.

*Shit.*

The last thing I need to do is to text Trina and ask her for the key to take my drunken best friend back to our room after staying out all night without even telling her. No, I could use a little more time before facing that roaring lion.

I check another pocket and luck out. Slipping the key in the lock, I pause, unable to contain my vitriol any longer. I turn back to Charlie ready to unleash the rage threatening to take over, but she glances up at me, softer now, all her bravado and strength gone.

Her eyes dip to my mouth, and in turn, my gaze shifts to her cheeks, her lips.

Not willing to go down that path, I swing open the door, the remains from the previous night's celebration apparent all around the room. Charlie walks right past me to her suitcase, fiddling with it. She's avoiding me.

But two can play at that game. I swipe my ditty bag and a change of clothes from my duffel and stomp off toward the bathroom. Flashes of her face so close to mine, the feel of her thumb dragging across my mouth flood my brain, but the thought of losing Charlie to a low has completely engulfed the memories of seeing her for the first time without her firewall up.

And the fear of her taking it back.

I open the bathroom door and, before her brooding can stop me, I turn and spew, "Charlie, you are the most selfish person I have ever met," and I punctuate it with a deafening door slam.

She never thinks of what all this shit does to me. She just does whatever the hell she wants.

Drinking alone? Sure.

Putting herself in a place to be…

*Fuck.*

I spin on the faucet in the shower and jump in. The cold blasts my skin, and my heart, already pounding, throws itself into a whole other gear.

*How am I supposed to keep pretending to be your friend now? I could do it before when I thought that was what you wanted. When I knew you thought I was too stupid. Too screwed up. When I didn't want you to be saddled with my own shit on top of yours.*

I reach for the square bar of hotel soap and send it flying from my shaking hand before I can scrub anything.

I slam my hand against the fancy marble tile, sending small cracks along the grout around where I make contact.

Who the hell would want any part of my screwed-up life? Any part of me?

*But maybe that's it. Maybe you know I'm too stupid, Charlie, too screwed up to ever make you happy.*

*Maybe you want me, but you know better. And all my shit is what is keeping you from having what you want.*

*Just one more thing I've screwed up.*

I press my hand against the wall to keep it from closing in any more.

Lines of water stream down my face and I haven't even dipped it in the spray of cold coming from the showerhead.

*Shit.*

*I'm sweating in a cold shower.*

*That's not good.*

*No. It's bad.*

*Really bad.*

*Like heart attack bad.*

*Fuck, I'm gonna die in this lousy hotel shower, totally naked.*

I rip back the curtain and snatch a towel while I leap over the edge of the tub, the dingy white bath mat sliding under the force. My shoulder crashes into the wall, my body following right after.

I let my head fall to the brown marble floor and drag the corner of the towel over my bare ass.

*This is how they'll find me, dead in a little puddle of water and tears.*

*You're so fucking weak.*

*Can't even shower.*

*Can't protect her.*

*And you're a total asshole.*

*No wonder she doesn't...*

"You okay?" she yells through the door.

I sit up to check the lock on the door behind my feet. It's locked.

"Yeah," I bark, putting way too much force into it.

*She can't find me like this.*

*Four, Steele. Get to four.*

I start to inhale, counting in my head, *one... tw—*

*You can't will yourself out of a heart attack, dumbass.*

I try again, one... two... th—

*Shit.*

*You are an asshole.*

*It's not even her fault.*

One... two... three... four. And exhale for four.

*You attack her for blowing off steam like you've done thousands of times.*

In to four. Out to four.

*For trying to save your friendship without having to tell you what a fuck up you are to your face.*

In. Out.

*She did it to save what we do have.*

In. Out.

*If we still do have it.*

My pulse finally slows.

*You smell like shit again.*

I step back in the shower, warming the water this time before hopping in. I lather and rinse in twelve seconds.

*You have to make this right, Steele.*

I turn off the water and take the dry towel from the rack, stepping out carefully this time.

I wrap the towel around my waist as I open the door. "I didn't mean it, Sands..."

"Charlie?"

Nothing but an empty room.

# 22

## GREYSON

When I finally make it to the restaurant downstairs, I find everyone at a large table next to the wall of windows, opened to let the cool ocean breeze in. The adrenaline surge from earlier has left my body, and, in its place, is a sickly fatigue poured over a giant helping of guilt.

Searching for Charlie among the group, I only find an empty chair.

Makes sense. I wouldn't want to see me right now either.

I lean down to give Trina a kiss. She gives me her cheek.

Great. Let's just add that to the list of Steele Screwups. The small chance of her overlooking this just evaporated with the clouds.

She leans over to me, "Where'd you run off to?"

"The bartender called me about Charlie. She was drunk and needed help getting back."

Shit. I shouldn't have said that; I can see Trina throwing that in Charlie's face. "But please don't tell anyone. I know she would be horribly embarrassed if people knew."

"Yeah. She'd be embarrassed."

Trina turns her back to me to talk with Tank. I guess that one's over.

"Where's Charlie?" Indigo asks. "I thought she was coming with you."

With me? She'll never truly be with me.

"I think she went for a walk. She'll meet up with us later, I'm sure."

I hope.

I order a plateful of pancakes, hash browns, eggs, and bacon, hoping to wash away my fatigue and guilt with salt and syrup.

Charlie slips into the empty chair across from me, refusing to look my way. Her hair is wet and her cheeks are flushed pink. It's what girls try to make their faces resemble with makeup and whatever else it is they do in the bathroom for hours. Charlie does it by going for a swim.

And I know she swam; that's where she works things out. She once told me it was the place she goes to cry because the tears just fade into the ocean.

Indigo rests her hand on Charlie's arm and asks her something I can't make out.

Charlie plasters on her bogus Party Smile and shakes her head.

"You want to order something? We can wait," Sonny asks Charlie.

Pancakes or toast, Charlie. Order something to soak up the stomach acid that's been swirling since you rolled out of my arms this morning.

She turns her way and gives her a bogus Party Smile, too. "No thanks."

Dammit, Charlie. You've got to eat. If not for the hangover, for the diabetes.

Tank shoves a whole piece of bacon into his mouth. "We were thinking of doing the Makamaka'ole Falls hike. You know, go swim in the pools and stuff."

Trina lays her hand on Tank's arm. "Ohmygod. I read about that one in the guidebook, and it's like..."

I can't stand to listen to that girl babble. Not when there is still so much to say. Stuff that matters.

Charlie's nearly silent now, which is usually a bad thing. The more she has to say, the quieter she becomes.

I slide the remains of my pancakes and hash browns her way, a white flag of sorts, but make quick work of the eggs and bacon, trying to fill the cavern in my belly, while not making any headway on the cavern in my chest.

She meets my gaze and wrestles out a fraction of a Real Smile. I'd take a fraction of Charlie's Real Smile over the forced Big Party Smile any day.

"I'm an ass," I mouth to her.

She raises an eyebrow as if to say, You think I don't already know that? as she pours a layer of syrup over her feast and scoops up a huge bite.

After breakfast, I pull Trina aside. I know we have to get it over with eventually, so I man up and take my medicine.

"Something's wrong, huh?" I ask trying to give her an easy way in.

Her face is devoid of any emotion. "You could say that."

"You're done with me." More of a statement than a real question.

"Completely."

She scurries off to join Indigo and Tank who have wandered off to the hotel store to buy preparations for their hike. She turns back to me, her face softer now, almost pitying. "You really should avoid letting anyone else fall for you before you get your shit with Charlie sorted."

I think I just did. I finally got my shit with Charlie sorted. Fully.

I laugh to myself. Shit With Charlie. I like that way better than Poe Friends.

Halfway up the Makamaka'ole Falls Trail, Charlie is dragging behind, weighed down by her first hangover and the weight of my asshole ways.

The alarm from her Dexcom shouts at her that she's high. I check to make sure she's dealing with it.

Her face is screaming red and her lips are in a tight scowl like she's trying to kill someone with a look. Not me, this time. The trail.

She hates appearing weak, and if there has ever been a time she's felt weak, it's right now. She's taking small steps and has both hands wrapped around the straps of her pack, a move she usually reserves for mile fifteen of a twenty-mile hike, not the first five hundred yards of a pleasure walk through a beautiful rain forest. She must really be hurting.

I turn back around before she catches me. I don't need to heap any more anguish on her shoulders which already have to bear more pain than she deserves.

Forty minutes later, her Dexcom is still hollering, "You're fucking High!!!" or at least I wish that is what it would say so she'd actually do something about it.

You may not want me or even need me, Charlie, but I sure as hell need you.

And I need you to at least stay alive.

I turn back and hike to where she is straggling behind and hand her a Gatorade Zero. It's one of the few things she can drink when she's high. I hate that shit, but I pack it anyways, along with the pocket full of energy gels, just in case.

I had no idea what a hangover would do to her blood sugars—she's never had one before—so I filled my pack with stuff to fix her whether she went high or low.

She shakes me off.

Seems I forgot to pack something that might fix her pride.

"You have to hydrate," I scold.

Dex yells again and she removes it from her back pocket to silence it.

I swipe it the moment it's visible. 345, double arrows up. That's even higher than I thought it might be.

And it's still rising.

The heat and humidity combined with a nasty hangover and a giant hike? Stupid plan.

She should have sat it out.

I should have made her sit it out.

"Did you fix it?" I demand.

She lowers her head, "Not yet."

"Fix it."

She pulls her pump from her waistband and dials up a bolus, showing me before putting it back in place.

"It's bad enough you went out drinking with no one there to watch your blood sugars. You could have...You don't get to check out on this."

Asshole just keeps pouring out of me. I sorted out my Shit With Charlie; this shouldn't still be happening.

She steps towards me and slips the Gatorade out of my hand and downs half of it, before nodding an apology.

I turn and run back up the trail, hoping the pain of an uphill sprint will burn out any more asshole I have left.

By the time I catch up to everyone, they have gathered motionless, heads craned upwards.

The Makamaka'ole Falls pour water over the edge of a rock channel in the black mountain after drifting from the Eke Crater and tumbling down some two hundred fifty feet of falls.

Charlie's breathing has become more mellow as she slides in next to me. I study her face as she takes in the falls; she's miserable and beat down and most of that is my fault.

I slide my pack off my shoulder and snag another Gatorade. I wish I could take some of the weight off her, make her lighter, but every time I open my mouth I only add more to it.

I hand her the drink and take the empty. She struggles with the top and returns it to me without taking her eyes off the falls. I turn to her, refusing to hand it back until she acknowledges me.

She looks at the drink, and finally up at me.

"Wipe that last twenty-four hours?" I plead.

"Sure." She downs the whole bottle and hands it back to me with a full Real Smile across her mouth, that sumptuous mouth I want so badly to feel against mine.

Fuck.

Knock that shit off, Steele.

One second into a clean slate and I am already screwing this up again.

# 23

## CHARLIE

After the hike from hell, where I attempted to pay my penance through high blood sugars and regret, we jumped a flight back home. I slept the whole plane ride home, trying to avoid the hangover from my wild night and from the things I said.

I spend the next week avoiding Greyson and the memories pricking my conscience.

He doesn't get the memo.

**Greyson: I've had a crap day. Fish tacos on your deck tonight?**

**Charlie: I'm still really tired from that trip.**

Avoiding him sucks, but I don't know how to be around him now.

And the guilt is bad. Like, really bad.

I broke my own rule. I crossed that line.

And I should know better.

A week later, I try for a saltwater rinse to cleanse myself from the guilt starting to turn my insides brown with purple smudges. I paddle out under a blotchy grey sky, with an off-shore wind. Typically, a wind like that will hold the waves up longer before they break, making them a surfer's dream.

But, today, they are a nightmare.

I paddle into a four-foot wave breaking left and miss it by inches. My reward? A face full of spray from those dreamy off-shore winds.

I spend the next thirty minutes missing waves and enduring a water flogging each time.

With my stomach in knots—I haven't eaten right in days—my paddling is weak and I can only endure so much thrashing before even my spirit has been licked. I paddle in and sit on the stairs leading to the deck in my wetsuit, too beaten up to even shower. I toss my board in the sand, wrap my arms around my legs and rest my head on my knees.

How do I navigate the aftermath of the Hiroshima-sized bomb I detonated?

Saltwater from my eyes merges with the ocean water on my face.

How do I make this go back to normal?

My phone buzzes me from the railing.

**Greyson: You up for lunch?**

How is he ready to see me? Is he that much of a masochist?

I make up another lame excuse.

**Charlie: Nah. Working on Nudge. I got to get this thing done.**

I'm not ready to see him until I figure out how to make this right. How to make my head right.

I force myself up and through the shower, giving myself a few more weak moments to cry as the water rushes over my head. If I give it enough time, maybe the guilt will wash off, too.

Dragging myself upstairs, I throw on my fuzzy skull pajama bottoms and my favorite coastal blue Wears Woody hoodie with a watercolor picture of a Woody under palm trees on the front. I trip over my still full suitcase spilling out of the closet into the bathroom.

Not only am I avoiding Greyson now, I'm avoiding anything to do with that ill-fated trip. If I'm going to fix any of this, I might as well start there.

I clean my room and bring my suitcase out to the garage laundry. This place was built as an artist studio so it doesn't have a laundry room, but our landlord is kind enough to let us use the one in the garage.

Maybe if I don't think about him, the guilt will vanish.

But it's damned near impossible not to think about Greyson. Flashes of him pop into my mind at the weirdest moments.

As I dump my suitcase into the washer, my white jean skirt falls out on top of the pile and I instantly feel the warmth of his hand as he slid it onto my ass, tugging me closer that morning.

I shake my head like I'm trying to fling the thought out of my head.

I walk back into the house and try to distract myself by tidying up. While scrubbing the morning's dishes, I'm instantly reminded of a stupid joke he used to tell to get a rise out of girls.

"What do you do when the dishwasher stops working?"

His bimbo would search both of her brain cells for the answer.

"Kick your wife and tell her to get back to work."

She would then play her prescribed role, act in outrage, and hit him playfully.

Every.

Single.

Time.

It's like they have all been reading out of the same playbook.

I toss the last clean plate into the dishrack and search for a more effective distraction.

"Holy Kubric" comes from the back deck.

Indigo shakes her hand then plunges her pinkie finger into her mouth.

I nod to the old jimmy-rigged fire pit staged temporarily on the sand. "You finally replacing that disaster waiting to happen?"

I commandeer the pliers and sit down next to the pieces scattered around the deck. Indigo can run a film set like SEAL Team leader, but, with a huge propane tank involved, I want to make sure we don't end up with a month-long explosion of Kilauea on the back deck.

And a fire pit with a direction book thicker than Indigo's next movie script is exactly the distraction I need.

Before I realize it, the sun is headed into its saline grave and Indigo has lit up her fairy lights in the Banyan tree. I collect the leftover pieces and hope this is the type of fancy contraption that includes extra hardware like high-end shirts with a few spare buttons on the underside of the hem.

I turn on the propane and click the starter. Flames slowly rise from the crushed glass covering the gas pipe. No more dodging mini-fireballs required.

Indigo covers the table with a tapestry of the British flag with the words "Punk's Not Dead" painted haphazardly across it and arranges plates of marshmallows, graham crackers, and an assortment of bite-sized candy bars on top. "You're doing s'mores with us right?" she asks.

I'm not in a social mood, but with a plate of 3 Musketeers and marshmallows staring me in the face, I really can't say no. "Sure. But I should probably put some protein in my belly before the onslaught of sugar."

I'm still cooking up an omelet when the sound of my phone strangles my stomach. I slide the omelet onto a plate and sprinkle Cheddar cheese on it before returning the package to the fridge and taking my plate to the amber driftwood table in the adjoining dining room, plunking my phone on the table.

I demand my stomach stills while I read the text.

**Greyson: Let's try to forget about Maui. I am sorry if I came off like a jerk. I was just worried about you and all. I hope you understand.**

I scan the room, trying to quell the tears forming. Above the sliding doors, a surfboard-shaped chalkboard brandishes a Jeff Spicoli quote. "All I need are some tasty waves, a cool buzz, and I'm fine."

I rub the heel of my palm over my right eye before it betrays me.

*You are so clueless, Sands. You made a pass at him when he has a beautiful girlfriend.*

Like he'd ever go for me.

And, damn, he was so pissed.

So. Pissed.

I'm not even sure I meant any of it either.

I will never let that happen again.

Never.

Finishing my protein, I clear the dish and head outside. I drop onto the bench and try to reply, but my fingers hover over the keyboard deadlocked. My brain has no directions for them either.

*Miserable Brain. You've had control of the English language for nearly three decades. Say something.*

"That Greyson?" Indigo asks as she closes the sliding door behind her.

I momentarily abandon my self-flagellation. "It's the first time I can't figure out how to text him back."

"Makes sense. Maui was..." she walks to the cooler, removing two bottles of beer, "...a development?"

She hands me one of the beers.

"A development? What does that mean?" I tip a little of the beer into my mouth, afraid of the insight she may lay down.

"The prevailing ebb and flow between the two of you has expanded to a new wavelength since then. It went from around a 520, a cool blue, to a 590, a golden yellow."

I wait for her to continue, to tell me what that means, what she saw, what Greyson told her, but she doesn't. She allows the silence to nudge me.

But how do I explain something that I can't even decipher?

A squeal from the sliding door cuts through my attempts.

"Spartans! Prepare for battle! For tonight, we dine in Hell!" Tank bounds through the door, brandishing a fistful of metal sticks like he's a gladiator fending off a Coliseum full of ravenous rhinos.

"You found them. Thank Spielberg." Indigo takes the faux swords and lays them next to the marshmallows on the table.

When I turn back to the fire, Occy has materialized on the bench next to me.

"It's Charlie, right?" His eyes crinkle at the corners.

I bite down on a smile.

"Yep. And you're the wannabe Occhilupo?" I tease.

"So I hear you've been doing a little acting."

Indigo hands each of us two skewered marshmallows to roast. Setting my beer on the back of the bench, I take the offering.

Occy dips his into the pit until they are engulfed in flames of their own. He blows out the inferno while he waits for my answer.

"I did Indigo's short in Maui." I slowly twirl my mallows safely above the flame.

"And?" he prods.

"And?"

"What'd you think? Of the whole acting thing?" He slams one entire, blackened treat into his mouth.

"Honestly, I loved it. I didn't think I would, but it was so freeing to be someone completely different from myself."

After all the quagmire I created in Maui, I hadn't taken the time to realize I thoroughly enjoyed acting. I could try on new personalities without anyone judging me. I never had to worry I had the right words or that the person across from me understood what I was saying. And I could fully embrace my sexy side without losing the respect of colleagues or confusing friendships.

"You were wonderful, too." He taps my knee with his finger. "You have a future in this business."

He downs the second mallow in one bite.

Boys. Always trying to butter girls up with their lies and fake compliments.

"And how exactly would you know?"

With his thumb, he swipes a stray blob of white fluff from his lips into his mouth and I am enthralled.

"I've been working with Indigo on the rough cut."

It takes me a minute to rip my thoughts from his tongue running over his lips searching for leftover marshmallow to process what he says, but when I do, my eyes go wide. He's been watching hours and hours of me acting badly, messing up lines, and cussing out loud when I did.

Out.

Loud.

"I'm so sorry you had to watch that."

"Sorry? It's been awesome." He leans in closer and lowers his voice. "But I have felt like a bit of creeper watching you make out with Tank over and over."

I hide my face behind my hand.

"And a bit jealous," he confides shyly.

Jealous of what exactly? I am horrified at the memory of take after take after take of my pathetic stage kissing. "I swear I don't kiss that badly."

His glance dips to my lips, lingering there for a moment before rising to my eyes again. His voice turns dark and smooth. "I'm open to any proof you want to convince me with."

Hoping the blush that must be spreading across my face will be hidden by the flames, I focus on perfecting the bronze on my marshmallows in the fire.

When they're perfect, I gingerly remove them from the skewer and lean over to the table to lay down my skewer. When I sit back up, Occy is still focused on me. His devilish face is making me wonder what exactly he is playing on the movie screen in his head.

He steals one of the marshmallows precariously perched on my fingertips and pops it in his mouth and I am praying he misses some so I can watch him swipe his thumb over those inviting lips again.

A flirty voice from across the fire interrupts my daydream. "Are you going to introduce me to your friend, Charlie?"

*Narcissistic Infringer, meet Cute Boy who is actually flirting with me. Cute Boy, meet my ex-friend.*

But, instead, I choose to be civil. "Bex, this is Occy."

Bex sits on the other side of Occy grabbing his arm. "You must surf, huh? These are surfer's arms, for sure."

Tank glides into Bex. "You think those are arms? There's a reason they call me Tank."

He offers Bex his arm. "Two reasons actually," he says with an evil grin.

Occy takes the opportunity to remove his arm from my Ex-Friend's grasp.

Bex, in heaven in her boy sandwich, has turned her flirting up to full power, making me invisible again.

Accepting my fate, I pick up my nearly full beer and head to the kitchen.

# 24

## CHARLIE

After my foray into drunkenness and bad decision-making, it will be a good, long while before I drink again. I know Greyson would kill me for wasting such a choice beer, but I pour the Sculpin I.P.A. down the drain and toss the bottle in the recycling bin, then retrieve a Diet Dr Pepper from the fridge and crack it open.

Leaning back against the white laminate on the kitchen island, I reluctantly reread Grey's last text, hoping it will inspire a coherent response this time.

**Greyson: Let's try to forget about Maui. I am sorry if I came off like a jerk. I was just worried about you and all. I hope you understand.**

Maybe I don't have to figure all this out. Maybe we simply forget it ever happened.

My thumbs hover above the screen as my eyes drift to the surfboard chalkboard again.

**Charlie: Forgetting sounds good. Especially since it's all a little hazy anyways.**

But is that really true? The details are etched into my mind like the first copy of the Ten Commandments into stone tablets.

I erase it and try again.

**Charlie: Forgetting sounds good.**

*Great, Charlie. Three whole words. You're the next great American novelist.*

"Wow. That Bex girl sure has to be the center of attention." Occy's Australian accent rouses me from my emotional dissertation.

Before I realize it, "Your accent is so sexy," has slipped out of my mouth.

"Okay. What do you want me to say?"

There's a reason I usually think about what I say before letting uncensored drivel leak out.

"Sorry. I just thought it sounded refreshing. Different."

"No. I mean what stupid phrases do you want me to say?" He thickens his accent. "Shrimp on the barbie. G'Day Mate. Budgie Smugglers."

"People actually ask you to do that?"

He points outside towards Bex. "Why do you think I am in here?"

"Sorry about her."

I lift my soda stopping halfway to my mouth. "Budgie Smugglers? Is that what I think it is?"

"Banana Hammock? Scrote Tote? Marble Sack? Or my favorite, the Daytona Dong Sarong?"

I knew I shouldn't have taken a sip right then. I nearly douse Occy in soda, running to the sink to spit it out before it comes out my nose.

So much for having a cute boy flirt with me. Still batting a thousand on that front.

"That's way too many names for a bathing suit that absolutely should not exist," I say when my mouth is free from any more liquid ammo.

"Only time you'll catch me in one is paying off a lost bet."

I picture that as my eyes scan his budgie.

*Crap. Charlie, eyes up top.*

He leans up against the counter next to me. "I actually love your accent. The way you said surfer last time we met." He strikes the R really hard. "Surf-eRRRR. That was the greatest."

So he remembered my name and me saying surf-eRRRR. That's kind of sweet.

In return, I put on my best Aussie accent. "There's nevaah been a bettaah surfaah in the waddaah than the one wearing budgie smugglaahs."

Occy spits out a puff of beer midst before buckling down his lips. "Okay. *That* was the greatest."

We make our way back outside and catch the last half of Tank regaling everyone around the fire pit. He's lit up by the dancing flames like he's on stage at the Gershwin.

"So I yell at my dad, 'Fish on.' I set the hook and I can feel the weight. This thing is huge. Like white whale huge."

He runs to one end of his stage, "The way this thing was pulling, it had to be from here," he gallops to the other end, "to like here. At. Least."

Each time I turn to Occy, who is still standing mere inches from me, he is smiling right back at me.

"And I get it closer to the boat, but I still can't figure out what it is, but I know it's gargantuan. So I net it and pull it up and realize it's a freakin sixteen-inch dong. I caught a sixteen-inch dildo and that thing fought me like an eight-foot marlin."

I am in awe of Tank's ability to entertain anyone.

The purple-haired girl who showed up with Tank lets out one explosive, "Haaaaaaaaaaaaaaaaaa," followed by percussive cackling. Indigo's holding her sides in pain. I would expect her abs would be up to this kind of workout hanging around Tank so much. Tank's shaking so hard he's going to piss himself. Bex is looking down her nose at us heathens who appreciate dildo humor.

Occy kindhearted chuckle reminds me of the slow warmth of whiskey, or at least how I've heard Grey describe it.

"Oh. My. Gosh. I forgot to tell you." Bex grabs my forearm to twist me towards her. "Greyson totally..."

I watch as Occy drifts away from me, taking a seat on the opposite side of the fire. He gives me a *See what I mean?* nod towards Bex.

I laugh and shake my head in agreement.

"Are you even listening? I just said Greyson totally propositioned me."

"Who propositioned you?" I reply, trying to give her my full attention to save us all from a Bex rampage.

She turns up the volume so everyone has to listen to her tirade. "Greyson did. Greyson totally propositioned me."

I let out a long sigh, waiting to hear how Bex twisted some little comment into Greyson coming on to her.

"You don't believe me!"

"Not really."

"Don't be a blighter, Char. I was telling him this story of how I bought new lingerie for Hunter and he's like, 'You should try it on for me. In your room. Right now.'"

"There's no way he said that, Bex."

I know there's no way that actually happened, but the picture it forms in my head makes me nauseous.

"Swear it, Charlie. That day he picked me up cause I had a flat tire. He trapped me on the side yard and pushed me up against the gate."

The thought of Greyson's hands on Bex.

Pushing her up against a gate.

Our gate.

Kissing her.

The marshmallows and candy in my gut threaten to show themselves again.

Greyson in our room gaping at Bex in lingerie, trying to have sex with her.

In our room.

In my room.

Every other guy has picked Bex over me. Why would Grey be any different?

"That's why the gate's broken. And thank God it broke, it gave me an escape from him." She captures my hands and puts on her best concerned face. "Please don't be mad at me because every guy wants me. I don't do it on purpose."

I know Grey will screw around with women he's not even into... if they're hot enough. With girls who can't string together words into anything resembling coherent sentences. With shallow girls who only care about their appearance and finding an equally hot man.

But, Bex?

He hates Bex.

I must be so incredibly revolting, even more than I realized if Grey is willing to pursue Bexley Liddell before he'd even take a second look at me.

He can't really be that myopic, that he'd screw someone he actively despises?

"I know you wanted him to be into you, Charlie, but he's just not. I'm really sorry."

It shouldn't come as a shock that Grey isn't into me, but I always figured if I was one of the last girls on earth he might consider me, but apparently, not if Bex was still alive.

The agony of that thought slowly mutates into a growing storm of rage until old words flash into my mind.

*I'll figure it out. You'll how he feels by the end of the week one way or the other.*

She set this up. She was testing Grey by trying to seduce him. Which means her story is nowhere near the truth.

And she actually thinks that in doing this, and telling me in front of a crowd, she was doing me a favor.

A favor!

"Okay..." I mutter.

It's best not to contradict Bex outright. It only incites her. I've found a well-placed 'okay' goes a long way without actually having to agree with her.

Without bothering to stop undressing Occy with her eyes, she says, "Your best friend is a total man whore, Charlie."

"Hmm," I mutter while Occy throws me another of his winning Aussie smiles.

She temporarily suspends her visual assault of him to turn her full attention towards me. She lowers her voice only the slightest bit. "I'm sorry, Charlie. I know you were hoping he was in love with you. But if he liked you at all, he wouldn't be trying to sleep with me."

There is so much wrong with every part of this statement, I don't know what to defend first. Not that she'd let me interject words into her self-serving display of phony loyalty even if I could find the right ones.

"Charlie, you haaaaave to distance yourself from that guy. He obstructs your baby duct on a regular basis."

"Thanks for the input, Bex."

I flee before she has a chance to go on. Swiping a handful of bite-sized candy bars from the table, I start towards the beach.

From over my shoulder, she calls out, "I always have your back, Charlie."

*If only that were true.*

I can't believe Bex is now lying straight to my face. She's always bent the truth to suit her, jazzed up a boring story to gain a bigger reaction from her audience, but she's never flat out lied to my face. She is so wrapped up in finding the 'perfect' men for us, or maybe I should say the perfect men for her, she is willing to lie and manipulate to get it.

She doesn't care about what is best for me, who is best for me. She just wants to make sure her guy gets along with my guy so she can continue to monopolize my time. She couldn't deal with me having a man of my own cause she wouldn't be Number One in my life.

Not that she's ever been Number One in my life.

But she wants that.

Needs it.

Demands it.

It's why she and Greyson have never gotten along. When he came around, I spent less time with her, told her less, trusted her less. And she can't handle not being the center of attention.

She hates him because she couldn't command his attention. She needs to know she can have any guy she wants, but she never could entice Greyson.

The worst part about Bex's lie is it's not even a believable lie. Greyson may take out bimbos, but he doesn't pursue girls he doesn't genuinely have some real interest in only to get them in bed.

He may say the Rule Book is my creation, but he has rules of his own. He never dates more than one bimbo at a time. He won't let a girl choose his clothes.

And he doesn't lie. Not to get ahead in life. Not to women about his intentions. And especially not to me.

By the time I finish my silent exoneration of Grey and our friendship, I have marched to where the lagoon pours out into the ocean. Unless I want to wade thigh-deep through the water, I have to stop.

I bend down to pick up a rock and try skipping it. The current from the receding tide has disrupted the surface enough the rock sinks straight to the sandy bottom.

I pull out my phone and try to type out what I have finally realized.

Grey is a great friend. He's by far the best friend I've ever had. Probably the best I ever will have. And I need to make sure he stays that way.

I pull up his last text, as my phone vibrates with a new one.

**Greyson: Charlie?**

*Dammit.*

My heart melts.

Every. Single. Time.

Even in text, when he uses my name, it does something to me I can't stop.

With words failing me, I text a gif of a sea turtle coming up for air in clear aqua water. It's the only thing I can find to express how I feel.

His reply comes almost immediately.

**Greyson: That mean you're done avoiding me?**

His second text comes even faster.

**Greyson: Btw...That email? Erased**

Email?

What email?

I faintly remember sending Greyson an articulate email about not assuming he meant anything when he kissed me.

I open the email app, scroll through the Sent folder, and find one addressed to Grey.

At 11:30 p.m.
*That night.*
I was a full three drinks in at that point.
*Shit.*
*Shit. Shit. Shit.*
Is this why he was so pissed?
What did I say?
*Shit.*
I gather the strength to open the email.

> From: Charlie Sands
> To: Greyson Steele
> Dear Greyson. That feels funny when I say it. Graaaaaaaaaaaaysonnnnnnn. Sonnnnnn. Sonny. Oooh I liek that one.
> Your my best friend. And you kissed me. Friends don't kiss. But you did. And thats baaaaaaaaaaaad.
> im in thiat bar now drinking cause its so baaaaaaad. You need stay my friend nevermore. All right? Poe friends.
> I love you.
> Charlie
> but totily dont tell ur girlfriend you macked on me

My breath grows deep and drawn out as I read the words I know Greyson read.
He read those words.
I told him kissing me was bad.
Like, baaaaaaaaaaaad.
What was I thinking?
Oh, yeah. That's right. I was three drinks in, I wasn't thinking.
At least I got one thing right. Friends don't kiss. Not like that.
Not with that look in his eyes like I was exactly where he wanted to be.
Not with the feel of his lips against mine...
*Stop, Charlie.*
If kissing a friend is baaaaaaaaaaaad, then reliving every

bewildering, brazen, breathtaking moment of that kiss is horrrrrrrrrrrrrendous.

We have to go back to before we both started breaking the rules. If we ever want our friendship to last, we have to follow the Rule Book. It's the whole reason I wrote it in the first place.

I palm my phone to share my new resolve, but it's not something I can do over text.

I need to do this in person.

# 25

## GREYSON

*I*t's been sixteen days since I kissed Charlie and told myself I was doing it for her.

Fifteen days since I let Charlie go out drinking alone when I told her I'd watch her back, but stupidly, foolishly, brainlessly, insanely let Trina distract me from my promise.

Fourteen days since I told her—sorry, make that yelled at her—that she was the most selfish person I had ever known even though I am the only one who was being selfish.

Thirteen days since the last time I've seen her.

Since we've been *us*.

We've never gone this long without talking. Even when I was driving cross country trying to lose myself, she made me check in with her every single day.

I never missed a call.

Neither did she.

But after twelve perfect years with my best friend, I fucked it all up all because I was stupid enough to think I knew more than she did about these things.

She wrote a fucking Rule Book because she knew I would eventually screw things up.

And she was right. Charlie Nostradamus called it years ago. Greyson Steele is a brainless, horny fuckup. I'm surprised I lasted this long without screwing it up. I don't know why I thought I could wipe the slate clean after kissing her and making her drunkenly admit things she would never have said if she was sober.

I did that.

And I spent the last five months trying to push her boundaries to coax her into loving me even though she has told me thousands of times, in no uncertain terms, it will never happen.

The realization sits heavy in my guts as I start my next shift. Not ten minutes into it, we get toned to a building fire in Leucadia.

When we arrive on scene fourteen minutes after the initial call, the colorful Marty's Cafe is fully involved, flames going through the roof, black smoke enveloping the prominent sign on the side of the building promising, "Good Food. Good Vibes."

The building also houses the Beachside Art Gallery and Reynolds & Sons T-shirts. It was built in the 1910s and is iconic as it sported the first exterior mural in Leucadia. I have been through the building many times. It's an interconnected maze of doors and hallways running through all three businesses, one of which regularly doesn't pass fire safety inspections.

It is filled floor to ceiling with t-shirts, vintage magazines, used books, and tourist knickknacks. It's also filled with handmade candles. Each time the owner failed inspection, he would remedy the violations before the reinspection, but no doubt, after he passed, he'd put everything back the way it was before.

Even though it's still early, a crowd is starting to form. After talking to the witnesses on-site, we know there is one cook who is unaccounted for so I take Junior to start a primary search for victims and the seat of the fire.

I open the air bottle on my SCBA and swing it onto my back, connecting the buckles and tightening down the straps. I slide my helmet and Nomex hood off my head and don my fire mask, replacing the hood and helmet when they're in place.

Before we step through the entry point, the anthem that plays in my head every time I head into a burning building starts.

Charlie's voice purrs, "You are Braver than you believe. Stronger than you seem. Smarter than you think."

Every. Single. Time.

I couldn't stop it if I tried, not that I really want to. It fills me with fearlessness exactly when I need it. Especially since that one call.

Junior and I leave our badges on a carabiner outside the entry point, signifying we're inside. We enter and start a right-handed search around the building. It's still dark outside and, with thick smoke billowing out of the building, I can't see my toes while standing, so we fall to our hands and knees and begin to crawl.

I run my right hand along the wall as I make my way into the building. Junior holds my left foot and searches further away from the wall behind me.

"Firefighter. Anybody in here?" I shout and then listen for any response.

The only sounds are the cracking of the fire and the sound of the engine to my right.

Continuing my search along the first wall, I come to a door. *Try before you pry.* I check for heat, then open it. I anchor the door, while Junior takes a search rope to explores the room. He is invisible the moment he moves past me.

The front of the kitchen is next. The register sits on a tall wooden counter, the large chalkboard menu usually sitting on the wall behind it is fully engulfed. The kitchen is tucked away so far into the building it is impossible to reach.

We turn to the left to enter the tourist shirt store. Totally engulfed, we can't even enter it.

The next room we search, the dining room of the restaurant, is filled with picnic tables painted teal and aqua with a huge mural on the back wall, not that any of that is visible now. The right wall of the room is lined with massive windows Mick broke earlier to increase the ventilation.

In here, Junior is barely visible as he conducts his search. He checks each picnic table, top and underside, progressing along the right-hand wall. When he comes to the bathroom door he passes it.

*What the fuck is he doing?*

"Check the fucking door," I shout at him through the intercom. "It's commercial. He's a cook. He's not in there."

That's a fucking rookie mistake. "Go back and fucking look!"

He goes back and disappears momentarily through the door.

Knowing I have only fifteen minutes of air in my tank, I take two slow breaths to slow my heart rate. Nothing will suck air faster than a speeding heart rate because I let myself get out of control mentally.

"No one in there, Steele," he reports when he reappears.

I crush my anger and continue our search. Ripping him a new asshole right now won't help anyone.

When we finish our search, I scan the scene for Captain Jameson, passing by Patrick who is still talking to witnesses. As I brush by his shoulder, he points to the guy he's talking to and shouts, "The missing cook."

Glad he's not inside the impenetrable kitchen.

"Steele. What'd you find?" Captain Jameson calls out when I'm still a good ten yards away.

"No one inside. But we need to get a backhoe in here to rip the face of the building off to get to the kitchen."

During a fully involved structure fire, temperatures inside a structure are often fifteen hundred degrees Fahrenheit. By cutting a hole in the roof and ventilating the building, the heat is allowed to escape through the roof thereby making it safer for firefighters to enter the building and apply water directly on the fire. The same holds true for walls.

"And the cook?" she shouts over the noise of the sirens and the howling of the fire.

"Talking to Hennessey."

Captain Jameson calls for a backhoe.

When she is out of earshot, I grab Junior by the coat and drag him behind the engine. I toss him up against the hard red metal and get right in his face. "You fucked up, Junior. You check everywhere, every fucking time. You have no idea where what people will do to hide. You always fucking look."

"Roger that."

Not letting up, I shove my gloved finger into his chest as my voice grows louder and louder. "You cost us time in there. More time means more risk for us and for survivors. And fuck if I'm gonna lose my life cause you thought you knew where someone wouldn't hide in a fire."

A hand shoves my arm from Junior. I turn to find Mick.

"He looked. And no one got hurt," Mick says.

If he wants to take the brunt of my rage instead of Junior, I have no problem doling it out to him.

I step into his personal space. "It doesn't fucking matter. He may have gotten away with it this time, but next time, it's gonna mean someone's dead."

He nods to Junior to leave.

"I get it, man. I do. But you need to bring it down," Mick says calmly which only serves to incite me more.

"Bring it down?" I jab my whole hand in the middle of his chest. "You said he was ready. He was your fucking responsibility and you're sitting here telling me to bring it down? This is on you, Mick."

Something over Mick's shoulder grabs my attention. Chief Trapp is taking in every single horrible word I spew.

*Fuck.*

I remove my hand from Mick and walk around the backside of the pumper, giving myself some space to cool off before Junior's fuckup becomes mine.

Junior's smart enough to keep his mouth shut on the ride back to the station. I'm not sure I could contain myself in the cabin of the pumper if he didn't.

*Fuck.*

He should have known.

He should have looked.

If he can't get the most basic of skills so ingrained in his head that deviating from them becomes impossible, then he'll become a huge liability.

He'll get himself killed.

Or one of us.

Or some totally innocent little girl with her whole life ahead of her.

And that will haunt him until the day he dies.

Trying to block out the face that haunts me, I stare out the window watching the dark as empty buildings on Highway 101 pass by.

A light is on in the window of the yellow, Victorian building housing Pannikin Coffee and Tea. I bet Renee is already inside cooking up her famous scones.

When we pass D Street and Kealani's comes into view, I still can't get the girl's face out of my mind. When we pass Cardiff Reef and the clouds form a wrinkled sheet of slate grey overhead, the sight of perfect, six-foot waves does little to distract me from her face. When we finally pull into the station, I hop out, take care of my duties, grab my radio, and stumble out to the small wooden bench overlooking the wetlands at the foot of the station.

The flood of adrenaline from the morning's call finally washing out of my system, I am completely spent with nothing left in me to stem the flow of tears constantly threatening to spill out when her face appears.

My first year on the job, we were toned out a little past 2:30 in the morning to a car accident on Highway 101 just north of Dip In The Road. The divided two-lane highway runs downhill with the ocean to one side and a twenty-five-foot cliff to the other.

It took us eight minutes to get there, but I kept tabs on what was happening on the way. It was a single vehicle flipped on its roof.

When we pulled up, there was one other fire truck and one ambulance on the scene. I checked in with the Officer-in-Charge who told me they weren't sure how many were in the vehicle and suggested I do a search of the area for anyone who had been ejected from the car.

The speed limit on this part of the 101 is fifty, but people regularly go sixty. I recalled the projectile stats we learned in the academy. A crash at sixty miles-per-hour will eject a human roughly one hundred fifty feet, with a max-height less than fifteen feet. A fifty-mile per hour crash, one hundred ten feet, max height less than ten feet.

Beginning my search at the wreckage, I searched north up the road from the vehicle. It was clear for the five hundred meters up the road visible before it leveled off, putting the road out of my field of view. To the south, a thousand meters was clear.

The cliff was at least twenty-five feet above the road at this point. No way someone made it up there. Much more likely they went over the ocean-side of the road. I pulled out my torch and began my search along the edge of the road, making sure to check carefully in the dark among the boulders bordering the road on the sand below.

They were clear to the north.

It's strange the details you remember in moments like these. To the south, there was a blue beach towel laid out on the sand with the words, "Dear Beach, I think about you all the time," in bright pink block letters.

I searched four hundred feet past it and found nothing.

Jogging back towards the wreckage, I found Captain Jameson. I needed to do something productive for the people we knew were trapped in the car instead of wasting time searching for nobody.

Jameson was dragging the jaws of Life out of the engine.

"No one has been ejected, Cap. What else can I do?"

"You looked for ejections?" she handed the tool to Thomas.

"Yes, Captain."

"Everywhere, Steele?" She grabs Yates by the jacket to get his attention. "Go with Thomas. Get them out of there."

"Everywhere in the ejection radius," I repeat.

"Top of the cliff? Did you look up there?"

"It's too high, Cap. At sixty—"

"Dammit, Steele. Go look on the fucking cliff."

I ran to the base of the cliff hunting for a way to scale it. When I tried, the walls crumble under my weight.

A hundred yards to the south, the cliff met the road. That's two hundred yards in heavy gear. To the north, the cliff meets the road in about the same distance, but that run is uphill.

I sprinted down the road to where the cliff leveled out and scurried up the side. At the top, I sprinted back to where the wreckage was, trying not to trip in the dark brush covering the cliff.

Two hundred feet from the wreckage, I pulled out my torch and began sweeping it back and forth as I proceeded. Every twenty feet I stopped to reorient myself to the wreckage and listen for any updates on the radio. During my second stop, a faint whimper captured me.

"Firefighter. Anyone there?"

The voice called out a few yards ahead to my left. I swept my torch in that direction and found something moving as I ran towards it.

It was a young girl, couldn't have been much older than five. She sat up when she saw me.

I scooped her up in my arms and began the long trek to a location safe enough for me to stomp down the incline with her in my arms.

"I got you, hon," I reassured her.

I found a tree on the side of the cliff and used it to scale the cliff, cutting down the distance to the ambulance.

When I made it to the road, the tiny figure in my arms became insanely heavier. She was limp and not breathing.

Squatting to lay her on the asphalt to start CPR, blood puddled beneath me. It was far too large a puddle for her tiny body. CPR would only serve to pump out the remaining blood even quicker.

I rose with her still in my arms. Her long blond curls, painted crimson, were plastered to her face. She was so small I could hold her weight with one arm, so I slid my hand along her back, freeing my other hand to push the hair out of her eyes with my thumb.

"I'm so sorry," I whisper.

Peering around the tree to the wreckage twenty yards off, a tall figure was screaming, "She was in the car. Where is she? My baby was in the car."

The moment her father saw his precious child in my arms,

his life would be forever changed. It would be over. I couldn't find the strength to impose that on him.

So I held her in my arms while I listened to the rhythmic roar of the ocean waves, while the acrid scent of gasoline mixed with the salt air, and dozens of red and blue lights ran along every visible surface.

*Stronger than you seem.*

The words drove my left foot forward. Followed by my right. My left. My right.

A few yards later, I knew my silhouette became visible to her father because he turned to me before collapsing.

*Stronger than you seem.*

Captain Jameson hauled him to his feet.

Still walking, I held tight the little girl in my arms.

A few yards from the wreckage, an ambulance crew met me in the street. Captain was still holding onto the girl's father who looked me dead in the eyes, begging me for good news.

I had none to give him.

And he somehow knew. He knew his life would never be the same.

I didn't see Thomas lift her from my arms and place her on a gurney, but I felt the weight of her small arm as it dragged along the top of mine.

The bus doors slamming.

Her dad wailing.

Sirens pulsating.

And then, silence.

My arms were still right where they were when I held her.

Only they were empty.

And covered in the same crimson I wiped from her forehead.

I tugged off my gloves and slipped out of my coat, leaving them on the asphalt where they fell.

I staggered to the engine and collapsed against the tall back wheel.

*How could I not have looked up there?*

# 26

## GREYSON

Y ou get your ass handed to you by Cap?" Mick dumps a pound of coffee grounds into the filter as I join him in the kitchen.

"Right on a silver platter. But, I deserved it. And she's right. I can't let my shit get in the way of being a better leader, especially with the younger guys. Did Chief Trapp say anything to you about it?"

"He asked me if you do that a lot."

I snag a glass from the cupboard and fill it at the tap. "What'd you tell him?"

"I told him I'm the only one you yell at like that cause you know it's the only way I'll listen. Told him you know the perfect way to talk to each guy to make the biggest impact."

"Thanks for covering for me."

He fills the coffee machine with water and turns it on. "It's true, man."

"I'm not sure Junior would agree," I laugh.

"He'll get over it. And he sure as hell won't ever forget to check everywhere, every fucking time."

I down the water and refill it. "By the way, I shouldn't have talked to you like that last night. There's no excuse."

"We're cool. But, look, I got to ask..." He pulls ten cups from the cupboard and rests them next to the coffee pot. "How are you feeling?"

"How am I feeling?" I scoff.

We don't talk about feelings here. It's a house full of men who have to put up their shields to deal with all the disturbing shit we encounter on a daily basis.

"I know. I used a four-letter word." He drags a chair to the breakfast table.

It's still early and Junior won't start cooking breakfast for a while.

Mick motions for me to sit next to him.

I hesitantly sit a few chairs away.

"How are you feeling?" he repeats.

"Fine."

What has gotten into this guy?

"Thirty-four percent of us have thought about suicide."

What? Why is he talking suicide?

And what the hell? That many?

He begins to spin the salt shaker on its edge. "That's ten times the national average."

"Where'd you learn that?"

"My therapist starts each week with a tasty fact like that."

Therapist? Each week? The department only gives us three sessions a year with a therapist.

The salt shaker falls to the table. He picks it up, spins it again, and goes on. "Eighty-five percent of us have mental health issues. 6.6% have attempted suicide."

"Shit. That many?" I blow on the salt spilled on the table. "Is anyone doing anything about it?"

"Come on, you think they notice? Even if they could figure out what to do about it, there'd be no money to do it."

Patrick sinks into the chair between me and Mick. "Money for what? You guys hitting the bars again tonight? I can pay if you guys are willing to show me some tricks."

"Money for programs or services to deal with PTSD among first responders," I correct him.

"Man. That would be great. I used up my three visits with a shrink by February."

"We'd need more than therapy time, though that would help," I say.

"Like what?" Patrick asks.

"How about training us to talk about it? With our brothers? You know how much worse this would have been to have a superior try to bring it up?" I suggest.

"And we should have a class in the academy on all aspects of mental health and self-care. My sister was telling me about how much guided meditation has helped her deal with her husband's cancer." Patrick takes a napkin from the dispenser on the table and wipes the scattered salt into his hand. "There's stuff out there that could help. Even if it's just to reduce stress."

He crosses the kitchen to dump it in the trash.

I motion to Mick for him to stop spinning the salt shaker. "You know the mess bugs him."

Mick slides the shaker across the table, far enough he won't be tempted to nab it again.

"So who's going to step up and demand they do it?" Patrick asks.

Patrick peers at me.

Mick stares at me.

That's the exact reason we're in this position. No one wants to risk their reputation to take on the higher-ups and ask for what we need. Ideas are great, but they're not going to fix anything unless someone steps up and makes them into reality. My mom always said, "If you don't have the courage to walk alone, others will not have the courage to walk with you."

"I will," I say more to convince myself than to announce my plan to lead.

"You can kiss Captain goodbye," Mick warns.

Patrick sits back in his chair. "You rock the boat, they'll blacklist you from every promotion, every transfer. The BigWigs in San Diego talk."

Now that it's in my mind, though, I can't ignore it. And I can't walk away from my duty.

"If I get blacklisted, that'll be my sign firefighting isn't for me," I offer.

"You know that's not true, Grey. You were made for this job," Mick says.

I recall all the calls we've gone on over the years, the fires, the traffic accidents, the good we've done. I know I can't walk away from this job.

"If it gets bad, I could go somewhere else."

Away from the blowback. Start somewhere new. Like Maui.

Away from Charlie. Get the space I need so badly so I can let her go.

Junior strolls in. He takes four dozen eggs out of the fridge and piles them on the counter. "You leaving us, Steele?"

"He's considering pushing for better PTSD support," Patrick fills him in.

Junior lays two packs of turkey bacon next to the eggs. "Shit. That would be great. If things get really bad cause of it, my old man is retiring as Chief back home and could put in a good word for you."

I just don't know if I can do this job without Charlie next to me, settling me, supporting me. That would be worse than not having any PTSD support from the department.

Which is exactly why I have to knock off this pushing the boundaries nonsense with her.

As if Charlie can sense that decision, my phone buzzes in my pants.

**Charlie: Can I stop by the station? I want to tell you something and it can't wait for lunch**

Tell me something?

I'm done with your confessions, Charlie. I'm trying to follow your Rule Book. It's about time you did, too.

*And, yes, you can wait for lunch.*

*Or better yet, tomorrow.*

I stall by filling a mug with coffee before even considering texting back. I offered up an olive branch last night and got back nothing. Now she wants to talk? Not gonna happen.

I pad over to the far side of the kitchen and stare out the wall of windows overlooking the wetlands. The spring wildflowers have filled the dry land with oranges and yellows.

My pocket buzzes again.

**Charlie: Fine then. . .**

I can picture the mischievous smile she must on her face.

*What are you planning, Charlie?*

I wait for her to make her move.

Nothing.

I call.

"Greyson. Long time, no see," she says like I called her out of the blue instead of her manipulating me to call her.

"What are you planning?"

"Nothing horrible. I promise."

"Then why are you being so coy?"

I hate that she still has the power to get me on the hook.

"I figure if you are too busy to text back, I should just stop by the station. You know, save you some time."

If she weren't so damn cute when she did this kind of thing, I might be tempted to call her manipulative. But she usually only resorts to these tactics if she's trying to persuade me to do something I should be doing already.

"How about I meet you somewhere for coffee in twenty?"

All the joy runs from her voice. "You are so weird about not letting me meet the boys."

She always gives me crap about that, but this time she sounds a little hurt.

"Kealani's in twenty?" I ask.

"Okay," she mumbles.

Now she sounds a lot hurt.

Fine.

If she wants to be thrown to the sharks, I'll toss her. I'm done protecting her if she's not willing to do the same for me.

Kealani's started serving breakfast a few months ago. They have pancakes and Belgium waffles piled with pineapple, bananas, mango, and coconut. Charlie is sitting in a booth next to the giant glass windows lining the front of the building. She is fiddling with a sugar packet, the hood of her navy blue sweater drawn low. She doesn't notice me until I tap on the window.

She smiles at me, but there's a tension and sadness to it. I'm not sure if she's upset I won't introduce her to the guys or about the conversation we simply *had* to have in person.

She meets me at the counter to order.

I order pancakes with all the fruit.

"Can I get a small black coffee, Leilani?" I flash her a grin.

"Sure thing, hon." She spins around to pour my drink.

Charlie is eyeing a huge piece of chocolate brownie in the display case a few feet away. She'd never eat something that sugary this early in the morning. It would be a Number Killer as she calls it.

She eats plenty of sugary food, but this early in the morning, her body is more sensitive to it. Her blood sugars would be all over the place for the rest of the day.

But there she stands, pretending to be undecided. She's stalling as if she wants to avoid me paying for her like I have nearly every time we've eaten together.

I pull out my wallet and remove a card. Charlie's still pretending to ignore me. "If you really want to meet the guys, we can do it on Poker Night next Thursday," I concede.

"Really?" She perks up and nearly skips over to me. "Can I host?"

What the hell; it will be a shit-show anyways. "Sure. But don't go overboard. I know how you always get with hosting things."

Leilani sets my drink on the counter, "Anything else?"

"Whatever the lady wants," I reply.

Charlie throws me a Thank You smile. "Can I have an omelet with bell peppers, tomatoes, and cheddar cheese, and a large Diet Dr. Pepper?"

We chose this as our place for that exact reason. It's the only breakfast place in this town that serves Diet Dr Pepper from a fountain and still lets you order coffee in English. No advanced degree in coffee ordering needed.

We slide into the booth and gaze out the window, each of us waiting for the other one to start. Guava Jelly by the Ka'au Crater Boys comes from the speakers in the kitchen.

Charlie fixes her gaze on me, brows pinched. It's her Serious Face.

I know I'm in for it. The legion of Satanic Leaf-Tailed Geckos are assembling.

"Do you really think he wants her to rub guava jelly on his belly or am I missing some sort of Hawaiian innuendo?" she asks.

I baptize the table with coffee expelled alongside my laugh.

Charlie rushes to the counter for napkins. She returns and begins cleaning up my mess. Her hand stops at the center of the table. She stares at the coffee-soaked napkin. "Clean slate?"

Relief flows through me at the thought of not having to hear Charlie say things I don't think I can hear right now.

To finally get back to the way things were before I was stupid enough to push it farther.

She finally lifts her gaze, begging for my answer.

I throw her a reassuring smile. "Clean slate."

# 27

## CHARLIE

The second week of February brings a heatwave like it does nearly every year. Though the water is still cold, the blazing sunshine on my back makes me want to surf forever. Lucky for me, I have come down with a cold— cough, cough— so work won't be in the way of me taking advantage of every minute of this respite from the shatteringly cold winter.

Well... cold for San Diego. I've had to wear a sweatshirt almost every day since the year began and that's just crazy. I've even had to put on a jacket a few times.

After six hours in the water with only a short break for a grilled cheese and soup for lunch, I take a twenty-minute blazing hot shower on the deck.

Once thawed, I head upstairs and change into a pair of boy shorts and a tank top and dive into my bed to let the late afternoon sun usher in a well-deserved nap.

I wake to Dex screaming.

Springing out of bed, I slam my shoulder into the door frame on my way to sugar. The stairs sway under my feet making it nearly impossible to make it downstairs in one piece.

With sweat gushing out of every pore, I tear open the fridge door, throwing aside milk and beer, seeking apple juice.

The pickle jar tips and spills nasty pickle juice onto the top shelf.

The fridge door is tugged back. "Can I get in there?" Indigo asks sweetly.

"Did you drink my juice!" I demand.

She steps back from me. "What?"

"Did you drink my fucking juice?"

"Hell no." Indigo tilts her head taking in the scene. "You're low."

"Yeah."

I need sugar.

There's no sugar.

Indigo walks outside.

I need sugar.

The shaking in my muscles has turned into a painful weakness.

I swing open the cupboard door and snatch the box of C&H brown sugar. Stuffing my hand into the box, it hits the bottom of the box before coming back up empty.

Crappity crap.

Tears pour out of my eyes as fast as sweat has been gushing from my pores. The weakness in my legs wins as I slide down to the ground.

Indigo breezes through the slider with an open Dr Pepper and wraps my hands around the can. "Drink," she commands.

I comply, fizz going up my nose.

"A few more sips," she urges.

I finish it, wiping my eyes with the back of my hand.

"How low were you?" she asks.

"I don't even know. The scary low alarm went off and I came right down."

Indigo slides the Dexcom receiver out of my hand. She flashes the screen in my direction "42. Double down arrow. You need another Dr Pepper?"

"I really want cheese."

"Okay. Like slices or something?"

"Bag of shredded."

Indigo locks the sliding door and pulls the curtain.

I thank God for her discretion at times like this.

She hands me the bag of shredded sharp cheddar cheese and lays a dishtowel on my chest. She knows how this turns out with cereal.

As I shovel the cheese over my open mouth, flashes of the last twenty-four hours come flooding in.

The low blood sugar has shut off my emotional filter, so I hurl it all at Indigo.

"Who the hell have I become, Indie?"

"You mean the Cheese Monster in the cutest pajamas I've ever seen? Where'd you get those?"

I let out a laugh and, with it, a few strands of cheese. I love it that, when Indigo laughs at times like these, I know she's not laughing at me. "I mean lately. Around Greyson. There's something so off. Wrong."

The sugar begins to leak into my bloodstream, bringing a bit more clarity to my reasoning. "It's like my brain is screaming at me what to do, the right thing to do, and there's an evil little Gremlin in there doing whatever the hell he wants, and for the life of me, I can't stop him. I can't even figure out what he's trying to do."

"I have a few ideas, but I think you might need some more brainpower to process what I have to say. That low wiped you out. Why don't you go throw on some clothes and come outside with us while you recover? It's such a beautiful night. Tank's telling us stories. It might be nice to drift off into someone else's stories right now."

Once strength has returned to my body, I head upstairs to rinse off the gallons of sweat dripping off my body and put on some clothes before returning downstairs.

"...so we throw it in this kid's bed." Tank, standing in front of the bonfire, pretends to drop something in an imaginary bed.

Occy's face lights up when I peek my head through the open

door. He slides over on the bench surrounding the fire, making room for me.

I return the smile as I sit next to him.

"So, four in the morning, out in the hallway, something lets out an ear-splitting squeal." Tank leans back and lets out a squeal that would summon every wild pig in a fifty-mile radius if there were any.

Occy leans over to me. "I was hoping you'd come out."

"Had I known you were down here, I would have come out a while ago."

This earns me a terrific Occy smile.

I don't know if it's the confidence I gained from repeatedly practicing scripted flirtation while acting or the immediate positive feedback Occy supplies, but for the first time, I am having fun with the whole flirtation thing.

"And we find him, butt naked, running down the hall screaming. It was so worth the three days of scrubbing toilets."

"What did you do with them after?" a girl from beneath her navy hoodie.

"We ate 'em," Tank replies like it should be obvious. "Can't waste good lobster."

"For the love of Spielberg. After being in sheets full of Kubrick knows what, you ate them?" Indigo asks.

"What? The hot water kills everything." Tank scans his rapt audience for someone to back up his disgusting theory. "Charlie, you're like a science person. Boiling water will kill cock snot, right?"

"Come on, Tank. You really have to say that?" Occy chides.

"Boiling water may kill them, but it won't remove their dead bodies from the pot," I say as sweetly as possible while discussing the viability of baby batter.

Tank holds his stomach as he doubles over onto the bench.

"Can we please move on from this topic," Hoodie Girl pleads as she reties her combat boots.

Indigo saves us all from further exploration of Tank's possible consumption of another guy's—

"Hey, Occy. When you heading out on your surf trip?"

"Next week," he says, beaming.

"Surf trip?" Now there's a topic I can get into. "Where you going?"

"Maui. A couple of my friends are stopping there on their endless summer surf trip, so I'm gonna meet up with them. Honolua. Pe'ahi. Olowalu. Eight straight days of epic waves, fresh fish, and a coldie to wrap up the day."

That's my exact definition of Heaven. Not that I'm in a rush to revisit the site of my last failure, but we didn't have time to surf a single day on my last trip, and there were a couple of reef breaks calling my name.

"That sounds amazing, Occy. You are so lucky."

"You should come with me. That would make it so much better." He lays his hand on my knee. "Come on. You have to come."

"I would so love that." I try to picture Glenn's face as I ask him for a full week off only days before Prick is due to be finished. "There's just no way I could get off work."

"Do the Harry and figure it out when you get back." He rests his beer on the bench and holds out his hand. "Here. Give me your phone."

I raise my brows as I hesitantly hand over my phone.

"Don't stress. I'm just putting my number in here for when you change your mind and realize life is too short to make a quid by working."

Did I just flirt well enough to be invited on a tropical vacation?

I bite down on a smile.

There might be hope for me yet.

Although there's no chance I could ever skip town with only six days' notice, I've been daydreaming of surfing tropical waters and eating fish straight from the sea ever since Occy invited me.

"What's with all the food?" Indigo's voice rouses me from the fantasy.

I come back down to reality and realize I've been stirring the onion dip for ten minutes.

I've spent the last four hours turning our kitchen and dining room into the ultimate Poker Room with anything these boys could want: snacks, desserts, finger foods, and a fridge full of every type of local craft brew.

"Poker Night," I squeal before I'm able to reign in my excitement.

I want every one of Grey's friends to beg him to have every single Poker night at my place from now on so even if he thought this would be a one-time thing, he will have no choice but to keep letting me play.

Indigo dips a carrot in the dip as I carry it to the island. "That's right. He's finally letting you meet the station boys."

"But he doesn't really want to. He's only doing it cause I pushed him so hard."

"It's about time he introduced you. I still don't understand why it's taken this long."

"He's embarrassed by his neuter-gender sidekick. He doesn't know how to explain me. And you know how those guys are, always giving each other crap. He doesn't want to give them any more fodder."

"First off, you are not neuter-gender, Charlie." She hops up on the island. "Have you ever thought he doesn't want to introduce you because he wants you all to himself?"

"Yeah right. What would he want that for?"

Indigo stares at me like it should be obvious.

I shake my head, hoping to wave off the subject.

She bounds off the island to pluck a beer from the fridge. "Has there ever been a time where you thought of Greyhound differently?"

"He's like a brother. I would never. I have never."

"So you never wanted to lean over and kiss him, to run your hands all over those abs? Hell, I do every time he's shirtless."

Yes.

So many times.

Every time he says my name.

For a split second after he complements me, before The Rationalizer has a chance to explain it away.

When he steps in to chase off some Delta Bravo who's trying to hit on me.

When he kissed me.

But all those were fleeting moments.

And way too recent and volatile to mention.

So instead I shrug.

"The last time you two went for a run and he stripped off his shirt, I remember thinking I should write a script where he could play a lifeguard just so I could spend a week leering at him shirtless, and then four more weeks salivating over all the footage."

If only she knew how right she was.

When Greyson turned eighteen, his shithead dad kicked him out. It didn't matter that he was still in high school or that he had no time for a job between school and baseball, his dad woke him on his birthday with the classified ads and said, "You're eighteen. Get a job and get out."

He got a job as a lifeguard and got his own apartment within a week.

That was a rough summer for me.

After he would finish lifeguarding all day in the sun, we'd go to his apartment every night to hang out and watch movies. He didn't put on a shirt until September.

And what the sun and lifeguard training did to his body was ungodly.

We'd sit on the couch and I could actually feel the heat radiating off his body. I don't remember a single movie we watched that summer; I couldn't drag my mind off his tanned, shirtless body just waiting there so close to mine.

Had I not been sixteen and so terrifyingly unsure of myself, I might have done something about it. But I knew, even back then, I had no chance with a guy like Grey.

I pour a bag of Fritos into a bowl and wipe away the crumbs. "Maybe for a second when I was sixteen," I admit.

I wait for her to freak out like Bex would if I ever admitted to even a fleeting thought about Greyson this way let alone a whole summer of lusting after him, but it doesn't come.

She simply nods silently and takes another sip of beer, which makes me want to keep talking.

"You've got a keen eye for casting. He was a lifeguard that summer. Definitely drool-worthy."

"And you've got a keen eye for quality men. Greyhound is compassionate, confident, protective, and brave, all wrapped up in a gorgeous, seductive, oh-so-lickable package. You become more confident when you're with him."

Lately, the last thing I feel around Greyson is confident. It's more like confused, anxious mush.

The timer on the oven dings. I fold a dishtowel over a few times before taking the last batch of cookies from the oven and setting them on the island.

"That's exactly the opposite of what Bex thinks. She's convinced he's a boyfriend roadblock."

I scrutinize Indigo's face for any indication she disagrees. I need someone to contradict Bex. To tell me I'm not crazy for believing I can keep him around and still find love.

Indigo takes her time considering my question. I'm so used to Bex shooting off her mouth before I've even finished talking, it's unsettling. I assume it's because Indigo has depths of wisdom to plumb, unlike Bex.

"It's possible," she says.

So much for holding out hope.

So I have to leave behind the only person who has ever truly known me in order to find someone who wants me to be his everything or I consign myself to going through this life without ever having it all.

"But not in the way you think," she adds.

*Not in the way I think?*

What other way is there?

# 28

## GREYSON

*O*ver the following week, things get back towards normal with me and Charlie, but they still aren't all the way there. We miss a few runs. She bails on Tuesday dinner. There's still a weirdness to everything.

I brought this on myself by trying to push that line. Charlie made the rules for a reason and she's always right. I was a fool to think I could simply turn up the charm and she'd fall into my arms.

But now that the thought of us together has sprouted, even though I haven't vocalized it, I am ever aware of the ghostly cyanide.

And it might be enough to poison everything we have. I can't be around her without all this turmoil in my head making everything gritty, like sand in our bearings.

On Thursday night, I walk through Charlie's open front door like I've been doing since I met the girl and stride into the kitchen. Charlie's unbuttoned, blue-checked flannel is flowing around her as she fusses with the food on the kitchen island. Sliders, mini pizzas, bite-sized sandwiches, and all the usual poker night food, pretzels, nuts, candy.

I don't know how she convinced me to throw her to the

sharks, I must have run out of the energy to fight her on anything anymore. But, now that it is happening, I am quickly regretting the decision.

"Don't even bother knocking anymore, do ya, Greyhound?" Indigo quips.

"And miss the chance to catch you running around here in less than you should be? No way."

I wrap her in a bear hug before moving past her to hurricane Charlie. "So what do you got going on over here? Feeding the lost children of Sudan?"

Charlie's hands stall over the m&m cookies she is arranging on a surfboard-shaped platter.

Indigo jumps in before she has a chance to answer. "Why don't we get Greyson's opinion on the roadblock thing? He certainly knows you the best. I'm sure he could give us some insight, a male's perspective," Indigo teases.

"No way! Indigo, we're not involving him," Charlie asserts.

I'm fully invested now. "Involving me in what?"

Charlie's death stare, a combination of sheer terror and rising anger, convinces Indigo to drop it.

"It's nothing. Just girl talk."

"Oh yeah? You know how to do that, Charlie?" I tease.

"You may not have realized, Greyson, but I am a girl."

*You're not a girl, Sands. You're a woman. You're all woman.*

"Greyhound, you know she's a girl," Indigo adds. "I've seen you checking out her rack before."

Indigo's keen observation surprises me.

"Don't you have somewhere to go?" I say, trying not to let her reveal anything else incriminating.

"I don't know, you've got three hot firemen coming over. I might stay."

"There's four of us, you know," I amend.

"I know, but only three of you are hot."

I pretend to be insulted.

"They might come through that door any minute. Shirtless. Wearing just their fireman pants and those hot red suspenders."

Indigo drifts off, fully immersed in the fantasy heating up her mind, as she begins to narrate the heat. "The really hot one would lift me up, throw me over his shoulder, and carry me up to my room to toss me down on my bed and have his way with me."

Indigo's really getting into this one, that I expected.

But Charlie sweetens the now shared vision. "And somehow his hands are soft and smooth as he grazes my bare back to lift me, pulling me under him,"

Charlie, beneath me, waiting for me to draw her closer overtakes my mind. And, as far as I'm concerned, the picture she has in her head, is of me too, but I'm careful not to let it splash across my face how much I enjoy that.

"So that's what does it for you?" I ask Charlie before I'm able to stop myself.

Charlie is shoved back into Silent Mode, embarrassed she was so easily drawn into the fantasy.

"Oh yeah. Big time," Indigo proclaims.

Thank God Indigo is here to take the heat off our brush with the outlawed.

"So how does Mark feel about this obsession with firemen?" I ask Indie, trying to ignore the desire on Charlie's face as she turns away from me, pretending to fuss with the cornucopia of food she has laid out.

"I don't know. I'll go ask him. You know, you might have just planned our role-playing for the night," she says with lust in her eyes, before flitting out the door.

Charlie, still trying to dodge me, continues to prep the table of snacks.

I snag a handful of pretzels, leaning in close over her shoulder. "Is that banana?"

"Where?" she says without moving.

I break the Half Foot Rule and she freezes like a deer. She thinks if she doesn't move, I won't see her. Like I could ever miss the sight of her in a room.

"You smell good," I let out before realizing what I've said.

She slides her shirt back, exposing a red shoulder with a thin white tan line. "I got fried at the beach this morning. It's banana and coconut from the after-sun lotion."

The peek of this usually forbidden breadth of skin, though innocent enough, is thrilling and perilous at the same time. I am trying so hard to get things back to the way they were, being this close to her is not helping at all.

I step back, hoping Charlie didn't sense my diversion into forbidden lands.

She flees the situation by sifting through a junk drawer for a deck of cards. She tosses them on the poker table without meeting my eyes.

A knock at the door gives me my much-needed escape. Hopefully, my boys will keep me a safe distance from Charlie so I don't wander down that dark alley again.

When I return to the kitchen with Mick and Junior, all signs of my misstep have vanished.

"Beer's in the fridge, feel free to help yourself," Charlie says.

"Whoa. Is all this for us?" Mick, the exact picture of Indigo's fantasy fireman, marvels at the spread.

"Dude, we should play poker over here every week," Junior adds, still waiting to fill out his uniform.

The boys settle into the table while Charlie takes out even more food.

"So, you ever ask Coffee Shop Girl out?" Junior asks Mick.

"Three days in a row now, and she won't budge. Every day it's the same thing. She's got this white tank on stretched so tight you can almost see through it. And she flirts with me like she's a camel in the desert looking for some of my..."

"Dude!" I shout.

He remembers Charlie's there. Not a stellar start.

"Anyhow, she flirts with me every morning. But when I ask her out, it's like she's offended."

Patrick, fair-haired and only bold when rushing into a burning building, knocks on the open door.

"Come in," I shout like I actually live here.

He hesitates.

"Patty, get in here," Mick yells.

Patrick peers around the corner, searching for a familiar face.

"Sit down, Patty. Mick was just telling us about Coffee Shop Girl," I instruct.

"That's the third time she totally snubs me. So I go in this morning wearing my station shirt. The old one, a little small, logo front and center. No way she'll turn me down in that. And I give her the business, you know, the smile, the charm, the 'darlin.' Everything she was impervious to yesterday."

"Did it work?" Patrick asks, taking mental notes to improve his own game.

"Get this. She says," he does his best wispy, flirty female voice, "'So, yesterday, when you said you wanted to get a drink, you meant like at a bar? Cause I thought you meant like here. But I would love to get a drink or even diner sometime.'"

"Makes sense. Charlie was just telling me, in surprising detail, how firemen are every woman's fantasy," I give her an impish grin.

Charlie tries to shut me up with her mind... or at the very least a vicious glare.

"Really? Yours too?" Mick asks.

Silent mode returns to Charlie. She dives into the fridge to hide.

"So when do we get to meet Charlie?" Patrick asks.

"Seriously?" Junior asks.

A dumbfounded Charlie retreats from the fridge and gives a passing wave. "Hi, Patrick."

"How did you not get that?" I say incredulously.

"The way you're constantly insisting she's only a friend made me think she had to be a dog. And you are not a dog," he adds in Charlie's direction.

Charlie slides into the seat next to Patrick, still a bit perplexed. "I'm not quite sure how to take that."

Patrick hangs his head. "Sorry, Charlie."

"What do you guys usually play?" she asks changing the subject.

"Poker," Patrick says sweetly.

"No shit, Sherlock. We are sitting at a poker table and all," she sasses.

That's enough to convince the boys she can hang, but she

really drives it home. "Five-card draw? Texas Hold'em? Blind man's bluff? Seven Card Stud?"

"Hold'em," Mick says with a frisky smile that Charlie totally misses.

She shuffles the deck expertly and deals. A few hands in, Mick is regaling us with another of his wild tales.

"So I take a swing at the guy and land it square in the face, which is surprising considering how much I've had to drink. He goes down, straight to the beer-soaked carpet. And the two girls he's with swarm him."

He tosses two quarters in the pile. "For a second I think, 'If he plays his cards right, he may actually get lucky off this.' And I'm feeling pretty good, proud I know how to throw a punch. And his friend stands up, now."

"And he knocks the shit out of you?" I toss two quarters in, too.

"That's what I think he's coming at me for. So I say, 'You really gonna step up to me after I knocked out your friend with one swing? I guess I'll have to knock the shit out of you too.' And he, calm as shit, says, 'Thanks. That's all I needed,' and lifts his shirt real sly to show me his badge."

"I don't remember you calling me to bail you out on this one," I lay down a full house.

"That's because I start apologizing and the storyteller comes out and I start weaving this tale of woe and misery and how he looked just like the guy who stole my wife." Mick waves for me to take the pile. "By the time I finish, he's taking the cuffs off and driving me home."

Charlie clears a few of the empty bottles on her way to the kitchen.

"You lied your way out of being arrested? I'd crap myself if I tried lying to a cop," Patrick chimes in.

"What about you, Charlie? You've got to have some great stories of flirting your way out of tickets," Junior says trying to steer the conversation her way.

"Only time I've really dealt with the cops, I was hanging off the side of a bridge in a bikini."

Thinking her story was over, she grabs a Diet Dr Pepper from the fridge and a pint glass from the freezer.

"Shit. Now I've really got to hear this," Mick pleads.

Charlie pours her drink while she returns to the table. "I was on a date with this guy I really liked. I hadn't been that into a guy for years. He was smart and funny, and God, was he hot," she starts.

"Who was this?" I demand.

"Blaze," she sits again.

I take a long drag from my beer, while I contemplate this new info.

"Anyways, we are on our second date, and we were walking back to his place after dinner. And I'm babbling because I'm so nervous about going back to his place, so I start telling him how the bridge we were walking over was the same bridge David Hasselhoff jumped off in an episode of Baywatch. You know real sexy talk," she lifts her foot onto her chair so her knee rests next to her chest.

"That sounds about right," I tease.

What was I so worried about?

"So, we stop to look at the water and it's a red tide. I figure I've already wowed him with my knowledge of obscure TV trivia, I might as well throw in some nerdy biology while I'm at it. So I tell him all about how the red tide fluoresces when it's agitated and how if you jump in it's bright enough to pass through your eyelids--"

"You can see it with your eyes closed?" Junior asks in utter disbelief.

Fed by the boys' attention, Charlie slowly shifts from self-disparaging to really telling this story. "If you jump at night, it forms this glow-in-the-dark ring around you. And it's like you jumped into another world for a few seconds. The warm, saltwater surrounds you and the world goes from dark to this most brilliant green. When you finally pop up, there's a remnant of that glow around you to remind you of the few seconds you were allowed in a world of light and warmth."

"Who thought a biology lesson could be this sexy?" Junior is enrapt.

"You told all of this to him?" I ask, suspiciously.

"Not with any grace. It came out more like, 'It's like green and glowy.'"

That sounds more like Charlie.

"Anyhow, he whips off his shirt and I'm breathless. This guy is the perfect specimen. My only recourse was to match his shirtlessness."

"There's no way you whipped off your top in front of this guy, in public no less," I call her out on her, let's say, embellishment?

"Well, duh. I had a bikini top on."

"You usually go on dates in your bikini?" Mick asks, a little too interested in her answer.

"I was wearing this top," she motions to where her shirt would have hit. "It was the only, um, top I could wear under it. And naturally, I wanted to match, so I threw on the bottoms as well."

"Naturally," Junior adds.

I shuffle the cards hoping to hurry up her story.

"So we're hanging over the side of the bridge and he jumps, but I can't let go. And he's encouraging me, shouting from the water, until I see my skin light up red and blue and red and blue."

"Finally. Cops. Can we get this story over with now?" I ask. Mick shoots me his *Quit Being a Shitty Wingman* look.

"I'm trying to explain to the cop that I'm not crazy and that my date is in the water, but he's nowhere to be found. So, of course, I look totally crazy. He slides his hand down to his taser."

"You didn't just flirt your way out of it? You. In a bikini. You definitely have the advantage," Mick says, motioning to her body.

I almost spit out a mouthful of beer at the thought. "Charlie couldn't flirt her way out of a paper bag."

# 29

## GREYSON

Charlie drops her eyes to the table, her lips pursed and one eyebrow up. Then she lifts that look up towards me.

Yeah, maybe it was a bit mean, but I say stuff like that to her all the time and she never minds.

"Damn. That's harsh," Junior chides.

Having to hear Charlie talk about herself in a bikini, flirting, has pushed me into full asshole mode, and I can't stop it from happening. "I've seen Charlie flirt. It's both hilarious and horrifying to watch."

If the looks she gave before were death stares, this one is a genocidal stare. The boys are smart enough not to step in the middle of the minefield I've created.

"Oh come on, you don't think it's true, Charlie?" I plead, trying to get her to lighten up.

Silence.

She won't even look at me. I know I've stepped in it when her anger and frustration drive her to Full Silent Mode.

I kick her foot under the table, hoping she'll see my 'What Do You Expect From an Asshat Like Me' look.

She gazes right past me, to the lights hanging from the Banyan tree outside while madly adding layers and layers of bricks to the top of the Fortress Wall.

When she's satisfied it's high enough, she says without bringing her gaze anywhere near me, "Who's bet?"

Always the one to smooth things over, Patrick throws in a quarter. "I think that's me."

"Ooh, big spender. I'll see your quarter and raise you a quarter," Mick says oblivious to the exchange that just took place in front of him.

I try again to catch her eye to offer my apology, but she's too busy rolling that insult over and over in her mind, letting her anger wash over every aspect, completely detached from the joking and betting going on in front of her.

They all pause as the bet rolls around to Charlie. Patrick taps her leg, trying to jar her awake.

She glares at me awhile tossing her cards to the table without a word, and walks to the fridge, falling back into her fugue as her hand rests on the handle.

I gather the cards and shuffle. "You want me to deal you in, Sands?" I ask.

No reply.

I deal her in while I wrack my brain for a way to set things right again. "Ante up." I say, but no one is paying attention.

When I follow their leers, I find Charlie hanging on the open fridge door, frozen. She steps back from the fridge with purpose, slips off her flannel, and tosses it on the counter. She peruses the fridge's contents a second time, bent at the waist, her lean frame stretched out in a short, pink, crop top and tight, threadbare jean shorts in full view.

My shoulders unwind and I drift back into my chair. Without adjusting my gaze, I take a long drag from my beer letting the cold alcohol fizz on my tongue as I fully absorb the view.

She reaches further back in the fridge for something, tugging her shirt up even more to reveal her back, tan and muscular from so much time on her surfboard.

My hand could run along her skin, sliding that shirt up further.

*Shit. Don't go there, Steele. Clean slate. Don't let the cyanide poison everything. Just. Look. Away.*

But I can't. I can't rip my gaze from her ass, from the line leading from her hips to her chest and up her neck. The one that curves in all the places a woman should.

She finally straightens up with a beer in her hand.

My brow raises, questioning her choice. We're only now getting over the misery she caused the last time she drank.

Charlie straightens up and saunters over to the junk drawer, setting down her beer.

Every head swivels to follow. It's like she almost knows all our eyes are on her, our minds each filled with our own set of lascivious thoughts and she's purposely giving us plenty of fodder.

She slides her hand up her neck, pressing gently while dipping her head to the side. I'd be happy to work that out for her later, on her couch, my legs wrapped around her as she sits in front of me.

*Fuck.*

She is not making it easy to maintain this clean slate.

Charlie opens her beer letting the cap fall into the drawer followed by the opener. When she turns around, we all quickly turn back to our cards trying to hide our filthy thoughts.

All except for Mick who is smiling right at her, the arrogant bastard. It's as if he wants her to know what he was thinking.

I turn back to her, anticipating her *No Way In Hell I'm Falling For That* look. It's one she tosses out often, and one he probably seldom receives.

But, instead, she's smiling at him.

Smiling!

Every muscle in my back tenses. I instinctively square off towards Mick like I might reach across this table and beat that grin right off his face.

What the Hell has gotten into her?

She holds his gaze the whole way back to the table letting her hand graze his shoulders when she slides into her seat next to him.

My ribs tighten like the first signs of a heart attack and my heart thumps against the inside of my ribs way faster than it should be.

Is it a heart attack?

I think my left arm hurts a little too.

Fuck, why is this so hard to watch?

"Sorry. Is it my bet? I guess I should peek at my cards first," Charlie says in a voice I've never heard before. It's softer and higher and definitely sexier.

She slides her cards off the table and pushes in two quarters.

"I'm out," Patrick mutters.

"Me too," Mick says.

Who is this girl? God, even her posture is different. It's like she's being held up by self-confidence and sex appeal she has no ability to contain.

"Greyson. Your bet," Mick jostles me out of my head.

"I don't know, I'm out, I guess."

"It's just you and me, Junior," Charlie coos. "You willing to go the whole way?"

"I'm in. Turn and burn, Greyson," Junior says.

I hesitantly oblige, laying down a two of hearts.

A huge smile swells over Charlie's face. I guess she's lost her poker face in all this. . . flirting?

"Let's go with a dollar," Charlie says.

Junior hesitates.

"Come on, Junes. Don't pull out on me now."

My mouth falls open. I slam the deck back onto the table trying to knock some sense into her.

She doesn't even flinch.

"I'll see your dollar and raise you a dollar," Junior says trying to show he's man enough.

"Looks like Junior grew a pair," Mick jabs.

"I'll see your dollar. Show me yours?" Charlie teases.

Damn, the innuendo pouring out of sweet, innocent, little Charlie makes me think she might be possessed.

"Two pair," Junior says proudly.

"So close," Charlie gives him a pitying smile while laying down her cards. "Full house."

Charlie pulls the pot into her pile, stacking the money neatly as she soaks in the attention of the boys. She looks up from her pile, catching Mick's gaze. Her grin is heart-stopping.

And infuriating.

She quickly knocks Patrick and Junior out of the game. The flop on the table, a queen of clubs and six of hearts laid next to the jack and ten of clubs, the nine of diamonds already on the table, Mick folds.

With Charlie and I the only ones left, she's got to acknowledge me now.

"So it's you and me, Chuckie," I say using the name I know she hates, trying to rile her up like it's always been so easy to do.

But I get nothing.

Charlie turns to Mick, who gives her the smile she's yearning for, and she folds, tossing her cards to the table.

While she's busy giggling at Mick again, her hand resting on his forearm, I check her cards. I know I shouldn't. I know it's a low thing to do, but it's unavoidable.

The Ace and King of puppy feet, as she calls them. She folded on a royal flush just so she wouldn't have to interact with me. Could she really hate me that much just for saying she can't flirt?

Which, by the way, I take back fully. She can flirt better than any woman I've ever seen.

The whole night continues with Charlie running the show, every guy eating out of her hand.

Well, every guy except me. She won't even glance in my direction.

And she doesn't warm to me at all as the night goes on. It's not like her to hold a grudge. We can hardly go an hour after a fight without hashing it out and moving on. This is something different entirely.

"It's the last hand of the night," Junior narrates in his best sports-caster voice. "Just Mick, the ever-aging bachelor with a few scattered dollars left to lose, against Charlie, the sexy shark with a full pile to mess around with. Will it be Mick the underdog who has never won a game of poker in the ten years he's been at the house? Or will it be the gorgeous surfer girl who just joined the team? It's a game of beginner's luck vs. the old man, struggling to get it up."

My jaw clenches at the word 'sexy' dripping out of Junior's mouth. I know where that mouth's been and I don't want it anywhere near Charlie.

I deal the last hand.

"Your bet, Micky," she nudges.

When she slides her hand onto Mick's knee, he's about to lose it. "It's okay to lose. I won't think any less of you," she continues.

The tourniquet that's been wrapped around my chest all night, contracts even more. I stand, sending my chair flying back to the wall and storm off to the fridge.

Fuck. I wish Charlie stocked whiskey in here. Maybe Indigo's stashed some good stuff somewhere. Or at least Bex has got to keep something stronger than beer. It has not been doing the trick tonight.

I slam the fridge door and start pillaging through the other cupboards. Nothing but boxes and boxes of her stupid Lucky Charms and spices up there.

"Uhh, we need another card. You gonna help us out any time soon, Greyson?" she commands.

"Yeah, I'll get right on that."

I give up my search for hard stuff, but I take my sweet time opening a beer and returning.

When I finally lay out a card, Charlie takes one look at it. "All in."

"You really think you have what you need to beat me?" Mick teases.

"Only one way to find out?" she nods to the pile.

"What the hell? All in." He slides his chips in.

Everyone is locked in on Charlie again. She giggles and a piece of hair falls into her eyes. She tucks it behind her ear.

I don't think I've ever made her giggle. I've made her chuckle. I've made her laugh, waiting for the perfect moment so she'd spit out her DDP. I've even made her laugh so hard she peed her pants, though she would never admit it.

But I've never made her giggle.

Her voice drops back to regular Charlie, giggle-less Charlie. "Think you could actually deal there, Sport."

So wrapped up in the memory of her face when she realized she pissed herself, the pride from knowing she thought I was that funny, it took a moment for me to figure out what her words meant. "Huh?"

"Steele. A card."

I lay out another card, matching her exasperation with my own spiteful look.

Mick flings his cards on the table. "Full house. Sorry, Charlie. I know you had your heart set on winning. Maybe I can make it up to you somehow."

Charlie smiles as she lays out a Queen of hearts and then the Queen of diamonds.

"Can I make it up to you. . . somehow?" She bites her lower lip seductively.

Mick, the best player I've seen play the game, is so drawn in, he's without a retort. I don't want to know what he is dreaming up to answer that 'somehow'.

"Damn. Four of a kind? You really do have what it takes to beat ol' Mick," Junior says.

Charlie pulls the pile towards her.

She puts on her contrite face, the one she uses to get out of detention and arguments with me. "Sorry, boys. I didn't mean to end your poker game so quickly."

"You did it with such style, I think we can forgive you," Patrick says.

Not one to let the night end early, Mick adds, "Did I see a ping pong table on the way in?"

Charlie high-fives Mick and leads her throng of admirers to the game room.

I sit, trying to figure out what I just witnessed.

But I can't. I have no idea what this was. Who this was.

After twelve years of thinking I knew everything about her, Charlie goes and completely blows up any notions I had of who she is and what she's capable of.

Not ready to watch round two of the dance she and Mick seem to be entangled in, I go to the head, close the door, and lean my head against it.

All this because I said she couldn't flirt. I don't know how many times I've said stuff like that to her before. It has to be in the thousands.

If you asked her to consult her Rule Book, you'd see it was a perfectly acceptable way to enforce the Half Foot rule. Sarcasm, put-downs, harsh joking all acceptable ways to enforce the distance.

She's done it, too, called me a man-whore, a player. She accused me of studying the RomComs she forces me to watch so I'd know exactly how to play on a girl's need to have those scenes recreated.

Sure, I had memorized certain lines, had a system set up so I could create poems involving their names on the spot, and knew how to pack a particularly effective picnic, but I never took offense when she pointed out my slightly sleazy ways. Why was she getting so high and mighty now?

If I had a hard copy of that damned Rule Book of hers, I could step out of the bathroom and chuck it right at her head, remind her of the stupid rules she has been doing a shit job of holding up lately.

With no book to throw, and in no mood to play, I leave the head, and lean up against the corner of the open doorway to the game room, sipping my beer and calmly observing this new Charlie in what appears to be her natural environment.

After each game, they switch teams giving each shark a turn on her side. She and Mick are currently destroying Junior and Patrick, congratulating each other after each point with a high five that is more like their hands are making out than slapping.

Halfway through the first game, Indigo comes through the front door, dragging Mark, now in bright yellow fireman's pants and red suspenders over a navy blue shirt. They are so enthralled in their foreplay they don't even notice us.

They tumble to the foot of the stairs, kissing and twirling and pushing each other against the wall. When they hit the bottom of the stairs, Indigo stops, takes Fake Fireman's hand, and leads him up to her room.

Charlie spins towards me and laughs; a momentary truce.

"Did she just grab that guy off the job?" Mick asks.

When they win the last game, Charlie wraps herself around Mick in a celebratory hug. He doesn't miss the opportunity to slide his hands down her back.

My whole body heats up more with every inch they slide. Rising from the wall, I size up Mick like never before.

Charlie twirls out of his grip, beaming.

I relax again into the wall. Guess, there's no one to protect if this is what she wants.

"Three games each for Charlie and Mick. Looks like we have a tie-breaker for the win," Junior announces.

"Sounds good. Let me just grab my drink. I need a break after that one," Charlie calls out as she floats by me, close enough to smell her banana lotion, to see the image she inserted in my mind earlier of her underneath me, waiting for me to pull her closer.

I follow her into the kitchen.

It's time to end this shitshow.

# 30

## CHARLIE

*I* swing open the fridge door, the cool air billowing over my feet, and rest for a minute. It's hard work proving a point.

I've always believed people should constantly be improving, reforming. It's the reason that, out of the six doctrinal statements I incorporated into my tattoo, Semper Reformanda has resonated with me the most.

We're all flawed human beings. The good ones, though, they spend time finding their own weaknesses and attempting to improve on them. I know I have not always been top of the class in feminine skills, but I have spent this last year attempting to improve. From trying new clothes to experimenting with roles that stretched my skill set to flirting in real life with Occy, I now feel like I am not a complete failure in this department.

But Greyson, still cannot see the change. And, if he can't see it, has it really happened? He has always been able to look beyond my outward attempts to fit in, to the real me. If he doesn't realize how far I've come, maybe I'm still just playing the part of a sexy leading lady.

I retrieve a Diet Dr Pepper from the shelf, slamming the door a little too forcefully.

I slide my old pint glass off the table and pour my drink, letting the sight of the huge pile of money in front of my seat refill my energy tanks.

Greyson rounds the corner, determined to empty it out again. "This has got to stop, Charlie," he growls.

Most times I love hearing my name come out of his mouth, but this one is like a smack of a breaking wave on a frigid morning ushering in an ice cream headache like I've never felt before. He's furious.

I'm finally letting loose and enjoying the fruits of my hard work, and he's mad. We used to be so in sync, always reacting the same way to any social experience, and here we are now having the polar opposite reaction.

"This has got to stop," he snarls even slower as if I didn't hear him the first time.

I take a sip of my soda, studying the tangerine-orange Ripper logo on my pint glass, while I let the bubbles of the soda distract me from his anger, if only for a moment.

"I get it, Sands." He steps up like he could stop me from going back to continue playing with his friends. "You made your point."

*Yeah... I don't think I have.*

"You're making a fool of yourself, Charlie."

Oh, really? A fool? I finally have the guts to flirt like I've always wanted to, like the feminine woman I am, and I'm a fool? They haven't taken their eyes off me for a second, and I'm a fool? I've proven your callous assessment of me so totally, absolutely, completely, brutally wrong, and I'm a fool?

Something in me clicks and I finally see with total clarity.

This isn't about me.

I rest my glass next to the stacks of money I won from the boys. "Ohhhhhhhh, I get it."

I begin to close the distance between us. "You're pissed cause I'm focused entirely on them," my finger taps his chest, "and not giving you any attention."

*Shit! I broke the Half-Foot Rule.*

*We have rules for a reason, Charlie. They keep this relationship working. You can't break them and expect everything to keep humming along the way it always does.*

I begin to lift my finger, to change tack from my current course.

Although... if I've already broken the rule... I might as well go for broke and let him feel the full force of my point. I let my whole hand rest against his chest and his hard muscles under my palm flood me with confidence.

And a plan.

With my palm still on the valley of his pecs, I push him up against the wall. "I think we can remedy that predicament," I say in a sultry voice I've never heard from my mouth before.

I let my fingers brush slowly down his chest, meandering along his stomach, lingering momentarily in the space between each defined ab.

He follows my every movement with his eyes.

I take my time until one finger rests tucked just inside the top of his jeans, giving him a small tug to ensure he knows who's in charge now.

He searches my eyes for an explanation.

Confidence from my successes earlier has me buzzing with boldness, as I answer him with a grin that says, *You're in for it now, Bucko!*

His hands slide onto my hips, as he draws me towards him.

I steady myself with my other hand on his chest and the center of gravity shifts into the wall behind him, enticing me to explore what I shouldn't.

What I can't.

But, I'm unable to pull my gaze from his lips and, slowly, the warning cries of the inconceivable are being drowned out by the strengthening pull of...

*Damn. Those lips are begging to be kissed.*

I know I downed that beer earlier, but that can't account for feeling this off-kilter.

He lifts his head from the wall behind him and lets his tongue sweep across his lips.

I follow its every movement, mesmerized.

*What was that?*

*Did he just...?*

*Does he want me to...?*

My mouth opens with that glimpse behind the stone wall.

His smile broadens like he can read my mind and knows the indecent thoughts running around in there.

*You're proving a point, Charlie, that's it.*

Grey draws my hips closer until I'm pinned against him.

*He's just calling my bluff.*

His gaze dips to my lips again as his head begins to close in.

*Shit. What is he doing?*

*Oh my God. What am I doing???*

Panic sets in and The Rationalizer, in a particularly foul mood, begins barraging me. He starts with the most obvious.

*You just threw it all away. All of it. You can't expect Grey to keep forgetting every time you feel like crossing the line. Once is an accident. Twice is rude. Thrice is a twatable offense.*

I argue back.

*This isn't on me. He was the one who couldn't imagine in his wildest dreams I could possibly be sexy.*

He slides his hands around my back, enveloping me in his arms. The Rationalizer strikes back.

*You're not even drunk this time. There's no saying you didn't remember or you didn't know what you were doing. You did this on purpose because you had to prove to him you could be flirty. And we both know that is a fucking lie.*

*It's not a lie. And I didn't throw anything away. I may have crossed the Half-Foot Boundary, but I didn't cross The Line,* I scream back, not that The Rationalizer ever listens to any of my excuses.

"You coming, Charlie," Mick calls from the other room.

"Mmm, hmm," is all I can muster, never drawing my eyes off Greyson.

*You didn't cross the line?* The Rationalizer picks up his berating. *Then what exactly are you doing wrapped in his arms fantasizing over gravity and his chest and his fucking lips?*

I muster all the strength I can find to overcome my paralysis.

"Give me a second, Mick," I say barely loud enough for him to hear.

I indulge in one more moment of Grey's embrace before I push away and try to salvage what's left of our relationship. "I guess I proved my point."

I storm off leaving him plastered to the wall.

Around the corner, I pause, taking a moment to compose myself before returning to the game room, but not before screaming at The Rationalizer to shut the hell up. I cannot take one more moment of his berating.

Walking to my side of the table, I try to figure out how that got away from me. I was only showing Greyson how wrong he was about me. That I was more than his neuter-gender sidekick.

That's it.

He was the one to fling us across The Line. I put my hand on him—just a hand—like he's done plenty of times with me, and he goes into full player mode, pulling me into him, bringing out his pre-makeout warm-up.

As I consider, the ball goes flies by me.

"Come on Charlie, you're not gonna let me win are you?" Mick pokes.

"Huh?" I try to pull the room into focus.

Patrick jumps up from the couch to retrieve the ball, placing it in my hand. "Please don't let him win. The last thing he needs is another reason to be arrogant."

"I'll try."

*Focus, Charlie. Deal with that other stuff later.*

With the spin I put on my next serve, the ball twists off course when it hits the table, sending Mick diving. "One, nothing?" I taunt.

"One, one, babe," he throws back.

"That first one was just you getting the ball to me so I could serve first, like a gentleman would," I argue.

*There you go, Charlie. That's more like it.*

Greyson leans up against the wall farthest from me, beer in hand, pure hatred pouring forth from every ounce of his body. He may have pushed it way too far, but I started it. If I wasn't so incompetent at this girly crap, if I didn't need so badly to prove to Grey that I could be just as flirty as all the bimbos he dates, none of this would have happened.

Maybe he was right. I have so little experience flirting I didn't even know how to manage it. It really was hilarious and horrifying. Only problem is, no one is laughing now.

"So what are they playing to?" Greyson asks, concealing the hatred so obvious to me.

"Eleven?"

"So ten, then." He arrogantly raises his beer to his lips.

Patrick, always missing Grey's sarcasm, corrects him. "Eleven."

"Win by two, though," Junior adds.

"So nine, then," Greyson grunts, looking straight through me.

Mick holds the ball he's about to serve and turns to Greyson behind him. "What's up with you, man? He said eleven."

"Oh... you don't know about Charlie's theory on beating guys," he drawls.

Of all the people I could have angered, I had to piss off the one with every piece of ammo he needs to hurt me back.

"She had no problem beating you in poker, did she?"

*Oh, Mick. This isn't your fight.*

Greyson still hasn't taken his eyes off me. "We don't play those kinds of games. Do we Charlie?"

That one pierces my armor and explodes like a hollow point bullet blooming inside my chest, tearing through flesh, pulverizing organs, liquefying bones, until there is nothing left but a mass of ooze searing my skin, trying to escape.

I can't tell if the tears screaming to break free from my eyes are from the pain or the anger, but I know I cannot let them fall in front of him.

I serve the next one right into the net.

My second attempt? I miss the ball completely.

Bending down to retrieve the ball gives me a moment to reinforce my defenses. Shaking off my confusion, I replace it with the stoicism that is my ever-ready companion.

"You got this?" Mick peeks under the table and asks with a sweetness that almost breaks my defenses.

"Yeah. Sorry. I'm ready."

My next few rallies improve. I'm back to slamming a few of them. I even send one off the table and over the railing to the sunken living room.

"You hit it, you get it," Mick bellows.

I'm more than glad to put some distance between me and the newly incensed Greyson, if even for a minute. I keep my eyes on Mick as I pass him on my way to the stairs.

Once in the relative privacy of the lower room, my body relaxes as I attempt to reassure myself nothing has changed. As I round the banister again, rising up the stairs, Greyson is joking with Patrick, looking so much more like the fireman in my fantasies than the comfortable best friend I've known for the last twelve years.

I swear sometimes he must hear what runs through my head because his face falls from laughing with his bros to, I don't know... maybe... derision? Is that actually something he could be feeling for me now, after all those years, with everything between us?

"Nine, six." Mick is ready to win.

I've won my game to nine. Now I'll let him win his game to eleven to save his ego. I let my play diminish to allow Mick to take the lead and eventually win.

Mick offers me his hand beside mid-court.

I shake it with a "Congratulations."

He holds my hand softly, leaning closer, and whispers in my ear. "I have to ask. Is all this flirting because you're actually interested in me, or is it just to get someone's attention?"

I was so intent on proving Grey wrong, I never even considered how my actions tonight would affect these guys. So, in addition to screwing up the most important relationship in my life, I also screwed over three people I have been begging to meet for years.

Great work, Charlie.

"I, uh.." I've never found a way to reject a guy without feeling horrible.

He lifts my hand and kisses it sweetly. "Got it. It's fine if you don't want to admit it to me, but you should probably admit to yourself who tonight was for."

I'm so stunned, I can't do anything before he spins towards the couch. "Junior. Thank Charlie for a wonderful evening and let's get out of her hair."

Patrick picks up the dishes and empty bottles and disappears into the kitchen.

"See ya, Junior. It was great to meet you," I say as I retreat to the kitchen after the safe and ever-clueless Patrick.

As I make my way past Greyson, he doesn't move from his post, except to follow me with his head, glaring at me as if he isn't just as complicit in creating this shit-storm.

Patrick pumps soap onto a sponge and starts in on the dishes.

I hop up on the counter next to the sink.

He stares intently at the already clean plate he is scrubbing. "I know you like that geeky, biology stuff. Have you seen the new coral reef exhibition at the Scripps aquarium?"

He rinses the plate while he waits intently for my reply.

"I read about that one, but I haven't had a chance to check it out, yet."

"You know they are starting to use coral reefs to develop medicines for Alzheimer's?"

"I heard that. It's crazy how much can be cured by using real stuff instead of so many chemicals."

There's nothing like a little scientific talk to get my mind spinning back on its axis.

"So, you think you'd want to check it out sometime? With me?" He puts the plate in the dish rack, conveniently hiding his face from me. "Maybe we could grab some dinner before?"

"That sounds like a really nice offer, but, I don't think I'm in that place with you."

He scrubs my empty pint glass. "I understand. I had to take a shot."

"But, Patrick?"

He stops madly washing dishes. "Yeah?"

"The washing the dishes is a really good move. You have to keep that one."

"Really?" He appears shocked to hear the compliment.

"Oh yeah. It puts the picture in her head that you're the type of guy to take care of things. You know, considerate and caring. It's the perfect move before you ask her out."

Greyson rounds the corner and rests against the wall, once again, staring me down in this strange sullen gaze.

I can't match his gaze for more than a moment or my head will start spinning again so fast it might actually spin off my neck right into the ceiling fan, shredded into a violent burgundy mess all over the ceiling, dripping in giant globs back onto the tacky linoleum floor.

"That makes me sound like a pussy—sorry—like I'm weak. Why on Earth would a girl ever go for a guy like that?"

Thank God for innocent Patrick grounding me again.

I hop off the counter just to move. "If she's just looking for a quick hookup, she probably won't." I rest my hand on his shoulder. "But if she's looking long-term? You're the guy she's looking for."

"Thanks, Charlie."

I check if Greyson's face has softened at all, but the wall is now holding itself up without his weight to help.

Patrick gives me an awkward side hug and I follow him to the door, taking note of the empty room. I lock the door behind Patrick and head upstairs. Three steps up I freeze.

He might be up there, waiting to unload. My heart, the one recently pulverized by that hollow point, is somehow back together and pounding at my ribs like the one-armed drummer of Def Leopard.

I lower myself one stair.

This is not a conversation I can have right now. How am I supposed to speak when I can't even come up with words for what's going on inside my brain right now?

The brain-fan-spectacle flashes back in my head when I spy

the couch downstairs. I could sleep there. Not have to face the Greyson ambush waiting in my room?

But, in this state, I could not handle a Bexley talk when she comes home tonight. The only place safe from that misery is my room.

*Please, God. Please don't let him be up there.*

# 31

## CHARLIE

*I* push my bedroom door open to a deserted room. My comforter, covered in images of waves, lays crumpled on the dark blue sheet. My white mesh desk chair sits empty. The navy and white sea star and turtle-covered area rug surrounding my bed is uninhabited.

Instead of relief, I am met with tears. Grey is not here. That's the only thing I know. Grey is not here.

I don't know why I want to punch my fist through a wall and at the same time collapse against that same wall. Why I want to hit him and to hold him. I can't even tell if sadness or anger or frustration or some other emotion with unidentifiable origin and purpose is driving the tears spilling over my cheeks.

I get into bed and drag the comforter over my head, letting the tears guide me to a tumultuous sleep.

Well before my alarm blares the next morning, the tears fill my eyes again before I can even open them. I bathe in the heartache for a minute, grieving the loss, before it is drowned out by a grip of rage driving my eyes wide open.

Needing to kill time and kill the emotions threatening to detonate my body, I decide to bike the twelve miles to work. I stuff a change of clothes into a backpack and forgo breakfast, the punishment of hunger feeling appropriate.

Halfway there, Dex screams.

*Shut up. I don't need you yelling at me, too.*

My legs start to shake on the peddles. My useless and incapable body gives out on me.

*Thanks once again for failing me. You were the one who convinced me last night I had to touch Grey, that I had to hold him. You were the one who completely ignored my flawless rules to keep our friendship functioning. You had to have more, you selfish, riotous, insubordinate bastard.*

I stop at the bottom of a hill next to the water and throw my bike into the ice plant on the side of the road. I fling my traitorous body in the sand a few feet farther and dig through my backpack for the Gu energy gels I stash in the small pocket.

I empty two into my mouth and wait for the sugar to hit, welcoming the brutal feeling of my heart slamming against my ribs and the ferocious falling sensation of dropping in on a massive wave. It seems appropriate for my body to feel as rotten as my mind.

When my blood sugar dips lower waiting for my stomach to wrestle sugar into my veins, I lose all ability to control my emotions and I disintegrate into a screaming, blubbering mess.

"Fuuuuuuuuuuuuuuck!," I howl at the ocean.

I mash my teeth together as the pain I had restrained earlier floods in unbridled. My body shakes uncontrollably, burning up even more of the sugar my brain hungers for to detain my free-flowing emotions so I can actually get up and make it through this shitty day.

Fuck. This hurts.

My muscles hurt.

My skin hurts.

My brain hurts.

My heart hurts.

If I have to endure this much longer, I won't have anything left in me to do anything except lay here in the sand and wait for high tide to wash me away.

I lay back in the sand, knowing the sweat I am bathed in will make it stick to every part of me when I get up. I close my swollen eyes and use the crook of my elbow to block out any remaining light.

*I can't do this.*

The falling sensation fades away.

*How am I supposed to finish a full day's work in that Hell-Hole when I don't have the energy to move?*

My heart begins to slow.

*One thing at a time, Charlie. Just get there.*

My legs cease shaking.

*You'll feel better in a few minutes.*

My muscles grow stronger as the sugar rises in my blood.

*Wait for your strength to come.*

I wipe the last tears from my eyes and press on the surrounding skin, hoping to relieve some of the swelling.

Pushing myself up, I watch as small waves sweep onto the sand and retreat into the sea. The sound of the small pebbles at the waterline as they are pushed up and pulled back again fills my mind with the first moments of peace since last night. When the spring sun dries the sweat from my skin, I stand and dust the sand from my arms and legs. On the bike, the wind will remove anything I missed.

The Big&Lime logo high on the side of the dark wood-paneled building taunts me as I peddle across the bridge over the train tracks. It's hard to believe no one saw that logo and thought to themselves, with the ampersand so prominent in the design, it screams BadSlime. What idiot signed off on that?

I can almost hear the response in the board room as a stoned Glenn says, "Let's call it Bad and Lime," his bros erupting in a cacophony of chortles that could give Beavis and Butthead a run for their money.

I take the last hundred yards of my ride to shove my

treasonable emotions deep down and plaster on the hardened mask it takes to endure another day here.

Dirk's blood-red Tesla whips into the parking lot and comes so close to hitting me I can feel the wind off his micro-dick-compensatory automobile.

"Watch it, Dick," I scream, slamming my hand onto the trunk.

I toss my bike on the bike, skateboard, and scooter rack on the entry wall and say hi to the only other woman in the office. They call her lunch girl. Even Glenn does, and he's her uncle. I once asked her what her name was. She replied, "You can call me Lunch Girl. Everyone else does," and added a giggle.

She is in charge of a few trivial tasks besides retrieving lunches for the crew, like restocking supplies, ordering, and giving the guys something pretty to leer at upon entering the building. At least that's how it appears, watching them file in past her each morning.

On my way to the bathroom to change, I glance at the black and white pics on the Big&Lime Greatest Moments in Sports Wall. I study what men think are the best humans have to offer in sport. Brandy Chastain shirtlessly celebrating winning the World Cup, is missing. Nadia Comaneci, at fourteen years old, scoring the first-ever 10.0 in Olympic gymnastic history and a total of seven perfect scores in the 1976 Games. There is no picture of Katherine Switzer hiding her gender and outrunning an attack by the race director when he found out a woman dared to run in *his* Boston Marathon. Gertrude Ederle's successful first female swim across the English Channel and Billie Jean King beating the crap out of Bobby Riggs in the Battle of the Sexes are both missing, too.

"You left your sweaty handprints all over my Tesla!" Dirk's annoying voice pulls me out of my contemplation of Big&Lime's skewed view of sports history.

I don't bother acknowledging him. I shove open the bathroom door to find Thad G, aviator glasses perched atop his head at the sink picking at his face. "Don't you knock?"

"Get out," I growl.

He drops his hands from his face, sticks them in the pockets of his jeans so tight only his fingertips can slide in, and slinks out.

I lock the outside door and whip off my shirt. Wetting a wad of paper towels, I wipe down my skin, before drying off with another handful of towels. I change my shorts and realize in my scattered state this morning, I forgot a clean shirt.

I hang my damp tank under the hand dryer they installed before they realized the energy to run it did more environmental damage than paper towels, then slip on the less-damp top and stare at my reflection. Purple smudges hang below my eyes. Red splotches cover my skin. My blond hair is in knots from wind whipping through it for twelve miles.

I splash my face with cool water, hoping to erase the purple and red, and finger comb my hair before tying it up again. Who even cares if it's good enough?

I trudge to my desk and sink into the chair ignoring Dirk who has been lurking there while I changed.

He leers at my chest. "Shit, Charlie. Did you just come from a wet t-shirt contest? Your tits stand out so much in that tank top I almost believe you're a chick."

What. The. Fuck.

I stare at him as I replay what he said. My face burns. I rock back in my chair and cock up my brow waiting for his apology.

No apology comes.

All the fury and rage bubbling below the surface begins to rise. He doesn't even make an attempt to hide that he's still staring at my chest.

I let my head fall back to my chair, avoiding the sight of the dipshit in front of me, trying to steady my nerves and keep my job.

The basketball hoop my colleagues use at will entices me to scan the office. I notice the giant penis sketched on the wall with "Fuck The Competition" scrawled beside it. The wall of jerseys comes into view, once again not a single woman represented. My gaze settles on the scoreboard that punctuates every afternoon with forced humiliation from boys I outperform every day.

When I return my gaze to Dirk, he is flanked by the Thad known to grab the last 5 beers in the company fridge and hide them in his desk drawer so he won't be without and the Thad who claims he only eats protein because he is absolutely clueless about the carbs and fat in each bite of bacon, eggs, and steak he eats.

These are my colleagues. Boys who think it's perfectly acceptable to not only ogle a woman's body but to come right out and comment on it. These are the guys who are still trying to outcool the jocks who tortured them in high school by being just like them. The problem is, these dipshits think the only people here lower on the social totem pole are women.

"You on the rag or something?" Dirk asks.

I wait to discover if either the Thad on his right or the Thad on his left has the balls to call Dirk on his shit.

They don't.

"You know, I've always been aware that you're a dipshit, Dirk. But until now, I wasn't acquainted with the colossal depths of your dipshittery."

I rest both hands on the edge of my desk, while I survey the poor excuse for boys in front of me. I rise in one movement, sending my chair flying backwards. After it slams into the wall with a noise that silences the whole office, I place the mango-colored coral and Shrinky Dink turtle from my desk into my backpack, hoist it onto my shoulder, and walk right through the wall of Dick and Thads on my way to Glenn's office.

I slam open his door into the filing cabinet behind it, making an even louder metallic clang.

"It's time for you to do something about your brogrammers out there," I holler.

He calmly shuts the lid of his laptop and sneers at me. "Are you having some sort of problem getting along with your colleagues, Charlie? How can I help you make some changes to fit in better?"

"Me, change? You have got to be shitting me, Glenn. They are the ones who need lessons in how to be decent human beings."

"This is the first I'm hearing about it."

"That's bullshit, Glenn. You know exactly what goes on out there and you do nothing about it. You even warned me before you hired me, basically announcing you are perfectly fine with the completely illegal, sexual harassment culture you have not only condoned for years but have actively nurtured." I stalk out of the room, slamming my hand into the beige filing cabinet beside the door. "Fix. It," I shout as I reach the door.

"And if I don't," he asks arrogantly.

I turn slowly and look him dead in the eyes. A grin slowly spreads on my face for the first time today. "Oh please, please, tell me this is you refusing to fix it because that is all I need to make sure you and Big&Lime are finally a name that everyone will know."

I trudge to the front of his desk to emphasize my point. "You'll be infamous for being the stupidest asshole in tech for admitting to an employee who brought you a sexual harassment claim that, on top of the fact that you have been aware of the problem for years, and sought to blame it on her, you intend to do nothing about it."

I place my palm on the stack of paper in a tray next to his laptop and slide the top sheet onto his desk in front of him. "Can I get that in writing so it will make the trial that much easier?" I slap a pen down on top of the paper. "You seem just stupid enough to do that."

Glenn sits stunned while I tower over him and glare. When he finally makes an attempt to speak, I turn on my heels and exit.

On my way out the door, I stop in the kitchen to fill up my backpack with the giant glass jars of candy and chilled Gatorade Zeros Lunch Girl began stocking once she noticed me bringing my own from home. I throw in a few full-sugar Gatorades, too, in case I get low on my ride home.

I lift my bike from the wooden rack on the wall, tossing aside the helmet some Thad was careless enough to hook onto my bike and walk past the front desk when I'm stopped by the sweetest voice. "Can I run out and grab something for you, Charlie?" Lunch Girl asks.

She is so much more patient than I could ever hope to be.

"That's okay, but you could do one thing for me." I walk my bike back to her desk.

"Anything."

"What's your real name?"

She glances around to make sure there are no Thads lurking around. "Jamie. I'm Jamie Yates."

"Hi, Jamie. You are one of the most organized office managers I have ever worked with. Everything you touch becomes so pretty and colorful."

Her eyes become glossy and I know she hasn't heard a compliment in this place for as long as she's been here. I won't leave here without giving her as many as she can take.

"I always smile when I see the way you set up our lunches with a color theme for each day. And how you noticed what I would bring in and then stock it for me in the fridge. That was the sweetest thing."

She replaces her watery eyes with a smile that wrinkles her otherwise smooth skin. "They give you such a hard time, I wanted you to have something for you for once," she whispers.

"I totally appreciate that. Please know, you don't have to put up with their crap to have a place to use your skills. You deserve better than this place. Promise me you'll look for one."

Jamie nods and I can tell the wheels are beginning to spin with plans of leaving Big&Lime.

As I bike home, the spot where I collapsed this morning calls out to me. I have to hop off my bike and rinse off in the ocean. I slip off my socks and shoes and pull off the tank top that started my 'hysterical' grasp at freedom, revealing my sports bra underneath. I toss the white top to the sand next to my bike and sprint full speed into the water.

The water is barely sixty-two, but the shock against my skin is invigorating. I stroke past the breaking waves and float with my toes peeking out of the water in front of me.

The sun has warmed since this morning and is beating down on my face, my smiling face. Finally free from that crappy job, I begin to wonder what else I could ditch to keep this sense of freedom coursing through my veins.

Bex's ludicrous Summer Goal?

*Gone.*

*I quit.*

And damn, that feels amazing.

No more awful dates surrounded by three people I have nothing in common with. No more wasting my Friday nights with strangers pretending to be someone I'm not. No more strapping myself into her hideous clothes and then feeling uncomfortable in my own skin even when I change back into my normal clothes afterward.

What else?

Trying to figure out what is going on with Grey?

I wouldn't have to find a way for my heart and my head to agree anymore. I wouldn't have to analyze everything he does to see what he's thinking anymore. I wouldn't have to think that miserable thought that has been pinging around in my brain since last night.

If he's the person who knows me best in this world, and he's attracted to any moderately pretty girl on earth but honestly thinks I have no flirting skills, that I am not girly enough, that I'm not attractive, then it might be true.

Maybe I'm not attractive, not because I couldn't care less about pursuing it like I've always told myself, but because I don't possess the requisite attributes. This entire attempt to figure out how to be girly is just a waste.

A waste of my time.

A waste of my energy.

I mean, what is the point of putting in all this effort, if I am just going to be unattractively girly in the end anyway? Wouldn't I be happier if I stayed the adventurous, athletic tomboy I have always been? I'll be alone either way, so why bother?

I close my eyes and let the saltwater splash along my face as I sink with every breath out and rise with each breath in. I take a few more breaths as the cool water steels my resolve.

*I quit.*

I quit listening to Bex prattle on about everything I should be and correcting me when she thinks my behavior will drive away boys.

I quit trying to be like the skinny, dressed-up Barbies I see in every movie and TV show.

I quit pretending to be sexy for any more of Indigo's films.

I quit trying to flirt with the firehouse boys to prove an impossible point.

I quit trying to flirt with Greyson and destroying an entire friendship in one night.

I quit trying to be something I can never be.

On the sand again, I strip off my wet shorts, replacing them with dry ones from my bag, and dry my hands on my tank top. I pick up my phone and fire off a quick text.

**Charlie: You still headed to Maui on that surf trip?**

**Occy: Yeah. Why? You thinking about coming with me? It'll be a beaut. I'll even promise not to wear my budgie smugglers...**

**Occy: Unless you like them... Then I'll wear them all day.**

**Occy: If you can get your plane tix, the rest will be my shout. We got Mate's Rate on the house. Just need to harvest a few fruit trees for Finn. You have to come, Charlie!!!**

I let the Freedom Train steam on.

**Charlie: Why not! I'm in. Email me the deets.**

His response is a gif of a bearded bald guy in a blue and red tank top I assume is a rugby player, celebrating whatever it's called when they score a goal. He raises his arms, gives a few high fives, and skips off the field.

I guess that means Occy's happy I'm going.

I think I am, too.

# 32

## GREYSON

Thursday night, after Charlie decided to fuck with my heart just to prove to me she could, I pointed my pickup north and drove, stopping when the roads became so familiar I would have known them blind. With all the grinding of my palms against my eyes on the drive up, I wasn't far off.

I drove around the streets of my hometown on autopilot, ending up in front of Charlie's childhood home. The light in her old bedroom is out, but the street lights illuminate the light blue waves on the fabric of her curtains.

"I can't believe you would fuck with me like that, Charlie," I shout at her ghost taunting me from behind the window. "With absolutely no regard for my heart."

She knows.

She knows exactly how I feel.

She has to know.

And she still fucked me over just to prove to me she could.

I let that abomination dwell with me as I lay my head on the steering wheel and let the weight of the long night force sleep upon me.

The clatter of metal on glass pierces my sleep, the early

morning light seeping in through my closed lids. Connor's voice drags me the rest of the way to fully conscious. "You finally go full stalker?"

"What?" I mumble.

He mimes rolling down the window, so I feel around on the door for the handle only to remember my truck was made in this century. I press the ignition button and roll down the window.

"Everything okay with Charlie?" he asks.

"God. I don't know," I grumble.

His head swings to her house. "Is she okay? What happened?"

"She's fine. We... I don't know... had a fight?"

The last thing I want to do is recount last night to Connor. I try to change the subject. "What are you doing home?"

"We had to make some wedding decisions yesterday and Bethany wanted to make sure I didn't let my mom turn our little wedding into a huge production."

"How did a bonehead like you end up with such a great girl?"

"She says she liked my laugh."

The glowing appreciation on his face replaces my jealousy with pure joy for my friend.

"You laugh like the Pillsbury Doughboy," I mock.

"Nothin' says lovin' like something from the oven. Hoo hoo," he giggles in a helium-altered voice.

Bethany is in for a lifetime of laughs with this guy.

"I know you look like shit and all, but you up for a run?" he asks.

Thank God I keep a pair of running shoes and shorts in the truck at all times. "Flogging my body with a few, fast miles sounds perfect."

After our run and a burrito at Nick's Deli, we spend the afternoon drinking on Connor's parents' porch and hitting golf balls onto the elementary school across the street. Four beers in, we get the inspired idea to relive our glory days by sneaking into the site of countless hours of training and torture, Los Al High's pool.

"Shit. He's coming back," Connor whispers and we both

duck our heads below the edge of the pool hoping like hell the security guard won't be able to spot us from this distance.

When he leaves, I stretch out my arms behind me on the edge of the pool gutter, letting my head fall back against the cement edge.

The pool is so much smaller than I remember it. When we had to jump in fully clothed the first day of water polo practice, I thought I would never make it to the other end. Now, I could put in a hundred laps without breaking a sweat.

Connor is just as lost in nostalgia as I am. "You remember the look on Coach's face that first day Charlie showed up for polo practice?"

Our high school didn't have a girl's water polo team, which obviously wasn't going to stop Charlie. She hadn't told anyone she was trying out. Not even me.

First day of tryouts, she showed up in a ball cap and huge swim parka. When Coach told the guys to strip down, grab a cinder block, and tread water with it above their heads "until the first pussy pukes," she dropped her parka, grabbed a brick, and jumped in the water as everyone else on deck stood gaping at her.

Connor shoots water out of his mouth in a neat stream. "He nearly shit bricks. He couldn't imagine a girl could be named Charlie."

"She was so bold back then. Took whatever she wanted."

Charlie at fifteen was a thing to behold. I wish I had had her fearlessness when we first met so I could have pursued her before twelve years of inaction dug the groove so deep neither of us has the strength to extricate ourselves.

Connor's still treading water in the middle of the pool like he's testing himself to see if he still has it. "Things had smaller consequences back then."

I know I owe Connor the truth about why I'm up here, but I am in no mood to have a heart-to-heart. "Fuck consequences. If she wanted something, she'd have taken it by now."

"I'm not sure that's true."

The last time he gave me that line, he screwed up my mind enough I slept with Charlie in my arms. No fucking way I'm going back there. "Sure or not, it's fucking true."

Connor breaststrokes to the side of the pool. With a voice laced with kindness, he points out, "She's just as scared as you are."

He lifts himself out of the pool like he's done a thousand times before and scales the high dive in seconds.

Charlie doesn't do fear.

"Double Gainer?" Connor calls out from twelve feet over my head.

"You crack your head open, you're on your own."

After crashing at Connor's parents' place late Saturday night, and a visit to our old church Sunday morning—a requirement of anyone staying the night at Mrs. Holmes' place on a Saturday night—I take my time driving home down Highway 101.

Tuesday morning, I get a text from an unknown number.

**Unknown: Any chance I could tap those doctoring skills of yours?**

I scan my memory for the last girl I played doctor with, coming up blank, and, right now, I really don't care enough to avoid offending her.

**Greyson: Who is this?**

**Unknown: Only the best director you know.**

Of course.

**Greyson: What can I do for you, Indie?**

**Indigo: My last few films haven't been enough to offer medical insurance to myself so I was hoping you could come over and check something out. Just reassure me I'm simply being neurotic and it's nothing that can't be fixed with some Vitamin C and whiskey.**

The last place I want to be is Charlie's. If I can't hold back my asshattery with Connor when he merely alludes to my Shit With Charlie, there's no way I can avoid unloading on her if she were actually in the same room.

But Indigo has always been good to me and I owe it to her to help.

**Greyson: I'm at home. You can come over.**

**Indigo: Not sure I can drive. Come here?**

I let out a long sigh.

**Greyson: Sure. Be there in ten.**

Ten minutes later, I put my hand to Charlie's front door and pause. If she's there...

I raise my hand to knock when my pocket buzzes. Probably Charlie telling me to stay the hell away.

I pull out my phone to confirm my fears, but it's not her.

**Indigo: Don't worry. Charlie's not here.**

I walk in the door and up the stairs to find the back half of Indigo sticking out of the fridge.

"Stone or Lagunitas?" she asks.

"I'm good."

"Or is it a whiskey kind of a day? That sounds like a whiskey voice." She glides to the other side of the kitchen, opening a lower cabinet, returning with a bottle of Jameson Irish Whiskey and two coffee mugs. So that's where she hides the good stuff.

"Here," she sets a glass down in front of me.

"You said you weren't feeling well," I prod.

"You and Charlie had a huge blowout last week?"

I study the amber liquor in my glass and take a sip. "She told you about it?"

"Not really, but I can tell. She's different when you're not around, balancing her out," she throws back the whole glass and pours herself another. "She tends to, what did you call it in Maui? Spin out?"

"Yeah." I take another sip. "Did she tell you what it was about?"

"How about you tell me," she says, grabbing the bottle and stepping into the sunshine on the deck.

I'm starting to see what Charlie meant when she said Indigo has a way about her that makes you want to talk about things you'd never in a million years want to talk about.

As I follow Indigo outside, I silently recount the Poker Night debacle. Me being a total ass to Charlie when it came to her flirting ability, cutting her where I know she is most venerable. The flirty looks she gave Mick, looks I've always craved. My stupid assumption that her pushing me up against that wall meant she finally wanted me.

The ache in my chest when she told me that would never be true.

"I wish I could tell you what it was about." I finish my mug of whiskey and hold it out for another pour.

Indigo picks up the bottle, and with it suspended above my glass, asks, "How many times have you two fought in the last year?"

My gaze drifts past the big Banyan tree to the ocean as I try to recall. I can't see past this last fight, though. It's as if everything before that night no longer exists.

Indigo pours me a tall one and pushes it back to me.

I empty it. "I don't know. We have spats all the time, I guess."

"No. I'm talking big fights. Like you don't talk to each other for a few days, or you can't sit in the same room without wanting to murder each other. Really think about the last couple of fights you've had. When were they?"

I lean back against the railing. I can still hear Charlie's voice, soft, plaintive, *I guess I made my point.*

"The last big one was the night we played poker," I offer.

"And before that?"

Me roaring, *You are the most selfish person I have ever met.* "In Maui."

"And what happened both of those times?" She's leading me somewhere, but I have no idea where.

"We made up?"

She laughs like she's saying, "Stupid Boy."

She offers me another pour. "I mean what happened right before both of those fights?"

Any more whiskey and I won't be able to grasp the insight Indigo is offering.

I stall. "Right before?"

I can almost feel Charlie's thumb on my lips, confessing how she thinks of me when she takes care of herself. And Charlie's hand on my chest again, pressing me up against her kitchen wall, the way she leaned in when I licked my lips.

Right before?

We cross that line.

Because I can't follow simple rules.

I push.

I fuck it all up.

I send the mug in my hands sailing across the deck.

It cracks into rubble, leaving the shard with the handle still attached lodged in the trunk of the banyan tree in the middle of the deck.

Indigo just laughs at my outburst.

"I'm sorry. I'll pick it up," I apologize.

Indigo begins picking up pieces of the mug. "I had this brindle Labrador when I was eight. When we went to pick out our dog, all the puppies played together, soaking up all the attention. But Nike sat off at a distance. He was small and couldn't keep up. He stole my heart that day. I begged and pleaded with my parents to let me keep him."

Indigo grabs the trashcan from the kitchen as I eradicate the wreckage of my tantrum. "By the time he was one, he was the strongest and friskiest dog I had ever seen. If I tried to go swimming in our backyard pool, he would attack me, barking and jumping all over me. I had to sprint to get in the water before he could get to me. Eventually, I learned I could trap him in the garage so I could take my time getting into the pool."

Am I Nike in this story or is Charlie? Or has Indigo simply switched topics with no warning?

"On the hottest day of my thirteenth summer, the garage door broke. But there was no way I wasn't swimming."

I pull the wedge of broken mug out of the Banyan tree and toss it into the can.

Indigo awards me with an approving smile as she drops onto the bench around the cold fire pit.

I recline on the bench next to her as she forges ahead with her baffling story.

"I mustered up all the courage I had and stepped outside. Nike sprinted across the yard and knocked me to the cracked concrete patio. I thought I was a goner, but do you know what he did? He immediately stopped barking and licked my face, then he laid down, cuddled right up against my side, calm as I have ever seen him."

She sips her whiskey proudly like she just concisely elucidated the meaning of life.

But it flew way over my head.

"So the moral of the story is..." I say, no clue where she is going with this.

She takes pity on my poor, dense soul. "I wish I found Nike's bark translator before I wasted years thinking that distance was the only solution to our problem."

If distance isn't the answer, then what is?

No distance?

Isn't that what I've been trying for the past year? That has only made everything worse.

I desperately need a Charlie bark translator because I have no clue what the hell she wants from me.

Or maybe I just need Charlie to use her human words.

Is it possible she's barking this loudly not because she wants to keep me at a distance, but because she really wants to cuddle up with me?

The old rationalizations playing on repeat through my skull quickly drown out that hope.

It's not like that with us.

She's way too smart for me.

She deserves a guy who is way better than me.

She shouldn't have to take on all my mental shit.

We're just Poe Friends.

Poe.

Friends.

Fucking stupidest phrase I've ever heard.

But...

What if...

"So, now that we got that cleared up." Indigo picks up her glass and walks inside, setting it in the sink.

I follow her wanting to soak up all the wisdom she possesses.

"My throat's been killing me for about a week and I have

these weird growths under my chin. Right here. Feel them." She grabs my hands and puts them on her lymph nodes.

She changes topics like what she just proposed was the simplest concept ever.

It's taken me twelve years to even consider the possibility.

# 33

## CHARLIE

On the fifth day of my new Life of Freedom, I round the corner to the kitchen to find Greyson leaning up against the kitchen island, staring into Indigo's eyes. The waves of pain I left behind yesterday wash over me again all at once. And my ability to move flees.

How could I not have seen that? Indigo always spoke so highly of him. Said so many kind things.

He brings his hands to her neck, as he lifts her chin slightly. His hands still grazing her skin, they move... awkwardly.

I so don't want to be watching this, but my mind, however loud it is screaming, cannot convince my body to move. I have to say something, to make it stop. I'm not sure I could watch this and still manage to ever move from this spot again. I might be stuck here forever, like some weird living sculpture.

Grey keeps kneading at her neck, almost as if he were checking her lymph nodes. Maybe playing doctor is another of her role-playing fantasies. It wouldn't surprise me to find out she has all sorts of weird fetishes.

And maybe that's what Grey wants, a girl who—

"You know, I think I was overreacting," Indigo says, turning to me and throwing me a mischievous grin. "I actually feel fine now. I think I'm gonna get ready for Nick tonight."

She stops beside me, saying playfully, "I got him over here, you have to do the rest."

As Greyson leans back against the island and stares at the floor, I focus on the fridge. It's a safe place to hide while I gather my strength.

"You want me to go?" he mutters.

I want to yell, "No. Please don't go. I never want you to go," but I can't get my mouth to move.

"Yeah. OK. I guess I'm gonna go," he answers for me.

I turn and show him the two beers I pulled from the fridge. A faint smile washes across his face as a bit of tension flows from his shoulders.

He's wearing my favorite shirt. It's an old, navy blue shirt from his uncle's firehouse he got when he was fifteen. It's been washed so many times it's soft as an otter's fur, with a few well-placed holes here and there. It's a size too small now, the sleeves just short enough to show off his triceps as they flex to support himself as he leans back against the island.

He usually only pulls it out on rough days.

I pop the caps off the bottles and hand him one, taking a step back to give him some space.

He nods to my open suitcase in the dining room I've been packing with food. I haget nervous about not finding affprdable vegetarian food options and, although I think Occy offered to pay for me, I hate depending on someone else to do that.

He finishes his sip. "What are you packing for?"

Of all the things we need to talk about, this is not one of them. "Surf trip to Maui."

He squints his eyes and stares at me like he is trying to figure out who he is looking at as he growls, "When?"

I take a long draw of beer to put off answering, then gaze out the window. "I leave tomorrow."

I study his face for some sign that there's a possibility we get through this, but the distance between us is becoming glaringly obvious. The distance I had to put there to survive.

When I realized I could never be the girly girl he would want, it gutted me. I can't let him get that close again.

"I thought you couldn't get the time off," he snarls.

I hate not telling him stuff. Whenever something important happens to me, Grey is always the first person I want to tell. It's not real until I do.

The words under the tattoo on my bare foot seem to glow. *Semper Reformanda. Always Reforming.*

It's true of the church. It's true of people. Well, good people anyways. And it's true of relationships.

We're simply reforming our relationship.

"I quit my job last week," I mutter.

He slams his beer onto the counter behind him. "You quit your job. You're going on a surf trip alone. What else haven't you been telling me?"

His anger is ripping open a wound I thought had scabbed over last week.

It hasn't.

Although I've broken nearly every rule, I refuse to break rule #1.

He was the one who wrote it when he asked me to swear to always be totally, absolutely, completely, brutally honest with him. Before our very first surf together, we sat in the front seats of his broken-down, dingy white VW bug at the top of the Huntington Cliffs to check out the surf, when he turned to me and made me promise.

I close my eyes as I try to be as honest as possible without sacrificing my already damaged heart. "I'm going with Occy."

"Occy? Occy!"

He begins pacing back and forth in the kitchen, muttering Occy's name under his breath. "You're going away with Occy. What the hell, Charlie?"

"I need a bre—"

He stops and points at me.

"You're the one who made the Rule Book, Charlie. Remember? Poe Friends and all that shit. And now you'rE breaking all sorts of rules like there won't be any repercussions?

Like nothing's gonna change, and it's not the first time you've done it either. If it were the first time, I could overlook it, but it's not."

I slam my beer down next to his. "What Rules?"

My frustration is starting to rival his.

"I'm not having this conversation, Charlie. I'm done." He shrugs. "I can't do this anymore."

"Fine with me, I didn't want you over here in the first place," I shout.

He walks two steps towards the back door, then turns back to add one more stab to my already pulverized heart. "You know, Charlie, this is the most screwed-0up relationship ever. I mean what kind of relationship has a fucking Rule Book?"

He storms out the back door and down the beach.

This is exactly why I wanted to leave. It's gotten so bad between us we can't even be in the same room without shouting and purposely hurting each other.

What Rules did I break?

Besides the Half-Foot Rule that he's also broken too many times to count this year.

How about we talk about his kissing me in Maui? And falling asleep next to me shirtless in Santa Barbara. And all the flirty texts and looks he's given me over the past few months.

And let's not forget the whole Poker Night spectacle. He was not innocent in that. It takes two to tango.

So now he's pissed at me for trying to put some distance between us so we can hopefully salvage what little remains of this friendship before we have nothing left?

I think that will be my next rule. Rule # 72: When both parties have done a shit job of holding up the rules, and all Hell has broken loose, both parties shall give each other a sufficient amount of time to reset the friendship, so everyone can go back to following the rules.

I'm invoking Rule #72 right now.

I taking a Grey break.

# 34

## CHARLIE

*O*utside!" Occy paddles towards a massive wave cresting farther out than the set waves have been breaking. The Hawaiian gods have been blessing us with clean, head-high waves all morning. A few puffy clouds hang above Moloka'i at the far reach of the aqua-blue waters of Honolua Bay.

I pull my surfboard under me and paddle furiously.

Occy's a faster paddler than me so he makes it out in time to swing his board around and take off on a monster ten-foot wave. That's ten-foot on the California scale. Ten-foot Hawaiian is nearly double that and way too intense for me.

I watch as the peak of the wave crashes down on the water right in front of me. I place my hands on either side of my rail and extend my arms forward to shove the nose of my board under the surface of the water. I take a breath and follow the course of the board, pushing the tail down with my foot when we are fully submerged to bring me back to the surface once the power of the wave has passed.

I open my eyes, looking for the next wave. It's fifteen feet ahead of me and coming in fast. This one, however, I am close enough to pick off. I take three strokes towards it, knowing exactly the spot to catch it. I swing my board around, push the tail deeper in the water, and let it pop out beneath me, propelling me forward. With three strong paddles, the wave slides under me, driving me forward.

The moment I feel that push, I pop to my feet and begin pumping down the line. The lip in front of me promises to spill over as I tuck beneath it and drag my hand on the face to slow down.

As the wave wraps over me, I begin pumping furiously again to gain enough speed to get out of the barrel. The wave spits me out and I sail over the shoulder. Occy and his mate, Jax, pump their fists and hoot in celebration for me as they paddle back out to the lineup.

I ride the momentum of that wave until it releases me and my board sinks. Laying down on my board again, I begin paddling back out behind the boys, joy exploding in my chest.

*This.*

This is exactly what I needed.

In the lineup, there's none of that boy-girl nonsense. Just waves. Waves I understand. They're constrained by physics to always follow the rules. Everything else in this world refuses to play nicely. Which is why I took a break. A work break. A Bex break. A Grey break.

The only things I need are sunshine, saltwater, and fish tacos.

I sit on my board in the lineup. "You guys see that one?"

Occy and Jax are too busy chatting up a girl who's joined us in the lineup. Her dark hair has been lightened by the powerful Maui sun to almost white. It lays damp in perfect waves down her back. She is in fantastic shape, probably from all the surfing. She has the body I wish I would have earned with all my surfing if it wasn't for all the extra calories I have to stuff down my throat when I'm low.

She sits in a tiny, hot pink bikini atop a board painted with neon flowers and waves. While she scans the horizon for another wave, Jax paddles up behind her and tosses her off her board. She splashes him playfully and climbs back on her board while the boys watch intently. So much for none of that boy-girl nonsense.

When she looks my way, I give her a friendly nod. It's not as unusual as it used to be to see another girl in the lineup—it would sometimes be a year between surfer girl sightings—but we're still in the minority, so girls tend to support each other out here.

When she sends a nod back, Occy finally notices me. He points over his shoulder to my new friend. "Charlie, this is Billie."

Occy told me Billy would be joining us, I just didn't realize Billy was a her. "Oh. Billie, I.E.," I laugh. "How's it?"

"Hey, Charlie I.E," she calls over her shoulder as she takes off on a good-sized wave.

At least she can hold her own out here.

As we all shower off after another hour of perfect waves, I relive one of the best waves of my life while fresh water pours over my crispy skin.

"I'm hosting Game Night tonight. You guys are coming, right?" Billie's voice pulls me out of my reverie.

*Game night?* I haven't played board games on a Friday Night since junior high, but who am I to complain? I turn off the shower and grab my towel. "I'm down."

Occy takes my spot in the showers. Jax bumps Billie's hip, stealing the shower from her. She stares him down. "You were done. Weren't you?" Jax laughs.

Billie and I take advantage of the show going on in front of us. Jax tips his head back under the water letting it stream over his broad shoulders and powerful chest. His trunks ride perfectly low on his hips, showcasing the oh-so-desirable V in his hips. He turns and scrubs his hands over his short brown hair, flicking water on Billie as he does.

Occy is narrower but muscular. He runs his hands along his wavy blond hair pushing water through it before rubbing the salt off his shoulders and chest. "As long as we're playing strip poker, I guess I could be convinced," he mutters under the water.

Jax turns off the water. "Not gonna happen, Occy."

Jax being so overprotective of Billie reminds me of...

*Grey Break, Charlie.*

"Can we do food first? I'm starving." Starving can sometimes mean a low coming on, so I check Dex. A solid 135. Not bad for three hours in the water.

Billie points to Jax. "Ryder was going to grill up some yellowfin for fish tacos. We just need to stop by the store on our way."

With everyone rinsed off, we walk towards the parking lot.

"Ryder?" I ask Billie about the nickname.

"Ryder's his first name. Jax is his last. Everyone in his unit called him Jax, so it's what most people call him now, which is silly, cause he's way more of a Ryder."

Jax unlocks his army green 4Runner and I grab my clothes. After wrapping a towel around my waist, I slip out of my bikini, throwing on a pair of dry trunks instead. I'll wait till my top dries before I throw on my grey ringer shirt that says "Have a Crummy Day" in faded white letters. It's soft on my skin which is perfect after a full day in the salt and sun.

The boys don't bother changing, out here their trunks are already dry before we get back to the car.

Billie wraps a cotton candy pink skirt around her waist and tops it off with a lightweight, cream-colored button-down shirt. She leaves it unbuttoned over her bikini top. She runs some product through her wavy hair, using her towel to take out more moisture.

I frown at my solid brown trunks and the dingy, grey shirt in my hand. I've worn a pair of trunks just like these for the last three days. My hair, when it dries out here is a mess of half waves and half fluff, so I've been throwing it back in a sloppy bun.

Billie took the same amount of time to get ready as I did, but she's beautiful.

"Charlie's coming with me," Billie calls to the boys.

On the drive to Kihei, she fills me in on who will be joining us tonight. Piper works with her at Kaulike Hanai and grew up with her in Kihei. She'll be bringing her husband, Riley, who is a high school science teacher. JJ is a local cop and a huge football fan. He's originally from New Jersey, which explains the football thing. Finn is a real estate tycoon according to Billie and can be super quiet, but is hilarious once he gets a few beers in him.

"So is your place near here?" I ask.

"It is, but we do Game Night at Ryder's place."

"You host it at his place? So are you two...?" I wag my brows at her suggestively.

"No." She laughs. "We're just friends."

"I have one of those." Or, maybe, *had* is a better word.

Billie pulls into the parking lot of the Times Supermarket.

"I'm confused. Why do you host game night if it's at his place?"

"When you see his place, you won't be confused."

We hop out and meet the boys at the front door where Billie hands out our assignments like a troop leader getting her men ready for battle.

"Charlie, corn tortillas. Corn. Don't even touch the flour ones. Ryder, you're on cabbage and veggies for guac. Occy? Beer. Lots. Variety. Grab a cider, too. And stay away from the pissy domestics. I'll grab everything else. Meet up front in five."

I half expected her to make us put our hands in and call out a cheer on the count of three.

I wander around the store until I find the tortilla shelves on the back end cap of the last aisle and grab two packs of corn tortillas. Ryder stands in the middle of the produce section with a basket full of veggies. Billie gave him the hardest assignment. He's studying avocado after avocado. "I have no idea why Billie had me do this. She knows I can't pick a ripe avocado to save my life."

"You need some help," I offer.

Clang!

I whip my head towards the direction of the sound. A stack of metal crates that were stacked to the ceiling, now lay scattered on the floor. Next to them, a young boy dressed only in red trunks surrounded by hundreds of kiwis, mangoes, and blackberries.

He picks up a mango and holds it up to his mom. "I got it, mommy."

He squishes his way through the fruit to his mom who

sweeps him up in her arms and scurries off before an employee can see who caused the mess.

Hoping for someone to laugh with, I turn to Jax, but his face is far from amused. It is full of fear and fury.

He is scanning the produce section, eyes shifting from fruit to fruit, head swiveling from vegetable to vegetable.

I scan the store for the threat, but I am getting the feeling it's one I won't be able to see.

Jax's left hand holds an avocado against his chest, his right fixed on top, like a pitcher on the mound getting ready to wind up.

"Jax, you good?" I ask quietly.

He startles, then looks at me like he's seeing me for the first time. "Fine," he says sharply, then turns on his heels and bolts out the front door.

I've seen that look before. Greyson wore the same one the first time he had a panic attack. It freaked me out when I saw it—I had no idea what it was—but now, I've seen enough of them, and read everything I could on the subject, I am fairly certain that's what's going on.

Needing to make sure he's okay, I toss the tortillas in his basket and follow his path out the front door.

Outside, I find him sitting on a picnic table in front of the store, hunched over, staring at the avocado still in his hand, his thumb wrapped so tightly around the fruit it is pressing a divot into the thick green skin.

"Jax?" I ask softly, not wanting to jar him. "You mind if I sit?"

He nods, not pulling his eyes from the avo.

I know he's the expert on this. He doesn't need me to tell him anything. So I sit next to him in silence and wait.

I wait as he stops being an owl, looking every which way.

I wait as he struggles to slow his body down.

A breeze brings the scent of hibiscus our way. A '68 Chevy Chevelle piled high with surfboards glides into a parking spot. A half-dozen beach boys squeeze out like clowns from a clown car.

Hiss breathing steadies.

A group of teens rolls out of the store, hands filled with six-packs they had to have used a fake ID for.

Jax tips his eyes up to study me.

I hold up my hand with my thumb and finger touching. "Can I grab that?"

I slide an invisible pin into the avocado opposite the trigger he has trapped down and he releases his 'citrus' grenade.

I place it next to me on the chipping orange paint of the picnic table.

After a few moments, his gaze falls. He kicks at a Hawai'i Nui Brewing bottle cap on the faded asphalt.

"How many tours?" I ask quietly.

"Enough to send me back home with PTSD." He manages a sad laugh. "You don't look surprised by it. You familiar?"

I bite my tongue at his use of PTSD, but who am I to tell him what to call it? It's his after all.

"My friend, Greyson. He's a firefighter. Had a bad call a few years back. We were introduced to PTS then and learned to deal with it together."

"You two sound close." He picks at a callous on his hand. "You said he was just a friend?"

"Yeah."

He looks up at me as he struggles to ask, "Was the PTSD a deal-breaker for you?"

It breaks my heart to think Billie wouldn't love him because he has to deal with this. I turn to face him, to make sure he hears. "PTS never stopped me from loving him."

His confusion shows. "You keep missing the 'D."

"The D is a liar."

"What?" He laughs as if I'm crazy.

"The D, it puts the onus on you."

He's still not getting it. "D. Disorder, like it's a problem inside of you. Take away the D and it becomes the stress' fault, not yours."

He contemplates my silly theory for a moment. "Huh. It does make a difference."

A devilish grin radiates across his face. "So are we just gonna fly past the fact that you said you love your best friend?"

*Fuckaroo. Did I actually say that?*

*PTS never stopped me from loving him.*

Where'd that come from?

"You guys done? The Commander told us to meet up front," Occy jokes.

"I just needed some fresh air really quick," I say. "I can run back in and check out."

I leave Jax with Occy and Billie to finish our shopping. I grab Jax's basket from beside the avocados and make my way to the checkout as guilt begins to fill my chest.

I hope Grey hasn't had to ward off any panic attacks while I've been gone. He'd call me, wouldn't he?

I slide my hand in my pocket for my phone but pause when I hear his words in my head.

*This is the most screwed-up relationship ever. I can't do this anymore.*

He didn't mean that. He couldn't have meant that. He--

"You ready, Miss?"

It takes me a second to figure out where I am. I silently set my basket on the conveyor belt, not capable of moving my mouth under the weight of those words. I pay and gather my bags.

When the doors open and usher in the comforting aroma of guava and pineapple, I pull myself back into the present.

I am here now. I am not going to let something back home ruin one minute of this for me.

# 35

## CHARLIE

The sun is setting as we push through the side gate of a two-story Hawaiian bungalow. As we step out into the back yard the view opens up.

Jax lives on the water. His backyard is a Hawaiian beach.

Hawaiian.

Beach.

Sure you have to step down two whole stairs to put your feet in the sand, but the warm Maui water is only ten feet beyond.

That tops even my own living Nirvana.

A tan and ripped morsel of a man, covered in only low-slung trunks, is building a fire in the fire pit surrounded by weathered Adirondack chairs painted all the sunny colors of Maui; peaceful pink, sunny mango, joyous green, and an aqua rivaling the color of Grey's eyes.

"That's Finn. I'll introduce you two later. You can set the food down in the kitchen in here." Billie points to the faded, emerald-green house.

She leads me through the back door into a house matching every fantasy of the island house I will one day own. Soaring wood-framed ceilings, Brazilian walnut floors, and windows everywhere hold up the traditions of island living. A small living room looks out over the backyard, bordered by a bright kitchen that must have been designed by a world-class chef. Jax must know how to cook, or I may not believe in the fair hand of God any longer.

"This place is amazing, Billie. How have you not moved in and refused to leave?" I begin pulling the food out of the bags and setting it on the granite-topped island.

"Ryder is way too meticulous. I would drive him crazy." She hands me a small bowl for my guacamole, then pulls out a cutting board and knife without hesitation, like she designed the kitchen herself.

I begin peeling and coring the avocados. Billie goes to work on the block of aged cheddar.

Jax joins us, reaching for a chunk of cheese from her pile.

She taps his hand with the side of the knife. "Patience, RyGuy."

He shoots her a huge grin. "I can wait."

His words feel loaded with something that flies right past Billie.

She pours some gluten-free crackers onto a serving dish and lays the cheese slices next to them. Think I'll be skipping those. She lifts the platter and makes her way to the backyard.

I throw the cilantro and onions in the bowl and begin working on a tomato. "Jax, can I ask you something?"

"Fire away," he says leaning a hip against the island.

"You asked me if Greyson's PTS kept me from loving him." I swipe the diced tomatoes from the cutting board into the bowl. "Do you think that's what's keeping you and Billie apart?"

He laughs. "No. She's actually great about it." His smile falls a bit. "But we're just friends."

I laugh. "I know that phrase all too well."

Jax's gaze swings to JJ who just came through the door and his smile evaporates completely. JJ wraps his arms around Billie's waist as she passes by. She spins and kisses him.

I bump Jax's shoulder. "I know that all too well, too."

He studies my face. "It's no-"

I finish his sentence. "Not like that with you guys? Sure, it isn't."

His brow furrows.

"Don't worry. I won't say a thing. I know how delicate those things can be."

His shoulders relax. "Weird question, but what did you do with the... uhh..." he holds up his hand in an avocado shape.

I motion to the guacamole in front of me. "You sure know how to pick a perfectly ripe grenade."

He smiles. "I've had lots of practice."

Billie brings over another couple and introduces them as Piper and Riley.

"So, Billie tells me you work in tech. What do you do?" Piper asks.

"Right now? Nothing." A wave of pride washes over me remembering how I went out. "But, I was a programmer at Big&Slime for a couple of years before I quit."

"Why'd you leave?" Riley asks.

"It was a nightmare working with those guys. Just a sexual harassment lawsuit waiting to happen." I turn to Piper. "You work in tech, right? It's like that where you work."

"I've worked in a few places like that before."

"They harassed you?" Riley is getting heated. "Did any of those guys touch you?"

"A few of them would do totally inappropriate things, but no one touched me. You think I'd let anyone do that?" She lays her hand on his arm to allay his fears. "After working at a few bad companies, I wanted to build one that wouldn't be like that at all."

"So you only hire girls?" I ask.

Billie grabs a pile of warm tortillas from the oven. "The fish won't eat itself," she says as she makes her way outside.

Jax and Riley don't need to be asked twice. They are out the door in seconds.

I snag the guacamole and Piper takes the bag of chips from the counter as she continues. "If we did that, we'd be just as bad as the brogrammer frat house. I hired people based on their coding skills and their interpersonal skills. I want every person to be a part of the team."

We slip into the backyard. The ice-blue water laps against the sand as the sun rushes below the horizon.

Finn sets a platter of yellowtail on the live-edged koa wood table on the back porch. Piper, Billie, and I follow suit, laying down our offerings next to bowls of cabbage, white sauce, and shredded Monterey Jack, Cheddar, and Asadero cheese.

We all sink into chairs around the table and serve up our feast. I make sure to sit next to Piper so we can continue chatting. "How can you be sure they didn't just put on a good face in the interview?"

"Before I hire anyone, I get to know them first. We go surfing. We do a ropes course. We go to get drinks. And I see them respond to all these situations before I hire them." She picks up a piece of fish and lays it on a tortilla on her plate.

"Then I take the top five candidates and give them a twenty-four-hour team coding challenge and watch everything they do. I pick the person who brings the skills and talents and personality traits we're missing."

I take my first bite of freshly caught fish taco. The fish is so perfectly cooked, falling apart in my mouth, and impeccably balanced by the spice of the white sauce and the sweetness of the grenade guacamole.

I remember to finish chewing before I speak. "Do you still end up with people who are so good at what they do they start to get arrogant and demanding once they move up the ladder?"

"There's not a ladder at Kaulike Hanai. Everyone's on equal footing."

"Does that work?"

"Really, damned well, actually. Everyone has a chance to solve any problem we have even if they aren't in that division. At our weekly strategy meetings, everyone is in the room. From the night janitor to the CEO, well, me. Anyone who has a problem they can't fix shares it. Then we go to the question round where people ask follow-up questions. Sometimes those questions are what spur us to think differently and find the solution."

She pauses to take a sip of her white wine before continuing. "Can't figure out why your marketing isn't hitting? You ask everyone. Can't figure out how to get gum out of the carpet? You ask everyone. The knowledge of the collective is always better."

So, places like that actually do exist. I so badly want to be a part of that. "It sounds like heaven."

"It's not perfect yet, but I like going to work each day. And I love what we've been able to make."

Piper's phone blares the Clash's *Should I Stay or Should I Go* and she and Riley both hang their heads before she steps away from the table to answer.

When she returns, she says sadly, "That's Sperry."

Everyone must know what that means because they all stand to say their goodbyes.

I look to Billie to fill me in. "Sperry's their nine-month-old."

Piper gives me a tight hug and says, "I'd love to see what you're working on when you're ready for it."

"That would be great, actually. Thanks."

After Piper and Riley begrudgingly leave early, we sink into the Adirondack chairs surrounded by the smell of kiawe wood on the fire as Billie orchestrates a game of Two Truths and a Lie.

I learn Finn lived in his van for a whole year and used to own a pet cricket, a perfect pet if you live in a van.

Ryder always uses fake names in restaurants and wore the same red hoodie every day of seventh grade, which made a lot more sense when he shared that was his dad's before he died.

And I'm convinced Billie has got to be my new best friend. She is so incredibly happy and positive. The meanest thing I heard her say was how much she hated the color red.

When it's JJ's turn, I decide JJ most certainly wrote a play senior year of high school about a war between hard-boiled eggs and bacon while the sausages tried to be Switzerland and almost died from an allergic reaction to a banana slug he was dared to eat. There's no way he hasn't ever sung karyoke.

While everyone else deliberates, take a moment to myself. I am among interesting people who aren't trying to make me into someone else, crystal clear water whose warmth calls out to me even at night, waves that could keep me entertained for centuries, and fresh, healthy food everywhere.

Maui has everything I need.

Almost.

Maui has almost everything I need.

On my last night here, we plan to have dinner at a local pub. Occy and I follow Jax and Finn through Billie's front door without even a knock. It's a small board-and-batten-style shack with light yellow walls and a deep, comfortable couch that is perfectly designed for a post-surf afternoon nap.

"You ladies ready?" Jax calls to the other room.

Only the sound of giggles and laughter returns.

Occy nudges me. "You're a girl. Go check on them."

For the first time ever, I don't mind being grouped in with the girls. Billie and Piper don't act like the girls back home who are obsessed with their looks and in constant battle with each other for the nearest man's attention. They are beautiful without putting much effort into it. Two girls, who, like me, are rugged and bold and strong, and, yet, have found sweet, kind men who love them anyway.

It gives me hope that, as a girl who isn't a size double zero with a closet full of the latest designer clothes, one who would rather be in the ocean than a mall any day of the week, can still be seen by a guy as feminine, as worthy of pursuit.

I round the corner to find Billie and Piper in beautiful sundresses. Studying my blue and white striped trunks and white tee, I am so underdressed.

I've always thought clothes were a waste of decision-making brainpower. As long as all the right parts are covered, I didn't care what I put on. Unless it's a day that demands my Ren and Stimpy shirt.

But I'm beginning to think it's not an either-or kind of situation.

I've only known Billie for a couple of days, but she reads me pretty well. "You want to borrow something?"

Her question doesn't sound judgmental or passive-aggressive like when Bex says it. It's sweet.

"Sure, but I don't really know what," I admit.

I don't want to be wearing my own clothes, but every time I borrow clothes I feel like I'm playing dress-up.

"What are you in the mood for? A dress? Skirt?" Piper asks.

"I have no idea." The two ladies in front of me are so impressive, I hate to admit it, but I do. "I have absolutely zero style sense."

Billie pulls a sleeveless white dress made of lace over a solid white slip from her closet and holds it up to me. "This will make you feel sexy."

I don't hate it. It's pretty and fun, but it feels like me. A me I haven't met until now, but me all the same.

I hop out of my trunks and slip the dress over my head. It's soft and light against my skin. And I instantly feel more confident.

Billie digs through her jewelry box. "Let's add a little color." She holds up a few bracelets and necklaces for me to choose from.

I pull the one with bright orange string wrapped around a silver wave charm and slip it on my wrist.

Billie laughs. "You can wear more than one, you know."

I pull a few more and slide them on.

Piper holds out two closed fists for me to choose from. I tap her right hand. She flips it over to reveal a fistful of silver jewelry, one ring with an aqua turtle on it, and a matching pair of earrings.

Slipping them in my ears, I study myself in the mirror. I'm not sure I could have found a more perfect outfit. I'm almost... sexy.

And I definitely feel sexier. I wonder if acting like I was a sex goddess for Indigo's short has somehow rubbed off on me.

"Thank you so much. I wish I had your style. You think I could borrow it for a while?"

"Style isn't something you can borrow or even buy," Billie says. "It's about finding things that speak to you. Where you can say, "This makes me feel like my strong, amazing self, but an even shinier, happier version of myself."

I love how these girls view femininity. They see tough as beautiful. Not some skinny, size double zero, blond dummy.

Their beauty comes from knowing themselves and taking charge of their sexuality. A sexy woman is a woman who knows what she wants, not an emaciated robot who fits into whatever stereotype society has deemed beautiful that year.

"You should tell that to the girls back home. They are killing themselves trying to buy the latest whatever." I think back to how many times I have found Bex crying over her credit card bills after mortgaging her soul to buy boots she swore would secure her next boyfriend or a cut and color costing more than my rent for the month.

"It's not about fitting into some mold," Piper continues where Billie left off. "Expressing yourself through the things you wear is like another way of producing art. You have to wear things that bring you joy and declare on the outside what you already are on the inside."

I've never thought of style like that. I just knew I hated the pressure to fit into the box, so I refused to do it. I never knew I could create my own box and decorate it any way I wanted.

I hear Bex's rules in my head. *Fashion is about more than the bare necessities needed to cover your jubblies and jay-jay. It's about the extras, the flourishes. The bracelets, earrings, shoes that showcase what you have. Show it off.*

Her rules weren't wrong. Her hardware was. I can find pieces I feel confident in, that are totally me, and still follow the rules.

These girls have totally figured out how to do that and being around them has helped me figure out how to do it, too. To find the items that make my outsides match my insides so I can advertise the amazing mint-n-chip ice cream I have inside and the right guy, the one who loves mint-n-chip ice cream, will know he wants to bring me home.

"So, you're a big Jimmy Buffett fan?" Finn says as he jumps over a lava rock submerged in the sand. I think it's the first thing I've heard him say all night.

My last night in Maui, we all stroll along Ho'okipa Beach after we finished dinner at Mama's Fish house.

"What makes you say that?" I stall.

Either this guy has the strangest pick-up lines I've ever heard, or all his silence is really a decoy while he secretly delves deeply into the minds of the people around him.

"You were singing *I Have Found Me a Home* under your breath as we left."

Thank God he wasn't really reading my mind. I didn't want to have to explain my ever-growing list of Occy's shortcomings I was adding to during dinner.

"I may be a bit of a fan, but not in that over-the-top, only-know-his-worst-songs, buy-an-RV-decked-out-in-tropical-kitsch-and-get-so-wasted-in-the-parking-lot-so-I-don't-ever-make-it-inside-the-concert-arena kind of—"

"Swimming," Occy shouts like a four-year-old seeing the ocean for the first time. "Swimming. Now. Everyone."

And my Occy-Fault list grows.

He kicks off his flip flops, pulls his neon green leopard print shirt over his head, and sprints to the water's edge, leaping into the water with a belly flop.

Finn shrugs, defeated. He knows there's no arguing with four-year-old Occy. Jax, JJ, and Billie race to the water, now warmer than the air around us.

I may have felt sexier tonight than I ever have before, but that doesn't mean I'm ready to strip down to my skivvies in front of a group of near strangers. Instead, I meander towards Piper who is still on the sand, hoping I won't be the only party pooper.

Just as I approach, Piper sheds her skirt and top, revealing a huge beige bra and white briefs. "Aww, crab."

She glances left and right, then reaches down her bra and pulls out two round pads, and tosses them in her bundled-up shirt.

I raise my brows looking for an explanation.

"Nursing pads. When I'm not around Sperry, I still let down."

Well, shit. If Piper is bold enough to strip down to a beige nursing bra, complete with nursing pads, why am I letting my hang-ups keep me from enjoying the water?

I pull my dress over my head, fold it neatly, and lay it gingerly on my sandals before strutting to the water and diving in.

When I pop my head up in the shoulder-deep water, Occy wraps his arms around my waist. "It's about time. I was getting lonely in here."

"You know what they say about distance," I reply.

"Huh?" His eyes drop to my mouth. He's clearly more interested in kissing me than figuring out my reference, so he pulls me closer and does just that.

Occy is an exceptional kisser. He's so good, he could do it for a living. Great pace. Perfect pressure. Tangling his fingers in my hair.

But it's... missing something. Or maybe I'm missing something. That kiss won't drive me to push him against a wall, to cage him in, to slide my hands along his sides, and turn this into a full-body kiss.

It's a really good kiss, but it isn't...

"Wait till you get her back to the Ohana, dude. We don't want to see that," Jax shouts.

When we get back to the car, there are only two towels.

"Maybe you should have planned this a little better, Occy," Jax points out, handing the towels to me and Piper. Drying off quickly, I pass the towel on to Billie.

Before he is even dry, Occy starts bouncing like a small child. "Let's go hit Ambrosia. It's our last night here. I want to go big."

I've noticed in the last few days Occy needs to constantly be doing something. Keeping up with him has worn me out. When Grey and I grab tacos at a restaurant with a view, we sit for hours, drinking soda, eating chips, and talking. Occy sits only as long as it takes him to eat, and then we are off to do something else.

After two three-hour surf sessions today in waves at the outer edge of my ability, and a night out at the pub, the only thing I want to go big on is sleep. I desperately want to crawl into soft blankets surrounded by cool air from the A/C and drift off to sleep.

"Would it be a total bummer if I went back to Finn's? You guys should still go out, though."

"I'm starting to fade, too. I'm gonna pull the parent card and head home," Piper chimes in.

"You sure? It'll be epic." I don't know if Occy persists because he actually wants me there or if he's just reassuring himself he tried so he can party without remorse.

In my jammies and snuggled in bed, I scroll through the photos on my phone and find one of Timmy the Turtle.

While we were snorkeling the second day here, Timmy swam right up to me and stared at me for the longest time. I swear he then tipped his head for me to follow him before he lazily drifted towards the rocks at the end of the bay. I swam with him the whole way.

At the rocks, he lurched ahead to capture a fish in his beak before turning to show me his prized possession. I know turtles can't actually smile, but I swear he was smiling as he showed off his lunch.

I hit the share button on the pic to text it to Grey, but when I start to type, all I can think about is hearing him say, "I can't do this anymore."

I shut off my phone and try to ignore the churning in my stomach that's been building all day with the growing recognition my official Grey Break ends tomorrow, and I still don't know if the unofficial—and possibly permanent—Grey Break will take its place.

# 36

## GREYSON

*I* spent the first two weeks of Charlie's abandonment getting pissed. Pissed at her. Pissed at me. Pissed at the sweet lady next door for feeding the birds and encouraging them to sing at six in the morning.

Not too proud of that one, but grateful for it because it shook me out of my rage.

I spent the next two weeks trying to figure out how to fix us. I let things go so far it didn't matter if I was trying to pursue Charlie or trying to abide by her Rule Book, I would overreact to everything and cause even more friction. Then I'd pick a fight to release that frustration.

I pursued her and it made things bad. Or, as Charlie says, baaaaaaaaad.

I stopped pursuing her and it made things worse.

I've come to realize all the fighting and friction weren't from what I was doing or not doing. It was simply a result of not being the right guy for her. And she deserves to have the right guy. If that means I need to back off to let her make room in her life for the right guy, then that's exactly what I'll do.

As if she could sense I decided this, a picture of the proudest green sea turtle with a fish hanging out of his mouth flashes on my phone.

**Charlie: I'd love to tell you the story of my new friend, Timmy.**

**Greyson: Is that real? Turtles can't smile, can they?**

**Charlie: Meet me at Kealani's in ten and I'll tell you.**

**Greyson: I'd love to.**

When Charlie breezes through the door of Kealani's, she's wearing old jeans and a t-shirt, her hair in a ponytail. Even super casual, she is gorgeous. She leans into the counter and chats with Asa for a few minutes. There's a little of Flirty Charlie in there and she seems to enjoy the attention she's garnered from him. Maui has been good to her. She has a confidence I've never seen on her before.

Grabbing her cup from the counter, she turns and waves to me before filling it up. I can't pull my eyes from her as she bounces in anticipation of the caffeine hit or as she strides across the restaurant to slide into the booth across from me.

"Hi," I say, still gawking at her like a dumbass.

"Hi."

Our server, Asa, appears with two plates. He sets the steak in front of me and the other in front of Charlie. It's rare Kealani's screws up an order, but there's fish on that plate. I catch Asa before he leaves.

"Hey, I think this may be wrong. She didn't order fish."

Charlie waves me off. "It's fine, Asa. Thank you."

"It's not a problem Charlie. You can return it. I'm sure Asa will be more than happy to make you another if it gives him a chance to come flirt with you again," I say, caring a little too much about the way Asa glanced at the picture of a wave across her chest.

*Way to make space for another guy, Steele. Two seconds in and you're failing.*

"I ordered this, Grey."

"That's fish."

"I know what fish looks like, Grey. I eat it now."

"What happened to you over there? Flirting with Asa. Eating fish. What's next? You're gonna tell me you got a—"

She steps into my words. "Got a what? Sex change into a girl? News flash, Grey. I've been a girl this whole time."

"I didn't mean... I know you're a girl, Charlie." My voice trails off, "Believe me."

She stares out the window. With her hair up, her newly tanned neck calls out for me to plant kisses all along it.

Shit. Why can't she ever look bad?

Fiddling with my phone to escape the awkwardness, I spin it around towards her, her turtle pic now my wallpaper. "You want to tell me about this little guy?"

She offers me a hesitant smile that immediately turns real when she sees the pic of Timmy. "You made that your wallpaper?"

"It reminds me of you. So spill. Can turtles really smile?"

She skewers some fish and takes a bite. So weird to see her do that.

"I'm not sure if all of them can, but Timmy definitely can. He invited me to lunch and when he caught a fish, he turned to show it to me with the proudest smile I've ever seen."

It must rival the smile Charlie has on right now.

"Did you get any good waves?"

"Every. Single. Day. Occy knew these totally secluded breaks with no one around. It was amazing."

"Occy." I push some rice around on my plate afraid to meet her eyes. "You two a thing now?"

I look up to scan her face for a reaction.

She quickly shoves another bite of fish in her mouth like she's trying to buy time to decide if she wants to tell me. "Occy's nice and so much fun. He can make the most boring thing a total blast."

I dig my teeth into my bottom lip, willing myself not to say something mean. "So... nice and fun? That's it? Not the man of your dreams?"

"Well, he is freakin' hot. Like Greek God hot."

Maybe she thought my question was the green light to talk to me like a girlfriend or something because it all comes out in horrifying detail.

"Two weeks of seeing him in nothing more than trunks?

Damn. Even if I'm not madly in love with him, it sure would be fun to take a ride."

It's too much to hear her gush about that Vegemite-eater. I swipe my cup from the table and stomp over to the machine to refill it.

When I return, she's back to wearing a very different smile, one filling her eyes with spite.

"Sorry, Greyson. Was I being too girly for you?" she snarls.

Before I spit out something nasty, I pause.

I asked. I asked about Occy, and now I'm angry she answered? *Space, Steele. She needs space for the right guy.*

My anger reigned in, I try to smooth things over. "It's just weird, hearing you talk like that. You don't usually talk about guys like that."

"That's because if I ever showed even the slightest interest in a guy, you'd laugh it off or find some way to undermine me. So I stopped telling you that stuff ages ago."

"Well, maybe I don't want to hear about your love life."

"Oh, like I want to hear about all your escapades. The girls you think are dumb as a snail but you still have plenty of fun with? The girl who knew exactly how you wanted to be kissed. The girl who went crazy when you kissed the inside of her elbow. Do you think I want to be regaled with stories of your conquests?"

She still sees me as that guy. "When was the last time I told you a story like that?"

"Only because you've had a dry spell." She takes a triumphant sip of her soda.

*That wasn't a dry spell, babe. It was a choice.*

A choice she inspired.

"I sat and listened to your stories for years, Grey because I care. The least you could do is give me the same courtesy."

*The difference is, it kills me to hear about your dates. You couldn't care less when I share mine.*

I rake my hands through my hair. This is too hard. Creating space for her to fall for another guy is too hard. It's worse than the fighting.

But... I have to do better.

Be better.

Think about what she needs.

I draw in a long breath and say with a sigh, "You're right."

She scans the room for someone to tell her they, too, heard what I admitted, but there are no witnesses. The place is empty. "I'm right?"

I unfurl my fists under the table and wipe them on my jeans. "Yeah. You're right. I'm sorry."

And just in case she doesn't believe me, I pull out all the stops. "Look. To prove it, let's go on a double date."

"What?"

"I'll show you how okay I am. You and me and Occy and Brittany. What do you think?"

*Please say no. Please say no. Please say-*

"Okay. Sounds fun. Thanks, Grey."

*Shit.*

What did I just sign up for? I couldn't hold my shit together when she was merely talking about Occy. Now I have to sit across the table from him for an entire night without beating the shit out of the dude as he holds her and flirts with her and kis-

*Fuck.*

New Rule.

Rule #23. Greyson must think before he speaks.

# 37

## CHARLIE

The June gloom has hidden the waves from sight this morning, but not the sound of water dumping onto itself, starting from one end of the beach and moving steadily to the other. It sounds fun out there, but I may wait for the sun to peek out a little later; I need some time to figure out how I got roped into another double date.

After so many terrible double dates orchestrated by Bex, I promised myself I would never go on another one, but Greyson looked so sweet trying to make up for freaking out when I told him about Occy.

I mean, what kind of monster would I be if I didn't agree when he was so genuinely sorry?

I hate to say it, but I'm actually a little excited to go. It might be fun.

As long as Grey doesn't go all caveman on Occy. Most of the time I don't mind him scaring off the losers who try to hit on me, but Occy's not that bad.

I strain to see the waves while leaning on the splintery railing as Indigo's words roll over and over in my mind like the waves gearing up for me to play on later. *Greyson is standing in the way of you pursuing a romantic relationship, but not in the way you're thinking.*

How else could he be standing in the way of a relationship besides scaring guys off? I wish Indigo would simply come out and tell me what the hell she meant instead of talking in riddles.

I pick at a four-inch sliver of wood arched away from the rest of the railing.

Or maybe Bex was right? She has known me for longer than Indigo has. And she's known Greyson, too. It's possible he stood in the way of me finding someone and I was just too close to realize it. It has to say something that the first real relationship I've had in forever was when Grey was not around.

My phone rings out with another Jimmy Buffett ringtone.

Though we ended on good terms, it still feels unsettled between Grey and I, and I'm not sure I can take round two of a fight. I would so rather be going for the type of round two Indigo's got going on upstairs.

Right before Jimmy stops crooning, I pick up the phone and the memory of our tiff yesterday hits me like an eighty-foot wave at Jaws so that I can barely breathe out, "Hey."

After a torturous pause, I hear a quiet, "Hi."

I wait for him to fill in the empty cavern between us. He is the one who called after all.

"Charlie, are we good? I am really sorry. You have every right to tell me about your love life. I don't know why I overreacted."

I still can't figure out what happened. He asked about Occy. I was just answering his question.

"You did overreact, didn't you?" I say with a laugh as I sit down on the steps leading to the beach and bury my toes under the fine grains of sand.

"I think overreacted is a little strong. It's more like I had an unbalanced reaction."

That's the part that has confused me the most. Greyson has always been the most level-headed person I know. To the world, he can be gregarious and unpredictable, but with me, I can always depend on him being a steadying force.

And he was so not that yesterday.

He hasn't been like that for a while.

"Why..." I pause, wanting to make sure I get the words right. I want to know why things have been so different lately. Why we've been getting into these little fights over nothing. Why nothing is going smoothly anymore.

I pull a grey-blue stone from the sand and toss it down the beach. "Why exactly did you overreact?" I mutter.

There's no way it could be the same reason I'd been overreacting so often lately.

Could it?

"It was just... I don't know."

I can hear Mick and Junior chatting in the background while he hesitates. "When you were talking about Occy and all that, it made me. . ." he starts again.

I change my mind. I don't want to know where that sentence ends. It's territory we can't be in. "You don't have to answer that. It's fine. I'm fine."

And I was. It never took much to forgive Greyson.

"And I'm an ass. I know," he admits again.

"Oh, whatever. Get over yourself."

I lift my feet to the bottom stair as I turn to lean against the handrail post. "You're gonna miss a perfect session this afternoon. I can already hear the waves peeling off the point. What time do you get off tonight?"

"Not till five."

"We could push the double date back till eight? Get in a quick one after work?"

"I'm sure Occy might understand you blowing him off for some 'killer tubes, Dude'," he says in his worst waterlogged Aussie accent, "but Brit would kill me."

The clouds are showing streaks of light silver where they've thinned from the sun's heat beating down on their topsides, a hint of clear skies in about an hour. I should spend that hour looking for a new job so I can afford to live this close to the water, but I really don't want to hang up with Greyson. He'll probably call it anyways, we rarely talk for more than five minutes.

"My sister was showing me this personality test the other

day. It's supposed to show what kind of person you really are. You want to take it?"

I can hear him flipping through papers at his desk at the station.

"As long as it doesn't tell me I'm a psychopath destined to eat only the left pinkie toe of all my victims."

"The big toe would be fine? Or even the right pinkie toe? But the left pinkie is where you draw the line. Good to know."

"Whatever. You may start the test, Doctor Steele."

It turns out to be one of those silly tests you find in the teeny-bopper magazines Bex and I would read as kids trying to figure out our futures. Which Character on Dawson's Creek Are You Most Like? Or Which Jonas Brother Would Make Your Perfect Husband? You know, the ones backed by peer-reviewed science that show you things critical to your life's path.

But surprisingly enough, it was right on a couple of questions. Like the first two. You're supposed to answer question one with your favorite animal and three adjectives to describe it.

Of course, mine is the black-tipped reef shark because it is a fierce predator, and sleek as hell. And there's really no other animal who is going to give it a hard time.

Question two is your second favorite animal and three adjectives to describe it. Another easy one. The green sea turtle, or Honu to the Maui locals, because they live their whole lives just chillin' in the ocean or soaking up the sun's warmth on the sand and they're smart enough to eat food that doesn't feel pain and won't swim away from them, algae.

"Huh. I think that's true," he taunts me. I hate knowing he has the answer sheet in front of him and won't share.

"What's true?"

"I'll tell you what your answers mean when you answer all of them."

It takes another ten minutes of him asking these odd questions and then laughing about how accurate they are or how much that is 'so me' for us to get to the good part, the explanations.

"So the first one is about how you want the world to see you," he starts.

"So I want the world to see me as fierce, sleek, and top of the food chain? Where'd you get this quiz, the back of Dumbass Weekly?" I ask.

"Don't you though?"

*What?*

I want to be seen as fierce, sleek, and invincible? There's no way.

But then I begin evaluating my life, lately.

Fierce? My rules at work are all laid out so I won't reveal my weaknesses, so I can one day get to the top of the food chain, run my own company, call my own shots. No natural predators.

And I struggle socializing in big groups because I spend so much time editing what I want to say so I don't sound stupid, or step into some frat-boy sexual innuendo, that by the time I've figured out what to say, the conversation has moved on.

Sleek? I may want to be seen as sleek as hell, but I am so far from achieving it and my attempts only make me come across as boring.

And fierce predator? That couldn't be more unlike me.

I rise from the steps, dusting myself off, and pull a splinter out of my shorts.

I don't believe in a zero-sum game, there's room for everyone to succeed. I don't need to take anyone down to get ahead. I can't stand what seems to be the National Pastime of Females Everywhere, cutting each other down. I never learned to play.

Eat before being eaten, on the other hand, may be more like me than I am willing to admit.

Especially with guys.

I may have been quick to discount a guy before giving him a legitimate chance with me. It's much easier to doubt a guy's true intentions or downplay his character than to make myself easy prey.

This quiz is more insightful than I thought.

I drift inside to refill my pint glass with more ice and DDP.

"I may see what you mean," I concede. "So what's the second favorite stand for?"

"This one's perfect. It's who you really are, your true self. You're smart. I don't think that one needs any explanation, Mensa."

"Hey. I never joined Mensa. You remember that. Those geniuses are so weird."

"Eating food that won't feel pain. You are always thinking about how other people will feel about what you do. Not like you're worried about them judging you, but more that you can somehow predict how they will feel if you say something a certain way. Or you find stupid ways to make them feel cared for."

The sun has broken through the clouds and is beating down on the dark grey paint holding the deck together. I escape the heat under the roof of the screened-in sleeping porch wrapping around the north side of the house. "And you think I do that?"

"Of course."

"I'm gonna need an example."

While he grapples with my demands for authentic incidents over dubious platitudes, I toss three pillows covered in neon yellow pineapples to the foot of the bed and stretch out.

"Okay. Fine. I've got one." His voice is peaceful and unhurried in a way I've never heard him talk before like he is content to simply linger in this moment with me as long as he can. "You never take the dollop in a new tub of butter."

"Butter? That's the best you can come up with. Butter?"

"It's not really about the butter, Sands."

I lift my legs onto the white bar topping the chartreuse, neon yellow, hot pink spindles of the bed and bob my feet up and down. "So what is it about?" I prod.

"You know I get a small dose of satisfaction at being able to run my knife across a new tub of butter and picking up the little curly-cue at the top. So you always make it a point to leave it for me. It's really sweet, you know like I know you were thinking about me when you did it."

"It's fun to think about that tiny gleam in your eyes when you open the lid and see it's still there."

"See. Sweet. And you are the most chill person I have ever met. Like you have never known a moment of anxiety in your life. You're so chill it bleeds into the people around you and they soak it in. You know how important that is to me."

We finish the quiz explanations and he shares his answers.

Then we drift off into those questions you ask when you want nothing more than to do nothing with another person. I tell him about wanting to do more with my life than jumping into the next juvenile tech company that will hire me. He tells me about how he still has dreams where he's playing professional baseball and wakes up crying. We move on to talk of places we want to travel and how we definitely need another trip back to Maui to get time to swim with the turtles.

"And the sharks. Don't forget the sharks," I add, though I am feeling way more sweet turtle right now than callous shark.

He's in the middle of telling me about his favorite childhood memory—his last birthday party before his parents split up, the last moment he truly felt like a child—when the alarm in the firehouse blares. "Shit, really? Now? We haven't had a call in over thirty hours, and one has to come in right now."

I feel a stirring in my chest like I'm waiting for him to tell me he won't hang up. He'll skip this call and keep talking to me. I know it won't happen, but I really want it to.

"Go and save the world, Steele," I say, still holding out a school girl's hope he won't.

"I'll see you tonight?"

"See you tonight." I keep the phone pressed to my ear trying to suck out every last minute with Grey until the screen goes black.

# 38

## CHARLIE

When I finally hang up with Greyson, my phone says we talked for seventy-four minutes. That may be longer than the sum total of all our phone conversations during our entire friendship.

Seventy-four minutes. How did that happen? And why did it feel so different?

I stare up at the cracked white paint barely holding on to the boards of the porch ceiling and think about heading out to Maui again with Grey. Swimming with turtles, surfing until we can't lift our arms to paddle, Greyson with a deep, deep tan on his solid frame just like when he lifeguarded that one summer, and sleeping under those stars with Greyson's tan arms wrapped around me. Everything we could do, alone, under the stars.

The buzz of my phone jolts me awake before I drift too far down that fantasy lane.

**Occy: We still on for tonight? Pick you up around 5:45?**

Occy.

Occy is thinking about our date tonight and I'm sitting here daydreaming about sleeping with Greyson in Maui.

Tonight, I'll have to sit between these two men, the one who says I am his fate and the one with whom my fate has been inextricably linked since the day I met him, and I'll be expected to make polite conversation.

How am I supposed to do that?

On a regular night, I'd be lucky to pull off polite conversation. Tonight, with all these thoughts—these fantasies—floating in my mind about Greyson, it will be impossible.

I have to know what he's thinking. Did that phone call change things for him too? Could one phone call possibly change a lifetime of the way he sees me?

Or doesn't see me, as the case may be.

Either way, I have to know.

And I have to know before I go on this foolish double date. I have to ask him straight out what the hell is going on between us.

And it has to be in person. Even if he's at the station, I'm going to march down there and ask him.

I fly off the bed and through the house, slipping on my vans next to the front door. As I reach for the door, it swings open, pushed by a frazzled Bex.

I try to slip by her. "Hey, I was just on my way out."

She steps in front of me. "But I need to talk to you, Charlie. You're the only one who can help me figure this out." She plops down on the couch assuming I will follow suit.

I don't move from the doorway. "Can we do this tomorrow? I have something really imp—"

"Brad dumped me. So there, my crisis is bigger than yours. And I need my best friend to console me."

I've never noticed before now that she only uses that phrase when she needs something from me. I'm pretty sure she's never said to herself, "You know, Bex, you're Charlie's best friend, you should put aside what you want and make sure you take care of her needs first." I'm not sure those words even exist in that order in Bex's vocabulary.

I'm tempted to turn and walk out, but I know the fallout from that would suck up way more of my time and energy. It's simply more efficient to give her what she needs now and take care of "my crisis" when we're done here.

I sit on the arm of the couch opposite her and steel myself for an hour of esteem-building talk and pats on the back. I will still have time to go talk to Greyson before I have to face him with Occy by my side.

"So Brad dumped me. Me. I know it seems like I am always talking about guys, but this is the first guy in a long time I would actually want to exclusively date. Like only him."

"That's big for you." I acknowledge hoping she gets through this quickly.

"I haven't been this whooped on a guy in a while. The weird thing is, and don't take this the wrong way, but I had six really cute guys all calling me to ask me out on a date for last Saturday. Six. And I didn't go out with any of them because of Brad. Does that make sense or does that sound arrogant? Because by no means am I arrogant."

*Just because you say it doesn't make it true, Bexley.*

"You don't sound arrogant," I drone. I swear I could do this consoling best friend job without even thinking. I just take the question at the end of every one of her complaining jags and reassure her of the opposite. "No, you're totally pretty," or "No, he's not good enough for you," or even "No, you're definitely not vain and petty and devoid of any thoughts deeper than a lake in the desert."

I think Bex may be the one person in my life with whom I am routinely dishonest. She's like my honesty superpower Kryptonite.

I hate the way I am with her. I lie to her straight out because she doesn't want to hear the truth. I learned long ago telling Bex the truth freaks her out. She is completely incapable of hearing it, and, so, I stopped telling her the truth.

"And then he tells me, get this, he tells me I'm not real enough for him." At this, she has gone from whiny and pitiful to fired-up and roaring at the thought of someone thinking she is anything less than perfect. "I just don't understand boys. How could he say that???"

You know what they say about insanity and doing the same thing over and over but expecting different results? Maybe if I change my input, try a little more truth with her, the output may change, because what I have been doing for the last twenty years isn't working for me any longer. "Were you being real with him?"

But she goes on as if she's listening to me as little as I have been listening to her. "And now our Summer Goal is totally screwed. Screwed. It's the first one ever we haven't accomplished by the end of summer and now we're not ever going to accomplish it."

Why am I wasting my time trying to talk to her when she is so clearly not hearing a word I'm saying? It's going to take more than one sentence of truth to change a relational dynamic that's been built up over twenty years. "Finding a real relationship takes more than surface stuff, Bex. More than clothes and appearances."

"And now you're going to end up with some loser that me and my future husband are going to hate," she says wrinkling up her face like she just smelled a week-old tuna sandwich found under the Seal Beach Pier.

She can somehow twist a guy dumping her because she's shallow into how I am unworthy of a decent man.

And I am sacrificing finding out what I have with Greyson for her to sit here and insult me.

Maybe she's the real cockblock in my life. All her digs at my femininity and her commandeering my social life and thinking she knows the type of man I need is what is really standing in my way of finding a man. And now she is literally standing in my way of finding out if that man is Greyson.

"Ugh. Like Greyson. I haaaaate Greyson. You can't marry him," she whines like a toddler.

Looks like Bex's taken some of my Truth Serum tonight, not like she needs it. She's never had a problem telling me exactly how she feels.

"I guess that makes sense. He's everything you're not," I reply. *Oh, shit. I think I overdosed on truth serum.*

And it's not stopping.

"Greyson thinks about what I need; you only ever think about yourself." I continue, unable to defend against the overwhelming power of the Truth Serum. "He finds ways to help me with my diabetes without making me feel like I couldn't handle it on my own; I don't think you've ever even asked me about it, even when I was in the hospital getting diagnosed."

That small leak of truth has broken down the entire dam. I erupt from the couch knowing if I don't get out that door, the flood of truth restrained for decades will crush her.

We might not recover from that.

I walk towards the door unable to stop my mouth. "You try to make me more shallow and petty and manipulative so you won't feel as bad about yourself. He has only tried to reassure me of my strengths and gently point out my weaknesses so I can work on them."

I stand in the open doorway for a moment, then turn back to her. "If it comes down to you or Greyson, I pick Grey. Every. Single. Time."

I slam the door behind me so she can't hear what falls out of my mouth next, then storm off to my Jeep, picturing Bex sitting on my couch dumbfounded.

Sliding into the front seat, I slam the door, hoping to send one last message her way. I cannot believe I have been friends with such a selfish bitch for so long. I don't usually like to use that word for women, but, in this case, it's the only one that works.

I check my pocket for the keys so I can drive off in a huff, and it's only then I realize I left them inside the house, the one I just stormed out of.

No way in hell I'm going back in there to witness the damage I've done. If I have done any damage at all. Bex may be sitting there on my couch laughing at the hissy fit I just threw. Who knows if that girl even has feelings to be hurt by a scene like that?

But I'm still not going back in to find out.

It's two miles to the fire station, a forty-minute walk, but I make it there in twenty, a personal best for a two-mile run. Walking up the driveway, I try to catch my breath.

The engine pulls into the driveway behind me. "Hey, Hottie," Mick calls from the driver's seat.

The boxer shorts and tank top I put on last night are clinging to my body from sprinting in the early May heat. I can't believe I'm going to ask Grey if he wants more than friendship dressed like this. Have I learned nothing?

"Hey, Mick. Is Grey around?"

"You finally done lying to yourself, I see." He parks the engine and hops out the door. "Glad to see it."

"Just get Grey out here, please?"

Patrick slides out the side door. "He left before our last call. Didn't he call you?"

I give Patrick a hug and glance down at my phone. "He didn't call, was he supposed to?"

"He spent ten minutes staring at his phone with your number on the screen," Junior chimes in.

I hug Junior and glance at my watch. I've run out of time. I still have to get home and change before Occy comes to pick me up.

"I didn't realize you were hugging the heroes. Where's mine?" Mick asks.

Mick wraps his arms around me and whispers in my ear, "You better hurry. He's headed out for a date tonight with the girl of his dreams."

*Girl of his dreams.*

My hands on his chest, I push back so I can see his face, his hands still around my back. "Did he say that, those words, or is that just you being you?"

His face is earnest, a face completely foreign to the Mick I've experienced. "His words. And the smile it brought to his face? I'd make my play fast if I were you, Charlie. I think this one might take."

I guess that's my answer.

I stare out the bay door and bite my lower lip, hoping the pain from my teeth will overpower the pain in my chest.

"Thanks, Mick. I needed to hear that."

I turn to drag my body, now heavy with defeat, the miserably long two miles home.

# 39

## GREYSON

Sitting at the bar at Nobody's Pub with Brittany in tow, I'm already at the bottom of my first of the many IPA's it's gonna take to get through tonight. After our phone call this morning, I don't know how I'm expected to sit across from Charlie while she makes googly eyes at that guy.

There was something so different in that call. We've never struggled for conversation—we've been talking constantly for the last twelve years—but I've never heard her like that.

She was tender. Sentimental. For the first time ever, Charlie wasn't protecting herself. She wasn't running every word past a filter to make sure I didn't misinterpret it. She just spoke.

It was like we had nowhere to go and all the time in the world to get there. When I got toned out, I nearly quit my job right then and there if it meant I could keep talking to her like that. Then she tells me to go save the world and, shit, it nearly broke me.

But she's coming tonight with him.

And it's killing me thinking about whether he gets to experience the softer side of Charlie, too. Has she bared her soul to him? Is she sweet with him? Does she make him feel like he could conquer the world with one little sentence?

Brittany is chewing on the straw of her bright pink drink, asking one moronic question after another. "So do you like being a fireman?"

Without pulling my eyes off the front door, I give her an unenthusiastic, "Why else would I do it?"

I know she doesn't deserve my contempt, but she has been trying to hijack my attention for the last twenty minutes while we wait for Charlie and Crocodile Dundee to grace us with their presence.

Charlie has never been more than three minutes late to meet me. Ever. But after a few weeks with this hippy, she's showing up twenty minutes late without even a text. I already hate this guy.

"So, do you want to, like, ask me something?" Brittany pleads.

"Yeah. Sorry."

I really should do a better job of being nice; my mom would be devastated at my lack of basic courtesy tonight. "You design dresses, right? How'd you get into that?"

She begins to answer, but the noise just sounds like rushing water as Charlie glides through the front door in a white sundress glowing against her bronzed skin.

There's my Charlie.

Her wrists are covered in bracelets of neon string and an aqua necklace draws my eye to her chest.

My heart pummels my ribs, pumping blood to places it should not be. Places that would torpedo my chances of holding onto whatever version of friendship I still have with the girl.

I set my pint glass on the bar and move towards her ready to wrap my arms around her until the Aussie version of Spicoli plods through the door and throws an arm around her shoulder.

My abs slam up against my stomach threatening to expel the beer sloshing in there now. Thoughts of pulverizing him, of crushing his skull, breaking his ribs, flash through my head. I turn back to Brittany, preventing Charlie from reading my face, and raise a finger to the barkeep while I gather myself.

A hand rests on my shoulder.

*She's just your friend, Steele. A Poe Friend. Nevermore.*
Shit. She's got you saying fucking Poe Friends now.
*Get your shit together, Steele.*

I throw an arm around Brit as I turn to Charlie and her current distraction. Brittany flashes me a smile. It's the most I've touched her since meeting her last week and she thinks it means something.

It does. Just not what she thinks.

"Hey, I'm so sorry I was late. I went to go talk to. . . Uh, Nevermind. I am sorry, though," Charlie says.

"No problem."

"Greyson, this is Occy. Occy, Greyson."

I take my arm off Brit to shake his hand and grip it like an ax I'm about to use to rip through the roof of a burning orphanage. He tries to answer back with a weak clasp feeling more like my four-month-old nephew trying to grasp my finger.

God, I hope Charlie doesn't notice the pissing match we have in this one gesture.

"Good to meet you, Mate," he says.

*Really? Mate?*

*What are you going to call me next? Chief? Or Sport?*

I step back and give him a once-over. He's wearing a navy button-down shirt, unbuttoned over a white tank top. An aqua necklace in the shape of a wave rests on his tank, looking awfully similar to the one on Charlie I've been trying to avoid looking at.

Oh God, they bought matching jewelry. And they both wore it tonight. How freakin' cute.

"And this is…" Charlie pulls me from my stare-down.

"This is Brittany. Brittany, this is Charlie and… What was your name again?" I jab.

"Occy. I *just* told you," Charlie scolds. "It's really nice to meet you, Brittney. So how'd you two meet?"

"Uh… It's Brit-tan-ney. Like a UK dude, the color of my skin, and my knee. Got it?"

Charlie cocks her head at me as if to say, "Where'd you pick up this delightful scholar?"

The hostess swings by, arms full of menus, and leads us

around the throng of customers to our table. Like the Silverstein poem that lent its name to this pub, there is somebody in each place that I look.

The dull roar of numerous conversations does nothing to drown out the voice in my head telling me to flee.

I slide into the stool opposite Spicoli so I can grill him without having to deal with Charlie staring back at me from across the table.

"Grey, Sweetie, I haaave to sit there," Brit whines. "There's sun on this side and I just got my roots touched up. The UV's will totally kill them."

"It's almost sunset," Charlie laughs.

"Yeah, exactly. The rays are, like, so much stronger before night. And, like, the green Flash and all that."

Charlie smiles, taking in the nonsense without needing to embarrass Brit. She can argue the crap out of any subject with a worthy opponent, but, she refuses to punch down.

I pull out the stool for her and Brit gives me a cocky smile, thinking she is well on the way to making me do whatever she wants with her childish fussing.

"Can I get you guys something to drink?" the waitress asks.

"I want a Piña Colada," Brittany commands.

"Sorry, hun. The blender's broken," the waitress picks up the drink list from the table. "But we have a list of—"

"Ugh. Fine. Then do you have a Cosmo? But, like, with none of that crappy Vodka. With the expensive stuff."

"Sure," the waitress says with a smile. This woman is a saint for not smacking the snot right out of Brit-Tan-Knee.

"I reckon you have Fosters?" he asks.

Of course, he asks for Fosters. Not an original bone in his body. I bet next he's gonna ask if they can whip him up a Vegemite sandwich.

"That is the sexiest way I've ever heard that ordered," the waitress coos. "Is your accent for real?"

Spicoli is basking in the waitress's attention as he rattles off whatever stereotypical phrase she can come up with. I think even Brit is amused.

Charlie uses his distraction to study me. I can see the wheels in her head turning as her face flashes between the emotions of whatever it is rolling around in there. Confusion, disappointment, hatred, and... possibly... lust?

It feels great to have her eyes on me again, even if she is only weighing whether or not I've turned into a permanent, full-time asshole instead of the nice guy with a few asshole tendencies she used to know.

The waitress interrupts my interrogation, "And for you two?"

I lift the beer I'm currently working on.

"I'd love an iced tea, please," Charlie says sweetly.

I love that she always treats every person she meets with kindness. She can instantly sympathize with however hard they have it and does whatever she can to lighten their load if only for a brief moment.

"So did you, like, lifeguard back in Australia?" Brit asks while twirling a lock of her hair.

At least she won't care when I have to break the news later tonight that this was our last date.

He starts going on and on about his bravest rescues and his lifeguard competition wins. Brit is enthralled, egging him on with 'ooh's and 'you are so brave's.

Charlie is doing an adequate job playing along, but it's only a Smile and Nod look he can pull out of her. There's not a speck of real admiration on her face.

"Oh my God. I forgot to ask, Grey, honey. Did you get the promotion? Are you going to be Head Fireman?" Brittany asks me.

My gaze shoots straight to Charlie. I haven't told her about applying. Hell, I haven't told her about getting my degree.

Her face hardens. "What promotion, Greyson?"

I can hear the fortifications going up around her wall.

I pick at the label on my beer so I don't have to meet her eyes. "Captain Jameson's retiring and wanted me to apply for the job."

"Good on ya', man. You'd be stoked to be Captain," Spicoli babbles.

Charlie's eyes haven't moved off my face.

"So, babe. Did you get it?" Brittany demands.

I can't believe I have to do this in front of two strangers. I have to tell Charlie, out loud, what she already knows.

I wasn't smart enough.

Not for them.

Not for her.

"They haven't decided yet." I'd rather lie than give Charlie one more reason to be glad she chose him over me.

Charlie starts to shake her head with every horrible thought that passes through her head.

*He's lying to your face.* Head shake.

*He's been lying to you about getting a degree.* Head shake.

*About the biggest chance he's ever taken.* Head shake.

*He's too stupid to even be friends with.* Head shake.

Each and every shake hits me square in the chest, but I can't take my eyes off her. It's all true and I deserve every shot she wants to fire.

Spicoli removes his hand from the table and slides it onto Charlie's thigh. And another blow strikes my chest.

He whispers something into her ear and she tries to reassure him with a smile. "I'm fine. I promise. Still a little jet-lagged," I can hear her say.

He appears sufficiently convinced. Stupid fool.

He should at least know by now when she claims she's "just tired", she is not just tired. It usually means she is feeling big things and is so busy trying to process them enough to put them into words she can't be concerned with trivial small talk and uninspiring conversation.

Ready to move on, I ask him, "So are you planning on making a career out of the lifeguard thing?"

Charlie is the only one to pick up on my slight.

"Nah. I've moved on to much bigger things. I'm studying right now to be an EMT so I can save lives off the beach, too."

I bite down on a smile as I realize this guy is just a shorter, scrawnier, dumber, Aussie knock-off of me. She's dating a flimsy imitation of me.

A copy of a copy of me.

Made on a really shitty copier.

"Sounds exciting," I bait him.

He takes the bait and is off on another story-telling jag. This time he's telling stories that aren't even his to tell.

How Charlie could have handled traveling with this douche for three weeks is beyond me?

Charlie's still sending daggers my way, trying to scold me for my bad behavior. I don't give her the satisfaction of acknowledging it. Maybe if she'd spend more time listening to him instead of trying to bore holes in me with her eyes, she'd have realized what a fraud he is four stories ago.

But, however much she is ignoring him, he is doing an equally first-rate job of actually paying attention to her. "Why don't we go throw some money into that jukebox and see if it has anything worthy of playing," he says with a smile that breaks her hold on me.

I watch as he takes her hand and leads her across the bar. She stands in front of the jukebox looking for songs. He lays his hand on her lower back as he says something in her ear making her smile and turn towards him.

He uses this moment to his advantage and leans in touching his forehead to hers as he says something else that makes her whole body relax into his arms as he closes the distance between them to kiss her.

That should be me.

I should be the one making her relax, showing her how stupid all this is.

I should be the one she is talking to in hushed tones so the weirdos around us don't hear us.

Not him.

"They forgot the bacon on my veeeegan burger," Brit announces, the table now filled wtih our food.

If Charlie brought a water-downed version of me, I think I brought the polar opposite of Charlie. I had no idea when I called her last minute, Brittany was so completely brain-damaged. Perhaps all the chemicals she uses to appear so perfect have seeped into her skull.

If only she just didn't open her mouth, she'd be great. But, alas, she does open it, and the shit that pours out frightens me.

"They probably don't get too many orders of vegan burgers with bacon," I say.

"Why?" she accuses, completely oblivious.

"Because most vegans don't eat bacon. You know the whole animal thing?"

"Bacon is totally fine for Vegans. It comes from a pig like milk comes from a cow. It doesn't actually hurt them."

There are so many things wrong with that statement I don't bother correcting her. Besides, Charlie is headed back our way, and I would hate to give her any more fodder to judge the intellect of my date.

"You guys up for black ball after we finish eating?" New Toy asks.

"Black Ball?" Charlie and I ask in unison.

"Sorry. Pool." He tips his head to the tables by the large window upfront.

"Why not. Let's play some "Black Ball'," I say, mocking his bogan accent which, delightfully, draws another scowl from Charlie.

I'm starting to get the hang of this new game. I insult New Toy, she feels a dose of my misery.

Let's get this game going, then.

# 40

## GREYSON

The waitress sets down a pitcher of beer before clearing our empty plates.

Charlie leans back, rubbing her stomach. "I forgot how amazing a tuna melt can be."

"Tuna melt? Didn't you see that TikTok that said that fish and dairy can cause dark spots on your face?" Britany warns.

"Who's ready for pool?" I say, more than ready to move this night along.

Brit swipes the pitcher from our table as we make our way to the other end of the restaurant. She fills her pint glass on the way over and downs the whole thing in one gulp, filling it up again before she joins us.

I should ask her if something is bothering her, but then I'd have to listen to her answer, and I'm not sure I could take another diatribe on animal rights or the beauty industry.

"Eight ball? Want to play couples?" Charlie asks sweetly.

Her words hit me like a forty-foot wave slamming down in the impact zone.

Couples? Is that what you're calling yourselves? A couple?

I decide I'm not done hurting her.

"Whatever you want, Charles," I call across the table as I arrange the balls in the triangle.

I can see my jab land as she slumps over as if I really did sock her in the stomach.

She turns her back to me and walks to where her drink is sitting on the small table nearby. Her hand moves to her eyes as her shoulders rise and fall in a controlled movement I have seen too many times. It's her, Please Don't Cry In Public move.

Shit. I know she hates that name and she knows I know.

It's a right hook to her soft spot, probably the only one she has. The one that says she is not pretty enough, not girly enough, which couldn't be further from the truth, but one she believes wholeheartedly anyways.

I want to go apologize. To wrap her up in my arms and tell her I didn't mean it. She is girly enough. To tell her every guy in this place has been watching her, wanting her, doing ungodly things to her in their minds since the moment she stepped in the door.

To tell her I have been watching her, wanting her.

She gathers herself again and grabs a cue off the wall, waiting for her turn.

Sppicoli comes up behind her, wrapping his arms around her waist and swaying with her to the beat of some overplayed pop song I'm sure he has memorized all the moronic lyrics to.

*Easy there Kangaroo Boy. Keep it in your pouch.*

He peers over her shoulder, making sure I see the display that's so clearly designed for me. "So, Charlie tells me you've been her friend for like over a decade?" he says, putting a snide emphasis on the word friend like he's trying to remind me of it.

So he has been paying attention to what's been going on here tonight. Maybe he's not as dim-witted as I first thought.

"Something like that," I say not lifting my head from the shot I am lining up.

I break and sink two balls. The moment I look up from the table, he spins her around and nearly inhales her mouth. I swear he's trying to eat her whole face in one big bite.

I hate seeing her kissed so badly, but I don't hate seeing that he feels the need to mark his territory. It means even he can feel the tension between me and Charlie.

Between us.

Brit steps up to the table and hits the ball closest to her which happens to be the four. She's now more sauced than an enchilada. "Babe, you have to hit the white one and make it hit the other ones," I say.

She sways to the other end and hits the cue ball with the side of her cue, then bolts upright like she's finally been hit with a clear thought. "So you two have never, you know...?" she asks.

"What?" Charlie asks.

The thought flies out of Brit's mind faster than it came.

Spicoli finishes for her. "You've never bumped uglies? Copped a root?"

Brittany lays her cue against the wall before spinning around to add, "You've never done the pants-off dance-off?"

Occy drops his arms from Charlie's waist. "Not even a slob job?" Occy presses.

Charlie's still trying to process his weird-ass language.

"You've never screwed?" he explains.

"Nope," Charlie says proudly like it's some big accomplishment.

"Have you ever been... physical?" he asks suddenly acting proper.

"No. Never," she answers.

I tilt my head as my mouth falls open.

*What exactly is your definition of physical, Charlie?*

"Never? Really? Like never kissed or run your hand over his chest? He's never grabbed your ass? Or you've like been laying next to each other and he's a little too excited and you just lay there enjoying it?" Brittany adds.

"We have the Half-Foot Rule for that very reason, it keeps out the confusion," she says like it should be completely obvious to anyone with half a brain.

"What's a Half-Foot Rule?" Brit asks.

Charlie's stare prods me to explain, but there's no way I'm going to defend that lunacy.

"I don't know. We don't get closer than half a foot," she explains weakly as if she doesn't even believe her own lies anymore.

Spicoli chuckles.

See. Even he knows how stupid that is.

"So there's no confusion, you know?" she adds.

*Totally. No one's confused here, Charlie.*

*Not you.*

*Not me.*

*Everything's crystal clear.*

She lines up her next shot.

"So what happens if you break the half-foot rule?" New Toy inquires.

What happens? What happens is the world as we know it would no longer exist. A giant chasm would open up underneath San Diego and release a swarm of demons and devils so fiendish humans could no longer exist in the same plane. All of humanity would perish, followed by every living organism on earth. The Earth would cease to spin and collapse into a black hole bigger than this universe if either of us would be stupid enough to break the virtuous, esteemed Half Foot Rule.

"It would never happen, would it Charlie?" I snarl.

Charlie fumbles her shot so the cue ball spins sideways and falls into the corner pocket.

"Great hit, Charlie," Brit cheers sincerely.

Charlie smiles to Brit, still somehow sweet to her. "Thanks, Brittany," she says pronouncing Brit's name like she demands. "I'm gonna grab another pitcher."

She takes the empty pitcher and vanishes into the crowd.

The bar's been slammed all night. I think we finally made it full force into tourist season. I love the heat of summer, but I hate the barflies it brings from out of town.

"You guys done with the table?" asks some kook wearing socks under his sandals.

Spicoli can deal with him, I have to go handle my Shit With Charlie.

I find her at the end of the bar, the locals-only secret spot for refills. She's on her toes leaning on the bar, trying to get Jimmy's attention behind the bar. It won't take long, looking like that.

Her long blond hair falls over her shoulder as she catches his eye. She holds up the empty pitcher and says, "Lagunitas?"

He smiles and is right on it.

I stand there watching her. I want to tell her to ditch Kangaroo Boy and to marry me. That I'm the only one who can make her happy.

But instead, I march up to her and demand, "When did you become such a liar?"

She swivels from me to Jimmy who sets down the pitcher. "Here you go, Charlie."

She pays for the beer,—tipping generously I'm sure—sets the pitcher back down on the bar, and turns to me. "Really? You act like a dick the whole night, and that's what you want to talk about?"

"It's never the whole truth with you. You shade the truth or only tell part of it, or flat out lie like you just did back there."

"That's total bullshit."

*Were you not there at that last conversation? We've never been physical? You've never broken the half-foot rule? What universe have you been living in?*

"So that line you were feeding your New Toy about us, that was being honest?"

"New Toy?" She's amused.

"Yeah, you know, Kangaroo Boy back there." She smiles again. I'm on a roll.

"Fine," she says with a shrug. "But I am always honest with you," putting an emphasis on always.

I drop my head. The memory of her thumb running along my lips and her mouth so close to mine soften my anger.

But the next memory flashing in my mind, of her taking it all back, reinforces my resolve.

"You've only been completely honest with me once. And you don't even remember it," I growl.

I study her face to see if there is any recognition of what I am really asking for, begging for.

She folds her arms in front of her chest defensively.

*Don't shut down, please.*

She digs her teeth into her bottom lip, slowly letting it slide back out.

*You have to know what I'm talking about.*

*You know, Sands.*

She sucks in a deep breath, letting it tumble out of her slowly.

*Charlie, I need the truth. One way or another, whatever it is, I need the truth.*

She covers her eyes with her hand, rubbing them before dragging it down her face.

"I..." she lets out, almost inaudibly, "...remember."

My ribs succumb to the magnitude of her words. I couldn't have possibly heard that right.

My lungs stop working. I am unable to make them draw breath. Because if I do, if I breathe my next breath, this moment will evaporate.

And it may never materialize again.

*You remember?*

"What?" I plead for an answer I can make sense of.

She lifts her eyes to meet mine. Her lips start to make the shape of a word and then fall.

*Come on, Charlie, don't back out now. I have to know.*

"What," I plead, "did I just hear you say?"

*I need to hear them, the words that will recolor everything I know. I have to know for sure you actually said them.*

"I remember, okay?" she spits out.

The ground shifts under me like the deck of a boat being tossed in a gale.

She remembers.

"You remember? You remember," I snarl. "You told me you drew a complete blank on that night. Those were your words. 'A complete blank.'"

I wait for an explanation. Something. Anything to justify the fact she knew all this time.

She knew she screwed with my head. With my heart. She put it all out there and then didn't even bother taking it back, she just pretended not to have done it. Like her denial of it would somehow change the fact I heard it.

But I heard it.

I heard all of it

I stare at her, begging her for something to make all of it okay.

"I was embarrassed," she says barely above a whisper. "Ashamed."

*Ashamed? Of what? Of feeling something for someone as stupid as me?*

"I know the rules, okay? I know what crossing that line does," she says gathering some steam. "It blows up everything, I get that. I thought it was just best if we both pretended it never happened."

I rub the stubble on my cheek, trying to process this.

Does that make it any better?

"And I know. I know! You don't have to tell me," her eyes plead with me. "Please. Don't say it. I'm not sure I could hear it right now."

She closes her eyes as she takes in a deep breath and covers her mouth with her hand as she gazes out the big windows leading to the sand, gathering strength from her favorite place.

"I already know..." she can barely get the words out, "...you don't think about me that way."

The words do physical damage to her as they leave her mouth. Like with each one, more of her spirit spills out of her body.

She drops her head.

Slowly, I make my confession. "But. I. Do."

I want her to hear each word, for them to fill her back up, to give back everything she just laid out for me.

She raises her brows in disbelief.

I take a long breath, wrangling the countless thoughts coursing through my head, groping for one that will make her understand.

When I lay down at night, I think about you that way.

When I wake up terrified and drenched in sweat because, again, *she's* screaming in my dreams, I want you next to me to hold me as I drift back to sleep.

When morning finally comes, I want desperately to go back to sleep where I can hold you without all this fear threatening us.

The fear of losing you.

Of wanting too much from this.

Of screwing up the only thing holding me together right now.

Shit.

My next words could finally shatter the wall between us or fortify it forever.

"I do think.." I scrub my fingers through my hair, postponing the possible extinction of us that might come from my ill-advised tack. "I think about you that way," I sputter.

She studies my face.

I scan hers for any sign I've gone too far.

No sarcasm. No rage. No crying.

All promising signs.

The pint-sized win of my first confession propelling me forward, I take a step towards her. She takes one back.

I can almost see the thoughts behind her eyes, flashing like the lights of my truck. Red. Blue. Red. Blue.

It's like she is brawling with herself and it's a complete toss-up who will prevail, the sweet, open Charlie who confessed so much that night, or the tough, damaged Charlie who has convinced herself she is not girly enough, not sexy enough, for me to love her like this.

"I've thought about you like that since I saw you in your little jean shorts and that black short shirt, the one with the zipper down the front."

She's still not getting it or, possibly, just not believing it.

I take another step towards her, trying to close the gap between us. Her evasion is weaker this time.

"And in Santa Barbara, when you spent the whole night in my arms, I thought all sorts of things about you that night," I say, an impish grin spreading across my face at the memory of it.

She takes me in like she's finally seeing the real me.

And she likes it.

It compels me towards her. I take one more step. She retreats, bumping up against the exposed brick wall.

"There has never been a moment since the day we met I haven't thought about you like that. That I haven't wanted you." For the first time in a decade, I feel free from the pressing weight I have been holding up all these years.

She drops her gaze to the ground where my feet rest a mere six inches from hers and then back up to me. I know what she's asking me to do. What she has already done three times. What I've been too terrified to try myself for more than a dozen years. I smile at her as if to say, it would be my pleasure. She lets her eyes drift down to my lips.

I move towards her, almost imperceptibly, overcoming a lifetime of conditioning to avoid this very move. She lifts her hand and rests it on my chest, her eyes begging me to kiss her, the warmth of her hand dissolving the last of my restraint.

I lay one hand on the wall behind her head, the other I slide onto her waist, over her dress, around her back, as I step closer. I move in to meet her mouth. She pushes on my chest to stop me, but she leaves her hand there.

*I'll wait, Charlie. I've waited so long already, I can wait a few more moments for you to catch up.*

Her hand goes soft on my chest and her Badass Smile spreads across her face as she leans in.

She holds my gaze as we move closer until...

...her eyes dart over my shoulder.

And her face drops.

"I can't do this ri.... We can't... Not with..."

Not a single full sentence to tell me what just transpired.

She drops her head as ice crystals spread through my body, starting where her hand rested on my chest. Painful, serrated crystals, hacking my body to smithereens.

Charlie slides from my grasp, without another word. I turn to watch her trek across the bar to Occy, taking him by the hand.

They slide out the door as I collapse against the very wall that, only moments ago, held her against me.

"*I can't do this.*"

She can't do this.

She can't love me.

The lights above the throbbing crowd bleed into a dark blurry grey. I close my eyes and lean my head back against the gritty brick behind me.

My world is gone.

My Charlie is gone.

I drag my chest up to let in the smallest puff of air, giving in to its crushing weight moments later.

I put it all out there, nearly sliced open my sternum to shake out everything I had been carrying around for her for so fucking long, and she does a complete about-face.

She doesn't love me.

She was just fucking with me.

And now she's gone.

I drag in another wisp of air.

*Gone.*

Brit takes this moment to throw in her two cents. "You've ignored me all night. I am way too awesome to be ignored. And you could care less."

I open my eyes, sluggishly pulling my head from the wall.

"Actually, I couldn't," I correct her.

She cocks her arm back and straight up punches me.

Not slaps.

Punches.

She hits me like a dopey, female Connor McGregor right below my left eye with enough force to slam my head into the brick behind me.

The thud of her hand hitting my eye socket is followed by another when my head hits the wall.

The fuzzy, dizzy feeling takes over my brain and I give in to my weakened legs, sliding down the wall.

"I'm gonna throw the fuck up," she whines as she struts out of the bar.

I wrap my arms around my knees and let my head fall onto my arms and welcome the pain beginning to permeate my face as the legs of countless bar flies swarm and flit around my carcass.

*Gone.*

# 41

## CHARLIE

*P*lease. Don't say it. I'm not sure I could hear it right now."

Confessing to Greyson that I remember coming onto him while I was drunk in Maui was hard enough. Though I already know it's true, hearing him reject me, hearing those words spill from his mouth would end me.

"I already know," I whisper. "You don't think about me that way."

He rubs his hand along the stubble covering his cheek, a cheek I know I won't get to touch again after the disaster I've orchestrated here.

The costume I put on tonight, the one deep down I hoped might provoke Greyson, should have been a hoodie so I could hide beneath the soft bagginess, pulling the hood low over my eyes.

He lays out each word gently, deliberately.

"But. I. Do."

*Stop lying, Steele.*

*You don't.*

*You can't.*

*I'm not that kind of a girl.*

But his aqua eyes delude me into thinking that maybe...just

maybe... he could see me that way. "I do think," he rubs the back of his head.

It will only take him a second to clarify what he really meant. He loves me, but not romantically. He wants me, but only as a friend.

"I think about you that way," he insists.

But... *Where's the but?*

He drifts towards me.

*Why won't you just say it? Say what we both know you are thinking. It will never be like that for us. I can never be one of the dainty wisps you want.*

I take a step back, the look on his face making me second guess myself.

*You think about me that way? That way, as in, a romantic way, a carnal, lustful, you want to jump my bones kind of way? I thought I was being clear. How could you be so confused?*

"I've thought about you like that since that first night we met when I saw you in your little jean shorts and that black short shirt." He runs his hand across his stomach where my shirt stopped.

*Why do you remember that?*

"The one with the zipper down the front," he says as a lascivious grin ticks up the corner of his mouth.

It's the same smile I've seen on his face as he drifts away from our conversations to watch a beautiful woman walk by. The one I have to wait for him to finish before he'll refocus on what I'm saying. But it's directed at...

*Come on, Charlie. You know better.*

He takes another step towards me.

I drift back again.

"And in Santa Barbara," he adds.

The feel of his hand on the bare skin of my back, the angles of his shoulders as he pulled me tight, the smell of his skin mixed with chlorine that morning streak through my head.

*Fuck. I need to feel that again.*

"When you spent the whole night in my arms, I thought all sorts of things about you that night." The impish grin he was trying to stifle broadens. He moves towards me, pressing me up against the dirty brick wall behind me.

I feel the urge to run my hands up his tight abs, taking his shirt with them. To feel his skin against mine, the warmth of his body.

His shoulders unfurl and I realize it's the first time in weeks I've seen him completely relaxed, like all the tension tweaking his frame, tweaking every one of our interactions, has evaporated.

"There has never been a moment since the day we met I haven't thought about you like that. That I haven't wanted you."

I wait for him to take another step, but he won't. I stare at his feet, willing them to move, to rush towards me. I behold his face, begging him to move, to press his body up against mine.

A grin spreads across his face as he finally obeys, crossing the half-foot line I fought so hard to enforce for far too long.

His lips scream at me. I need to feel them on mine. He closes the distance between us. He is so much closer than a half-foot and every ounce of me is screaming in response.

I need to touch him, but I need to be sure he is saying what I think he is saying.

I lay my hand on his chest, trying to gain some clarity before I drive off this cliff, but that point of contact sets him off.

As he lays his hand on the wall behind my head, I follow it with my eyes as his rocky biceps flex under his shirt sleeve.

Without my permission, my hand rises to grasp his arm.

His other hand glance along my waist pulling me into him. He rolls his tongue along his bottom lip and I cannot pull my eyes from the show. I am drawn to trace the same path with mine.

But if we go there, if I do that, I can't take it back. And I may not be able to stop.

He inches close enough I can feel his breath on my face. I push against his chest.

*Wait. Let me catch up a minute.*

I want him to stop moving so I can process what he has already said.

But I don't want him to ever stop.

Understanding I need a second, he waits.

*I think about you that way.*

He wants this.

And, Lord knows, I want this.

There's no cliff to drive off.

I lift my head from the bricks and reach for what I want.

For him.

His passionate gaze meets mine. My eyes drop briefly to those lips again before returning to his eyes, the same crystal blue shade as Napili Bay.

I wet my lips and drift towards my Grey as I see Occy walking towards us over Grey's shoulder.

Shit.

Shame forces my gaze to the floor.

I'm on a date with another man, a man who asked on the way over if I'd be introducing him tonight as my boyfriend.

There's no way I am having my last first kiss ever while I'm cheating.

"I can't do this ri...."

I step back.

Occy marches closer.

"We can't...

How do I explain?

He is mere feet from Greyson's back.

"Not with..."

I've seen Greyson throw a punch. If Occy wants to get physical, it's gonna get ugly and he doesn't deserve that. He doesn't deserve any of this.

I side-step Grey and grab Occy's hand, leading him to safety in the other direction.

Pulling him out the door, I try to figure out what to tell him.

Sorry, I've been leading you on, but I'm in love with my best friend?

I don't think I'm ready to call you my boyfriend since I have been harboring unchaste feelings for my best friend?

Or simply, I'm a horrible person for doing this. You deserve so much more.

The cool night air blows the hem of my dress up. I drop his

hand, catching my dress before it can make me feel any more bare than I already do.

Occy turns to face me, leaning up against the navy stucco wall. The aqua wave necklace laying on his chest catches my eye. When we bought the matching necklaces from Auntie Kina in the farmer's market after the best day surfing I have ever had, I was so sure I liked him. He was so kind and relaxed.

"I was wondering how long it would take you two." He shoves his hands into his pockets.

"Take us two?" I ask.

"You and Greyson." He nods his head towards the bar. "Sexual tension that fierce is keen to ignite."

"Oh."

I suck.

I feel awful I subjected him to a full night of having to watch what I now know was a glaringly obvious display. I know lying to Greyson hurt him, and lying to myself hurt me, but I didn't realize, in the process of lying to myself, I hurt Occy, too.

"I am so sorry. I really did like you. It's just that Grey—"

He cuts me off. "No worries, Charlie. It just took you a bit to suss it out."

He wraps me in his arms. "He's a good dude. I know he'll treat you right."

"Thanks, Occy," I say into his chest.

Out of the corner of my eye, I see Brittany stumble out of the bar. She slips off her heels and staggers our way.

"Occy, did you see that?"

She stomps off.

He turns to me, silently asking permission.

I'm a bit surprised. "Really? Huh." I nod for him to follow her.

"She may be a few kangaroos loose in the top paddock, but I kind of dig that." I watch as he jogs up to Brittany and throws an arm around her shoulder. He heals up pretty quick.

With the last obstacle between Greyson and I removed, I race back into the bar to find him. I scan the tall tables by the pool tables, but they're only filled with tourists and guys from San Diego State looking to score with whatever they can find tonight.

I check the table we sat at earlier, but it is occupied by two toddlers far too young to be in a bar this late at night accompanied by two parents too strung out from too many all-day Sea World and Legoland trips to realize that fact.

I hurry to the bar and get Jimmy's attention. He's filling up a pint of Bud Light.

"Did Greyson close out his tab?" I ask.

"Yeah. Never seen him look so bad." He slides the pissy yellow beer in front of a slim girl barely old enough to vote, let alone drink crappy beer.

"Bad? Greyson, about this tall, brownish hair. That Greyson?"

"The Greyson who had you plastered to this wall back here just moments ago? Looked like shit."

What could have possibly happened between then and now to make him look like shit?

"You didn't happen to see which way he went?"

He swipes the bar with his damp bar rag. "Out the door. Can't really see past that."

"Thanks, Jimmy."

I step outside the bar and search my pockets for my keys.

Shit. I must have left them... at home... with my car.

I stupidly check the street where I last saw Occy racing to catch Brittany. It's not like they'll still be there.

I pull out my phone to text Grey.

**Charlie: Where are you?**

I wait to see the Delivered notification.

It doesn't show.

*Seriously, Grey? You spill your guts, pin me up against the wall, and then disappear and shut off your phone?*

With no other options, I start walking home. The second I get there, I swipe my keys from the counter and take off towards Greyson's house.

*Why would he do that unless he meant it?*

*He did mean it.*

*He did.*

I jump out of my Jeep and pound on his front door.

"Greyson!" Listening closely for any movement, I text again, hoping to hear his phone inside.

Nothing.

*He did mean what he said, right?*

*He had to.*

*Unless...*

No. *He meant it.*

"Greyson, come out here!"

*Unless... fuck.*

*Was he just getting back at me for poker night?*

The thought too much to withstand, my legs go weak under me. I crumble to the ground in front of his door as fat tears chase each other down my cheeks.

*He didn't mean any of it.*

# 42

## GREYSON

So what's my tack? My opening line?"

The last place I want to be is back in Nobody's Pub, one short week after having my heart ripped out in the far corner, but after weeks of putting off my promise to act as Patrick's wingman, I couldn't bail again.

Without Charlie around anymore, and after slamming my fist into Mick's face for saying I was a total pussy for giving up on her, Patrick may end up being the only friend I have left. And I have a feeling bailing on my promise for the fourth time may be the final nail in that coffin.

I've spent the last thirty minutes trying to give Patrick enough courage to approach the cute redhead at the far end of the bar, but he's still stalling.

"So once I get her talking, is that when I start lying?" he asks.

"What makes you think you should lie to women?" I swirl my pint glass. It's more foam than beer.

"Not actual lying," he backpedals. "But, like, resume lying. You know. Making everything sound way better than it really is."

"Don't do that shit." I push my glass forward on the bar. "Be real. That's what girls really want. It's the fastest way to know if someone's right for you. Don't wait till you're ten years down the road, and all the lies you've told trying to make it work come back to strangle any happiness you've been able to build."

"That's easy for you to say. If I were like you, I wouldn't have to pad my resume. You have girls lining up for you. I've spent the last half-hour trying in vain to get one girl to look my way."

"Girls are not lining up for me, Patty."

Who the hell would line up for a lying dumbass who couldn't get his shit together enough to be honest with a girl before a decade of lies drove her to give her heart to someone else?

Even if girls fell for my crap in the past, the six days of unkempt scruff covering my face, the unidentifiable brownish stain on my shirt, and the swollen eye behind a halo of fading blue and dingy yellow would certainly make them think twice tonight.

"Oh yeah?" He points behind me, and for a nanosecond, my heart thinks it might be Charlie, but I promptly extinguish that spark. Before I have a chance to turn and see who is approaching, a feminine screech tightens the shackle that's been crushing my chest for the last week.

"Blimey O'Reilly, Grey." Bex sounds like a complete moron with that stupid British cursing she claims makes her sensational. "Did you hear what Charlie did to me?"

Patrick pokes me in the ribs, smiling and nodding his head towards Bex.

I shake my head. No way I would ever release the demon spawn on sweet Patrick.

Bex doesn't notice I have no desire to listen to her warp the situation to get whatever the hell she is trying to get out of me. "She kicked me out. On the same day I broke up with my boyfriend. I had to sleep at my parent's place. Had she just done it a day earlier I could have just moved in with Brad, but she waited until she knew I had nowhere to go."

In my current condition, I have no patience for this woman. I am dealing with real Shit With Charlie, and Bex is here trying to garner my sympathy with lies and manipulation because, no doubt, she pushed Charlie too far with the same lies and manipulation.

"That's bullshit. Charlie doesn't do shit like that."

"It's true. After being best friends with her since we were, like, zygotes, she just shoved me out. Like a giant heap of smelly trash."

"You're lucky you got one day of Charlie's friendship, Bex. You know how much she values honesty. You wouldn't recognize honesty if it bought you a drink and felt you up in the back booth."

I turn back to the bar. I am done with her bullshit.

"I wouldn't be sitting there so cocky, Greyson. If she could throw me out for what you call lying— "

I step into her words. "Fuck, Bex. Did you ever stop to think that if you didn't hold on so fucking tight and try to control every damn thing, that there might actually be room for you in her life?"

Her silence compels me to face her. Knowing Bex, she'd sucker punch me from behind.

But instead of an angry Bex, I find a dejected child, mouth agape, plastered to the floor. Every few seconds her lips twinge as if she yearns to speak, but words are too heavy for her broken spirit. Then her lips slowly come together as her eyes go red and glossy.

Looks like my Charlie-fueled, Granny-Attacking rage is back. I rub my fingers into my eyes as I try to quiet the storm in my head. "I'm sorry, Bex."

Her silence persists.

I drop my hand from my face to find her nowhere in sight.

Unable to face Patrick, I glance to the barkeep, Jimmy. "Whiskey?"

He pours a shot. "It's the only one you get. So nurse it if you need to."

I toss it back in one motion. "What the hell, Jimmy. You're cutting me off?"

"Sorry, Greyson. Charlie's rules. She made me promise years ago never to serve you more than one whiskey."

I can't get away from this girl.

Patrick motions to his lady. "I'd better try my luck before she leaves."

I can't figure out if watching me launch myself off the pedestal he put me on finally gave him the confidence to approach the girl, or if the need to flee the resulting awkwardness drove him there.

Searching for anything to tamp down the raging inferno in my chest, I snag my pint of foam and tip it into my mouth, waiting for it to slowly trickle out. It's not whiskey, but it'll do the trick.

I turn back to the spot Bex vacated and realize that's the first time Bex and I have ever agreed on anything.

Poe Friends is absolute bullocks. Always has been.

Agreeing to it is a Bex-sized lie.

I raise my pint glass to Jimmy hoping Charlie's ban doesn't extend to beer as well. He slides another IPA my way. "Charlie may not have rules on beer, but I do. Take it slow, Greyson."

Over the rim of my glass, the redhead motions to the empty stool to her right. Patrick sends me a grateful look as he slides in next to her. If anyone deserves to find love, it's that guy.

And Charlie.

I lower the glass to the table, letting it fall heavily. Charlie deserves to be with the right guy.

And that's totally, absolutely, completely, brutally not me.

Even if it isn't Occy, I know it's not me, and Charlie deserves the space and support to find Mr. Right without me getting in her way.

I've spent the whole last year trying to nudge her or entice her or outright shove her towards the place I wanted her to be and it did nothing except scorch our friendship. How is that any different than what Bex does?

How the hell did I become just as bad for Charlie as fucking Bex?

I finish off the pint in one gulp.

There's no way I will let that stand. I'm done putting my needs ahead of hers. It's time to be the Poe Friend she needs.

I motion to Jimmy for the bill, while searching for the words I want to say when I find Charlie.

Jimmy lays the bill on the bar. "You're not driving, are you?"

I toss him my keys. "Can you hold onto these?"

"Smart choice. Didn't want to have to fight you for them; you look beat up enough as it is."

I lay a few bills down. "On my way to fix that right now."

He swipes the money off the bar. "Tell Charlie I said hi," he says with a smirk.

# 43

## CHARLIE

When the first rays of sunlight illuminate the horizon outside my window, my mind begins churning again. With no possibility of more sleep, I head downstairs ready to start another wretched day of my new Greyson-free reality.

Rubbing my eyes, I load my arms with Cookie Crisp and all the fixings and head to the deck. I toss my breakfast on the bar and stare at the water, still unable to believe that Grey could be that cruel.

Hoping a bottle of IPA will lubricate the gears of my mind that have been grinding all week, I return to the fridge, grab one, and pop off the top. Taking a long draw, I revel in the cold liquid burning its way deep into my stomach.

I fix up my Cookie Crisp and dive in, praying the sugar will kick the bleak mood lingering since Greyson got even.

**Bex: You up? I wanted to return the key.**

Just what I need. A Bex nightmare. There's no way I'm inviting her in. She can give me the key on the deck. That way if she wants to get hysterical, I can escape inside and lock the door.

**Charlie: Out back. Come around.**

Right after our fight, without the slightest amount of fanfare, Bex moved out. No note. No call. Nothing.

I finally told her what I thought, stood up for what I needed, and she bails without a word.

I came home from moping around the beach the next day to find an empty room, an empty closet. She didn't even have the decency to text me. I had to hear it from Indigo that she left.

I know I said some mean things, but it was all true. For the week before our fight, I had been thinking a lot about how my relationships with Greyson and Bex were so different. When Bex brought up how much she hated him, all those thoughts came spilling out.

"Hey Charlie," Bex says barely above a whisper.

She sure is skilled at faking remorse. Probably still looking to get something out of this. Without acknowledging her, I shove another bite of sugar into my mouth.

"Do you think you could turn around? I need to, like, say something."

If she didn't have the decency to tell me she was moving out, I sure as hell am not going to be the more unselfish friend today. After a lifetime of doing just that, I'm done.

"I can hear you just fine from here," I grumble through a mouthful of the only pleasure I've found this week.

"That's okay. Maybe it will make this easier." She leans up against the bar, sighing deeply as she studies the water.

"I'm sorry. I'm an absobloodylute bugger."

Stupefaction forces milk and cereal from my mouth. I was not expecting that phrase.

Wiping the milk dribbling down my chin, I turn my head her way. Her apology deserves at least that much.

Bex picks the polish from her acrylic talons. I guess that's all the remorse I'm gonna get from her.

A seagull inches his way towards the sand grave of my expelled cereal, eyeing us carefully.

"I'm afraid you'll leave." She kicks her foot towards the gull, before continuing. "If you're with Greyson, you won't want to be around me and you'll leave."

I am stunned.

But when I really think about it, it makes sense. When her dad left, I spent years telling her it wasn't her fault, and, even when she finally started agreeing with me, I never knew if she actually believed me or just agreed to get me to stop talking.

And every time she screwed up at home, her mom would withdraw all her love and give her the silent treatment until Bex fell in line and became the perfect little daughter her mom demanded.

Everything Bex does is to ensure that the people she loves won't leave her. And in the process, she becomes someone she's not. Obsessed with appearance, striving to gain a guy's attention.

It's the reason why so few people get to see the real Bex. The one who volunteers at the animal shelter and rescues puppies and builds playlists for all her friends so they won't ever miss out on a song that would be perfect for them.

I never realized she was doing the same thing with me. She spent the whole year setting me up on more blind dates than a seeing-eye dog, trying to fix me up, driving Greyson as far away as she could send him. All in the name of accomplishing her goal this year.

But our summer goal wasn't to find matching husbands. It was to reassure Bex that, even if I got married, she would always be in my life.

And it's time to achieve that goal right now.

I turn in my chair. "How long have we known each other?"

"Pretty much forever."

"And how many times have you selfishly put yourself before me, or demanded my attention no matter what was going on in my life, or taken out all your frustrations with life on me?"

Her head drops. "I know Charlie. You're the good friend. I know I have been a bloody rubbish friend. I understand. I just had to tell you the truth. I know you don't want me in your life anymore."

"I'm not making a list to justify cutting you out of my life, Bex."

A spark of hope fills her voice. "You're not?"

"After all that... rubbish," a nod to her favorite expletive, "you're still my friend. I'm not your friend because you do stuff for me. I'm your friend because you're family. Plain and simple. You've been there for every single big moment in my life. And I want you to be a part of every future big moment for the rest of my life."

I rest my hands on her shoulders and say as gently as I can, "I'm not your dad. And I'm not your mom. I'm not going to leave you."

Tears start to fall as I see the impact those words have on her.

"But, Bex?"

"Yeah," she says through soft sobs.

"I need you to start thinking about me, too. Not first, but just somewhere in there. What I need has to be factored into your thinking."

"I can do that." She wipes a ring finger under each eye.

"Good." Surprisingly, some of the misery that has framed my day abates.

"I know you're not a hugger, but is this a hug kind of a moment?" she pleads.

I wrap my arms around her and give her the reassuring hug I know she needs.

"I should go, Paul is waiting in the car."

"On a Saturday morning, huh? Call me later to dish?"

"For sure." She crosses the deck with more zip than she arrived with.

I settle in again at the bar and take another bite of The Crisp. Soggy. Is there anything worse than wasting a bowl of cereal because you let it grow soggy?

Feeling charitable, I toss it in the sand for the hungry gull, and pour myself another, laughing to myself as I play that scene over on my head.

Bex was totally, absolutely, completely, brutally honest. Which is crazy. I've never seen Bex anywhere near that genuine. And it got her exactly what she really needed from me.

All our tension, our anger, our pain, was created from her

trying to manipulate and lie to get what she needed instead of just telling me. All of that could have been prevented.

And I've been doing the exact same thing with Greyson.

I've been lying about who I am.

I haven't been the totally honest tomboy I claim to be. The one who is so brave for being completely herself. Not even close.

I've been denying my girly side because showing it makes me a sitting duck for pain. I've been afraid to try to find what my own girly style is because I am afraid to get it wrong. Putting on this mask of being a tomboy, or just one of the guys, is only my way of protecting the delicate fragile part of me that wants a man to share my life with and to open my heart to, but is terrified of being rejected and told I'm not good enough.

And it's even worse with Greyson.

So much worse.

I have been so totally, absolutely, completely, brutally *dis*honest with him since the day I met him. When I somehow convinced myself that I outplayed all the other girls because I got to be his neuter-gender sidekick when, in reality, I never even stepped on the playing field.

Because I have never, not for a single moment, lived up to that promise he begged me to make so long ago; to be totally, absolutely, completely, brutally honest.

I have been denying that I need him.

I've been denying that I want him.

That he makes my body light up.

That I want to show him every single part of me.

Even the girly parts that I hide so well.

And I want to show him right now.

Slamming my hands on the bar to propel me into this new future, I flip the cereal bowl and watch in slow motion as milk and tiny bits of cookie flow over the edge of the bar, landing on my legs before I can react.

"Towel," I squawk at Mr. Gull.

I rush to the sleeping porch to grab a towel from the shower instead of dripping my breakfast through the house. I step through the door to find Greyson framed in the early morning light, rubbing his neck.

His Station 6 shirt pulled tight across his chest, and his hair scrambled like my heart lately, suck away all my bravado. The rambling honesty that flowed unrestrained only moments ago has dried up.

Without any other words, I mutter a feeble, "Grey."

# 44

## GREYSON

*D*id you ever stop to think that if you didn't hold on so fucking tight and try to control every damn thing, that there might actually be room for you in her life?

The words taunt me all night as I lay on the bed Charlie and I dragged ten blocks to this porch when she first moved in until my tormented sleep is interrupted as a delightful voice entices me into consciousness.

Fuck. I've missed her voice, its absence, a torture inflicted by my own greed.

That stops now.

Though I failed to tell her last night that I am ready to be the Poe Friend she so rightfully deserves, today is a new day. This is a conversation best had sober, anyways.

I grind my palms into my eyes and enjoy the dull ache lingering from Brittany's well-deserved jab.

Drifting to the screen door, I reach for the handle as it whips open.

"Grey." It sounds more like she's letting out a breath than an actual word.

I raise my head to take her in. Her hands drop from swiping

away something from her grey wife-beater and threadbare denim shorts.

The offshore breeze tosses a piece of hair in her face. She pushes it off her bronzed face, revealing those sharp green eyes that always see the deepest parts of me. The parts I try so hard to hide.

*This is it, Steele. Time to tell her.*

I try to speak, but it comes out rusty. "You sleep too hard."

She laughs, "What?"

The sound of her laugh soothes the decay in my head.

I point to her window watching over us. "Seriously, Sands. You sleep right under that thing. How could you not have heard?"

Her sight moves from the window above, back to me, and then to the multitude of pebble landmines covering the deck around her bare feet. I can see her mind struggling to put the pieces together until her searching gaze hits my hand. Her brows sink in concern as she draws my hand forward, flipping it over to assess the damage.

When I got here last night, filled with alcohol and romantic notions, I tried to wake her by tossing beach pebbles at her window. When the first round didn't work, I went searching for another handful of ammunition, driving my hand into the sand, and coming up with the butt end of a broken Corona bottle wedged into my palm.

After washing my hand in the shower, I tore up a towel to stop the bleeding. Supposing it was a sign I should delay my proclamation, I crawled into bed and waited for the spinning to stop.

Still holding my hand in hers, she runs her fingers along my palm. "What is going on with you, Grey?"

Her touch evaporates the heartache that has been my loyal sidekick for the last week.

*Tell her, Steele.*

*I'm here to support you, babe. I want you to find love. You deserve it. Whatever you need from me, it's yours.*

*Say it.*

I shrug.

Shrug!

I can hear the words run through my head, but I cannot convince my mouth to utter them.

She doesn't rush me or demand I spill. She never did. Instead, when she drops my hand, she refuses to drop the connection, keeping her pinkie wrapped around mine, beckoning me to share, but I can't. I cannot get myself to tell my best friend that I want to support her in finding her own love. A love who is worthy of the amazing woman she is.

She tilts her head to the barstools overlooking the sand. "Can we talk?"

As she draws me over to the bar, she wraps her entire hand around mine, resting our joined hands on the bar as we sit, her hand looking perfect wrapped in mine.

I turn her hand over and begin to trace delicate lines along her palm, my fingers trying to share what my words cannot.

*If the only thing you can give me is friendship and never more, I am completely grateful. It is more than I deserve.*

I run my fingers from her palm to the tips of her fingers.

*And I will do everything in my power to make sure you get everything you deserve. Everything you ever want.*

We sit in silence as she watches me touch her so innocently and, yet, so intimately. She watches my face like she understands my finger message—she doesn't pull away or hesitate at my caress—and that little point of contact lights up my whole body, drives away the fogginess in my head, and soothes my heart until it's trembling.

How can I tell her to go find love in someone else when her touch is everything? Doing that would be like signing my own death warrant.

We sit at the edge of the deck overlooking a reticent sea. Nothing but ripples at the shore tipping onto the sand and retreating peacefully.

The wind brushes past Charlie and brings with it the scent of bananas and possibility.

Neither of us speaks.

She pulls her hand from mine to fidget with her hair, wrapping the blond strands around her finger. She turns to me, trying to speak, but fish bubbles come out instead.

I can't put this on her. I am the one who came to make proclamations. It's time to proclaim.

I turn to her, hoping that if I open my mouth the words will come, but she spins in her barstool to face me and her knees graze my thigh, which nearly guarantees I won't be able to say a thing.

I study her knees, then her face, and I can't read her expression. For years we could have entire conversations without a word. Now, I have no idea what she is thinking.

Scrubbing my hands through my hair, I spin back to the sand hoping to be inspired, to find my strength.

A seagull hops along the sand towards us, soliciting a handout, but we have nothing to offer him.

I am incapable of telling Charlie to find Mr. Perfect. I am totally, absolutely, completely, brutally powerless to make myself do it. I'm not good enough for her and I'm too weak to tell her to find someone who is, leaving me forever tethered to this endless anguish.

But as long as she's here next to me, it's a delicious torture that I will happily endure for the rest of my life.

# 45

## CHARLIE

Totally, absolutely, completely, brutally honest.

You can do this, Charlie.

Totally honest.

I turn my head towards him as he leans to put his elbows on the bar, pulling his sleeves further up his arms.

And. Triceps.

Flexing, solid, tan triceps. They steal all my words. All my thoughts.

He lets his head fall onto his hands as he tugs at messy strands. It's no wonder he is frustrated; I tell him I want to talk and then can't get out a single word.

*Absolutely honest.*

I try again, spinning on my barstool to face him. My knees graze his thigh as I turn, igniting my body. I sink into eyes the deep blue of a blazing flame, summoning all the courage I can muster.

He turns away and lifts my beer to his mouth.

I stare at the beer running over his lips, riveted, as he slowly pulls the bottle away and licks the nectar from his lips just like he did on Poker Night. Oh, how badly I want to be that beer bottle right now.

*Completely honest.*

If I'm ever going to say what must be said, I can't look at him. Glancing up the beach towards the lagoon, I let my words sail back towards him on the wind. "You said a bunch of stuff back at Nobody's."

*There's that poetry you wanted to share, Charlie.*

He seems to be trying to decide whether to take it all back or scream at me for not ripping off his clothes right there at the bar. But, instead, he rivals my poetic proclamation. "You said a lot of stuff, too, Sands."

No matter what he feels about me, or doesn't feel, as the case may be, I promised to be honest, and it's about time I lived up to that promise. I owe him that.

*Brutally honest.*

"I need you to know something Greyson." I take the beer from his hand and take a long draw, before setting it down again between us.

I turn to face him, stronger this time, ready to live up to my words.

He tilts his head, resting his cheek on his hand to consider me and it's about the cutest thing I've ever seen. The contented, intoxicating, Private Greyson only I get to see.

A patient smile spreads across his face. "I'm not a mind reader, Charlie. Haven't the last few months told you that?"

Distance. I need distance to get this out.

Swiping the beer from the counter, I stand, hoping to let out the building nervous energy. "Did you know you've never laughed at me when a low makes me act like a toddler?"

He spins around, leaning back against the bar, my squirming now entertaining him. "You sure about that?"

"Okay. Maybe near me, but not at me," I concede.

Taking a long sip of courage and a deep breath, I roam, bare feet patting along the deck. "And you're always with me when I have to face a world I don't know how to navigate. Even when you're not actually there."

My confidence grows as words finally come, "You put me back together when I fall apart."

Spinning on my heel a few paces later, I shake the bottle at him, "And you always protect me from the delta bravos of this world, but you never make me feel like I couldn't do it myself." I let the bottle fall to my side. "And you always push me to not put up with anyone's—"

"Fuckaroo," I scream while my foot reflexively pulls up, searing pain careening up my leg.

Looking down, I find shrapnel from Grey's assault on my window last night.

"Damn, Sands. Such language," he laughs out. He lifts his hands in defense. "Don't worry. Not laughing at you. Just near you, I promise."

Scanning the area for more landmines, I lower my foot gingerly to the deck before my gaze is pulled higher.

He was tossing pebbles at my window last night. After avoiding me for days, he shows up in the middle of the night to toss pebbles at my window.

I drop my gaze to his face. "Why were you here?"

"When?" he answers tenuously.

I give him my Stop-the-Bullshit look.

"I dunno. I forgot. Just the moron brain over here malfunctioning again."

"You know, you're one of the smartest guys I know, and you still believe you're this huge moron."

"Now you're just getting carried away."

"I know you don't see it, but the way you can read people immediately, and, no matter the situation, you know exactly how to talk to them and--"

He steps into my words. "That doesn't mean I'm smart."

But I'm on a roll. "You can keep up with me in any debate. And watching you spar with me? It's so damned..." I want to say sexy, but I'm working my way up to this full honesty thing?

*Screw it.*

"Sexy."

I wait for his retort but come up empty. Instead, he's staring at the pebbles scattered around me, while he rubs at the back of his neck.

With all my words out in the open, the motor driving me to pace, slows. I turn to face him. "Grey?"

I pause until he meets my eyes. "You're the best man I've ever known."

I take one more drag from my beer, trying to steady my resolve, and step forward, closing that once insurmountable divide. Leaning over him, I set my beer on the bar behind his broad shoulders and shatter the Half-Foot Rule one last time.

He lifts his head like my movements have injected his languid body with the smallest amount of strength.

Stepping closer, I tug at the bottom of his soft, navy blue shirt, lifting it just enough to slide my hands beneath, letting them glance across chiseled muscles.

Grey studies my hands as I savor his body.

I've spent countless hours next to his abs, but they've always been out of focus, obscured by that damned wall. With nothing blurring them now, I can see clearly and I finally get what those girls were talking about at last summer's party, what every girl discussed in high-pitched wails and moans whenever Greyson came around.

Without lifting his head, he accuses me. "You're toying with me again."

I wait until he lifts his eyes to find my response. "I'm not toying with you," I reply steadily, with the confidence I have been searching for my whole life.

I raise my hands to his arms, dreams not holding a candle to the feeling of running my fingers along the sharp angles of his triceps in real life.

His forehead crinkles. I can almost see the gears churning away in his head, processing, trying so hard to figure out what the hell I want. "Then you're trying to get me to cry chicken."

This one makes me let out a laugh that can almost be called a giggle.

A giggle. Who knew I even had one?

His eyes fall to my lips and in turn, my gaze drifts down his face and then back to those eyes that, in the clearing haze, have turned the same blue as my dress vans. "I'm trying to get you to see the truth."

I run my hands up his shoulders and down his chest. He follows their every move with his eyes. "Yeah? And what's the truth?"

I'm not sure he'd believe me if I told him, so I lean in closer, patiently waiting for him to let down the last of his defenses. He straightens up, little by little, bringing his lips closer to mine. His eyes scan my face for any sign of hesitancy. There are none. I have not even the shadow of indecision on my face. I think my assurance lends him the confidence he needs to move closer. His "I-Got-the-Answer-Before-You" smile shows up and he draws his lower lip in with his tongue, biting on it a bit to try to hide the smile he knows I will recognize.

My gaze fixed on his lips, I inch forward, pulled by gravity, which has once again moved from beneath my feet to where I hope it will remain forever, right behind Greyson.

He frees his lower lip and matches my movements. I suspect gravity has moved for him, too.

My incredulous expression asks if he's sure. His fearless smile answers.

So I press my lips to that smile. Slowly. Cautiously. Each kiss lending more and more confidence.

He runs his hands through my hair as our kiss becomes inebriating. Walls, fortified by twelve years of following the rules, slowly crumble under the weight of this new closeness.

I thought I knew Greyson through and through, but it feels like I am meeting him for the first time, exploring parts of him I never knew existed.

A raucous thumping followed by a squealing sound from the kitchen door sobers me up. Indigo and her faux fireman, both nearly naked, descend from their love den above to fortify themselves with food before a second round.

Greyson and I both freeze.

Indigo giggles as she pins her faux hero against the open fridge door.

Greyson awaits my guidance. It's one thing to finally be ready to tell each other, but I don't think either one of us was ready to share with the class. I want more time with our secret. I want to share this one thing with him and him alone before we let other people dissect our relationship. I hunt for a place to hide.

The sand at this hour is already filled with families and beach-hound tourists looking to soak up the San Diego sunshine. No privacy there. The only way inside is through the kitchen and I don't think either one of us could hide our smiles. Around the side of the house, past the outdoor shower, the daybed proclaims itself to be the perfect place to continue this conversation.

"We should go wash off our feet."

Greyson raises his brow like the simple act of kissing him has completely destroyed my brain, leaving me senseless.

I take his hand and pull him to the covered porch, stopping only to slide the curtains along the wire at the top of the porch roof.

Feeling more like an outdoor room, the porch is filled with tropical plants, a few hanging wetsuits, and the daybed layered with pillows. I lead Grey to the edge of the bed and sit. Just moments away from him and my lips already ache for his.

"You are way better at this than I ever imagined," he whispers as he sits next to me and I can almost taste the lust in his voice.

My lips descend on his and I kiss him with all the hunger twelve years of denial have built within me. He slides his hand along my back, lowering me onto the bed, pressing his electrifying body against mine as he does the same to my mouth.

I lift his shirt ready to enjoy the solid, toned body I ignored for so long. He lifts his body off mine, reaches back, and grips the collar of his shirt. It gets ripped off with one deft move.

He slides his hand under my back and pulls me under him, craving in every move of his body. He presses himself against me and I rise to meet him, tasting the hops still lingering in his mouth.

His hands, skillful and sure, glide to my hips, then deliberately skim my skin as they move up my stomach, bringing the hem of my shirt up with them.

He lifts his head away from me. "Wait," he exhales.

Wait?

He lowers his head onto the mattress beside me and pulls his body away from mine.

I freeze, my head still lifted.

He slows his breathing.

"I need to do this right," he whispers.

*Just say it fast.*

"When we do this..." He loses his thought and scrubs a hand through his messy hair.

"I know that you want Office Sp..." He stops again and scratches his stubble with the back of his fingers.

"You're not making any sense, Grey."

He notices the fear that must be written all over my face.

"We need to save that for our wedding night," he whispers.

My breath catches.

Our wedding night?

The words breeze out of his mouth like it's something we have discussed for years.

I ask with a look, Did I hear that right? He answers me by kissing me softly.

I kiss him, my hands sliding over his arms, my hands raking through his hair, hungry for him in a way I've never known, ready to devour him.

He lifts his lips from mine and breathes into me, "You should probably walk me out if I'm going to keep that promise."

"You really promise?"

"Totally, absolutely, completely."

His desire to do right by me giving me the courage, I drag myself from his grip.

He stands and pulls his shirt on. With his head in his shirt, he says, "So I'll call you later?"

I wait until his head pops back out. "You think after twelve years of waiting for this I'm gonna let you out of my grip now?"

He scampers over, wrapping me in his arms, and kisses me again, "Kealani's," and again, "for," and again, "breakfast?"

I only have the strength to pull away from him long enough to get out, "mmm-hmm," as he advances across the deck with me still in his arms, his lips leaving mine only as long as absolutely necessary to stay upright.

I pull away. "Keys."

"Hurry."

I dash inside to retrieve my keys from the kitchen island and turn to find Greyson framed against the clear, blue ocean, dancing, arms raised like he's giving thanks to God who was powerful enough to knock us both from our folly and give us the strength to finally be honest with each other.

That man out there, that adorable, brave, intoxicating, broken man, the man who could have any girl he wanted, he chose me.

He really is My Greyson now. Totally, absolutely, completely, brutally mine. And I never have to share him again.

He turns to find me leering. And this time, I don't try to hide it. I don't stifle the urge to jump him and never let him go. I give in to every single girly need that he fills me with.

When I walk out to him, he immediately draws me into his arms and sets his forehead to mine.

"I love you, Sands," he coos.

"I love you, too, Grey."

# 46

## CHARLIE

*I*always thought that playing the tomboy let me be more honest with the boys, let them be more honest with me. But staying in the safety of that role, the one I clung to so tightly, only showing a small part of myself, was simply dishonest.

And how can you be totally, absolutely, completely, brutally honest with another person if you are not first totally, absolutely, completely, brutally honest with yourself?

I slip on my new mango-yellow strappy dress and survey myself in the mirror. The deep V-neck and fitted body panel above a sun-ready skater skirt need more adjusting than one of my old t-shirts. I really don't need a wardrobe malfunction stealing the spotlight from Indigo tonight.

*"Take it from me 'cause I found, If you leave it then somebody else is bound, To find that treasure, that moment of pleasure, When yours, it could have been,"* Jimmy Buffett's mellow music fills my room from the deck below. I think Indigo is trying to get her guests in the island mood for Promises, her fourth indie film, the one she was wise enough to cast me in.

Not that she was oh-so-wise to showcase my limited talent, but her foresight in what the experience would teach me was brilliant. The confidence it would give me, the chance to explore a whole new side of myself without any risk, it changed me.

Once I know my girls are situated, I add a little color to my face. A touch of tinted moisturizer that I won't even feel after it soaks in, unlike the layer of spackle Bex prefers. Some black eyeliner—I love the little punk rock edge it gives me—and purple shadow. And some banana-flavored lip balm to keep my smackers soft and kissable.

I take one final peek in the mirror. My outsides match my insides, and they're both feeling amazing.

The island music hits even louder as I pass through the kitchen, "*Some people never find it, Some, only pretend, but me: I just want to live happily ever after every now and then.*"

Out on the deck, it's a smaller crowd than usual for one of Indigo's premieres. The tone of this movie naturally lends itself to a less raucous group. Indigo is talking with Sonny, Tank, and some girl that Tank is clearly trying to impress. From the look on her face, he's doing a poor job.

"Where's Grey?" Indigo asks when I join them. "I didn't know you two were capable of survival if you were more than thirty feet apart."

"We're not that bad."

I would try to convince her that we aren't attached at the hip, but over the past three months, not a day has gone by that I didn't see him. Any day he had off we would spend in each others arm's from sun up to sun down. He even lets me stop by the station now.

So, instead of trying to convince Indigo of something she will never believe, I just give in. "He's out front on a phone call."

"That's what I thought. Less than thirty feet."

Two quick beeps ring out and my hand instinctively flies to my waist. At the same moment, Sonny's hand does too.

She pulls her pump from her pocket. "Not me."

My hand rests where my pump is tucked inside the band of my undies under my dress—I've had to get more creative with my pump placement since I have branched out from jeans and jean shorts—but I have no idea how I am going to silence the alarm.

Sonny must notice the confusion on my face because she leans in, "You have the app? Silence it from there."

I pull out my phone and fire up the app for my pump. It's a high alarm—180. I silence the alarm and give myself a bolus. I think the nerves of having people watching my performance are making me high.

"Thanks. I don't know how I've gone so long without friends who know diabetes."

"Me either," she says as Tank pokes Aggravated Girl in the ribs trying to get her to laugh.

"I'm just gonna have to tickle you until you agree," he taunts.

"You're barking up the wrong tree," the brunette grunts.

"I'd move on Tank. Harley was my technical director when it came to the FBI stuff on Promises. She could make you disappear fourteen different ways and no one would be the wiser."

Dressed in a black hoodie over jean shorts and a pair of combat boots—exactly what that I would have worn to this event last summer minus the boots—Harley gives me a nod.

Woman of few words, my kind of person.

Tank finally gets the hint and moves on to his next target, me. "So, Charlie, I think it's about time we revisit that kiss. I know you've been thinking about it ever since Maui."

My teeth hurt in remembrance of that awful kiss. "Not ever gonna happen again. Sorry, Tank."

Harley looks at me like I was smarter than that.

I raise my hands in defense. "Indigo made me. It was in the script, I swear."

"Holy Spielberg, Tank. You always pick the worst women. Charlie's not single."

"Hey, I don't see a ring on it."

I lift my hand, showing off the titanium and koa wood band wrapped around a Moissanite stone, and I don't hate the ooh's and ahh's that the girls give me.

"That wasn't there yesterday," Indigo says.

"Last night," I boast.

After a perfect three-hour surf session at Swamii's, Greyson had pizza delivered to the beach. He sat on top of the cement table, I reclined on the bench overlooking the water as the sun sank into its salty grave.

"Do you remember that first night we had pizza?" he asked.

"Sure. When you told me you thought of me like a sister? Now that we're together, does that mean you're a fan of incest?" Leave it to me to bring up incest when a guy's trying to propose, but how was I supposed to know?

"I'm serious, Sands. Do you remember that night?"

"Every single moment," I whispered.

"We promised to be totally, absolutely, completely, brutally honest, so I know you'll believe me when I tell you that I knew that night," he said proudly while stuffing a huge bite of pizza in his mouth.

"Sure you did."

Sliding another slice onto my plate, I took advantage of his refusal to talk with food in his mouth to get in one more shot. "You knew nothing."

He slapped his plate down on the table and wiped his hands on a napkin. "You really do make everything difficult, Sands." He tossed the napkin into the trash. "We were five frames into our second game of bowling that night, and I was just sucking. What kind of sport is bowling anyways?"

"One you suck at?"

"So my dad calls and the last thing I want to do is talk to that bastard, but if I don't I know it will be that much worse when I get home. I walk off to do damage control and when I get back you had bowled my turn. Got a strike, of course."

"So you knew you liked me because I was a magnificent bowler?"

He rose from the table, driven by the anxiety response he always has when the subject of his dad comes up. "Oh my God, Charlie, will you let me finish?"

"Come here," I coo.

He steps to me.

Planting a kiss on his cheek, I say, "I'm sorry. I won't say another thing."

"Thanks." He kicks at the husk of a seed dropped from the

palm tree framing our little view of paradise. "I don't know how you knew, but when I asked why you bowled for me, you said, 'It looked like you could use a win.' No one has ever read me so fast—I put a lot of work into making sure no one could—but it was like that shield was invisible to you. All the shit with my dad, the constant anxiety, all my fears, you knew them instantly, and you had this amazing way of taking away all the pain without a single drop of pity."

He shoved his hands into the pockets of his jeans, letting the memory of that day wash away any thoughts of his dad. "I knew right then I had to do whatever it took to keep you in my life in the biggest way possible. And right now, the only way I know how to keep doing that," he freed his hands from his pockets and kneeled down. "I want all of you, Charlie, for the rest of my life."

He opened the small koa wood box, held out the ring, and stared at me. I may not know much about girly things, but I do know there's supposed to be a question involved in proposals. His face began to fall.

"Are you trying to ask me something, Grey?"

He suddenly remembered the end of his speech. "Charlie Sands, will you marry me?"

"I would have married you the first day we met, no reason not to now."

He slid that perfect ring on my finger and wrapped me up in an embrace I hope will last the rest of my life.

And as happy as I was, beneath it, if I was willing to admit, there was an undercurrent of sorrow. Sorrow for that little girl twelve years ago who was too afraid to play a game she was sure she would lose. Who spent twelve years underestimating herself, believing she wasn't nearly as worthy or as girly as all the beauties around her.

Had she just been smart enough to listen to Grey when he asked her to abide by his one rule twelve years ago she could have saved them both so much pain. The pain she caused him by making him believe he wasn't smart enough or good enough. The pain she caused herself by holding in too much for too long.

The pain from preventing him from doing the one thing that his nature was constantly driving him to do, to be absolutely honest.

I want to shake that little girl and tell her to be brave. To be honest. That the parts of her she thought were unappealing and wrong, the ones that she thought were the one mistake God ever made, giving her so many male traits, the ones that gave her a secret superpower, a backstage pass to Guyland, that those were the very things that made Grey love her. I want to save her from taking twelve years of happiness from her and Grey because she was too afraid.

I'm pulled back from the memory by Greyson's strong arms lifting me up and spinning me around before setting me down and giving me a big kiss.

"Good news, I take it?" I ask when my breath returns.

When Grey got passed over for Captain in Del Mar, we jumped on the next plane to Maui. Junior set up an informal interview with his dad who was building the groundwork to find his replacement as Captain at the Paia Fire Station. There were a few other contenders, but none as smart or as disciplined as my Grey, though trying to convince him of that was nearly impossible.

While we've been waiting for official word of what I knew was a sure thing, I have been laying my own groundwork. After thoroughly enjoying a few weeks without work, I got the itch to start working on Nudge again. I sent it off to Piper, the only other female programmer I know, to get a fresh pair of eyes on it and to find the holes in my work.

Instead of feedback, she wanted to buy Nudge to add to her Boardroom App. "I have people in Kaulike Hanai who I know have great ideas—I can see it on their faces—but they don't know how to speak up," she told me. "And if they're having trouble in this inclusive environment, I can't imagine the barriers people are facing in less welcoming companies. I think Nudge could give them the words to speak up."

She only had one condition. I had to move to Maui to finish Nudge and integrate it into their platform.

"You want to share what's got you two so giddy?" Indigo interrupts.

"Grey just became Captain in Paia. We're moving to Maui," I squeal.

As the deck lights dim, leaving her face glowing from the warm yellow twinkle lights filtering through the leaves on the Banyan tree, Indigo steps in front of the giant screen that will broadcast my debut as an actress.

"Nine years ago, my father sat me down and told me that he wasn't actually a civilian IT security specialist for the Navy. After the shock wore off, he told me the real story of his work and how it led him to meet and fall in love with my mother. I remember thinking how badly I would have loved to watch the two people I loved most in this world fall in love with each other."

On one of the many sherbet-colored floor cushions disguising our deck as the set of some MTV reality dating show, I snuggle in closer to Grey, breathing in the scent of caramel and peace.

"But in Promises, I get to see a little snapshot of the love story that made me. My wish is that it gives hope to those who have yet to find love and a sense of urgency for those who have. Remember, life is short. Savor every minute you have with each other."

The screen jumps to life as a giant me, walking along the lapping waves, slowly comes into focus. Steel drums back a mellow voice, "Beneath the moonlit sky, Shadows walk beside the water," as the woman on the screen stops being me and becomes simply a character in a great story.

I glance across the fire pit at Bex, who's a little too comfortable sharing a cushion with Patrick. Her pink bohemian wrap top over a pair of jean shorts and simple sandals let her fit in perfectly with the Hawaiian vibe Indigo has created tonight.

Since Bex moved out, we've had an easier friendship. She's even started to value my insight into boys and relationships. And clothes. Who would have thought it possible?

She seems happy next to Patrick like she's finally relaxed. Herself. She glances over at me and I mouth the words, "Summer Goal?"

She shrugs a cool Why Not?

Onscreen, Wells stands from the grassy hillside overlooking the building waves beyond. The camera pans down as he dusts off his trunks, following his hand as it lays a single sunflower on the engraved stone.

The camera focus pulls from the distant waves to the inscription, "SUTTON MARIE WATERS. 1962—1995. Her husband's greatest adventure. Her daughter's greatest example." The steel drums swell and the last sad lines ring out. "Wait for me 'til I return, Though she never will, He waits for her beside the water, Faithful still to California promises."

Before this acting gig, I clung so tightly to my rules. What I could talk about. What role I had to play. Who I had to be. Hell, I even had a stupid rule about the physical distance I had to keep from Grey. It wasn't until I decided to break every one of them that I truly found happiness.

Grey leans over and, right before he kisses me, whispers in my ear, "You are amazing, Sands."

I mentally toss that Rule Book in the one place it belongs, the blazing fire pit, and watch it burn, knowing that I only need one rule going forward.

Perhaps not even a rule. A promise.

I look over at my Grey and smile, silently promising him to always be totally, absolutely, fully, brutally honest for the rest of our lives.

# DIABETES APPENDIX

## CHARLIE

Thanks so much for reading my story and wanting to know more about diabetes.

I know diabetes or any chronic condition you don't personally have can sometimes be confusing. When you get diagnosed with diabetes or any chronic condition, you have to learn a whole new language and set and people try to simplify their explanations of the disease so inexperienced people can understand it without having to take a college course on the subject. But that sometimes can lead to confusion and incorrect conclusions.

The best way to really learn about what it is like to live with a chronic condition is to listen to those who have it. Be willing to learn with each new experience. Ask good questions. And realize that, although you will never fully know what it is to live with any condition you don't have yourself, you have a vast well of empathy that will allow you to be compassionate and informed about another human's experience.

To help you out, I have written out a little appendix to explain some of the situations you may have found me in while I was being a stubborn, boneheaded girl trying to find my way to love. They are all in chronological order with links to products mentioned in this appendix at the end of the chapter.

## A DIABETES PRIMER

Here are the basics of Type 1 diabetes. It's a lot like the speech you would hear from a doctor in the fifteen minutes he spends explaining a disease that can take years to fully master.

Something in your body—a virus, an out-of-balance gut, excess stress—causes your body's immune system to go a bit haywire and start attacking the beta cells of your pancreas, thinking they are a foreign invader. The beta cells of the pancreas, along with a few other organs and hormones, help regulate the amount of sugar in your bloodstream by producing and releasing insulin.

The amount of sugar in your bloodstream needs to be tightly regulated. A lot like a thermostat in your house keeps the temp between 68 and 72, your body needs the blood sugar to be between 80 and 120 mg/dl (or 4.45 to 6.67 mmol for you metric folks). Too much and you begin to destroy the other parts of your body leading to long-term complications. Too low and your brain and muscles can't function.

Since the pancreas stops being able to keep up with the insulin demands, a person with type 1 diabetes needs to give themselves insulin via a shot or insulin pump. Adam Brown, author of Bright Spots and Landmines, has compiled a list of 42 different things that can affect the amount of insulin needed at any one time. Things like food composition, caffeine, alcohol, stress, sleep, illness, other medications, altitude, and sunburn. And each of these factors can have a different effect on the same person at different times.

With that number of factors, dosing insulin can be a very difficult and dangerous pursuit, which is why a person with diabetes will not always have blood sugars in range, no matter how diligent and wise they are with their diabetes care.

## CHAPTER 5, PAGE 39
### Avoiding a piece of glass in the sand to avoid a lecture from my endocrinologist.

When I was diagnosed with diabetes in 2009, my very first endocrinologist warned me never to walk barefoot again. He pretty much guaranteed me that years of bad blood sugar control would destroy my nerves, one little glass landmine would cut my foot, and I'd never be able to feel it. It would end up infected, then the gangrene would set in, and I would have to have my foot amputated.

The only problem with this theory is that it was based on old data and old technology. Now, with the state of the art technology available and diligence and consistency, a person with type 1 diabetes can live a happy, healthy, barefoot life without the fear of one cut taking off their leg.

### CHAPTER 5, PAGE 41
#### Pretending my insulin pump is waterproof.

An insulin pump is a small device about the size of an old-school pager that delivers a steady flow of insulin, a basal rate, through a tiny tube inserted below the skin. It also can be programmed to deliver a bigger, quick amount of insulin, a bolus, often needed food eaten, or to correct for a higher-than-desired blood sugar reading.

I use the Tandem t:slim X2 pump with Control IQ technology, which is so freaking cool. It goes beyond the old-school pumps because it can interface with my Dexcom CGM and actually increase my basal rates of insulin if I am going high. It also can suspend my insulin if it sees that I am going low. This has prevented so many more lows than my old pump.

A good portion of people with an insulin pump or other diabetes devices find a way to make it fun, often naming them and giving them a personality. It's a great way of coping with the fact that we have a medical device attached to them at all times.

### CHAPTER 7, PAGE 59
#### Hiding my pump beneath a dress.

Finding an inconspicuous place to hide your pump can be difficult. Most times, in a dress, I place it inside my bra between my girls, but with Charlie's dress being a low-cut V top, it would be totally, absolutely, completely, brutally visible. The backup for me is tucked inside a pair of undies with a wider band, but it does make access limited and takes a trip to the bathroom to give a bolus.

### CHAPTER 11, PAGE 91
### Sugar is not only bad for people with diabetes
### but unhealthy for regular people too.

It is commonly thought that only people with diabetes need to worry about the amount of sugar they consume. But sugar is a major contributor to obesity, inflammation, and most of the chronic disease that we see in America. It is a good idea for all humans to reduce their consumption of sugar.

### CHAPTER 12, PAGE 101
### Getting low at Greyson's place.

Dosing insulin is a very difficult process. A normal functioning pancreas will adjust the amount of insulin in the body on a minute-by-minute basis based on a minute-by-minute assessment of the current amount of sugar in the bloodstream, current use by muscles and other organs, stress hormones present, and a host of other factors.

The insulin we inject lasts in the body for two to twenty-four hours depending on the type. To keep blood sugar levels steady, we need to calculate our body's future insulin needs, even though we may not know what kinds of stress, exercise, illness, or food we will encounter in the future.

When that calculation is too high, blood sugar drops. Hypoglycemia. We call it a low. It feels different for each person and each low.

Most of the time it is accompanied by a strong drive for food. Nothing else in life matters. Not social conventions. Not table manners. Not what other people might think of you.

Only sugar.

It's a lot like a zombie's drive for brains. And since, during a low, the brain is being starved of its only energy source, you often think like a zombie, too.

### CHAPTER 17, PAGE 143
### Facing TSA at the airport.

Some of the diabetes technology we wear is not cleared to go through the x-ray scanner at the airport, we often have to ask for a pat-down and visual inspection of our carry-on items. And since insulin can't go into the checked baggage because it would freeze, we have a lot of carry-on items. This whole process tends to extend the time it takes to clear security at the airport.

## CHAPTER 17, PAGE 144
### Focusing on insulin calculations

There is a ton of math involved in figuring out exactly how much insulin my body will need. Usually, I can do it in a split second, but every now and then there are enough factors in the calculation that I have to stop and think about it.

Flying can complicate the normal routine of insulin administration. Sitting still for long periods will often increase insulin needs, so some people with diabetes need an increase in the basal rate on the insulin pump. Sometimes it can even affect the amount of insulin needed to cover the food you eat during that time.

## CHAPTER 18, PAGE 158
### Traveling and meeting Sonny in Maui.

The amount of insulin needed throughout the day varies. A basal rate is the amount of insulin that drips continuously into your body from a pump. It is usually lower when you sleep, higher in the morning when the hormones that wake you up are higher, and then stays moderate throughout the day.

Just because you have changed time zones or the clocks for Daylight Savings Time, doesn't mean that your body automatically changes what it is doing. It takes a while for your body to adjust to the new time. Along with that, your basal rate needs will change over the course of a few days. So some people wait a few days to adjust the clock on their insulin pumps to match this slower change.

The Dexcom CGM is a device that measures blood sugar every five minutes via a small sensor and transmitter worn on the body. It then sends that data to an insulin pump, phone, or handheld receiver. The sensor is worn on the stomach or sometimes the upper butt.

The sensor has integrated tape to hold it on the body for ten days, but when you are in the ocean as much as I am, that tape can fail earlier. So I wear a water-resistant tape over the sensor to keep it in place.

I've tried many of the tapes on the market, putting them through their paces with countless hours in the ocean, and have found ExpressionMed's tape is the highest quality and has the cutest designs.

The Tandem pump will alert you if you start but don't finish the process of dialing up a bolus to correct for a high blood sugar or to cover food. This world is incredibly distracting and it happens more often than I'd like to admit, so it comes in handy to have Tex reminding me when I am.

### CHAPTER 19, PAGE 161
#### Greyson's first-hand experience with a severe low.

If a person's blood sugar gets too low, they may lose consciousness, have seizures, go into a coma, and die. Because of that, many people with diabetes carry around Glucagon. Glucagon is a hormone normally made by the pancreas to tell the liver to release glucose from storage.

When it is injected, it can prevent a scary low from becoming the dead kind of low. There are a lot of companies out there who make a glucagon emergency kit, but my favorite by far is Xeris Pharmaceutical's Gvoke HypoPen for the exact reasons why Greyson likes it. It's super easy to use, even when totally panicked. And when I have it with me, I feel like I am in control, not some stupid low blood sugar.

### CHAPTER 19, PAGE 162
#### Sleeping through low alarms

Sometimes, I sleep deeply enough that I don't hear the alarm that sounds when I am a little low. So I have rigged up my phone to use the fire truck siren when I am really getting scary low.

### CHAPTER 20, PAGE 174
#### Cravings from lows

Sometimes I have the weirdest cravings from lows. Lately, it's been shredded sharp cheddar cheese. But every now and then I crave a 3 Muskateers. I figure if I get to eat sugary food without guilt, I might as well make it count.

### CHAPTER 21, PAGE 184
### Drinking with diabetes.

Don't take Greyson's protective vibe the wrong way. People with diabetes can drink. Diabetes is not the reason I don't really drink. You saw how I speak without thinking when I've had one too many. But to drink safely with diabetes, it is important to do a little planning. You need to learn everything you can about what alcohol does to human biology. Amrita Misha at Beyond Type 1 wrote a great article on it here, https://beyondtype1.org/alcohol-and-diabetes-guide/. Alcohol can cause a low blood sugar, and a low often looks just like being drunk: slurred speech, acting goofy, passing out, seizures. Those around you may assume you're just drunk and that you'll be fine when in reality a low could kill you without them even knowing.

If I do drink, I always make sure I have someone sober who knows about my diabetes and what to do in case something happens. It's usually Grey, but we all know how that one turned out.

### CHAPTER 27, PAGE 321
### A surprise low during a nap.

Everybody feels lows differently. And every low can feel different. For me, when it's a bad low, I can get hypoglybitchy, I lose my manners, and any semblance of being kind. The filter that usually prevents me from saying exactly what's on my mind ripe with expletives shuts down. And I have some weird craving for shredded sharp cheddar cheese or Lucky Charms cereal. Who knows why?

Then the sweat starts pouring out of every pore in my body. And I get shaky and uncoordinated making finding sugar and getting it in my mouth a herculean task.

Luckily, I have some really cool people in my life who can recognize when I'm struggling and help me out. And they do a good job of shielding me from making an absolute fool of myself around people who haven't gotten to know me as well.

### CHAPTER 31, PAGE 268
#### Low from unplanned exercise.

Another low. Are you starting to notice a pattern? I've heard it said that war is long stretches of boring with a few moments of sheer terror thrown in. That's a lot of what diabetes feels like. Long stretches of ordinary, boring care, then random moments of sheer terror when a low hits without warning.

Once I get enough sugar into my stomach to fix my low, I still have to wait for it to get absorbed into my bloodstream and muscles to fully recover. And those can be the longest, most torturous moments. But it is the greatest feeling when the first drips of sugar hit my blood, the brain fog lifts just a bit, and I know I have escaped death yet again.

Then I only have to deal with the hanglowver that can sometimes follow a bad low.

### CHAPTER 34, PAGE 270
#### Weigh gain from treating lows.

I've calculated how many calories I've had to drink or eat to treat my lows in a year. It is astronomical. And sometimes I wonder how many pounds I carry because of it.

But before I bother calculating that, I remind myself that I would so much rather live my amazing life than worry one more second about a few extra pounds on my frame. I point out that I love my body for what it allows me to do, surf warm waves in Maui, run with Grey, comfort my friends with a hug, and certainly not for what it looks like or what size it is.

My body does way too much for me daily for me to judge it on such a meaningless and superficial characteristic.

I've also been trying to share this with Bex, who, surprisingly, has been starting to absorb it. And I think it's helped her a ton.

### CHAPTER 46, PAGE 381
*Pump apps.*

Finding people who also deal with your chronic condition can mean the world. It allows you to feel normal again. And it gives you the chance to trade tips and tricks that typically doctors haven't figured out yet.

BOOK TWO OF THE
WARRIOR WOMEN SERIES
coming Summer 2022.
For updates, go to
SeaPeptide.com/SaltiesScoop.

# ABOUT THE AUTHOR

*E*rin Spineto started her writing journey in 2011 with Islands and Insulin, her memoir of sailing solo 100 miles down the Florida Keys with type 1 diabetes back in a time when doctors were foolish enough to recommend against this kind of wild adventure with diabetes. She followed it up a few years later with Adventure On, a nonfiction book on using adventure to increase motivation to take care of chronic conditions like diabetes. Since then she has moved on to fiction and is currently working on Warrior Women, a three-book angsty RomCom series full of female surfers who happen to have diabetes and other autoimmune issues.

Erin's journey with autoimmune conditions started in 1996 with type 1 diabetes. She added hyperthyroidism to the mix in 2007, and has rounded out her collection with a little Anti-Synthetase Syndrome, which she thinks is so appropriately abbreviated ASS. Not letting anything slow her down, Erin is also a long-distance endurance adventurer and autoimmune advocate who uses stories to encourage others with chronic illness to go big.

Erin started surfing at age five when she stood up on her boogie board and realized waves were so much more fun to ride standing up. Since then she has had a love affair with empty beaches, warm water, and a post-surf lunch of fish tacos and Diet Dr Pepper (though she's had to give that up to fight the ASS) eaten on a patio in the sun with her own real life hero, Tony, and their two surfing teenagers.

You can learn more at SeaPeptide.com.

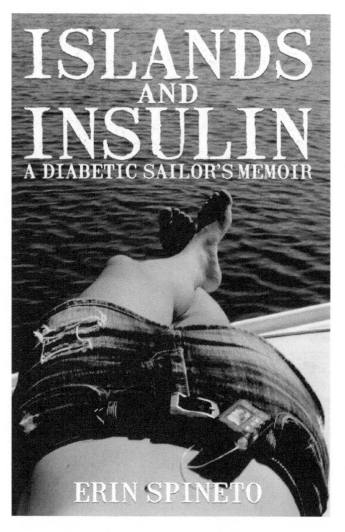

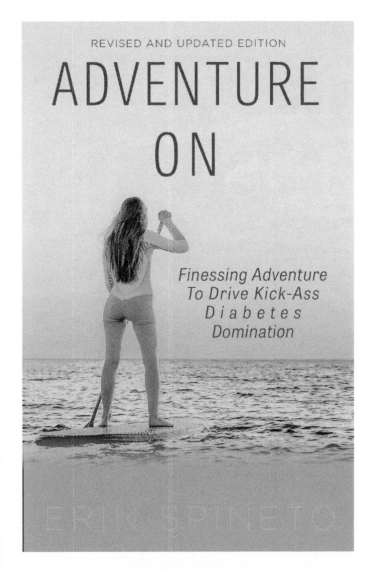

Mäde in the USA
Las Vegas, NV
13 July 2021